Mike Ripley has twice won the Crime Writer's Last Laugh Award for comedy crime and his *Angel* novels have been optioned by the BBC. He has written for television and radio and is the crime fiction critic for the *Birmingham Post*, as well as co-editor of the *Fresh Blood* anthologies which promote new British crime writing talent. He lives with his wife, three children and two cats in East Anglia.

Also by Mike Ripley

LIGHTS, CAMERA, ANGEL

Mike Ripley

ROBINSON
London

Constable & Robinson Ltd
3 The Lanchesters
162 Fulham Palace Road
London, W6 9ER
www.constablerobinson.com

First published in Great Britain by Constable,
an imprint of Constable & Robinson Ltd, 2001

This paperback edition published by Robinson,
an imprint of Constable & Robinson Ltd, 2002

ISBN 1-84119-465-4

Printed and bound in the EU

A CIP catalogue record for this book is
available from the British Library

10 9 8 7 6 5 4 3 2 1

For
Bill, May and Pierce
– with great affection,
and for
Denise 'Hotwire' Danks,
the Techno Queen herself,
and Walter Satterthwait,
without whom . . . it would have
been much funnier.

Author's Note
This is a work of fiction and no person depicted
herein actually exists or even comes close to any
real person involved in the world of Film, or any
part or constituent thereof by any means whether
now or hereafter invented, or any form of television
(whether now known or hereafter invented)
including, without limitation, standard television
and/or non-standard television, videograms and/or
videodiscs whether interactive or otherwise.
(Taken, without apology, from a standard BBC contract)

1

STARRING . . .

To be honest, by the time it got to New Year's Eve I was party-ed out and didn't mind driving the cab. After all, no other vehicle was going to get to move through the London traffic on the night of The Big One and, in any case, I had a big movie star in the back.

I'm not a real cab driver, but it was a real black London cab – an Austin Fairway – and it really was me driving it through Dome City on the last night of the century and I did have that Ross Pirie on the back seat. He didn't want to be recognised that night, so he sat back in the offside corner away from the pedestrians sandwiched alongside every inch of pavement on the assumption (false, so watch it) that no one recognises anyone in a black London cab after dark. I wasn't keen on being recognised any time, so I drove a black cab in London.

The cab was called Armstrong II. Ross Pirie was called Ross Pirie. It was his real name and it seemed to fit him well enough. He hadn't had to change it like a Michael Caine or a John Wayne or a Cary Grant. Ross had been cool enough for his parents, though I've no idea whether they even considered Maurice, Marion or Archie, and it was cool enough as a name these days to pass muster, maybe even try for a comeback.

Not that Ross was up there with the Caines, Waynes, Grants and the other movie greats, well not yet anyway, but he was getting there. His big break had come in an all-action World War II movie, *Six Men Dead*, despite the critics saying the genre was buried. And he'd followed that with a low-budget black comedy, *Treble & Bass*, about rival disc jockeys feuding on a local radio station in a small town in a part of northern England which time and the economy had forgot. Those two movies had made him a bankable star, though he'd been around for a while and some of his earlier films had achieved STV status (Straight To Video). But now he was a Name and a Face and being with him in public

7

made you feel like one of those gophers who trails around behind members of the Royal Family picking up the bunches of flowers.

He was rich, famous, handsome, obviously good at his job and had never given me a cross word or slanty glance, or dissed me in any way.

So I decided to dislike him, just as soon as I could find a good reason.

'We're going to be cutting this fine, aren't we, Roy?' he said in his deep, mid-Atlantic measured voice which women found incredibly sexy and I decided was going to irritate me.

'Keep your hair on, there's no need to panic,' I said irritably. 'I warned you what it would be like. Every drunk in town and a few million part-timers shipped in for the occasion, all out on the streets and it's not as if the pubs have shut yet.'

'You said that, Roy, you did and you were absolutely right,' he said smoothly. 'I'm in your hands completely.'

There were women who would have sold their souls cheap, and thrown their bodies in for free, to have had Ross Pirie say that to them. I lived with one of them.

Ahead of me three women in sleeveless sparkling party frocks and high heels took a chance from the traffic island and ran across the road in drunken girlie fashion, feet flapping to the side, dresses riding up, giggling insanely. All three clutched open bottles of champagne and they'd left their coats at home (or in the last wine bar but one) just to show how hard they were.

I braked rather harshly to allow them to get on to the pavement in one piece. Or rather three very attractive pieces.

'I wonder what they'll feel like in the morning,' said Ross behind me.

'I was wondering that too,' I said, along with: where did they live?

'"Drunks – those angry penguins of the night,"' he quoted, in a voice which was meant to remind me he was an actor. 'That was a line from a play I was in, I think. Can't remember what it was called.'

It was from a poem actually, but I didn't want to show off. Scoring points off actors really was picking low-hanging fruit.

I had picked him up from a do at the Dorchester, a charity

do for something called Opportunity 2000 which helped under-privileged kids. Whilst waiting for him near the sign saying Trader Vic's, sitting in Armstrong II with the engine running, I was approached by a dozen angry penguins of the night offering large amounts of cash, sex and/or Class A drugs for a ride south of the river. Turning down such offers started to get to me after about two minutes and I wondered how I could apply to be adopted by Opportunity 2000.

One of the uniformed doormen wandered over to me at an angle in a sideways, crablike fashion and I thought for a minute he was trying to clock Armstrong's number plate or check whether he had a hackney carriage licence on the rear. Then I saw the neck of a bottle of Glenfiddich sticking out of his overcoat pocket and I made the fair assumption that the seal had been broken.

'You the one for Ross Pirie?' he asked when I lowered my window. He looked down at his boots when he spoke so I wouldn't smell his breath.

'At his beck and call,' I said cheerfully like this was always the way I had planned to see in the twenty-first century, forging a bond with another unfortunate who had to work that night.

'What's he like?' asked the doorman confidentially.

'Oh, if only I had a pound for every time somebody asked me that,' I said, calculating that I'd have enough to buy a packet of cigarettes. Just.

'No, really, what's he like? I mean, he always comes across as quite a nice guy – on the screen that is.'

'Ah, the magic of the silver screen,' I said wearily, as if I knew *the truth*.

Then I saw his face start to fall in disappointment and his right hand flutter towards the bottle in his pocket like an ageing gunslinger.

'Actually, he's a diamond geezer, a solid citizen. He really is. Nicer bloke to run into in a pub you couldn't hope for. No side on him, no airs and few graces. What you see is what you get. A regular guy.'

'I knew it,' he beamed, his faith in human nature restored. 'Told the wife as much.'

'Generous, too,' I added straightfaced. 'Me and him, we're the same age, you know.'

'Oh, sorry about that,' he said.

I thought that was a tad uncalled for but at that moment the doors of the Dorchester opened enough to allow out the high frequency sound of female voices raised in excitement and Ross Pirie appeared at a brisk walk, slowing only to sign autographs. In one case, he signed the arm of a woman wearing a low-cut ball gown and enough jewellery to fill a safe on the *Titanic*. All that money and not a scrap of paper on her. She was probably telling him she would never wash that arm again, but the expression on the face of the dinner-jacketed man with her said she would.

Ross disentangled himself and flung a wave at the rapidly growing band of spectators, dodged a couple of camera flashes (which showed that the paparazzi didn't get time off for good behaviour either) and strode towards Armstrong.

The doorman drew himself up to his imperious height and almost saluted as he opened the door for him. With a sleight of hand worthy of a conjuror, Ross palmed a £5 note out of a pocket and into the doorman's hand.

'Thank *you*, Mr Pirie,' he boomed.

'Told you so,' I said to him as I took the brake off.

The doorman stood there, slightly drunk but happy with the world, his faith in human nature reaffirmed. I had helped there, brought a little sunshine into somebody's life. That was my New Year's resolution taken care of. Done and dusted.

The rest of the twenty-first century was my own.

There was no way we were going to make it. There were too many streets cordoned off, too many diversions, too many cops on the street and too many angry penguins wandering around looking for a good time and not recognising it when it hit them on the back of the head. Why wasn't I in Edinburgh, where they knew how to organise a street party?

A firework exploded way above us and the crowds of civilians paused to look up and go 'Ooooh!' It was like a scene from *Day of the Triffids* and for a minute I considered suggesting that Ross did a remake, but being eaten by a giant vegetable probably didn't fit his image.

'Was that the Queen?' he shouted in my ear, leaning forward on the rumble seat behind mine.

'No, it was a firework,' I said. 'Unless of course the revolution's started.'

'Right. Good one,' he said and he laughed politely but I could hear him thinking: Smartarse.

'I think it's amateur night, that one,' I said. 'The official River of Fire display doesn't kick off for half an hour. I don't know how much you'll see of it though.'

'Aw hell, I'm not worried about that. It just reminded me, I have to buy some fireworks for Chinese New Year.'

'That's not till February, is it?' I said unhelpfully.

'February 5th. Year of the Dragon. It's also the projected wrap date for the shoot, so I'm expected to throw a party. Thought I'd combine the two.'

There was a superstar for you. On his way to the biggest – or at least the first – party of the new century and he's already planning the next.

'You won't have a problem buying fireworks in Chinatown,' I told him. 'They sell them all year round.'

In fact the laws about selling fireworks had been relaxed for the Millennium celebrations so lots of places, from corner shop newsagents to supermarkets, were selling them. Even garages, which struck me as odd but then again they also sold charcoal briquettes and lighter fluid for barbecues so they were used to dealing in incendiaries. Some of them even had off-licences nowadays, selling booze and thus making them *the* place to visit in the middle of the night if you were an insomniac arsonist with a drink problem.

'You reckon?'

I sneaked a look at him in my mirror. He had his elbow on the armrest, his chin cupped in his hand, staring thoughtfully out into the night and the street-crawling crowds, probably counting his fans. He had automatically presented me with a profile which was famous enough already but destined to appear on the stamps of some obscure Pacific islands in the future. He could also check if any single hair on his head was out of place from the reflection in the window.

'Sure. Lin will know where. She'll get you a good deal.'

The fearsome Lin was Ross's personal assistant, or at least one of them. She was British Chinese, hard as nails and awesomely efficient. She could get him a good deal on a small war if she put her mind to it.

'No, I can't ask Lin,' Ross was saying dreamily. 'It's to be a surprise for her as much as a thank-you to the crew. It's been a pretty intense shooting schedule and she's worked her socks off, so I want to show her she's appreciated.'

'I'm sure she knows that,' I said, trying to keep the edge out of my voice. She was the sort of woman who would have had it written into her contract. Clause 2(a): I WILL BE APPRECIATED AT ALL TIMES.

'Normally, I'd ask Frank to fix things . . .'

But he couldn't ask Frank, his regular driver, because Frank had gone and got himself put in hospital.

And the top-of-the-range BMW he had been driving at the time had gone to the terminal ward of the nearest garage, where it was not expected to recover, suffering from that rare automobile disease of car-hits-wall-at-high-speed. There are some solid objects even a BMW can't drive through.

Which was where I came in.

Actually, it was Amy who had got in there first and on a strictly professional basis.

She had come home to the house in Hampstead about eight thirty one night four months back, dumped a heavy briefcase on the floor, thrown her coat on top of it and stomped straight through into the kitchen.

'So you've already eaten?'

She must have found the empty Domino Pizza packaging. I wondered if she knew I had an account with them.

'There's a slice in the oven,' I yelled over my shoulder.

I fumbled the remote control and turned down the volume a notch on the large flat screen TV, whilst popping the ring pull on another can of lager. West Ham had just gone into a 2–1 lead, but then they always played better when they appeared on satellite TV rather than when you turned up to watch them.

Amy shouted something which sounded like '. . . fancied going out . . .' but West Ham had just managed to string eight passes together without losing possession and I was trying to remember if this was a record or not.

'Huh?' I said, or something similar.

Then she was standing right in front of me, blocking off most of the television apart from the West Ham goal which I could still glimpse between her knees, a good three inches below the hem of her black leather skirt. I considered telling her that the sparkling silver tights she was wearing (which I had said looked like chain mail when she put them on that morning) really did go with that skirt and those shoes. But then she would have known that.

'Had a good day at the office, dear?' she said with more than a touch of venom.

I took this to be a reference to me sitting on the floor with my back against the four-seater sofa she had paid over two grand for, surrounded by a dozen or so CD-Roms, a discarded Play Station (I had won the Battle of the Bulge for the Germans in fifteen minutes, which couldn't be right, so I'd blamed Glenn Miller going missing), two or three empty beer cans, an ashtray, an empty tub of Ben and Jerry's Cherry Garcia, the new Harry Potter novel and a two-month old copy of *Country Living* which had an article about Amy in it I would one day get around to reading. I hit the Mute button on the remote. It seemed only polite and anyway, it was almost half-time.

'So-so,' I said, my eyes distracted from the triangle of screen I could still see, up her body, over the tight leather skirt and the pale blue ribbed polo-neck sweater with, at her throat, an amber brooch big enough to supply Jurassic Park with fossilised DNA.

She held a sheaf of A4-sized paper in one hand and a glass of wine in the other. On top of the wine glass she had balanced the last slice of pizza; didn't even thank me for saving her the last anchovy.

'You didn't forget to take the Freelander in for its service, did you?'

She transferred the wedge of paper to between her knees so she could hold her pizza and take a swig of wine. I could see that the papers were comb-bound with a plastic cover, like a presentation or a manuscript, because they were now at my eye level, which under normal circumstances was a pretty good level to operate at given Amy's legs.

'I didn't forget,' I said carefully, 'I just remembered too late for the garage to be still open.'

'That's OK,' she said, taking a bite of pizza. 'I forgive you.'

'I'll whip it over to Duncan tomorrow for the once-over. First thing.'

Duncan the Drunken was not exactly a registered Land Rover specialist but he did have a large collection of rubber stamps, one of which said he was, and I had long rated him as The Best Car Mechanic in the World (Probably) and he owed me a favour and it would be good to see him again. It would be good to get out of the house again.

'It's still under warranty, you know.' She licked her lips.

'Don't worry, there won't be anything wrong with it.'

That was why I liked dealing with Duncan. He ran one of the last remaining garages where, if you wanted it, they would find absolutely nothing wrong with your car.

'Fine.'

She took another bite and a drink, just standing there in front of me, knees clenched around the papers. Then she started noisily sucking each of the fingers of her left hand, but I was tough. I wasn't going to ask.

The hell I wasn't.

'What have got between your legs, dear?'

I said it innocently enough, but I didn't like the way she smiled all-knowingly as if she'd had a bet with herself and had just won.

She widened her knees and the bound papers fell to the carpet with a thump. Through the gap in her legs I could see a 3–1 scoreline flash up.

This had better be good, I thought as I stretched out a hand to turn the manuscript the right way up so I could read the words on the cover sheet. It said:

DAYBREAK
by
Walter Wilkes Booth
16th Draft

14

'Very interesting, dear. What is it?'

'It's a script,' she said with a squeak. 'We're in the movies!'

'We?'

'Well, me primarily, but I'm sure there must be something for you to do.'

We had been together for nearly two years and I still wasn't one hundred per cent sure when Amy crossed the line between patronising and sarcasm. Sometimes she zigzagged back and forth across it like a bootlegger during Prohibition.

I picked up the script and weighed it in my hand.

'So how big's my part?'

She glugged back the last of her wine before looking down at me, head on one side.

'Don't tempt me.'

'So how big's your part?' I leered.

'Don't be thick, Angel, you know I don't like it when you break into a sweat. They've asked me to design the costumes.'

'Who have?'

'Some big agency who are putting the production together at Pinewood. I've got two weeks to come up with some initial roughs. You can help me with the research.'

I looked at the title again.

'*Daybreak*? What's it about?'

'Dunno, haven't read it yet, but I have to look up American civil war army uniforms. The blue ones.'

'Naturally. The grey ones never did catch on. Grey is never going to be this year's black, is it?'

'Be serious,' she said, lashing out at me with a square-toed black shoe. I could tell she didn't mean it, though; she didn't use the heel.

'So they're seriously filming an American civil war movie at Pinewood? That would be just after the Bull Run service station on the M40 would it? I often nip in there for a Gettysburger and chips.'

She raised her heel, so I quit whilst I was ahead.

'It's not a war movie, it's a sophisticated, very stylish black comedy set in New York. It's just there are flashbacks to the hero's youth as a civil war cavalry officer. And, anyway, that's the only bit I need help with research. The modern day stuff I have a free hand with.'

'Hang on a minute,' I said, waving a beer can at her. 'The hero of this film was a young cavalry officer in the American civil war. On the Union side. Right?'

'Yeah, that's his backstory.'

Backstory? Guess who'd swallowed the film-buff's dictionary.

'So how old is this guy now?'

'I think he's 157 or maybe 189, I forget.'

'Amy, my sweet, are you sure this isn't a wind-up?'

I had been tempted to suggest it might be a porn film, but then porn film scripts don't go to the 16th Draft and who the hell needs costumes?

'No, it's a genuine . . . Oh, the age thing, I see what you mean,' she said, light dawning. 'It's because the hero is a vampire.'

Well of course he was.

Now it all made perfect sense, didn't it?

2

SCRIPT CONFERENCE

Of course Amy had every right to be in the movie business. She was, after all, one of the most sought after names in British fashion and I don't mean the catwalk, Britfrock scene which gets all the publicity and is basically the unwearable modelled by the uneaten, where everything above a size 8 comes with a special 'Blubberbutt' label. Amy had never experimented with plastic, rubber, tinfoil, feathers, pieces of Axminster and Wilton, fur fake or real, or metal chains – well, not in her designs. She was that rarity in the whacky world of women's clothing: she made things they actually wanted to wear and *could* wear without a second overdraft or the need for liposuction.

She specialised in blouses and tops – a one billion pounds a year market in Britain alone, of which she'd be quite happy to command a humble one per cent – and had been more than happy to sell out the business she co-founded to one of the national store chains. The two other co-founders hadn't objected. One was dead following a tragic road accident in the middle of an East End flower market. The other was doing three years at one of Her Majesty's stricter holiday camps for girls for a selection of offences under the Race Relations Act (the loony Nazi sub-clause) and conspiracy to cause explosions. It's a tough business the fashion business, like no business I know.

Their initial idea – *concept*, darling – was an all-purpose top which, with a series of drawstrings, could be made to be long or short-sleeved, round or plunging V-necked. The gimmick – *unique selling point*, sweetie – was the way they had sold them, to batches of office workers meeting in the local pub or wine bar for a girlie night. Except they hadn't really been there to 'sell' them, merely do market research, gaining instant feedback from their main target audience. Of course, the tops were snapped up but the idea of giving customers something they actually wanted

17

was so foreign to the High Street stores that Amy was able to command a premium price for her brand.

The *real* selling point, however, was the fact that the early versions of TALtops (named after the three founders: Thalia, Amy and Lyn) were *all* size 12, whatever it said on the label – which was invariably 'Size 10'. When you could pick your customers, targeting individual offices in the West End where more than sixty per cent of the staff were female and aged between twenty-one and twenty-five, that was fine and dandy. Everybody looked good in a TALtop, not just those with eating disorders.

Once the TALtop went national in shops, though, the concept started to get diluted. For a start, the national average size is 14 going on 16 (I had suggested a new '15' size to her but she'd treated that with the contempt it deserved just as if I'd suggested having 65 MB of RAM to a computer geek). So the idea of a 'Super TALtop' was born, then an 'Extra TALtop' and gradually – well, within a few months actually – the 'TAL' bit got dropped altogether and they became own-brand 'tops' for the store chains.

But the product was a good one – once Amy stopped using various dodgy sweat shops in the Brick Lane area – and sold itself. Even if her name wasn't on the label any more, Amy's future was assured on the bigger stage. She had had an idea and it had worked. There are very few people in business – any business – you can say that about.

Nowadays she was a designer, a consultant designer, a buyer, a consultant buyer, a non-executive this, an adviser on that. She wasn't a household name, she wasn't a brand, but she could make or break either when it came to clothes. She avoided the trashier end of the fashion press and certainly had a bigger selection of cuttings from the financial rather than the society pages. She liked it that way and so did I. It gave me a goal in life – to find out how much she was worth. I'd been on her case for two years and I still hadn't cracked it.

So when she came home that night and said she was going into the movies, it hadn't really surprised me. If she had said she was designing a Royal Wedding dress, then yes, I would have been impressed unless, that is, it had turned out to be for the Albanian Royal Family. If she had declared that she was reinventing hot pants and had signed up the Spice Girls to model them, then I would have had to query her sanity. If she had said she had the job of designing the costumes for one of the circus acrobat acts booked to open the Millennium Dome on New Year's Eve, I might have raised an eyebrow.

'So you're designing the costumes for a cowboy-vampire movie being shot in Buckinghamshire?' I asked, just to make sure I had got it right.

'No, you're not listening properly.'

I hated it when she said that. How could I not be listening *properly*? I mean, I was or I wasn't.

'It's a modern comedy set in New York among rich, smart thirtysomethings,' she said, putting her hands on her hips which I recognised as a Danger Sign (but only a Level 3 one). 'But they all happen to be vampires.'

'So it's a sort of *Friends With Fangs*?'

She smiled down at me, which is often a Level 2 Danger Sign, so I smiled back up at her. Endearingly. Charmingly. Warmly.

'I'm only smiling because you've driven me insane,' she said. 'What's your excuse?'

'No, no, I'm really, really interested,' I said.

Well I was. As soon as she got this off her chest she'd move so I could see how West Ham were doing.

'What exactly do you have to do for this film? Will you get a credit up there on the screen?'

'Damn right I will,' she growled, though I bet she hadn't thought of that until then. 'But I'll know more when we have lunch with one of the associate producers.'

There was that 'we' again.

'And when exactly will that be?'

'Tomorrow at one. Zoe's in St Christopher Place. The sooner I get a full brief the better. They start shooting over here in January. It means I'll have to rush through a few jobs in order to clear the decks.'

'And I suppose I'm driving you up the West End tomorrow?' I said.

'Why, how kind, darling.' She bent over and stroked my cheek with her hand and I hardly flinched at all. 'But you're coming to the lunch too.'

'I am?'

'Too bloody right you are. It'll get you out of the house for one thing. And give you something to get excited about. You don't seem to get as excited as you once did. . . Plus, somebody's got to read that fucking script by one o'clock tomorrow and I'm busy. Fancy a glass of champagne?'

I did a rapid mental stocktake and was pretty sure I had put a bottle in the fridge to replace the one I'd had whilst waiting for the pizza delivery.

'Yeah, love one.'

'I'll get it.'

She stepped over me and headed for the kitchen again.

West Ham were now losing 4-3.

Bugger. You take your eyes off them for a minute . . .

From the kitchen, a cork popped.

'Oh, by the way, did I tell you I've got the job to design the acrobats' costumes for the opening night of the Millennium Dome? We'll be invited of course, so we won't have the usual fight about where to see in the New Year.'

I raised an eyebrow.

The associate producer lunching us at Zoe's (one of several associate producers I was to discover) was a middle-aged woman called Gloria-Maria van Doodler. And I thought I had a weird name. Unfortunately, Amy couldn't resist introducing me in full.

'This is my partner, Fitzroy Maclean Angel,' she said maliciously. 'But he answers to the name Roy – or just Angel. Actually, he usually answers to the sound of a bottle opening.'

Gloria-Maria took my hand in a death grip. Up close I realised the 'middle-aged' tag was down to the plastic surgery. Her handshake was down to steroids, there was no other explanation.

'Great name,' she said looking me over. 'Great guy?'

'They're like cars,' said Amy casually as if I wasn't there. 'Look great in the showroom but after the first couple of thousand miles you begin to notice the bumps and the rattles and the uncomfortable bits.'

'That's when you should start thinking about a trade-in,' said Gloria-Maria with an evil little smile which said: I've got one at home too.

'Scots–Irish?' she said to me.

'No thanks, just a beer,' I replied, keeping the eye contact, not backing down. Women like this; they can smell fear.

She left it hanging between us for what seemed like an hour but was actually no more than thirty seconds.

'Sure you can have a beer, Fitzroy. Amy, you sit next to me. We need to talk while we eat.'

Amy scraped her chair out to break the tension and as we sat down I caught the eye of a waitress and ordered a Hoegarden wheat beer because it was the most expensive beer on offer. Gloria-Maria added a bottle of Swedish sparkling mineral water to the order and produced two packs of Marlboro Lights from a handbag the size of a suitcase, slapping them on the table.

'I *love* England,' she shmoozed, 'because you can still smoke in restaurants and bars. In Hollywood, it's like farting at a funeral. You know, Amy, some corporations not only have no smoking offices, they have no smoking sidewalks for fifty feet either side of their main entrance. You Brits are so lucky, being behind the times like you are.'

Not lucky enough. We've stopped burning witches.

She smoked three cigarettes whilst reading the menu and trying to persuade Amy to try the Thai crab vol-au-vent with the raspberry *coulis*. I double checked the menu just to make sure she wasn't inventing that and then searched in vain for steak-and-kidney pudding. That usually puts Americans right off, but I was out of luck and had to settle for the double-baked goat's cheese followed by the smoked duck breasts with parsnip compote and a spicy sweet corn cake. The menu might have been eclectic but the prices were anything but random. I wondered what the poor people were eating today.

Gloria-Maria ignored the wine list and demanded more mineral water for everybody, giving me the evil eye while she did so. Amy was glaring too and I couldn't work out why. I hadn't suggested having wine (though I would have liked to see the prices to use as a threat), as I was driving and therefore taking it easy and making my murky wheat beer last as long as possible. Then it clicked. I had ordered a main course *as well as* a starter. Oops! That was my card marked.

'So what do you think of the script?' Gloria-Maria asked Amy, blowing smoke out of the side of her mouth away from Amy. Towards me.

'Fascinating,' said Amy. 'It's funny, it's sharp, it's genuinely scary in parts and yet it manages to say an awful lot about love, and the loss of love.'

Gloria-Maria looked impressed and so did I. Amy had remembered everything I had told her on the way there.

'And it's *modern*,' Gloria-Maria enthused. 'It doesn't go for the Gothic, it's *relevant* to today's young audiences. Sure, it's funny but it's serious too. This could be a class act of a movie, maybe the only V-movie to be in serious contention for an Oscar – ever. The studio has high hopes for this one. No way is this not a good career move.'

'V-movie?' said Amy, puzzled.

'Vampire,' I said without thinking, then gave Amy a way out. 'You know, in the script you read to me. They never say the 'v' word to each other. I remember you laughing when you read that bit out.'

'Oh yes of course,' she said catching on. 'That was one of the nice touches which appealed to me. It was . . . clever.'

'I knew it would appeal to you Brits,' gushed G-M. 'Brits like clever. I thought it was almost cute the way the six main characters don't allow the use of the 'v' word.'

'What do they call themselves? The mortality challenged?' I asked innocently.

'They don't call themselves anything,' said Gloria-Maria, 'they just want to be left alone to live their lives.'

'Their very long lives,' I said, still with a straight face.

'But without ageing,' said Amy, almost dreamily. 'Without a single wrinkle.'

'Exactly!' breathed G-M, grabbing Amy's wrist. 'Tell me about it, sister!'

One of the scenes I had read to Amy in bed last night was where the thirty-five-year-old female lead saw the main advantage of becoming a vampire as being the fact that she could dump all her vitamins, creams, treatments and exercise regime. It struck me as a nicely ironic comment on the American obsession with physical beauty and vanity, but Amy and Gloria-Maria seemed to be thinking of it as a viable alternative to hormone replacement treatment.

22

'What wouldn't any woman give to stay looking like Zina Ray for the next two centuries?' said Gloria-Maria as if she was working out how much she had in her savings account.

'Zina Ray?' said Amy nervously, flicking me a glance.

It was my cue to come to the rescue.

'Wow! You've got Zina Ray to play Norma?'

Gloria-Maria let a smile crack her make-up as she stubbed out a Marlboro.

'That's quite a coup, isn't it?'

Amy nodded slightly. She'd got it now. 'Norma' was the female lead I'd told her about, obsessed with skin creams and vitamins and exercise, who eventually finds the best way to prevent ageing is to be killed by the bad vampire and then revived by the good, hero vampire – thus becoming a vampire herself.

'Zina Ray as Norma? That's brilliant casting,' Amy said, thinking commercially. 'She'd be on anybody's wish list to design clothes for.'

At least she knew who Zina Ray was, but then it would be hard not to if you had read a magazine or the gossip columns in the last twelve months. Talk about a hot property. She was certainly on my wish list to design clothes for, but not the sort Amy had in mind.

'Of course she has some sort of deal with Versace for her own clothes,' Gloria-Maria said with just a trace of envy, 'but I think Donatella does her proud. Did you see that gold sheath number she wore at the Golden Globes? No, you wouldn't, but trust me, Amy, it made her *shimmer*. I agree, the woman could wear a mail bag and still have every red-blooded male in the city beating their meat.'

'When do I get to meet her?' Amy asked, though funnily enough only just before I could.

'Oh, you'll probably meet her out at Pinewood when we start rehearsals in December.'

Gloria-Maria loaded another cigarette into her mouth and snapped her lighter.

'Not before?' asked Amy, and I was interested in the answer too.

'But you won't be designing for Norma, my dear. Most of the movie is present-day New York and so will be most of the

23

clothes. You know, Klein, Armani, Karan – the biggies with a worldwide rep. This will be an international picture after all, so we'll use brands people can recognise from Thailand to Timbuktu. Oh, and China. Big market for vampire films, China.'

That put Amy in her place. Being known from Stockport to Stoke Newington just didn't cut the mustard compared to Thailand or Timbuktu.

'So what exactly am I designing?' Amy said with a glint of steel.

Unlike me, she wasn't used to being given what she saw as the run-around.

'Your job is quite specific, Amy, my sweet. The pivotal scene in the script is a flashback featuring Jason and Amanda as they were, when they were in love, a hundred and thirty – or maybe forty, I forget – years ago.'

Amy looked blank.

Angel to the rescue again.

'We don't remember that scene,' I said. 'Do we?'

'Ah, well, it's being written as we speak. You must have gotten an old draft of the script. It's where Jason looks at the old sepia photograph of his long lost love which he keeps hidden in his apartment. Well, the director wants to expand that moment into a flashback – shot in sepia – to show Jason and Amanda as they were back in the 1870s, with Jason in his army uniform.'

Amy let this sink in then turned on me, just as our food began to arrive.

'You never mentioned an Amanda,' she hissed. 'Who the fuck is Amanda?'

I knew it would be my fault.

'Oh, she's dead before the movie starts,' I said.

I should have made her listen more carefully; told her there would be questions asked afterwards. But that was the trouble with today's go-getting businesswomen. If it didn't fit on one side of an e-mail (whatever) then it didn't get read, or if it did, it didn't sink in.

Basically, the plot of *Daybreak* revolved around NYC, the Big Apple, being able to support six vampire 'families' each with their own territory, living by rules laid down two hundred years before which were known as The Rules. But the families are not really families, they're just six individual vampires because vampires can't breed and The Rules say that if they fall in love and 'convert' a partner to vampirism, then they only have a limited time together before they have to part. Plus, the vampire who has converted the other one (cue here cries of: 'I vant to drink your blooood!') starts to fade away and die, having weakened himself – or herself – in the converting process.

It sounds better in the script; trust me.

So you have these six New York vampires, all looking smooth and thirtyish though in fact they're all at least a hundred and thirtyish, who are all cool and really successful and driving Porsches. They all have jobs, like literary agent, lawyer, public relations consultant and – best of all – tax inspector, but the key one is Jason, who just happens to be a bestselling author of horror novels.

The reason the vamps can do all these things is because they made some shrewd investments back in the Forties in pharmaceuticals and ophthalmics. This means that with a combination of appetite-suppressing drugs, special contact lenses and Sun Block Factor 95, they can exist in daylight and go about the city, day or night, not frightened of 'daybreak' as vampires of the old school were.

So they come across as a really nice bunch – one black, one gay, one a computer nerd, two women plus the die-hard romantic Jason – going to bars, going to work, screwing up relationships, cracking jokes, pulling strokes on each other. A regular cross-section of human life, except that they are all undead. But then, I've heard the population of Hackney described like that.

And life is fine and dandy because – plus point here in the campaign for audience sympathy – these vamps have worked out that with drugs and mental discipline (they've probably been to a shrink – they are American) they don't actually have to kill any more. A few sips here and there is necessary, but we're talking teacups of blood drunk holding the cup with the pinky extended rather than the buckets of blood on draught required in the old horror movies.

Then – cue dramatic music – a real vampire of the old school starts snacking on unsuspecting New Yorkers, leaving drained corpses, ripping off heads, baffling the NYPD and, naturally, giving rise to an angry village mob (or maybe Village mob) which is going to make life – or the afterlife – pretty tense for our vamp friends. So our hero, Jason, has to go out and find this rogue vampire and dispose of him, helped and occasionally hindered by Norma, his non-vamp journalist girlfriend who you just know is going to trip and sprain her ankle in the final chase sequence, because she's a girlie and that's what girlies do in movies unless they're played by Susan Sarandon.

It turns out that Jason's first love, when he was a Union army officer just after the civil war, Amanda, was a vampire and the vamp who converted him. Under vampire rules, she then does a bunk after their allotted term (I think a thousand days, but maybe I skimmed that bit), leaving him to pine away lovelorn for the next century or so, thinking she's gone away to die. But Amanda doesn't die, she finds another love, typical bloody woman, and converts *him* and they go into hiding in upstate New York in a small town called – wait for it – Daybreak.

It's *this* vampire – a guy called Victor – who comes looking for Jason a hundred and thirty years on, after Amanda has been decapitated (it's the only way to be sure with a vampire) by . . .

But I won't spoil it. Go see the movie.

'So basically, I'm designing the clothes for one flashback scene set in America in 1870, right?' said Amy after I had rehashed the plot for her.

'It's a crucial scene,' said Gloria-Maria who had, I think, realised that Amy was just as tough as she was. 'Isn't it, Fitzroy?'

That's right, drag me into it.

'Pivotal,' I said.

'It's a great script, isn't it?' Gloria-Maria said to me, waving a Marlboro in her left hand and a forkful of crabmeat in her right.

I felt that if I didn't get the answer right she would stab me with one or the other.

'Wonderful. Funny, compassionate, thrilling and –' I wondered how far to go here – 'very cleverly postmodernist with lots of beautifully crafted homage notes.'

'Homage notes?' Gloria-Maria said uncertainly.

Amy looked down at her food, but she was smiling.

'Oh yes, the critics will pick up all the postmodern references,' I said confidently. 'For example, calling Norma's boss, the newspaper editor, Edward J. Harker, I mean that's brilliant – a straight narrative line back to Bram Stoker and Jonathan Harker in the original *Dracula*.'

'You mean Coppola's film?' Gloria-Maria said uncertainly.

'Even further back. Back to the original text,' I said, open-eyed and keen.

I could see her thinking: Text? There was a text?

'And then there's a reference to a delicatessen, where two of the killings take place, which is called Murnau's. That's brilliant. Right back to the director of the original *Nosferatu*, almost as if it was completing a circle. A circle of homage.'

'Uh-huh,' she said slowly, not moving. Her crab had gone cold and her Marlboro had almost two inches of ash on it.

'Not forgetting the fact that there are *six* vampire families in New York, which is clearly a reference to the *five* Mafia families in the *Godfather* movies. That was Coppola again.'

'Mmmmm,' said Gloria-Maria, clinging to the one name she recognised and by now totally regretting she'd asked my opinion.

'But the clincher is Jason himself,' I said proudly.

'It is?' she echoed.

'His name – Jason Neville. Neville as in the hero of *I Am Legend*, the best vampire book ever written and made as the sci-fi movie *The Omega Man* with Chuck Heston. And those are only the things I've spotted. There are probably loads of other references I've missed. Wonderful stuff.'

I hoped Charlton Heston didn't mind me calling him Chuck.

'Yeah. Right,' said Gloria-Maria uncertainly. Then she dropped her fork with a clatter on to her plate and stubbed out the Marlboro. 'Wow. Your guy knows his movies,' she said to Amy.

'He has his uses,' said Amy, but before I could bask in reflected glory, she was back to business.

'So who's playing this Jason character?'

Gloria-Maria narrowed her eyes, put a hand on Amy's arm and played her trump card.

'Ross Pirie,' she whispered, knowing this would put her back in control, and sure enough, it did.

Amy's eyebrows did a little tango all to themselves and, though I'd never seen it before so I couldn't be sure, her cheeks began to blush pink.

'Oh well, that's all right then,' she said.

I didn't like the way her voice had gone quite husky all of a sudden.

Amy didn't get to meet the big guy himself for another two months and then only by chance. He had been 'passing through' London and decided to drop in on a pre-production meeting called by the art director and the set designer. Coincidentally, Amy had been invited to do a two-minute presentation on her costume designs, but she must have made an impression.

Her voice on the answerphone told me she was going on to have dinner with them in a private room at the Ivy and I wasn't to wait up.

3

TRANSPORTATION CAPTAIN

I got to meet Ross, as we now called him, three weeks before Christmas at what turned out to be the first of nine parties we were to go to with him before New Year's Eve.

Now I'm not one to turn up their nose at nine freebies in a month, especially not top-of-the-range quality freebies a couple of divisions above the usual Chilean Sauvignon and frozen canapés ones I got to gatecrash. Being with Amy hadn't improved the standard of party I attended, except that the women were a stunning cut above average, being mostly models. But models don't eat anything except flavoured air and they never drink in public, though I'm told their drink of choice is vodka and cranberry juice because it's the only thing which tastes as good coming up as it did going down.

But I knew the only reason I was tolerated was because of Amy and Amy was only tolerated, given her lowly status as a junior consultant assistant costume advisor, because Ross Pirie had the hots for her. When I'd raised this with her, she'd laughed and told me not to be ridiculous because 'Ross has the hots for every woman, that's his appeal.'

Well so did I, but nobody ever called it *appeal*. They'd called it lechery, lewdness, stalking, seven pints of lager syndrome and lots of other things, but never my *appeal*.

Still, it was a chance to rub shoulders and other body parts with the glittering souls who created the magic of the movies and get to find out what exactly a 'best boy' did, which was something that had troubled me ever since I first saw it on the credits of a film.

OK, so I did enjoy myself. Too much on more than one occasion, according to Amy, but I didn't see her stinting herself. And, best of all, the bills were picked up by Ross Pirie, so why stint myself?

It seemed only fair then that we should repay his hospitality in some small way and Amy had wangled two VIP invitations to the Millennium celebrations in the Dome down at Greenwich in the company of every Royal who could be prised out of Sandringham and every politician who wanted to be photographed with them.

When she'd given him the tickets, he had gone:

'Wow! A royal invitation! Two of the hottest tickets in town!'

'The second prize was four,' I'd said, but he hadn't been listening.

Instead, he had put his hands on my shoulders and looked into my eyes with the sort of sincerity which only comes from a theatrical background, and he'd said:

'Roy, can I borrow your wife – as my escort for the night?'

If Amy hadn't been standing next to him I might have tried to negotiate a price, but as she was, it was a done deal and he got no argument from me.

As it turned out, I was driving him to the New Year's Eve party to end all New Year's Eve parties, or so the papers said.

This wasn't because I didn't trust him – or Amy – it was because his regular driver was in hospital.

Because somebody had tried to kill him.

Trouble was, we weren't going to get there at this rate.

I had decided not to even try and get over the river anywhere near Westminster because of the crowds gathering in and around Trafalgar Square, as was normal, plus the extra bodies flocking to the Embankment for when the Queen touched off the River of Fire fireworks display to start the evening's entertainment. She was supposed to do it by activating a laser beam which would ignite the first fuse, but with a bit of luck she'd have a box of Swan Vestas in her handbag just in case.

I had heard that in the rehearsals held over the last few nights, the trial laser beam blasts for the fireworks and for the giant 'London Eye' ferris wheel had dazzled airline pilots coming in up the Thames on their approach to Heathrow. You wouldn't read that in the newspapers, of course. Nothing was going to be allowed to go wrong with the government's official celebrations to see in the next thousand years. That was why all police leave had been cancelled in the Met, although every copper I knew had put in for leave as soon as they heard the pubs were going to be allowed to stay open all night. But to be fair, the London Eye was the one cool thing about the whole mega-million-pound event and just as soon as they got it working I was determined to have a go. I was already trying to rehash the Harry Lime speech from *The Third Man* about peace, brotherly love, the Renaissance and cuckoo clocks.

Of course I would have to be with a film buff in order for it to work, because if you started up a conversation like that with a complete stranger, they'd have the padded van and the hypodermic waiting for you when the wheel finished its circle. But then I did have a film buff with me, in the back of Armstrong, who was loving the whole idea of meeting the *crème de la crème* gathering down at Greenwich that night. Even when I'd told him that he could make his current movie *Daybreak* twenty-six times over for what the Dome had cost, it hadn't spoiled his evening. And the Dome only got one year of life, not even a second chance when it went to video.

It was Amy, who had been down in Greenwich with several changes of her own clothes since breakfast, who had told me not to try and cut south of the river in Armstrong but to head instead for Stratford station in the East End, where special trains for VIP guests were being run to the Dome. The plan was to leave the West End north by north-west, then turn east down the Euston Road, zip through Islington and cut a way through the badlands of Hackney, then dump Armstrong in a side street and hop on the VIP special.

That was the plan. Amy's plan. All I had to do was stay sober until I had dumped Armstrong and make sure I didn't leave Ross Pirie locked in the back like a forgotten dog, or if I did, then at least crack a window open for him.

I was beginning to get an awfully bad feeling about it by the time we got to King's Cross. Just by the station entrance, stopped at the lights on York Way, the revellers were out in force, many of them committing lewd acts with the sole intention of frightening the horses, or whatever the local by-law called the offence these days. One young(ish) woman was leaning over the railings, laughing at the traffic and taking long pulls on a bottle of Diamond White. Her partner, standing behind her, had his long

31

white raincoat spread over her hips and buttocks so whilst you couldn't actually see anything from road level, the way his knees were going like pistons left little to the imagination.

'Are they doing what I think they're doing?' asked Ross from the back.

'They're doing what *I* think they're doing,' I said. 'And I hope the working girls on York Way don't spot them. That's the trouble with New Year's Eve; too many amateurs on the street.'

'Well, I've never seen anything like that before,' said Ross.

Then you can't be as old as you look, I thought but didn't say it. We were, after all, the same age, almost exactly. He had international stardom, an income measured in millions, a house in Los Angeles, a chalet in Switzerland, a personal hairdresser and a large chunk of the world's female population willing to throw their underwear at him.

And I was the one driving the cab. But I honestly didn't mind.

Nobody was trying to kill me.

Well, nobody I didn't know.

I had underestimated the number of cars on the roads that night and the number of streets cordoned off for parties, not to mention the number of cars simply abandoned in side streets as the owners hoofed it down towards the river to see the fireworks. And we heard the fireworks, like a creeping barrage in the distance, before we saw them.

'You guys declared war on anyone today?' Ross asked me.

'Dunno,' I said over my shoulder. 'Day ain't over yet.'

He thought about that, trying to spot the reference.

'John Wayne?'

'Jack Palance,' I said with a smile he couldn't see.

'That wasn't *Shane* was it?' he tried for a consolation point.

'*City Slickers*,' I said smugly.

'Damn,' he said quietly.

That made it 9–nil to me.

The sky began to light up with Technicolor explosions, the full widescreen treatment with a soundtrack of machine-gun rattles, deep booming thumps and an almost continuous rolling echo swelled by a deep-throated roar from a crowd of who knew how many.

'Impressive,' said Ross, but he wasn't that overwhelmed. He hadn't been recognised by anyone for nearly fifteen minutes and it was starting to grate on him. 'Where are we?'

'Islington,' I said, 'then we cut through Hackney and come out at Stratford.'

'I guess that was a dumb question,' he said. 'I'm no wiser. Hey, didn't you tell me that Hackney was your old stomping ground?'

I hadn't, not that I could remember, but Amy might have. I had once overheard her pointing me out to a fashion journalist as something she'd found in a skip in Hackney. As the journalist in question was so dense that light bent around her, she probably believed it.

'I used to live there,' I said cautiously. 'In my carefree musician days.'

In fact my cat, Springsteen, still did. Amy knew that and even allowed me visiting privileges. What she didn't know – I hoped – was that I was still paying the rent on Flat 3, at 9 Stuart Street. It was a peppercorn rent by London standards, fixed years ago in repayment for a favour I had done the landlord, Naseem Naseem. (No one could pronounce his surname so, like New York, we first-named him twice.) Amy thought the other people in the house were looking after Springsteen to avoid the disruption of moving him to her house in Hampstead, but if she'd thought about it she would have realised that not even I was cruel enough to leave Springsteen with a bunch of unarmed civilians.

'Were you ever in a band?' Ross sounded genuinely interested and I almost felt sorry to have to disillusion him.

'Not really. Sidesman, session musician, second trumpet on the backing track of something you'll only hear in a lift – an elevator – the odd club here and there. Mostly jazz.'

'But not any more?'

'Not for a while. Jazz became fashionable again.'

'And that was a problem?'

'Sure was. People took it seriously, started listening to CDs of people who really could play and realised how crap I was.'

I looked in the mirror and saw his brow creasing and then his

33

eyes widen. It was exactly the look he'd given in *Six Men Dead* when he'd finally worked out who the traitor was on the suicide mission to rescue the nuclear scientist from Japanese-occupied Java in 1942. I wondered if he knew he was doing it.

'So you only liked playing jazz when jazz was unfashionable, right?' he said slowly.

'That's about it.'

'I'll never understand you Brits.' He shook his head, making sure I could see him in the mirror, using it like a camera lens.

'I've never understood Canadians,' I said.

I could have said never understood *the need for* Canadians, but I just wanted him to know that I had checked out his basic CV, not start a fight.

'Me neither. That's why I moved to LA.'

'I think you should count that as a good career move,' I said and he laughed.

'Tell me about it. In a parallel universe I'm still playing rep theatre in Calgary, winter season. Jesus!'

The exclamation came as the sky lit up with a fresh bombardment of pyrotechnics; multiple starbursts rolling across the clouds, followed by the dull roar of the crowd's appreciation.

'I guess it must have been like this in your Blitz,' Ross said.

'I don't think the populace were out there cheering on the Luftwaffe,' I said, 'but I get your point. The shared danger. The community spirit. The prospect that the world might end at midnight, so there's just time for one last shag and two last drinks. The friendly London bobby walking out of the smoke, flagging us down with his bicycle lamp . . .'

'What?'

Actually the policeman didn't have a torch at all. He was wearing a fluorescent yellow jacket to reflect my headlights – and thus remove the alibi that I never saw him if I ran him over. But he was waving us over to the side of the road in no uncertain terms.

'What have we done?' asked Ross anxiously.

I should have realised that he would be nervous. As an American – OK, a Canadian who lived in America – when you were pulled over by the cops it involved flashing lights and sirens, then sitting nervously in your car like a good little citizen

34

while a cop with his hand on his gun took his time walking up behind you, willing you to make his day.

Ross Pirie had forgotten he was riding in what looked like a black London cab. All cabbies need is a cursory flick of the hand from a copper and they pull over. Why shouldn't they? They don't have anything to worry about. When did you last see a black cab getting a ticket?

'Relax,' I said out of the corner of my mouth. 'Let me do the talking.'

I'd always wanted to say that. No, actually I hadn't. *Wanting* to talk to the police is a concept I had never really got my head around, but it sounded good to be able to say it to someone like Ross Pirie.

''Appy New Year, officer,' I said as miserably as I could. 'You enjoyin' yerself as much as I am?'

'Oh, bundle of laughs,' said the copper, putting a hand on Armstrong's roof and leaning in towards my window as a multithunderflash went off somewhere above us. 'As if we didn't have enough on without somebody re-enacting the Gulf War up there.'

He jerked a thumb skywards just in case I had missed the fireworks display.

'Where you heading?' he asked, peering into the back of the cab.

'Stratford station.'

I hoped he hadn't noticed I was wearing a suit. I wanted to bond with him: cab driver and copper, both mugs for having to work on New Year's Eve.

'Forget it.'

'Why?'

'It's solid. They're even parking on the Bow interchange. We couldn't shift them even if we wanted to, but we've got orders to be all sweetness and light.'

'But what about the trains to the Dome?'

'Piss-up in a brewery springs to mind,' he said ruefully. 'You won't get near. They've screwed up the ticketing and the security searches are taking forever. Nothing's moving and there's a lot of people been there for hours getting really pissed off.'

'So what d'you reckon?' I asked, spreading my palms upwards.

'Go home and watch it on telly. Wish I could.'

He turned around so he was facing Armstrong's front and lowered his head until it was next to mine.

'Is that Ross Pirie in the back there?' he asked quietly.

'Yes,' I whispered.

'What's he like?'

'Top man. Good guy. Real gent. Generous with his tips.'

He leaned in even closer.

'You have to say that, don't you?'

'Until he's paid,' I said with a wink and the copper nodded his head.

'I think he's a tosser,' said the policeman quietly. 'But the wife likes him.'

'So what do we do now?' asked Ross once we were underway, though we weren't going anywhere fast. The copper had been right about the traffic and the parked cars and he hadn't even mentioned the impromptu street parties made even more dangerous by the fact that someone seemed to have armed all the drunks with sparklers and party poppers.

'We get as close to Stratford as we can, dump the cab and hoof it. I'll see if I can blag my way through security so we can jump the queue.'

There was a silence from the back which I took to mean he wasn't that keen on my plan.

'I'm not keen on that, Roy,' he said like a mind-reader. 'I don't want headlines saying I jumped a queue.'

He was right about that. The media were watching the opening night of the Dome like vultures following a limping elephant. Anything that could go wrong, would go wrong and magnified a thousand times.

'Fair point,' I said. 'It wouldn't look good if you were held up in a security check either, but I reckon they'll be pretty tight, what with the Queen leading the community singing and all.'

He leaned forward, resting his elbows on the back of my seat. I could smell his aftershave even though it was several hours since he could have shaved. How much did he use?

'I can't get out and hoof it, as you say, either.'

'Why not? I know I'm breaking the First Commandment of

Black Cabs when I say it, but sometimes *walking* is actually the fastest way of getting round London.'

'It's in my contract,' he said sheepishly. 'With the production company.'

'What is?' I asked stupidly.

'No walking.'

'You have a 'no walking' clause in your contract?'

'Not in urban areas and certainly not after dark. Not until the film wraps. Not without an escort. '

'You mean your bodyguard?'

'Yes. It's to do with the insurance cover for the movie.'

Now he tells me.

Though it was a fat lot of good expecting his bodyguard to be here tonight.

He was in hospital in the next bed to Ross's driver Frank. Somebody had tried to kill him too.

So there we were, another back street rat run cut off by the residents spilling out of their houses, drinks in hand, looking up at the night sky and going 'Ahhhhh!' in unison like they'd rehearsed it. A couple of them had wheeled their televisions outside and you could see far more of what was going on that way.

Ross Pirie thought that too. As I cursed and slammed Armstrong into reverse to try another side street, he said:

'Can't say I'm enthused about fighting my way on to a sub-way full of angry people, Roy. I think I'd almost be happier nursing a beer and watching CNN bring in the Millennium.'

'Seems reasonable,' I drawled.

He waited a beat, then tried:

'Jack Palance again?'

'Richard Widmark,' I said.

'Damn!'

I eased Armstrong towards Hackney proper. It was roughly on the way.

'You serious about holing up somewhere with a few beers, a TV, good music and some people who won't bother you?'

I almost said, who won't recognise you. Or even if they did, wouldn't give a shit.

37

'What about Amy? Won't she be pissed if I don't show?'

'Yes, but with me, not you. Hey, come on, it's not like you were on the Queen's personal guest list, so *she* won't miss you. And you can see the Dome any time. In a coupla months they'll have turned it into Disneyland anyway.'

'What about this open air concert?'

'Oh yeah, well you will miss Martine McCutcheon and Simply Red,' I said, conceding the point.

'Who?'

'Exactly.'

He thought about that for a few minutes while I found yet another street blocked by residents standing out with their kids in one hand and a glass in the other.

'You know a place with good booze, good music and good people and I won't see myself on the front page of the papers tomorrow?' he asked.

'Guaranteed.'

'Well, fuck it, I've got nowhere else to go tonight.'

'Good call, Ross,' I said as I turned Armstrong towards Stuart Street, where the party would be in full swing.

Number 9 was jumping. And so it should have been. I had, after all, personally invited some major party animals, given the benefit of my years of experience on the music choice and where to place my speakers, and had even supplied a thousand bottles of 'imported' French beer, a case of mixed spirits and a case of champagne. Actually, Amy had supplied the champagne although she didn't know it. She'd had five cases sent to her as Christmas presents by various buyers and department stores and there was no way she was going to drink all that lot herself.

Contrary to the scare stories six months before, probably spread by the champagne industry, there hadn't been a shortage of superfizz for the Millennium celebrations. Rumours had abounded about £4.99 bottles of eight per cent alcohol perry (made from pears) being passed off as £30 bottles of champers, but it hadn't happened on any sort of scale. Though there was one trick I had admired, when the bootleggers had not only added a fake champagne label to the perry, but had put on an extra neck label saying 'P&O Stena Line Duty-Free Sale Only'. Consequently, the people who had bought it had known that it was dodgy stuff, thought they were getting a bargain, and were unlikely to complain when they discovered it wasn't actually champagne at all.

But whatever they were drinking, the party-goers at Stuart Street had started drinking it early. Tuesday 28th December, I would have said if I'd had to guess.

The front door was ajar and green and purple flashing lights lit up the edge in time to the bass beat of the music belting out on to the street. The song was a club remix of 'It's Raining Men' and it was on the max.

The rest of Stuart Street looked deserted; locked up, no lights on. Everyone who hadn't been invited to Number 9 had wisely gone to a party somewhere else, or left the country, or rented a nuclear shelter for the evening.

'You know the people who live here?' said Ross, a slight hint of doubt in his voice.

'I live here,' I said, then quickly corrected myself. 'Well, I used to, before Amy and I . . . moved to Hampstead.'

He looked the place up and down, taking in the broken glass, the piles of cigarette ends and the half-empty bottles of French lager on the steps, the flaking paintwork on the door and windows and the handwritten notice on a postcard thumb-tacked to the door frame which said: BEWARE OF THE CAT.

'I get it,' said Ross thoughtfully. 'This is a stealth house.'

'A what?'

'A stealth house. Dennis Hopper's got one in the rough end of LA.'

I looked at him carefully, but he seemed to be deadly serious.

'You make the front of the house look like the back entrance to the projects after the graffiti artists have called,' he explained. 'That way people drive by never thinking that behind the door is a really cool pad designed in exquisite taste and which houses a superb collection of modern art. It wouldn't occur to anyone to burglarise it. It's a magnificent condo masquerading as a slum. Dennis is a really hip guy again, now he's been in detox,' he added as an afterthought.

I just looked at him.

'This is just a house, Ross,' I said flatly. 'Don't get your hopes up. Oh, and if anyone inside asks where you got that suit, just wink and say "Brick Lane". OK?'

'This is an Ungaro original,' he said indignantly.

'Yeah, well round here we buy them on Brick Lane, right?'

Well, at least we buy the labels which say Ungaro down Brick Lane.

He fingered his tie nervously; it was silk and probably an original as well.

'Should I lose the tie? This is informal, isn't it?'

'Hopefully this will be so informal it could be illegal in forty-eight States. Leave it, it's fine.'

On the doorstep the music changed to Shania Twain's 'That Don't Impress Me Much' but it didn't seem to make Ross feel at home. He grabbed my arm, clutching at straws as well as material, looking for a way of bottling out.

I was beginning to understand what was bugging him: people. He simply wasn't used to being with people. Now that's pretty loopy for someone whose face is known to millions the world over, but this was real, not stage-managed and he had no script, no minders, no public relations people and only me as a director.

'Shouldn't we have brought a bottle or something?' he tried.

'It's taken care of,' I said. 'Relax. Go with the flow and take your cue from me.'

He took a deep breath and nodded for me to push the door open.

The hallway held enough people to make the walls bulge and the staircase looked like a holding station for walking wounded, but I knew the main thrust of the party would be upstairs in Flats 2, 3 (mine) and 4. That was because Flat 1 on the ground floor was occupied by the reclusive Mr Goodson who was something, but not a lot, in local government. He kept himself to himself and everybody else in the house respected that. If he hadn't gone away for the Millennium, he would have bolted his door and put his ear plugs in like he always used to do when we had a house party. I only hoped somebody had remembered to tell him we were having one tonight.

'Angel!'

The scream stopped me before I could find an inch of space on the staircase. I was treading carefully because I didn't want to step on someone I didn't know and with the flashing disco lights it was difficult to tell.

'You made it!'

An arm encircled my neck and a pair of lips damp with gin squelched against my cheek.

'Said I would, Miranda, didn't I?'

Miranda lived in Flat 4 with Inverness Doogie. She was small, dark, humourless and Welsh, which was a bit like going through life firing on only two out of four cylinders. Doogie, on the other hand, ran on six. During the day he was a chef in the West End, working his way up the sugar strand career ladder through the kitchens of the posh hotels. By night he was basically a freelance football hooligan. Freelance in the sense that he didn't support any particular team, he just liked the prospect of a punch-up and football provided a universal excuse. Around Miranda, he was a lamb. After seven or eight pints on his own, he was a street fight waiting to happen. They were an odd couple, but they'd been a couple for quite a while now. If they ever formed a band – and it would be folk music, bet on it – I would call them The Celtic Twilight.

'You didn't have to put a suit on, you know. Or are you just showing off?'

She didn't give me time to answer, just linked arms with me and tried to steer me up the stairs. She needed the support more than I did.

'The vegetarian nibbles are in with Lisabeth and Fenella,' Miranda went on. They would be; meat had never crossed the threshold of Flat 2. 'The proper food's up in our place and Doogie's set up the bar in your place.'

'Why am I worried about that, Miranda?' I asked.

'Don't be. Mr Goodson is head barman.'

'Really? I didn't think we'd ever turn him to the Dark Side.'

'He's really loving it. Doogie showed him what to do before he went to work.'

'A Scotsman working on New Year's Eve rather than running a free bar? Now I do need a drink.'

'Oh don't worry, Doogie was only doing some poncy charity do up at the Dorchester. He got back half an hour ago with ten pounds of canapés. It seemed a shame to waste them.'

I hoped Ross didn't mind seeing them again. I looked over my shoulder to make sure he was still there.

'Who's your friend?' Miranda shouted at me as the music segued into some classic Sixties soul.

'Oh, that's Ross Pirie the actor and international superstar,' I said.

Even above the digitally enhanced boom of Detroit's finest, I could hear Ross groan 'Oh, no.'

'Yeah, right,' shouted Miranda. 'And I'm Kate Winslett. You always did think I was fucking stupid, didn't you?'

Sometimes it was just too easy.

4

SOFT FOCUS

'I know I haven't got over here as often as I should, but Amy's been keeping me busy. No, not the way you're thinking. Busy as in she's busy so I have to drive her here, there and everywhere, pick up that, take something somewhere, check the answer-phone, answer her e-mails for her, that sort of thing.'

It wasn't going down well, so I took another pull on the bottle of Jack Daniels and moved further over on the bed, patting the duvet next to me.

'I have tried to get away more – honest – but since she got involved in this film thing, life's been a bit strange.

'Yes, it really is Ross Pirie out there dancing with Miranda, though she thinks he's one of those professional lookalikes and I've hired him for the evening. I know Amy fancies him like mad and I know *that* sounds like sour grapes but it's not, really it isn't. I can't blame her, I mean he's a very handsome man – we're almost exactly the same age, you know – and I think he fancies her and he's rich and he's available, I mean like he's not married at the moment. I don't know why, but Americans seem to have a hang-up about things like that and maybe the same goes for Canadians . . .

'Oh God, I'm waffling aren't I?'

I put out an exploratory hand. It wasn't rejected.

'All I'm saying is that things have been mental lately. Amy's been doing these costumes for the opening circus down at the Dome, whilst getting her feet under the table with these film people. I know, I know, I'm talking about her again, but I'm just trying to say that she's had a lot on her mind and so she dumps all the stuff she can't handle on to me.

'Fair enough, we've had a laugh out of it so far. Young Ross is a bit of a party animal, you know, even though he usually behaves himself in public. We've been to the pre-production party, the get-to-know-the-second-unit party, the special effects unit's Christmas party, two at the BFI and he even flew us over to his place in Switzerland for three days of skiing . . .'

It was like talking to a Buddha. I took another pull on the bottle despite the severe look of disapproval I was getting.

'That's why I couldn't get over for Christmas,' I said weakly. 'Sorry, it sounds like I'm showing off but I'm not really.

'When I first met him, I thought he was a complete prat, all good looks and nothing up here.'

I tapped my forehead with the bottle, harder than I intended. It hurt.

'You know, like the models Amy deals with. Look under that immaculately coiffured hairdo and what do you find? The wheel's still turning but the hamster's definitely dead.

'But I'm coming round to him. Sure, he's got too much money and women throwing themselves at him, but, sod it, we all have a cross to bear in life. And I don't think he actually has much of a life, you know. Not a real life. Not a bugger-it-let's-go-down-the-pub-with-your-mates sort of life. In fact, I don't think he has any mates in that sense.

'He knows a lot of people – important people. And probably twenty per cent of the world's population knows him from the films or the gossip columns. But all that fame and fortune don't amount to much, not even a hill of beans, if you can't go off the rails once in a while.

'I suppose I feel a bit sorry for him, really. I mean he doesn't seem to have anyone he can trust, really *trust*. Not like I can trust you to be here when I decide to bother to turn up. There, said it before you could. I do miss you, you know . . .

'Shit!'

The door to the bedroom opened suddenly, boosting the sound of the music from the party and lighting up the bed like a prison spotlight.

'Angel? You in here? There's a phone call for you,' said Fenella primly.

'Sorry, kid, it looks like Amy's found me,' I said.

Springsteen jumped off the bed, casually slashed at Fenella's ankle with a paw as he passed her and slouched off to rejoin the party.

*　　*　　*

The communal house phone at Stuart Street is nailed to the wall by the front door. It still has an 'honesty' book hanging on a string, though the last entry in it was from over two years ago because everyone in the house had a mobile phone these days, even Mr Goodson. Amy had given me one, along with a pager (and she'd talked about electronic tagging), but they were in Armstrong's glove compartment, switched off.

I've never really seen the need for one as, statistically, every third person in London carries one. All you have to do is ask politely if you could borrow their mobile, as it was an emergency, and they'll all let you because otherwise it might look as if they didn't have one. And that would never do. It was a good system. You never paid for calls, you made new friends who felt superior because they had a mobile and you didn't, and – best of all – there was no itemised phone bill so Amy didn't know who I was phoning. And, of course, you were not at anyone's beck and call. You could drop out of circulation for up to several hours at a time, which is a radical concept for a lot of law-abiding citizens these days.

Unless you were being tracked by Amy.

I checked my watch with difficulty as I went down to the phone; having trouble focusing on the watch face and the edge of the stairs at the same time. It was almost 2.30 a.m., I had a half-empty bottle of bourbon in my hand, no idea where my suit jacket was, what appeared to be a salmon vol-au-vent smeared down my shirt and the music thumping out upstairs was purple patch Rolling Stones from the *Let It Bleed* era.

On all counts I reckoned I'd escaped the Millennium Bug.

I picked up the house phone which was dangling from its wire coil.

'Happy New Century, dear,' I said into the mouthpiece.

'What the fuck have you done with Ross?' shouted Amy.

Ross had actually been having the time of his life. When he realised that a quarter of the people there didn't know who he was, a quarter couldn't give a shit, a quarter thought he was a lookalike and the other quarter were too drunk to notice whether the roof was still on, he relaxed.

He not only relaxed, he mingled, he danced, he helped Mr

Goodson serve drinks behind the bar, he chatted indiscriminately with the riff-raff of Hackney who had nowhere better to go to see in the new century.

Fenella, who lived with Lisabeth in Flat 2, called him 'a sweetie' and asked me what he did for a living. I told her he was an accountant and she went away happy and impressed. I expected Lisabeth to hate him on sight, or as soon as she saw him talking to Fenella, but she actually warmed to him. I found out later that when he'd gone into their flat to watch the opening ceremonies from the Dome on TV, he had commented on the crystal she wore round her neck and noticed that the flat's layout conformed to feng shui best practice. Lisabeth, not used to having an interest taken in her, went all coy and almost blushed. At least she didn't hit him, something most men she's been in contact with would call a result.

Mr Goodson came up to me at one point and asked:

'Did that friend of yours say he was an actor?'

'He's done a few telly commercials, mostly for cars,' I told him. 'I'd say he was more of a male model with attitude than an actor.'

Inverness Doogie, thankfully, was well smashed and, as was usual in such circumstances, believed everything Miranda told him without question.

'Yon lookalike you brought, Fitzroy, he's pretty good,' he slurred, leaning on me for support. 'But I was cooking for that Ross Pirie today – yesterday – last night – up at the Dorch at a charity do he was swanning it over. He's much taller than your lad in real life, but it's no a bad likeness.'

My favourite car mechanic Duncan the Drunken dropped by with his wife Doreen sometime after midnight, but left after an hour as they'd had a better offer. On their way out, Doreen gave me a hug and breathed second-hand gin in my ear.

'Had a lovely chat with your friend Ross. He's a dead ringer for the real one, you know. I think he's a tosser meself, but Duncan fancies him.'

She must have caught the expression of stunned horror which shone through my booze-ridden features.

'Oh not like *that*. It's just that Duncan looks on him as a sort of role model.'

That left me even more confused. I couldn't for the life of me remember Ross Pirie playing a middle-aged, alcoholic Yorkshire-man who called his wife 'The Wife' and had the biggest collection of fake vehicle registration documents north of the river.

Whatever people had thought of him, Ross had liked them, though if he'd said 'they're my sort of people' I would have decked him.

I did notice that he stayed out of the way around midnight, or at least when anyone produced a camera to record the moment. He still wasn't sure that he wouldn't be in the gossip columns tomorrow. And he behaved himself from what I saw, which was not easy as at times the place was so crowded that moving from room to room was inviting a rape charge.

He didn't stint himself on the booze, tucking into double figures of bottled French lager and, at one point, sharing a bottle of twenty-five-year-old malt with Inverness Doogie, something which Doogie hid in the sink as soon as he saw me wander into his kitchen.

And twice I caught Ross down in Flat 2, his head pressed up against the television, trying to catch the latest news from the Dome celebrations, despite the music belting out and the crunch of people mashing bits of food into the carpet as they danced around him. When I got him alone I asked what he was doing and he said he was just trying to get an idea of what had gone on down in Greenwich, so he could have an intelligent conversation with Amy when he apologised for not making it.

I was impressed by that. It showed he was a true professional. I was also worried that I hadn't thought of it as well. I'd just have to wing it, as usual.

It didn't surprise me when Amy rang, though it had taken her longer to figure out where I was than I had estimated. I explained that I had left my pager in Armstrong and the mobile phone wasn't working because I'd dropped it and it was broken. And it hadn't been my idea to come here, we'd been stopped by the police and forced into a detour. And I hadn't rung her mobile phone because . . . because Ross hadn't wanted me to worry her on her big night and he knew how important a first night performance was and he'd watched every minute of it on TV and hadn't it all gone well and didn't HM the Queen look radiant?

I don't know whether she believed any of that or not, but at least it distracted her. Then she said she was coming round to Hackney and would be there in half an hour.

I thought: sure, and you're going to get a cab where at this time?

But I had learned not to underestimate Amy. So before I went back into the party, I checked I had my car keys in my trouser pocket and nipped out to Armstrong parked down the street.

Balancing the bottle of Jack Daniels on the roof I opened the front nearside door and reached into the glove compartment. I took out the mobile phone, dropped it on the pavement and brought my heel down on it hard – actually hitting it at the third attempt. Then I stuffed it back in the glove compartment and kicked the bits of plastic which had broken off underneath Armstrong.

There. My conscience was clear.

Amy arrived in style, stepping out of the back of a stretched Mercedes limo, the door opened for her by a large, well-groomed man in a tuxedo.

My first thought was that she'd somehow got hold of a car from Ross's movie producers but that didn't make sense because Ross himself had had to make do with me and Armstrong. It turned out that one of the guests at the Dome shindig was the Turkish cultural attaché and he had been so taken by Amy's pleadings that he had given her a lift in his limo, complete with teetotal driver and bodyguard, even though it was well out of his way. She can be quite forceful when she's pleading.

'Where is he?' she asked me before she was half-way up the stairs, though I had to lip read it above the music.

I jerked a thumb in towards Flat 2 and took a swig from the open bottle of champagne I had liberated on my last trawl through the party.

Amy peered into the gloom to see Ross in a clinch with Fenella. He appeared to be teaching her the Salsa to something mambo-Latino on the sound system.

'Well, he's safe enough there,' she said in my ear.

'Until Lisabeth spots them,' I said, handing her the champagne bottle.

She put it to her lips and took a toke, then snapped the bottle up to attention so that the wine fizzed and bubbled and foamed out.

'Where's Ross supposed to be tomorrow? I mean, later today?' she asked suddenly.

'I've no idea,' I answered honestly. 'Why?'

'Because I don't want the production company accusing us of kidnapping him, you dipshit!'

'He's old enough to look after himself,' I said, stung by her attitude.

'No he's not, he's a movie star!' she snapped back. 'If I get put in the doo-doo because of this, you'll be enjoying the rest of *this* as a suppository.'

She waved the champagne bottle in a threatening way, which was totally unnecessary as I was scared already.

We dragged Ross and Fenella into Flat 2's kitchen and closed the door, keeping the music down to a dull roar. Ross grabbed Amy in a big hug and started in on the compliments.

'Wonderful show, Amy. So sorry I didn't make it. It looked one hell of a spectacle. Jeesus, you must be shattered. I know how much nervous energy something on that scale takes. Did you get to meet the Queen?'

And so on. She loved it.

Fenella ran herself a glass of water from the tap then dipped two fingers into it and patted the fingers behind her ears. She gave me a wink and whispered out of the side of her mouth.

'Your friend Ross can certainly dance,' she said, with lots of raised eyebrows, patting water on to her neck to cool down. 'Says he learned on Broadway! If Miranda hadn't warned me, I'd have quite believed he was a movie star. You know what I'm like, I'll believe anything.'

She laughed and so did I, rather too loudly as she noticed I had been watching her chest heaving as she got her breath back.

'Who is it he's supposed to look like, anyway?'

I didn't get a chance to answer as Amy was thumping me on the shoulder trying to get my attention.

'Angel, listen up. It'll be best if we get Ross back to our place while one of us can still stand,' she said in her I'm-paid-to-speak-down-to-people-like-you voice.

'Which one?'

49

'Me, you idiot. Ross has to go to a party tomorrow night –'

'We invited?'

'I won't tell you again,' she said, waving the champagne bottle like she owned it.

Of course, technically speaking, she did.

'So I think it best if he comes home with us. We have a spare bedroom.'

'We do?'

'It's the place you sleep when you sleep alone.'

She said it like a line from *The Godfather* and it had an even more sinister ring than 'sleeping with the fishes'.

'Hey, I don't want to intrude,' said Ross.

'Please do,' I said, feeling I might be grateful for a buffer zone.

'Come on, Ross,' said Amy sweetly. 'We've had so much of your hospitality over Christmas, the least you can do is crash with us for one night. Look, I'm the most sober person you'll find in London, probably the only one. I've got champagne back at the house and Angel can cook us breakfast. He's good at breakfast. He watches all the cookery programmes on daytime TV.'

'They're really good, aren't they? Even though they do meat,' said Fenella.

I think we had all forgotten she was there.

'Well, if you're really sure . . .? I mean I only have an empty rented flat in Chelsea to go back to, so it's not like anybody'll miss me . . .'

'Then it's done,' said Amy and she held out her hand towards me. 'Keys.'

I handed over Armstrong's keys, hoping she would treat him gently.

The music stopped for a second then a Bryan Adams CD (definitely not one of mine) tracked in. Ross heard it too.

'One last dance before we go,' he said, grabbing Amy's wrist.

She shrugged after a nano-second's thought, like it had been a tough decision. Ross reached for the kitchen door then turned to me.

'If you don't mind, Roy, that is.'

I waved them on.

'Not at all, Ross. Greater love hath no man than that he lay down his wife for a friend.'

We made it back to Hampstead in one piece.

Well, Ross and I did, but I wasn't too sure about Armstrong's gearbox after the thrashing Amy gave it.

Once inside, Amy went to the fridge and cracked a bottle of champagne and I could tell from the look on her face that she was curious as to why there was only one left in there.

Ross went, like a homing pigeon, to our collection of movies on DVD, flicking through them, saying: 'Seen it, seen it, not interested, seen it, turkey, seen it, voted for it.'

When I asked him what he meant by 'voted' he said: 'For the Academy Awards. The Oscars. I'm a member of the Academy.'

'Cool,' I said. 'How do you get to join the Academy?'

'You have to be asked.'

There went another career window.

In the end we settled for a video of *Casablanca*, at which point Amy fetched a bottle of brandy to mix with her champagne. By the time Ingrid Bergman was offering herself to Bogart in exchange for the letters of transit, we were all drinking killer cocktails. When it got to the final scene at the airport, we were well down a bottle of Armagnac and we were all in tears.

Somewhere around 5.30 a.m. we showed Ross the guest bedroom. As he walked in unsteadily, he said:

'Great party, lovely people, great movie, good time.'

Then he fell, fully clothed, face-down on the bed.

Amy and I staggered over to him and leaned as close to him as we could without falling over ourselves.

'Do you think he's OK?' slurred Amy.

"Course he is,' I pronounced with perfect clarity. 'I saw his eye move.'

Ross had rented a small flat no bigger than a football pitch with a view over the Thames within inhaling distance of the Chelsea Physic Garden. He'd rented it on the advice of Gloria-Maria van Doodler, who lived in the flat below. It made me wonder just how much an associate producer got paid and whether there were any openings. I had no idea what they did, and didn't especially care.

I had woken up about 2 p.m. to find Ross already downstairs in the living-room, furniture pushed to one side, doing press-ups in the middle of the floor. He had a towel tied around his waist and his ankles crossed and was alternating his rhythm by moving from using two arms to just one. When he went one-armed, he would drink from a bottle of mineral water without a change in pace, then put the bottle down carefully and go back to two-arms.

Up and down, up and down, his flat stomach never closer than three inches to the floor, occasionally shaking his head to flick off the patina of sweat on his brow. I had no idea how long he had been there, but I counted forty-three press-ups on the trot before the strain proved too much and I had to go to the downstairs bathroom to throw up.

By the time I emerged and tried to scuttle by him and into the kitchen, he had his feet wedged under the sofa and was doing sit-ups, hands clasped behind his head. I kept my eyes to the floor and tried not to be noticed.

'Hi, there, Roy,' he said cheerfully without catching breath or varying his rhythm. 'I helped myself to juice but I couldn't find any decaff.'

'I'll tell Amy,' I mumbled.

'Hey, don't disturb her on my account,' he smiled.

It wasn't a problem.

When I took her a glass of orange juice and told her that Ross Pirie was downstairs in the lounge doing physical jerks, wearing only a towel, she was up and half-way down the stairs before I had one leg back in bed.

Not that I was allowed to stay there long. The film star and his costume designer had a power meeting over decaff and croissants and decided that I was volunteered to drive him home. His temporary home, as I discovered.

'Gloria-Maria found this place for me,' he told me as I drove, 'but I've only got it for a couple of weeks. She has an apartment on the floor below, though she's in New York until after the holiday, so it was kinda good you guys took me in last night. Could have been a tad lonely otherwise.'

The guy was amazing. There he was, a professional sex symbol, rich and fit enough to sweat off a hangover, complaining that he couldn't find a woman (or man) to drink or sleep with him on New Year's Eve 1999 in London. I reckoned I could have found about five million volunteers, give or take.

But then I was just jealous that he looked so good even in yesterday's clothes and so healthy on less sleep than I had managed. I was still having trouble talking. Fortunately, Ross was in chat mode.

'This is really good of you, Roy, driving me like this. I'd really like to drive old Armstrong here myself one day. If that would be OK with you, of course. I've never driven a London cab before, not even in a movie.'

Amy had wanted me to take the Freelander or at least the BMW but I persuaded her that nobody would notice Ross in the back of a black cab and even if they did, they wouldn't think twice about it. As far as I was concerned, in Armstrong I was less likely to be pulled by an enthusiastic copper (though there was little chance of finding one of those on New Year's Day) and given a breath test, which I would almost certainly still fail.

'You can take over now if you want,' I offered, thinking that way I could slump across the back seat and get some more shut-eye.

'My contract . . .' he said lamely.

Bloody hell, the guy wasn't allowed to walk or drive whilst he was filming. No wonder he was paranoid.

'So what are your plans for tonight?' I asked to change the subject.

'The director, Julius Cockburn, is sending a car for me about six.' He consulted his watch, which I estimated to be worth more than Armstrong. 'He's hosting a weekend at home down at his place in Surrey so we can go over the story boards of what we'll be shooting next week. He's trying to persuade me to rent a place in the country near Pinewood whilst I'm here. Gloria-Maria's fixed me up to see some . . . what do you call realtors here?'

'Thieving bastards,' I said automatically. 'Sorry, estate agents.'

'Right, estate agents. Well, I'm seeing one Tuesday to look round a place out beyond the Chalfonts of St Giles. Know it?'

I almost had a hernia suppressing a laugh at that one, but he couldn't possibly know what Chalfont St Giles meant in cockney rhyming slang.

'I know where it is,' I said. 'How you going to get there?'

I saw him thinking in the rear-view mirror and it wasn't an act.

'I hadn't thought of that. I just assumed Frank would be back from vacation.'

Except Frank, his regular chauffeur, wasn't on vacation, he was in hospital. Ross didn't say it, but it hung in the air between us.

'Why not take a cab?' I said foolishly. 'This one.'

'You volunteering?' he said with genuine, or well-acted, surprise.

'Doing nothing Tuesday,' I said with a shrug, which he took the wrong way.

'*That* was Jack Palance, right?'

'No, actually that was me, just now.'

I didn't have the energy to think up a con like, say, James Coburn in *The Magnificent Seven*, which would have sounded plausible enough.

'Well, I'd really like someone I could trust . . .'

It took me a few seconds to realise he meant me.

'Look, Roy, mind if I ask? What do you *do*?'

'This and that, stuff for Amy, bits and pieces, a consultancy here and there . . .'

'You haven't got a regular job, have you?'

'Have you?'

He smiled at that, making sure I saw it in the mirror.

'Good point. How would you like to be my driver on this shoot? Not as a favour, mind you, but professionally. You can use Armstrong here, I don't mind, or we can hire a car. I can pull down a top-of-the-range BMW or a Mercedes for the duration. The studio will pay. And they'll pay you. I'll get you on the studio payroll.'

And that was that.

The first day of the twenty-first century and there I was; in the movies.

5

CO-PRODUCTION

I didn't have to wait until Tuesday, I got the call on Sunday evening.

They were in trouble. Who else were they going to call?

Amy was in the kitchen trying to cook a turkey when I answered the phone. It was about eight o'clock in the evening and at the rate we were going, we'd probably eat about midnight. The problem was that she'd bought an organic, free-range, real meat turkey for us so we could have a nice, domestic Hampstead Christmas together. Then Ross Pirie had invited us to his 'little chalet' in Switzerland – which turned out to be about the same size as the set of *Where Eagles Dare* – and so the turkey had got stuffed into the deep freeze. Thinking about it, buggering off skiing in Switzerland *was* the traditional Hampstead Christmas.

Anyway, by some time mid-afternoon on the Sunday Amy had decided that the sad fowl had thawed enough to risk cooking, though our Estimated Time of Eating was constantly being put back as Amy couldn't quite remember the necessary weight-to-cooking-time ratio. When I suggested she converted pounds to kilogrammes, she just growled at me and muttered something about a roast turkey breakfast.

Normally, this extended waiting time would form a danger zone of temptation in terms of hitting the pre-dinner drinks, but I was taking it easy, sipping mineral water (Badoit, because it has a higher sulphur content than hell) and munching stuffed olives from the jar, laying off the alcohol. My Rule of Life Number 11 should have warned me: When your hangovers last *two* days, you're getting too old for them.

As it turned out it was just as well as I was sober when the phone rang.

'Twentieth Century Frocks,' I said automatically, thinking it would be one of Amy's mates.

'Hello, Roy? It's Ross Pirie, Roy. I'm with my producers and we need a meeting. It's kinda urgent. Sorry to disturb and so forth.'

'That's OK, Ross, you're not interrupting anything. I'll get Amy.'

'No, Roy, it's not Amy I want. It's you.'

'Me?'

'Yes, you. Can you come to a meeting right now? It's kinda important. Personally. You'd be doing me a favour.'

'Do I bring Amy?' I asked with my hand cupped over the phone.

'No. Let's leave her out of this.'

She was going to hate this.

'Where are you?'

'The Ritz. In one of the suites, registered to Don B. Sager.'

A suite at the Ritz? She was really going to hate this.

'And by right now, you mean like, right now?' I asked stupidly.

'Quick as you can. Is it going to be a problem for you?'

Cutting Amy out of the loop was one hell of a problem. This movie thing was all hers. She was the one wanted for her design skills, I was just there by accident. And yet I was the one being asked to meet the big cheese producer, Don B. Sager himself. It wasn't fair just to ignore her like that. Who could blame her if she went ballistic, thinking I was suddenly higher up the movie pecking order? This one needed a lot of careful thought, diplomacy and delicacy of touch.

'Do they still do valet parking at the Ritz?' I asked loudly.

There wasn't just one big cheese waiting for me at the Ritz, there were three. Plus two smaller cheeses. In terms of relative importance, I was the crumb left uneaten on the mousetrap by the mouse.

In fact a misplaced hand grenade in that hotel room would have taken out the star, director and producer of the movie *Daybreak* before an inch of film had been shot. I was quite surprised they were all allowed to be in the same place at the same time, a bit like members of the Royal Family never being allowed to fly on the same plane. Gloria-Maria van Doodler would probably have been missed by someone somewhere,

I suppose, and Lin Ooi-Tan, Ross's fearsome personal assistant, wouldn't have even been scratched. Shrapnel would just have bounced off her. No, it wouldn't have dared to come that close.

The two women glared at me in greeting, though I hadn't done anything to upset either of them this century – so far – while Ross thanked me profusely for coming then introduced me to the two men sitting on one of the three sofas in the room. Both held balloons of brandy and were smoking cigars, but there the similarity ended.

I had expected Julius Cockburn to be the archetypal producer from a thousand Hollywood clichés: small, bald, cigar-chomping, New York Jewish fast-talking, hustling here and scurrying there to do his quota of fifty different deals a day, but only after he'd fired three writers and slept with two starlets before lunch.

He was none of those. He was about fifty-five, had a mane of light brown hair framing a leathery face and wore a pink silk shirt with loose double cuffs turned out over the sleeves of a navy blue blazer which had leather elbow patches, something I hadn't seen for years. He wasn't even American, but quintessentially English and in fact he reminded me of my old English teacher, though I didn't think Julius had a record for fraud.

Julius also wasn't the producer, he was the arty one – the director – with a string of award-winning commercials, some worthy TV dramas and no doubt a few movies under his belt, though I couldn't think of one I'd seen.

Don B. Sager sounded as if he was a director of the carpet-chewing, God-dammit school, who had come up the hard way, learning his trade on location, mixing drinks for Peckinpah, blowing up trains for Frankenheimer, doing the second unit motor-bike chases for Sturges.

In fact he was the producer and he'd been too young to see a Peckinpah film on cinema release. He was about ten years younger but a foot taller than me, fit and slim enough to suggest he took his gym membership seriously and his suit looked like it was another Ungaro and a real one, from Milan, not Brick Lane.

He didn't come anywhere near my idea of a Hollywood producer, but then I hadn't actually ever met one before. I suspected, though, that when he went to all those power meetings with the studios, he had to produce his MBA in Film Production and wave it around before they took him seriously. At least he was American.

'Mr Angel, thank you for dropping by,' said Don B. Sager, holding out his hand for a shake which was much weaker, and damper, than I expected.

'I was in the area . . .' I said vaguely, knowing that anywhere in southern England and the Ritz were as good as next door to each other to most Americans.

'So was I,' he said pointedly looking at Gloria-Maria as he did so, '– fortunately. Gloria and I only flew in this afternoon, right into this.'

'Don, they had the apartment building staked out when I got there. What else could I do?'

Gloria-Maria spoke in a little-girl-lost voice I hadn't heard before. Ross had gone over to stand by the window, his arms folded, watching the reflected lights of Piccadilly in the glass. He said nothing, offered no clues. Lin Ooi-Tan just stood and stared at me.

'She knew Ross was weekending with me, Don. What else was she supposed to do?' Julius drawled in a cut-glass accent, staring deep into his brandy glass as if seeking inspiration.

Don Sager turned on Julius.

'Stalled. They wouldn't run anything without confirmation or denial and by tomorrow morning we could have got the lawyers and the public relations people on the case.'

'Tomorrow's a Bank Holiday,' I said helpfully. 'Nobody works in this country.'

'They do if they work for me,' he said, but it was an honest comment as far as he was concerned, not a threat.

'He doesn't,' said Lin, staring at me. 'There's no logic to getting him involved. No logic at all.'

I wasn't about to disagree with that. I would think twice before disagreeing with anything Lin said. She'd had me pegged as a disruptive influence from the start. And in any case, they hadn't even offered me a drink yet, let alone offered me a starring role so I was free to walk any time just as long as I didn't blow it for Amy.

But before I had to speak, Ross did.

'I trust him,' he said forcefully. 'I want him here.'

He said it without moving, still staring at the night through double-glazing, arms folded, a look of powerful concentration on his face. It was impressive.

'Well, that's settled then,' said Julius quietly, flicking an imaginary speck of ash from the sleeve of his blazer.

'Ross seems to think you can help us smooth over a little local problem which has developed,' said the young Don Sager, taking his cue.

He may be the big producer, but when his leading man spoke, he listened.

'Please,' said Ross, still looking at the window.

Sager didn't blush, just took it in his stride.

'We would like you to help us, please. If you can.'

I sat down in a leather chair even though no one had given me permission. I'm like that sometimes, impetuous as hell.

'So what have the newspapers got on him?' I asked, creaking my buttocks into a comfortable position.

There was an electric silence for about three seconds, then Lin and Don Sager spoke together.

'How did he know that?' said Lin.

'Who said anything about newspapers?' said Don.

They looked at each other, then both of them looked at me. Everybody was looking at me except Ross, who was doing his Garbo impression out into the night.

'You did,' I said, answering Don's question and ignoring Lin.

'I did?' Don said it like it wasn't actually coming out of his mouth.

'Gloria-Maria said her building – where Ross is staying – was "staked out". That means either police or the newspapers. As she's here and not down the Lucan Place police station, I assumed it must be the newspapers. Then you said they wouldn't do anything without confirmation, which . . . well, confirmed it. It also shows you're American if you think the British press waste time by confirming things like facts.'

I saw Ross smile at his reflection in the window as if I had just passed some sort of test. Or maybe he was just admiring his reflection. After all, he was an actor.

'So what have they got on him?' I asked when no one volunteered anything.

Don waved his cigar at Gloria-Maria, empowering her to talk. He didn't actually like cigar smoking, he just liked pointing with it.

'He didn't sleep in the Chelsea apartment on New Year's Eve,' said Gloria-Maria sternly, 'and was seen returning yesterday afternoon in a cab. I – we – suspect that the house manager of the apartment block is on somebody's payroll and he's the one who dropped the dime on Ross.'

'So he took a cab – mine, actually,' I said. 'It's not an indictable offence. Well, not yet anyway. And he stayed out all night on the biggest party night this century. Where's the problem?'

'Sometime this morning an eighteen-year-old punk whore rings the newspapers and claims that she saw in the new century in the back of a black London cab, having the ass screwed off her by none other than Ross Pirie.'

There was plenty of venom in Gloria-Maria's voice but I couldn't tell whether it was reserved for the punk, the whore or the fact that she was eighteen.

'So the story is: Love Rat Ross Doesn't Leave A Tip?'

No one laughed; not even Ross, though he could have been acting.

'They've even got the number of the cab,' said Don.

'K258 GPU,' I said.

Don looked at Gloria-Maria, who nodded.

'That's right,' he said.

'It's mine. I still don't see what your problem is, unless you think the story's true.'

It took a few seconds for it to sink in. That was exactly what they suspected even if they dare not think it aloud. I was there to back up Ross's story.

'Look, the whole thing's bollocks. Ross was with me and a houseful of people who will vouch for his whereabouts on New Year's Eve. Tell the newspaper he went to an unscheduled party in aid of a Third World charity. He was a surprise guest. Made their day. It's our word against theirs.'

I thought that sounded pretty good, or as good as anything their PR people would come up with. And as far as they were concerned, Hackney was the Third World.

'That might not be good enough,' drawled Julius in an accent which was more cut glass than the thing he was drinking brandy from. 'The young lady in question knew the cab's number plate and what Ross was wearing, even down to his tie, a Gianni Campagna original. And she's set a time frame for the alleged incident when Ross admits he was in the back of your cab.'

'That would be what? After we'd left the Dorchester and before we got to Hackney?'

'Exactly the time when we have no independent witnesses,' said Lin grimly.

'Except me,' I offered.

'*Reliable* witnesses,' she hissed.

'Which newspaper are we dealing with?' I asked Don, ignoring her.

'That's not an issue, I think,' he said crisply.

Because he didn't want me selling my story to them. So much trust in this business. (I'd already worked out that I wouldn't get much compared to the heartbroken girl, and anyway, Amy would kill me.)

'But it's one of the Red Tops,' I presumed.

'Red Tops?' Don looked puzzled.

'The tabloid papers,' said Julius as if talking to a child, which wasn't far off. He was old enough to be Don's father. 'In England they've got red mastheads.'

'Get it. Yes, it's one of your mass circulation tabloids. They can do a heap of damage to our image.'

'Sure, but they've got lawyers and they'll listen to your lawyers. They don't like showbiz lawsuits they can't win.'

'It's Sunday brunch time in California,' said Gloria-Maria. 'We can't find our lawyers.'

'But you have a line to the paper?'

Don nodded.

'I'm dealing with the features editor, I think he calls himself. I'm supposed to call him by his deadline.' He looked at his watch. 'Nine thirty.'

That gave us about fifteen minutes.

'Then here's what you do,' I said, sitting back in my chair. 'You call this guy and say you're a lawyer from the studio or the company, whatever, and that you intend briefing an associate firm over here in London to take out a restraining order on this woman while Ross is in this country. You believe her to be a known stalker who goes under the name of . . . let's say . . . Fenella Binks, and she's wanted by the FBI in America. And you ask them to fax over a photograph. They'll have taken lots by now. Get the fax number of the hotel.'

'We have a fax machine here in the room,' said Don.

They would have, wouldn't they?

'Then get it faxed here pronto. And don't forget to add, casually, that of course you'll be suing for libel as well.'

'Why not just threaten the libel?' asked Lin, determined to find a flaw in my master plan.

'Throw in the stalker element. The papers here are paranoid about stalkers and paranoid about anyone suggesting they are helping them. Stalkers give their own reporters a bad name. It might just spook them enough to miss their deadline.'

'Except we don't have a lawyer here,' she said with a sneer.

'I know. But you've got an actor,' I said.

Ross turned from the window, and he was smiling.

The boy did well. So well, we all gave him a round of applause as soon as he put the phone down. He had got the fast-talking lawyer act off pat. I was standing next to him and I didn't recognise him as Ross Pirie.

'They're faxing a photograph over any minute,' Ross said, flushed with modesty at his performance. 'This editor guy says she's called Kirsty Brown and she's British, but he said he'd send a picture just to jog Ross's memory. I almost barfed at that. Think it'll work, Roy?'

'We've sown a few seeds of doubt,' I said. 'And if they've tried to trace a real, licensed cab they'll have drawn a blank with the number she gave them.'

'But that is your number, right? Armstrong's number?'

'Who's Armstrong?' asked Don, sharp as a pistol.

We both ignored him.

'Yes, it's Armstrong's registration, so she must have seen us somewhere along the line.'

'What about your pad in Hackney? Can you trust the people there?'

At least he had the decency to look embarrassed when he asked.

'I'd trust them with your life,' I said.

Before he had a chance to think about how economical I was being with my certainty, a fax machine began to whirr and hum. We found it in the wardrobe which housed the giant TV and VCR unit.

Only one sheet came through: a head and shoulders shot of a girl in classic showbiz ten by eight pose, all eyes and teeth, looking up into the camera from under a dangling lock of hair. Ross ripped it out of the machine.

'I've never seen this girl before in my life,' he said, shaking his head, showing the others.

'Yes you have,' I said, even before it got round to me.

Now I really had their attention.

'Is there a fax number on the top, saying where it came from?'

'Yes. Why?' asked Ross.

'Give me a pen.'

I printed the message on a piece of hotel stationery and we faxed it through.

All I wrote was:

Is this the same 'Kirsty Brown' who appears on the external security camera film taken outside King's Cross station at 2210 hours on 31 December? If so, the police wish to interview both her and the man she was with.

'Now I remember her,' said Ross. 'She must have recognised me in the back of Armstrong.'

'She had quite an eye for detail,' I said with more than a little admiration, 'considering she had other things on her mind at the time.'

'How did you find out about the security cameras?' Ross whispered so the others couldn't hear.

'What cameras?' I whispered back.

Ten minutes later, the features editor rang and spoke to Don Sager.

It was, said Don, one of the most grovelling apologies he'd ever had the pleasure of hearing which, for a Hollywood producer, was really saying something.

From that moment, I was on the team and not just as a replacement chauffeur.

Don Sager sat me down on one of the leather sofas and explained it all to me while Gloria-Maria yelled at Room Service until they brought up champagne and smoked salmon sandwiches, partly to celebrate our 'public relations damage limitation victory' and partly because none of us had actually eaten anything for about eight hours.

I, of course, was still waiting for my Christmas turkey dinner. Don and Gloria-Maria had come off a long haul flight from LA and Julius had driven Ross up to London from his country mansion (I was convinced it would be a mansion, just as I was convinced he had labradors running around it) when he'd got the first panic call from Gloria-Maria. Lin had been spending 'vacation time' with her family and I almost said how noble it was of her to fly back from Hong Kong at such short – actually impossible – notice, when she let it slip that she'd been staying in Gerrard Street just down the road in Chinatown. Then I remembered what Ross had said about fireworks and that it wasn't Lin's New Year yet.

'You know what it takes to make a good movie, Roy?' Don asked me, pouring out the half-glass of bubbly I was going to allow myself.

'A big star?' I nodded towards Ross, who was deep in conversation with Lin. 'Who is also a really good actor?'

Don checked that Ross wasn't listening and said:

'Nope.'

'Thirty million dollars?' I tried.

'That would help, but not essential.'

'A talented director?'

'Jees-us, no!' Don laughed, not minding that Julius, supposedly going through some papers with Gloria-Maria, overheard him.

'A good, literate script?'

He stopped in his tracks at that one.

'Get real, Roy. No, what it takes is *trust*. I learned that very early in this business. If the money-men trust the producer and the producer trusts the director and –' He checked that Ross and Lin were still talking – 'especially if the star trusts everybody around him, then that old movie magic just seems to happen.

'Why do you think so many film makers use the same people over and over again? Same cameramen, same second unit crews, same supporting cast of bit-part players. You find somebody you can trust and you stick with them.'

'If they've got talent, that is,' I agreed.

He looked surprised.

'No, the talent thing comes later. The key is get a group around you so everybody's comfortable. The days when the director feuded with the producer, or when two stars hated each other on set, they're gone. Too expensive. Get your team together and keep it tight. Everybody one big happy family. No strangers unless absolutely necessary. Oh sure, you have to bring in a few new faces on screen to ring the changes and you have to work with new writers all the time.'

'You do?'

'Oh yeah, they burn out so fast. Name me a writer who's ever scripted *two* good films.'

'Raymond Chandler . . .' I started.

'Who?'

I should have known that Don was the type never to have seen a black-and-white film and it's pointless arguing with people like that. I didn't even bother telling him that Chandler had once described producers as 'low-grade individuals with the morals of a goat and the artistic integrity of a slot machine.'

'So you trust everybody except writers?' I said, to get him back on track. 'Where do I fit in?'

He glanced over at Ross, who was walking Lin to the door of the suite, hand on arm, whispering in her ear.

Don dropped his voice.

'Ross trusts you, man. For whatever reason, he's taken a shine to you and put his mark on you. And today you've come through for him big time. Stars like Ross, and he's gonna get bigger, they're up there on the screen and it's like everybody in the world owns a piece of them. They live in a closed circuit, a real Fantasy Island. They're in the public eye and that's what pulls them the big bucks, and they love that but what they hate is not being able to take a crap without worrying the toilet's bugged. They eat and breathe flattery to feed their egos, but deep down they know they shouldn't believe it. Trust, you see? On both counts. They need some people – just a few – around them that they can trust. Trust not to rat them to the media when they throw one on, or snort a line or screw somebody else's wife. And somebody they can trust to tell them the truth now and then, but not too often. Tell them when the bullshit really is bullshit.

'That's why Ross has his own personal entourage whatever the movie he's making. Gloria-Maria's worked on his last four pictures. Lin's been with him for five years now. He probably doesn't fart without checking with her. Marcus, his hairdresser, seven years. You met Marcus yet?'

I shook my head.

'There's a treat coming round the mountains when she comes,' he said with a snigger. 'Then there's Frank, who has always driven Ross when he's been in England, like forever. Until his accident, that is.'

'I'm getting the picture, Don,' I said. 'But tell me about Frank's accident.'

When I got back to the house in Hampstead, I found Amy in the kitchen slaving over a hot stove. Well, not so much slaving as leaning.

She had changed into a blue silk sheath of a dress and high heels, no doubt to give me some idea of what I'd been missing whilst I had been out playing with my new film industry friends. To protect it she wore a long butcher's apron with the Ram Brewery logo of Young & Co of Wandsworth, while she used a fork to prick the golden brown skin of the turkey resting in its roasting tray on top of the cooker hobs. She had a cigarette in the corner of her mouth (a bad sign) and a glass of red wine in her left hand. There was an empty bottle of an Australian Malbec on the work surface. (Very bad sign.)

'Isn't it bad luck to eat turkey now we're in the movie business?' I asked, sidling up to her from behind and putting my arms around her, feeling her spine stiffen like a ramrod.

'We?'

She said it like Lady Bracknell said 'handbag?' but she did it without dislodging a single speck of cigarette ash.

'I'm on the payroll, in the A-team, part of the great co-production of assembled talent which unlocks the sluice gates of creativity to produce magic up there on the silver screen.'

I ran my hands over her thighs.

'You're not wearing your Christmas present,' I complained.

'It's not your birthday, is it?'

She knew how to hurt, Amy did.

But the Christmas present thing was her own fault. She was the one who had decided to charge off to Switzerland to Ross's Christmas bash at the last minute, so I hadn't had time to do my usual Christmas shopping between 3 p.m. and 5 p.m. on Christmas Eve. A pair of genuine silk stockings, with hand-knitted seams, had seemed the ideal present and it fitted easily into my on-flight luggage. OK, so they were still in the Heathrow gift shop bag when I gave them to her, but it's supposed to be the thought that counted.

'But they're fashionably old-fashioned, aren't they?' I pleaded.

'No, just old. Fashion has nothing to do with it.'

She stabbed the turkey with the fork. Rather violently, I thought.

'Then how about these?'

I dug into my jacket pocket and came out with a small red box which those very nice people at the Ritz had gift-wrapped in shiny red paper with a silver bow. I curled it around her waist and held it to her cleavage.

'What's this? What have you done?'

'Nothing. Call it a late Christmas present or a let's-celebrate-my-new-job present. Whatever.'

She stuck the fork into the turkey, put down her wine glass and passed the cigarette over her shoulder for me to dispose of. Ash fell down the front of my shirt as I took a couple of hits before posting it into the empty wine bottle, the nicotine rush making me quite light-headed.

By the time I looked back, she had the gift wrapping in shreds at her feet and was snapping open the little box inside.

'They're gorgeous!' she breathed, then recovered quickly. 'I've got absolutely nothing to wear with them.'

'That sounds like a plan,' I agreed.

I helped her pull the apron over her head so she could try them on, which meant I could get back up close to her and actually see what was in the box myself.

They were ear-rings – single square-cut emeralds surrounded by diamonds, drop-shaped in a twisted pendulum. Amy ripped out the plain studs she was wearing and threaded them through her lobes.

'They must have cost a fortune,' she said as she rushed by me to find a mirror.

About a thousand quid, according to what I had overheard when Ross had made Lin go down to the shop in the hotel and buy them on her Amex card. Lin had complained saying it was 'too much', which I thought was a bit rich considering I had kept them out of tomorrow's papers. And then I'd heard Ross muttering that the production company would pick up the bill and anyway, they were for Amy, who was already on the production team, not me. He hadn't wanted to insult me by offering me cheap gifts for saving his bacon. I wish he'd asked me about that.

'OK, Angel, you've bought yourself some time,' said Amy, flouncing back into the kitchen and turning her head so that the ear-rings swung dangerously close to putting an eye out. 'But you'd better start talking about this new job you've got with *my* client.'

'Are we going to eat this?' I pointed at the turkey.

'While you talk. I'll carve us a chunk, you open some more wine. I couldn't be arsed to do vegetables and stuff.'

'Fine by me,' I said and walked across to the wine rack to select another Malbec.

Behind me, with her back to me, Amy sharpened the carving knife on a wooden-handled steel.

'Breast or leg? And, Angel, think before you speak.'

6

BACKSTORY

Frank Shoosmith had faced redundancy in the 1980s by ploughing his pay-off into an ex-demo Mercedes, lavishing it with tender loving care and registering himself as a luxury limousine with at least six different minicab companies.

Because he lived in Wimbledon he was one of the few drivers always on call south of the river and west enough to be available to do pick-ups from Heathrow and not mind the stick he got from the black cab drivers on the ranks there. It was also not much of a run up to Pinewood Studios, just round the M25 and off the M40.

The first time he picked up Ross Pirie, he had no idea who he was. But he did know the way to Pinewood and Ross didn't. He also didn't mind waiting around for a couple of hours to take him back to his hotel at Heathrow. This was before Ross was a big enough star to warrant West End hotels or rented apartments in Chelsea and, it being his first trip to Britain, he didn't realise that minicabs got paid waiting time and that Frank Shoosmith much preferred to stay out of central London in the rush hour. Add to that the fact that Ross didn't know many people here and Frank was a personable enough guy to chat to, and it was only natural that Ross asked for him on his next trip.

No errand was too much trouble for Frank to run and he never complained about hanging around or working late. He got on well with the other drivers who regularly worked Pinewood and realised they were testing him when they asked where Frank drove Ross after hours and if he was 'pulling anything' or 'playing away from home'. They also asked him if he kept a stash of cocaine ('they all use the old snow candy') for his passengers, or if he wanted some just in case. Frank kept his mouth shut on all counts, except to say that his beloved Mercedes was a drug-free zone. As far as the regular drivers were concerned, these were the right answers.

Within a year he was a regular himself, working for the production companies themselves, driving cars which they leased en bloc. Sometimes this meant no more than seven months' work in a year, but it was well paid when it happened and he always had his Mercedes back in Wimbledon and the Saturday afternoon wedding trade to fall back on if times got hard.

In the last stages of pre-production on *Daybreak* (and Frank could have told you exactly who was getting paid what on the picture, from conversations he'd overheard) in November and early December, Frank had been called up and had taken delivery of the new BMW Series 7 leased for the duration of the shoot.

As was normal before the actual shooting schedule of the film kicked in, things were pretty chaotic and Frank was here, there and everywhere driving not only Ross but also Gloria-Maria, Lin, Julius and just about anyone else as and when called on. Given the time of year, there had been numerous shopping trips up to town hunting for Christmas presents and, of course, there had been the parties, at least one, sometimes three, every night.

Frank didn't keep a detailed log of his movements, he didn't have to. As long as he was there on the end of his mobile phone, nobody really minded much what he did. Frank could be *trusted*.

But oddly enough, no one knew what Frank was doing out at the studios on Christmas Eve.

His last scheduled job had been to take Ross to Heathrow early that morning, where Lin, Amy and I and about a dozen other hangers-on had all met up for the flight to Switzerland and the Christmas party to end all Christmas parties. (Which, now I was on payroll and a trusted employee, I couldn't tell anyone about, though I think somebody got the incident with the flugelhorn and the Swiss-German oompah band on a camcorder.)

After waving us off at the airport, Frank had been expected to go home for the holiday, taking the BMW with him for safekeeping, maybe using it to drive the wife down to her mother's in Bournemouth on Boxing Day. Nobody would have minded. Frank, after all, could be trusted.

But instead he went out to Pinewood later that day, though no one seemed to know why.

Security at the gate clocked him in just after two in the afternoon and he was alone in the Beamer. They thought it a bit strange as there was nothing happening on the lot apart from the odd office Christmas party and those were mainly in the television production companies on Pinewood Road. There were a few people from the *Daybreak* crew around, but not many as shooting didn't start until the New Year.

One who was there for a fact was Bernie Brooks, which was a bit odd as there was little call for Ross Pirie's bodyguard to be there when the body he was supposed to be guarding was in Switzerland.

Not that Ross needed a bodyguard while skiing down a Christmas alp. (He was actually quite a good skier, or so it seemed to me from where I sat on the terrace bar.) What with Amy and Lin there, as well as several other adoring women, no harm-doer was going to get anywhere within range.

Which begged the question as to why he needed a bodyguard at all; a question I just had to ask.

Bernie Brooks was a recent addition to the team from November, when Ross started to come over from LA for the set-up of *Daybreak*, so he had only known Ross about four weeks longer than I had. There wasn't a problem there, I was assured, as Bernie had come highly recommended – *trusted* – by Pinewood Security.

Don Sager, Gloria-Maria, Ross himself, even Lin, had all seen his personnel file before he'd been given the job and his credentials seemed impeccable. He was thirty-four and had done ten years as a graduate entrant into the Met, including a spell with the Diplomatic Protection Group (they're the ones who drive round in red police cars and they're armed), before leaving to join a risk management company specialising in hostage negotiations, which had recommended him to Pinewood.

I had actually met him at a couple of the pre-Christmas parties Amy and I had gatecrashed as Ross's guests, but I hadn't registered exactly what it was he did. That wasn't saying much, though, as at parties with luvvies like the film business attracts I tend to switch off and just assume everybody is lying from the outset. I soon found that saved a lot of time in the long run. I just about remembered a tall, well-built bloke who looked as if he could handle himself, who spoke only when spoken to (which made him stand out like a sore thumb at those parties), always had his back to a wall and drank orange juice. He was balding – but then so was every male in London under thirty-five these days – and what hair he had was mown to a stubble which made him look harder than he probably was. Yet as he came with police firearms training and a black belt in Tae-kwon-do, maybe he didn't have to try and look hard.

As far as Gloria-Maria was concerned, and she was the one who authorised his wages, Bernie Brooks was off duty on Christmas Eve until we all got back from Schloss Petrie five days later. In fact he'd told her he was planning a trip up north to see his mum and dad in Sheffield for the Yuletide festivities and Yorkshire pudding served with a flaming sprig of holly or whatever pagan rituals they practised up there.

So what was he doing at the studios, with Frank Shoosmith, on Christmas Eve?

They had certainly met up there and had planned to leave together. We knew that because they were both in the leased BMW 7 when it shot out of the main lot and hit the brick rear wall of the old gatehouse doing – witnesses said – somewhere between fifty and ninety miles an hour.

The good news was that the gatehouse at least stopped the car's seemingly kamikaze rush out into the traffic on the main road. The bad news was that the gatehouse was more solid than it looked and the impact wrecked the car. The good news was that Frank Shoosmith's air bag worked perfectly. The bad news was that Bernie Brooks, sitting in the passenger seat, didn't have one.

The good news for both of them was that the production company behind *Daybreak* was willing, after Ross threatened to hold his breath until he went blue, to transfer them from the nearest Casualty to a private hospital in Slough and pick up the bills. The bad news was that both of them were going to be there for some time.

'So what was the cause of the crash?' Amy had asked me, just like I had asked them.

Nobody knew. Frank Shoosmith was suffering from selective amnesia and couldn't remember a thing about that afternoon.

Bernie Brooks was still in a coma. After nine days that was the really bad news.

'So what did the cops have to say about it?' Amy said, chomping into a turkey leg.

'Nothing,' I said, pouring more wine. 'Nobody told them.'

Technically, to cover themselves, Pinewood Security would have phoned it in to the nearest police station, probably Slough, keeping the details to the minimum. Car accident on private property – the BMW hadn't actually made it to the public road – two injured, already been seen off to hospital, studio security taking care of the wreck, no threat to any third party, no roads blocked, just thought you'd like to know. On Christmas Eve? Yeah, right. You're on your own, kids.

And because it was Christmas and Ross was out of the country, nobody else thought much about it either. Somebody had phoned Ross and told him but he hadn't said anything to us skiing groupies, except maybe Lin. It was only on the flight back to London that he had told me he was missing one driver over New Year's Eve and, like a shot, Amy had volunteered both Armstrong and me.

'So you're Ross's new chauffeur, huh? For you, that's a career move,' said Amy.

'Not just his driver,' I said carefully.

Amy waved the turkey drumstick like a switchblade.

'What do you mean?'

I told her about that evening's brush with the British press and how Don Sager now seemed to regard me as a bit of a fixer, a team-player and maybe a useful minder for Ross, who had already vouched for me as a driver.

It took a minute for this to sink in.

'You're not saying they want you to be Ross's new *bodyguard*, are you?'

'Not exactly. More a sort of personal assistant.'

'But Lin is his personal assistant.'

'I know, I know. How about second assistant assistant then?'

'But why? Why you? What do you know about movie making?'

'Nothing, but then I won't have anything to do with the filming bits, apart from making sure Ross gets to the studio on time.'

Now she was pointing the turkey leg like a gun.

'So how does the second assistant assistant actually assist?'

'Well, that bit's really a cover,' I said, a tad embarrassed.

'Cover for what?' she asked slowly, with menace.

'For finding out who has got it in for this film *Daybreak* and whether what happened to Frank and Bernie was really an accident or not.'

'You mean what happened to Ross's driver wasn't an accident?'

She wasn't going to like this bit.

'Only in the sense that it happened to Frank and Bernie and not Frank and Ross. Perhaps. Maybe. It's a mad idea Don Sager has. It's probably rubbish. Nothing in it. Fantasy Island stuff.'

'Oh my God.'

She leaned forward and began to stab me in the chest with the drumstick to emphasise her words.

'If you are responsible for Ross's safety, we're doomed. This film will never get made.' She paused. 'So tell me exactly what's going on. No, don't. I don't want to know.'

Then she stabbed me again.

'Yes I do. You'd better 'fess up and quick.'

I looked down at the front of my shirt. The drumstick had left an Olympic ring of grease stains across my chest, which would never come out of silk. Amy knew that. She was a woman; it was her job.

'It seems there's been a bit of a hate campaign going on ever since Ross signed to do this movie,' I said quickly. 'You know they don't say 'signed up', they say 'inked'. He 'inked' the contract, like with a pen –'

'Get on with it.'

'OK, there are two factions of Ross Pirie fans, it seems, and they've taken exception to this film *Daybreak*. One lot think it's really cool, being about vampires and all. They're the Goths – well, that's what Don Sager calls them. But there's another lot, which the studio calls the Moral Minority, and they think a film like this is messing with the undead, lacking Christian values and likely to upset Ross's fan base in Catholic countries, not to mention lots of little old ladies in Tunbridge Wells or wherever.'

'So what's this civil war between the fan clubs got to do with anything?'

'Maybe nothing, but it's certainly spooked Don Sager and the money men. That's why they insisted Ross had a bodyguard.'

'To protect him from what? Little old ladies in Tunbridge Wells?'

'No, not them, but the loony element, the stalkers among them.'

'Oh, come off it,' scoffed Amy. 'All film people are into this stalker shit. It's like a fashion accessory, they'd feel undressed without one.'

'The feeling is that Ross has got more than one, maybe a whole army of them, and they're threatening to picket the studios when filming starts. The other worry is that they seem remarkably well informed about what is going on. Like they knew Bernie Brooks had been made Ross's bodyguard, like they know when filming starts, and that Ross is looking to rent a house in the country.'

'How do they know all this?'

'We don't know,' I said honestly.

Amy couldn't resist that.

'Oh, so it's *we* now, is it? Well how do *we* know *they* know?'

'Apparently it's all on their sites on the Internet. They've got loads of stuff up there about *Daybreak*, have had for a month or so. Stuff that's not been made public. They seem to know everything about the production before it's gone into production. We could go have a look if you like.'

Amy dropped her skeletal leg of turkey on to her plate and threw the plate in my lap. She grabbed the bottle of Malbec from me and flounced off unsteadily towards the office where her computer lived.

Over her shoulder she said:

'Do they mention the costume design?'

The search engine turned up eighty-nine websites and 1,062 web page references when Amy typed in 'Ross Pirie'.

We discounted the obvious links to the various e-businesses trying to sell us the book of one of his films, the unauthorised biography, the watch he had worn in one of his early TV movies, the model of car he had driven in another or the beer he had once advertised in Japan, no doubt during a lean period in the script department.

Then we ignored the sites of the charities he had once supported, maybe still did, and then three sites in German, two in Swedish and five in Dutch. It was, I knew, quite rare to get a site in Dutch as nobody in cyberspace (or anywhere else) understands it except the Dutch, but understandable in the case of Ross Pirie as in his last hit, *Six Men Dead*, he had played a Dutch planter displaced from his coffee plantation on Java by the invading Japanese and so had been the obvious choice to lead the suicide commando mission back to the island to rescue the captured nuclear physicist.

(I don't care what the critics said, I liked it. It was a sort of *The Storm Jackal Has Landed South By Navarone Head* action thriller of the kind they didn't make any more, with an ironic, post modernist chess-playing scene which sent up *The Thomas Crown Affair* something rotten. Or maybe I was reading too much into it.)

That left twenty-one dedicated sites – shrines, almost – to the life, hopes, fears, ambitions and probably even inside-leg measurement of Ross Pirie.

Actually, there was one which gave his inside-leg measurement – thirty-one inches – and also listed every occasion (twice) when he had eaten sushi in a movie or TV show. It was called ROSS PIRIE: KEIKO'S PAGE, put up on a server neither of us recognised but we guessed was Japanese, and had a picture of him from an uncredited appearance in an early episode of *Hill Street Blues* where he was sitting in a restaurant eating something with chopsticks. There was also a reference to him eating sushi in a Tokyo restaurant whilst over there filming a Japanese beer commercial. And when in Tokyo, the beer's brewers had a suit made for him in the best 'Scottish tweed'. That's how his inside-leg measurement made it into the public domain, though how the adoring Keiko had discovered it remained a mystery.

'Can you believe this?' Amy said, shaking her head. 'Somebody's paid good money to put this up on the Net. So Ross twice ate sushi and got a suit made when in Tokyo. Is this what the information superhighway's there for?'

'We are,' I said philosophically, 'truly in the land of sadbastard.com.'

One of the more respectable sites, in that it at least attempted to look official, was called ROSS PIRIE HIS LIFE AND WORK, which had the faint whiff of an obituary about it. It was like people who got 'lifetime achievement' awards whilst they were still alive. It was a coded way of telling them they could stop now.

As far as I could tell, and I was no expert, it was an accurate summary of Ross's career.

Born in Vancouver, (late) only child of a pair of well-respected doctors. Went to medical school himself but got involved with a student drama club which led to street theatre, a stint as a stand-up comic (failed), a one-off summer engagement as a rodeo clown in Calgary (two broken bones and a cracked rib) and eventually walk-on parts with a touring rep theatre company, and no medical degree. Moved to Los Angeles and starved for four years doing bit parts in numerous TV shows, including thirteen out of fifteen episodes of the ill-fated daytime soap *Love Flight* about the private lives of airline pilots. Which made it all the more ironic that his first on-screen credit in movies was as 'Third Airport Hostage' in *Die Hard II*.

His filmography (that's what the site called it) nosedived after that, even though the parts got bigger. A couple of made-for-television suspense thrillers, *The House By The Shore* and *High Voltage*, where Ross played the suspicious-looking but actually innocent second male lead who ended up getting killed by the hysterical heroine. Then a low budget shlock-horror western called *Gravestone, Texas*, which featured a tribe of zombie Indians and, in my opinion, was worthy of cult status it was so bad. Then came what most actors regard as the kiss of death, the pan-European co-production *White Cut*, a murder mystery set in a Swiss ski resort, filmed in France, funded by Germans, directed by an Italian and edited and dubbed in a small office off Dean Street in Soho. But for Ross it was a bit of a hit, partly because he played the hero detective and partly because he could actually ski, which added a rare touch of realism to some of the exterior action sequences. It was also, for some bizarre reason, a major box office hit in Hong Kong and, of all places, China, although it went straight-to-video in Britain and straight-to-TV in the USA.

Somebody must have seen it, though, as Ross was hired to

play the heart-throb ski-instructor (who was actually gay) to a class of preppy female college girls in *The Colorado Thaw*, which showed he could do light comedy with a splash of pathos without leaving a dry seat in the house. That was his break-through in America, though it was dismissed as a bit of 'chick flick' over here.

From then on he moved inexorably up the billing until he was above the title. He proved he could handle himself as a tough guy private eye in *San Diego Story* and be slimy as a corrupt Congressman in *Pursuit Of Power*. Then came the wartime action thriller *Six Men Dead* followed by a complete change of pace (and rave reviews) for the low-budget British film – if that's not an oxymoron – *Treble & Bass*, where he played a talentless, big ego British disc jockey on a run-down Yorkshire radio station.

His latest film (so the site said) had him back in Eurotrash country in another pan-European production, though no low budget this time, where he reprised his role as the Swiss detective from *White Cut* in a follow-up sex, skiing and murder among the jet set mystery called *Side Edge*. Nothing much was known about this yet-to-be-released film, still being edited, except that the working title had been *Jagged Edge* until the writ had arrived from Joe Esterhas. Ross Pirie's next film, already in pre-production, was to be the modern-day vampire comedy *Daybreak* from the cult novel by Walter Wilkes Booth. Rumoured co-stars were hot babe and former model Zina Ray, black rap artist Bo Jay Roberts and Royal Shakespeare Company stalwart Alec Walters, with Walter Matthau, Anne Bancroft and Jack Palance pencilled in (not 'inked' you note) for cameo spots.

The site had last been updated on August 31st 1999.

'Nothing dangerous there,' said Amy, scrolling back to the top of the site and holding out an empty glass. 'Not even a snide remark about his divorce.'

'I'll open another bottle,' I said. 'I thought his divorce was well out in the open. And it's not exactly news any more, is it?'

When it had happened, Ross was only known to a handful of the people who know him now, or claim to. He had married a childhood sweetheart and fellow medical student at the age of twenty-one or twenty-two. She had stayed the medical course whilst he had gone off to do his theatrical basic training, and had qualified as a doctor. By the time Ross had moved to LA, she was supporting the pair of them and there was never a hint this was a problem to him. But she had wanted kids and he hadn't, or at least not until he had the prospect of steady work, so they had gone through that rare experience, an amicable Hollywood divorce with no money involved.

Later, after his hit romantic role in *The Colorado Thaw*, the divorce was dragged through the tabloid newspapers again, but even they had trouble finding something bad to say about him. It turned out that his ex-wife had remarried (another doctor back in Vancouver) and not only was Ross still in touch with her and her new husband, but he was godfather to both their kids.

Needless to say, what started as a juicy smear story turned into a massive boost for Ross's ratings among female movie-goers. Here was a thoughtful, caring, romantic hero for the Nineties. He was fit, handsome, had all his own hair and, above all, he was now single.

'There's no mileage in it,' said Amy, 'it's just interesting that none of these fan sites ever mention the private lives of their heroes if they can help it. Sometimes they actually say "so-and-so's recent change in their private circumstances will not be gone into on this site" like they were taking the moral high ground. The people who put these sites up do it for love, you know. They think they're protecting the stars, bonding with them, minding them. They like playing bodyguard. Bit like you, Angel.'

'I told you, I'm not a bodyguard,' I yelled from the wine rack in the kitchen. 'I'm a second assistant assitant.'

'Oh yeah, right. I forgot,' she yelled back. 'It's a thin red line between second assistant assistant and fucking groupie, if you ask . . . Hang on, here's one for you.'

'What you got?' I asked, though I was beginning to have trouble remembering what we were looking for.

'"This movie sucks",' she laughed.

'It probably does,' I said before I realised she was reading it off the screen.

The website she had called up had the address ross@day-break.piriefan.com and when the illustration on the title page eventually came up, it was a composite of Ross Pirie's standard studio glossy ten-by-eight photograph superimposed on the cover of the book *Daybreak*, with its full moon over the New York skyline. It was cleverly done and that catch line made you read on.

'No, not like that,' said Amy. 'These guys think it's a great idea. Listen to this: "Who better to play the smooth, sophisticated, modern vampire-about-town Jason Neville in the film version of Walter Booth's instant classic *Daybreak*, than pants-charmer Ross Pirie himself? Central casting have got it right for once! Shooting starts in January in England, where the SFX are cheaper these days before going on location in NY in February/March. All good Goths should book their tickets now and and added bonus is the casting of Brit actor Alec Walters, who played the Old Bloodsucker himself in the 1989 off-Broadway revival of *Dracula*. Memo to Gary Oldman: you were good, but Ross Pirie is the vamp we most want to get our teeth into." And it goes on – and on. there's loads of it.'

'The old pants-charmer. I like that,' I said. 'Try another one.'

Amy tried another eight, turning up information that seemed harmless in itself until you thought about how it got up there. For instance, three sites mentioned the fact that Ross was going to rent a flat in Chelsea pre-Christmas and then start looking for a house in the country near Pinewood in the New Year. In itself, that was logical and nothing to hold-the-front-page about. Most visiting film stars or rock idols rented places these days, ever since Madonna was virtually besieged in her hotel on one trip, and even though she'd rented an entire floor and went everywhere with twenty-six minders the fans and the press made life pretty hellish.

So that wasn't the sort of thing the production publicists would release, or if they did, Lin Ooi-Tan would take their livers out.

'How did they know about the Chelsea flat? And the country house thing? He's seeing an estate agent on Tuesday about that.'

Amy ignored me and scrolled on, still hoping for a reference to costume design.

She found two mentions of Ross's Christmas skiing trip, both dated before Christmas Eve, one of them suggesting that his Swiss 'hide-away' chalet (exact location unknown) had been a freebie from the producers of his skiing thriller *Side Edge*, and the other claiming that – 'sadly, for bachelor boy Ross' – actress Zina Ray would not be joining him for the festive frolics, though she was known to be on his wish list.

'Where do they get this stuff?' I wondered out loud.

'The sort of magazines you never read and the daytime TV shows you never watch, chat rooms on the Net where the fans swap info,' said Amy, eyes glued to the screen. 'Did you know there were *three* unofficial biographies of Ross already?'

'And him not even dead yet.'

There was a site dedicated to ten reasons why Ross Pirie was not a gay icon and then a really weird one, with excellent graphics, complaining that Ross had never appeared in uniform in a movie and here were a few examples of what he might have looked like. You got the nasty feeling that whoever put that site up regarded the fact that Ross had never played an SS officer as a definite negative, career-wise.

'Call me a Luddite,' I said wearily, 'but you know I'm really glad that only eighteen per cent of what's up there on the Net *ever* gets looked at.'

'There do seem to be an awful lot of people out there with time on their hands,' murmured Amy.

'Well, they're doing something with their hands, that's for sure.'

I yawned and contemplated calling it a day. After all, I was starting my new job in the morning, if I remembered to wake up in time.

'When was that car smash out at Pinewood?' said Amy, suddenly.

'Christmas Eve,' I said. 'Why?'

'Has it been in the papers?'

'I don't know. I got the impression from Don Sager that they'd managed to keep it quiet because it happened within the studio grounds. There were no police involved.'

'Insurance companies?'

'No idea. The car was leased, I know that, and the film people are picking up the medical bills. I can't imagine anyone would have done much over the holiday. Most companies aren't back to work until Tuesday. Why?'

'Because Pirie's Pets know all about it.'

'*Who*?'

'Pirie's Pets – it's a site and it's run by somebody called Pat. Here you are: Pat, The Premier Pirie Pet.'

'I don't believe it.'

But it was true.

'There's lots of it,' said Amy as the menu page illustration filled in to show Ross smiling and waving at the camera. 'Start with the News Update?'

'Why not?'

Amy clicked her mouse and the screen filled with boxes of type and a mugshot picture of Ross as he appeared in *Six Men Dead*.

'Here we go,' Amy read: ' "Pirie's Pets have never made any secret of the fact that we think Ross Pirie is a great human being, even if we have reservations about his latest choice of material. Over Christmas, Ross took time out from his much-needed Swiss break to send flowers to his long-time British driver Frank Shoosmith who was involved in a car accident while Ross was away. But that's the kind of guy Ross is." It says it was updated on 30th December. First with the news, or what?'

'Spooky,' I agreed. 'What else is there?'

Amy clicked on.

'There's a load of stuff about *Daybreak*,' she said, scanning the pages, 'and whoever Pat is, he or she has sure taken agin it. "This material is beneath him" – "a danger to his younger fan base" – "messing with dark forces" – "unchristian" – and then they start slagging it off. There's pages of it. Want me to print it out?'

'Yeah, go for it. This must be what Don Sager meant when he said Ross had a Moral Minority stalker on the Net.'

'Most of them are harmless,' said Amy, stacking paper to slot into the printer.

'I hope you're right,' I said, 'because they're certainly well informed.'

They were that.

The picture of Ross on the site menu page, him smiling and waving at the camera, had been taken no more than three weeks ago. I guessed from the background that it had been taken at Pinewood Studios – inside Pinewood Studios.

And I thought it a pretty safe bet that the middle-aged man holding open the door of the spanking new BMW 7 for him was Frank Shoosmith.

The very nearly late Frank Shoosmith.

7

PRE-PRODUCTION

Ross had gone back to Julius Cockburn's country pad for the night and I had arranged to meet him at Pinewood at 10 a.m. in order to get my security clearance and a full briefing on my duties, responsibilities, timetable, conditions of employment, dress code and, hopefully, claiming expenses.

I had been told by Don Sager to report direct to Gloria-Maria as he himself had meetings to go to in town rather than visit the studios. I got the distinct impression he didn't know where Pinewood was, and didn't particularly care.

So when I drew Armstrong up at the leafy gates and the blue-uniformed security man stepped out of nowhere to greet me, I leaned out of the driver's window and just said:

'I'm here to see Miss van Doodler. Is she here yet?'

The security man nodded seriously and leaned in towards me, putting one hand on Armstrong's roof and reaching to his throat with the other.

I had no idea what he was doing until he fumbled under his tie and collar to grasp a two-inch wooden crucifix on a leather thong around his neck. He waved it in my face and laughed.

'She's here, all right. Why do you think we're all wearing these?'

'That bad, is she?'

'She can be a right tartar, that one. You here to pick her up? She only clocked in about ten minutes ago.'

I realised he was seeing me as a cab driver, rather than an important new addition to the creative team behind the magic of the silver screen.

'I'm here to work for Ross Pirie, actually,' I said grandly. 'I was told Miss van Doodler would be on hand to welcome me.'

'Oh, right you are, sir,' he said, his tone changing immediately. 'I'll give her a buzz and let her know you're coming. What was the name, sir?'

'Angel. Just Angel.'

'Right, Mr Angel. I think she's over in the editing suite this morning. I'll get you a map so you won't get lost.'

He started to move to open the gates for me, then paused and stepped back to my side.

'The crucifix thing, sir . . .' He fumbled it back inside his jacket and behind his tie. 'That was just a joke. The assistant producer gave one to all staff here this morning as a sort of good luck charm. You see, we haven't done a vampire picture here for years.'

'Oh, I see,' I said, keeping a straight face. 'Isn't Miss van Doodler the assistant producer?'

'No, sir. She's the assistant executive producer. It was Miss Dulude who gave these out. She's the assistant *line* producer.'

'Of course,' I said as if I was any the wiser.

He opened the gate for me and I eased Armstrong in, pausing to grab a quick look at the scaffolding and the two builders with a cement mixer at the back of the gatehouse, who were trying to look busy repairing what I knew was a BMW-shaped dent in the brickwork.

The security man emerged from the gatehouse waving a photocopied map.

'That's OK, mate,' I said as I accelerated, 'I'll find her.'

Within five minutes I was totally lost. The windowless, concrete blockhouses formed a maze of streets hardly wide enough for two cars and cars were parked everywhere. If I had expected to come across streams of extras dressed as Roman soldiers, or alien monsters, or Hitler muttering, 'They lose me after the bunker scene,' then I would have been disappointed but I knew that only happened in Mel Brooks movies. There was little sign of human habitation, or any actors.

At one point, though, I turned right into a narrow alleyway and almost ran into the back of a fire engine.

My first thought was that it was a prop and somebody had just abandoned it, blocking the road. Then an upraised hand appeared out of the driver's window and the engine started up and the driver manoeuvred the machine into the side of one of the buildings so that Armstrong could pass.

I tooted the horn in thanks as I overtook him. The driver was dressed as a fireman and the tender, although smaller than the ones I was used to coming at you down one-way streets in London, looked realistic enough. It had Buckinghamshire County Fire Brigade on the side in gold lettering, which I thought showed a nice attention to detail.

At the end of that block I flipped a mental coin and turned right and at the end of that one, left, and still had no idea where I was. Then, up ahead at the next corner, I saw two young guys pushing a trolley across the road and into an alleyway to the right. The trolley was loaded with metal urns of tea or coffee, tins of biscuits, big plastic bottles of milk and waving fronds of piled-up styrofoam cups.

I had them now.

Armstrong followed them at a speed which would have had us pulled for kerb crawling in a decent neighbourhood, but the guys pushing the tea trolley didn't look behind them and made no effort to get out of the way. They stopped outside a large metal door with a 7 painted on it and a set of wall lights, one red and one green, with a notice saying DO NOT ENTER WHEN RED SHOWS. Neither light was on.

The guys with the trolley didn't have to knock on the metal door or anything. The people inside sensed it was time for a tea break and out they poured, half of them lighting up cigarettes as they emerged from the dark interior, half of them reaching for mobile phones as if their lives depended upon them.

One of them had to know where I was, and I struck lucky because the first person I asked when I climbed out of Armstrong also knew who I was. And very lucky as she just happened to be about six foot tall, with long, swept-back blonde hair and a strikingly beautiful mouth, highlighted with pale gold lip gloss. She wore a white shirt under a leather waistcoat, which emphasised one set of contours, and tight denim jeans which emphasised the other. She had her mobile clipped to a belt which seemed to be made entirely of beer bottle tops and she held a clipboard to her chest. I hoped she wasn't short-sighted.

It was just lucky that she was the nearest person to me, but then my Rule of Life Number 1 is that it's better to be lucky than good.

'Talk's free. Costs a dollar to look,' she said to me. She was American. I could tell that from the accent. The attitude just confirmed it.

'Sorry, was I staring?' I smiled, hoping my jaw wasn't actually scraping the floor.

'You must be the Angel guy we've been told about,' she said coolly.

'I'm impressed.'

'Don't be. We were told about the cab.' She nodded to Armstrong behind me. 'Plus Security called everybody on the lot about five minutes ago to say you were probably driving around lost and we had to watch out for you.'

'You found me. I'm Roy Angel, here to work with Ross Pirie.'

'I know.'

I thought she might shake hands like polite Americans do and, hopefully, this would progress to big hugs on our second meeting. Instead she put the clipboard between her knees and reached to her neck with both hands to undo the top two buttons of her shirt. Maybe Americans had loosened up for the new Millennium.

She fingered something around her neck then bent her head down and a mane of hair fell over her face as she pulled something over her head.

Straightening up she handed something to me.

'Have a crucifix. Welcome to *Daybreak*. I'm Burgundy Dulude.'

'Thanks,' I said, taking the small wooden cross on its leather thong and noticing, quite by accident, that she had at least another three round her neck, nestling in her cleavage. 'You're the line producer, aren't you?'

'Assistant. But you'll find that the people called assistants are the ones who do the work around here. Come on, get back in the cab and I'll show you where to go.'

'I'm not taking you away from anything?'

'No, we're doing some blocking for the first set-up tomorrow. I'm just making sure everyone we need has survived the holidays and remembered where they work.'

She snapped the mobile off her belt – it *was* made of bottle

87

tops and I recognised Budweiser, Miller, Schlitz, Moosehead and Genessee – and speed-dialled a number.

'Paul? It's Burgundy. I've got him and I'll bring him in. Tell Gloria-Maria, will you? Ten-four, good buddy.'

Then to me, she said: 'Shall we go? Or do you want me to strike a coupla poses for you?'

'I'm still staring, aren't I?' I admitted.

'Bug-eyed, I'm afraid.'

'I'm sorry, but you don't half remind me of somebody I used to know.'

'Yeah, right,' she drawled.

'And I bet you wish you had a dollar for every guy who said that, and a pound for those who asked if you were an actress?'

'You bet.'

I dug into the pocket of my jacket and produced a pound coin to offer her.

'Are you, by any chance, an actress?'

She had to smile at that, but she didn't take the pound.

'Burgundy Dulude is my stage name,' she conceded.

'And you're just doing this job to fill in between roles, right?' I beamed.

'That's right. I keep the stage name just in case I run into a casting director,' she said innocently, giving me an up-from-under look.

She really was an actress and I was aware that there was a sucker punch coming soon. Even so, it took my breath away.

'Plus, my real name is such a no-no, I actually prefer Burgundy Dulude. After all, you don't forget it easily, do you? It has so much more class than Burgundy Luger.'

She smiled sweetly, waiting for it to sink in.

'I used to know somebody called Luger,' I said slowly, my mouth drying. 'She was an American too.'

'That's right,' she said brightly. Too brightly. 'Lulu Luger. She's my sister. She still remembers you.'

She said it like it was a sentence.

Burgundy climbed in the back and told me to take a left at the end of the block.

'How is Lulu?' I asked hesitantly, checking her out in the mirror. 'Still in the music business?'

Her eyes stared back at me, unblinking; like a cat with a snit on.

'Yeah, still drumming. She has her own band now, called Dakota Sioux. They're kinda cool. Hang a left.'

'She used to manage a band when I knew her,' I said as I turned the wheel. 'A really loud Heavy Metal mob called Astral Reich, but I think they sort of ran out on her. What happened to them?'

In those days I had been much more involved in the music business myself, although Lucinda L. Luger and I went back a ways before that. She had taken time off from managing Astral Reich on their debut (debut and only) British tour to help me get a mutual friend of ours out of a spot of bother over in France. When we got back, she found the band had gone on without her and signed a recording contract. But I'd never heard of them since.

'Oh, she found them,' said Burgundy casually.

That explained it, then.

'This is it.'

I pulled up outside a double set of glass doors which could have been, probably were, modelled on cinema doors from the 1940s. I half expected a uniformed usher to appear and ask to see our ticket stubs. I had driven about a 150 yards in all.

'We could have walked,' I said.

'This is a movie lot, nobody walks anywhere,' said Burgundy as she opened her door. 'You're a driver. Wanna put yourself out of work?'

She pointed towards the doors where a stocky, totally bald man in a well-filled charcoal suit and white polo-neck shirt was waiting for us, hands behind his back.

'Paul Brettler,' said Burgundy, introducing us. 'Head of Pinewood Security. This is the Roy Angel we've heard so much about.'

'Very pleased to meet you,' said Brettler with a South African lilt and a handshake which suggested he wrestled wildebeest for relaxation. 'Ross is in the editing suite looking at a title sequence. He shouldn't be too long. Please, follow me.'

He lead me down a corridor, windows to one side looking out

over the lot, the wall on our left decorated every three feet with a framed poster of a movie shot there. All the *Carry On* films were there, plus the Bond films. I wondered if the posters were originals. If they were, they were worth quite a bit nowadays at auction, and there didn't seem to be any security cameras here.

'Whilst Ross is in the studio,' Brettler was saying, 'he is, of course, my responsibility. I understand that you will be looking after him once he leaves the area and that you'll report to Miss van Doodler.'

He pronounced it *ven Du-erdler*.

'I'm not actually sure what my responsibilities are as yet,' I said as he held a swing door open for me and we started down another corridor.

The gorgeous Burgundy was keeping in step with us, not saying anything, just listening. I kept one eye on her at all times, partly because it was good use of an eye but also because I knew her sister and it was possible she shared some of her more violent genetic traits.

'I presumed you were replacing Frank as Ross's driver,' said Brettler.

'Yes I am, I think, but Don Sager suggested there was a subtext involved in the job. A sort of keeping-my-eyes open role.'

I must have flashed a look at Burgundy or maybe Brettler just sensed something. He was probably good at tracking spoor. He seemed to catch on quickly enough.

'Don't worry, Burgundy is in the loop,' he said. 'She has to be while film is actually being shot here.'

'I get to see all the weird mail, too,' she said drily. 'It's one of the perks of the job. Not!'

'Crank mail?' I asked her.

'Off the friggin' sanity scale, and it's been arriving since late November. Not just letters, you always get those. People wanting jobs – actors, agents, writers – and the fan mail stuff, mostly for Ross and Zina Ray. That's OK. It's the other stuff that's a tad sicko.'

'What other stuff?'

I held another swing door open for her as we entered another corridor. I was even more lost now than I had been outside. Burgundy paused next to a poster which showed Barbara

Windsor losing her bikini top in *Carry On Camping*. I averted my eyes.

'Crucifixes, rosaries, bibles – seven of them so far – cloves of garlic, little leather pouches stuffed with really stinky herbs, hen's feet with little red ribbons tied in bows and on one breakfast-churning occasion, a fresh dead chicken complete with head, feet and feathers.'

She put two fingers into her mouth and made a retching sound. Brettler and I winced.

'What did you do with it?' I asked, which was a pretty dumb thing to ask.

'I gave it to Lin along with the garlic so she could stir-fry it. What the fuck you think? It hit the trash.'

Yes, I could definitely see the family resemblance.

'I mean, what colour was it?'

'Colour?' She looked at me as if I would be the next thing to hit the trash.

'What sort of a chicken was it?'

'Hey, I may look like a farm girl, but my interest in the country stops at line dancing. It was a white chicken. What other sort are there?'

'Black ones and brown ones, but you were lucky to get the white. The other sorts know fuck-all about voodoo.'

Brettler laughed.

'Voodoo? That's crap.'

'Real freaky crap,' added Burgundy.

'You're the ones who are making the film about vampires and giving out crucifixes,' I said reasonably. 'You're bound to attract the weirdos.'

'You think somebody's putting a curse on this movie?' Brettler said, eyes wide in disbelief.

'No, I think the garlic and the hen's feet and all that stuff are probably good luck charms from the fans who think vampires are really cool. The bibles and the crucifixes are from Ross's fans who don't think he should be messing with the black arts and making this film.' They had stopped walking and were both looking at me. 'All I did was surf the Net. It's fairly obvious you've got two sets of fans out there: the ones who approve of this vampire movie – the Goths – and the ones who think it's unholy and messing with the devil.'

'Vampire hunters in cyberspace,' breathed Burgundy. 'Just what we need.'

'Hey, they're just fans with access to a computer. I brought some print-outs with me of some of the latest websites.'

'So that's what you do, is it?' said Brettler.

I looked at him blankly.

'What?'

'Hack into websites and computers and things. That's what you're going to do for Ross? As well as drive him?'

'Oh no, I'm no computer geek. Don't really know how to turn one on.'

His bald, sunburned brow wrinkled at that.

'So what – if I may ask – special skills are you bringing to this job?'

'Er . . . none, I suppose,' I said, which I thought was fair as I didn't really know what the job was. 'No special skills, no experience, no expertise.'

I was being honest with them. Why didn't they look as if they believed me?

'So why are you taking the job?' Brettler asked, not aggressively, just curious.

'I wanted to be in movies?' I shrugged.

'You'll fit right in,' said Burgundy, hitting the next set of swing doors like she had a grudge against them.

The editing suite had a boardroom-size glass-topped table, ten trendy, bendy metal chairs, a four-seater leather sofa, a leather captain's chair on wheels, a computer control panel which could have brought back Apollo 13 by itself and one of those huge flat screen monitors which the BBC can't afford to buy and have to hire in.

Ross was saying goodbye to a scruffy, pot-bellied bearded guy with Coke-bottle glasses who was clutching a black metal briefcase to his chest. The guy had a grey, deathly pallor on the bits of his skin you could see through the facial hair and though he was probably under thirty, he looked well along the early coronary time/space continuum. From the number of times Ross said it, I gathered his name was Stefan.

'Great job, Stefan,' he was saying, 'as usual. Cuts as sharp as a pistol, Stefan. The music'll fit like a dream. You take care, Stefan.'

I had long since noticed that when people say your name back to you over and over again it means they have a serious attention deficit problem. It's just like people who say 'I hear what you're saying' when in fact the last thing they've been doing is listening, or when they're in meetings they say 'I'm not sure I've got the final version of that' which means they haven't got a fucking clue what's going on.

Still, Ross probably had a lot on his mind.

'Angel, welcome!' he beamed once Stefan had squeezed through the door. 'Just going through some edits for the title sequence of *Side Edge*. Never know where you are in this business: always finishing off one picture whilst filming the next and planning the one after. Come in and meet people. You don't mind if I call you Angel, do you? Amy does.'

Amy could call me what she liked. She could make my life hell, all Ross could do was fire me.

'That's fine,' I said.

'Great. Now, you've met Burgundy and Paul, I see, and you know Gloria-Maria and Lin, my right-hand girl.'

'I'd rephrase that in public if I were you,' I said.

Behind me I heard Burgundy choke on a snigger. Then Ross got it and laughed, which meant they all could. All except Lin.

'I will, Angel, I will.' Then he turned to the one man in the room I hadn't met. 'If you want a job in public relations, though, you'll have to get rid of Tony. This is Tony Lovisi, who's been looking after my image for years.'

Lovisi shook my hand firmly but gave the impression he didn't want me standing too close to his suit. He was friendly enough, though.

'I hear you were doing my job for me yesterday, Mr Angel, and that you did it very well,' he said with a faint accent I put down as posh Edinburgh, which is just about the poshest English you'll ever hear.

'Shall I send you a bill?' I asked as if surprised.

Ross laughed at that too, allowing nothing to dent the good mood he'd put himself in, or was acting out.

'No you don't, Angel, you got the wrong person there.' He put a hand on my shoulder and made the final introduction. 'All bills, claims, receipts, slush funds, so on, so forth, go to Alix here. She's our production accountant and keeps track of every cent. Alix Tse, this is Angel, your latest addition to the payroll.'

Alix Tse was a smaller version of Lin Ooi-Tan and I don't mean that it was just that they were both Chinese. I could swear there was a family resemblance there, or maybe I was just imagining things after meeting Burgundy and suffering hot flushes about her sister and worrying needlessly about how far cloning had gone.

Both Lin and Alix wore pinstripe trouser suits, grey and blue respectively, of different cuts but possibly from the same designer and Alix sported a TALtop with the latest silver thread weave. They both wore the little wooden crucifixes which Burgundy had been handing out.

'It'll be a pleasure taking money from you,' I said to Alix with a big grin.

She put her head on one side and looked away, as if I had insulted her mother.

'Don't joke with Alix about money,' said Ross, slapping me on the shoulder. 'She has one rule: Spend the company's money like it was your own.'

I hadn't been joking, but I laughed politely and sat down next to Ross. Gloria-Maria took the head of the table and tapped it once with a long pencil which she held like she would hold a cigarette.

'Shall I proceed, Ross?' she asked, not expecting an argument.

'It's your meeting, Gloria-Maria,' said Ross charmingly. 'I know it's for my benefit, but it's your meeting.'

G-M fought the urge to put the pencil in her mouth and draw on it.

'Actually, this is mostly for Roy's benefit,' she said in a tone which made me sit up straight. 'In effect, Roy, you are working for Last Ditch which means –'

'Excuse me?'

'Questions usually come at the end,' said Burgundy, her eyes on the ceiling.

She had nice eyes, just like her sister.

'What is it?' growled Gloria-Maria.

'Who or what is Last Ditch?'

'Last Ditch is the name of the production company which owns *Daybreak*,' she said and I got the impression that this meant Ross Pirie and everyone working on the film as well. 'And as I am Last Ditch's representative on earth, or at least here in England right now, that means you report to me in the final analysis.

'For day-to-day operation, reporting and responsibilities are as follows. Once shooting starts the day after tomorrow, you go through Burgundy whenever Ross is here on set in front of camera. She knows where he is and what he's doing. You do *not* attempt to find him when he's working without clearing it with Burgundy. Now when –'

'I'll need the number of your vibrating pager,' I said to Burgundy, hoping to impress her with the fact that I had noticed it on the rear of her jeans.

'Surprised she hasn't given it to him already,' Lin hissed to Alix.

'We'll come to questions at the end,' said Gloria-Maria. 'Anything to do with Ross's personal security whilst he's in the studio is, natch, Paul's area with Pinewood Security. He can also supply extra bodies as and when needed for crowd control.'

'Can I talk to you about Frank Shoosmith?' I asked Brettler across the table, much to G-M's annoyance.

'It'll have to be tomorrow,' said Brettler, looking at his watch. 'Call into my office whenever you like.'

'And Mr Lovisi here,' G-M said loudly, 'is to be informed of any journalist you might come across. He and he alone deals with the press. Is that understood?'

I ignored her and turned to Lovisi.

'I need to talk to you about coverage on the Internet. Do you check the websites?'

'Not on a daily basis,' he said slowly, which translated as 'never'. 'But it would be good to talk offline, see who owns it.'

And that 'talk offline, see who owns it' was genuine management gibberish for 'let's have a chat after the meeting and decide who is going to do it'.

'Afterwards would be good,' said Gloria-Maria, the nicotine stress really getting to her now. 'Whenever Ross is not on the set, even if he's just taking a pee, he's Lin's responsibility. She'll tell you where he has to be and when, and you take your instructions from her. Starting this afternoon.'

'He's going for a pee this afternoon?' I asked Lin innocently. 'Wow, that's what I call organised.'

There were more sniggers around the table.

'Tony and Paul agree that Ross shouldn't go back to his flat in Chelsea,' Lin said seriously. 'So your first task is to go and get his stuff for him and take it down to Julius's place in the country. I'll come with you.'

'To count the spoons?'

'Something like that,' she said, keeping eye contact longer than was necessary to make me nervous of her.

'And Alix,' G-M ploughed on, now with the pencil clenched between her teeth, 'will make arrangements for your pay and expenses, insurance, tax, so forth and issue you with a phone and a pager.'

Alix had not, as far as I knew, even so much as glanced at me during the meeting and even now she had her eyes fixed on an indeterminate spot in the middle of the table.

'Do you handle petrol receipts?' I asked her and only then did she look at me.

I got the distinct impression that she was nervous for some reason, as if she'd been dreading being asked anything. Maybe she was just shy, or maybe it was because she was sitting next to Lin, or maybe she just didn't like me.

'Of course,' she said with a slight shrug of the shoulders.

I didn't get a chance to say why I wanted to know. Gloria-Maria had had enough.

'Right, that's my piece said, eventually. Everybody knows everybody, right?' Her voice was becoming rather shrill. 'Are there any questions?'

No one said anything, but they all looked at me, even Alix.

'Not now,' I said sweetly.

8

LOCATION SCOUT

For someone who had decided to hate me on sight because it saved time in the long run, Lin Ooi-Tan spoke more or less non-stop as I drove her down the M25 to the M4 then into London as far as the Hammersmith Flyover before dropping down into Chelsea. Admittedly, she wasn't so much chatting me up as issuing instructions, some of which were really frightening.

Picking up Ross's luggage and taking it down to Julius Cockburn's pad in the country somewhere near Horsham in Sussex, that wasn't a problem. A bit menial, perhaps, but that was what second assistant assistants were probably for. And then tomorrow's main duty seemed to be taking Ross out with an estate agent from Slough to look at houses to rent. Another nice little drive in the country and more money for old rope.

Then Lin put the boot in with Wednesday's schedule: picking up Ross at 5 a.m. in Horsham for the first day's shooting.

I asked her if she'd got that right and she really did mean 5 a.m. as in 'in the morning' when it was still dark.

'Welcome to the movies,' she'd said. 'The stuff we're shooting here at Pinewood is centred around Ross's main scenes so he's on call most days, 5 a.m. to around 6 p.m. when you take him home or wherever he wants to go.'

I did some basic maths, working out driving times and getting home, and realised that I was facing up to a nineteen-hour day, even assuming Ross didn't want to go clubbing after work.

'Is that, like, every day? Five days a week?' I had asked.

'Six,' she'd said gleefully.

But then she'd tempered that by explaining that *Daybreak* was very much a studio-bound production due to the special effects and the minor fact that it was supposed to be set in New York. Consequently, all the exterior shots would be done in the Big Apple. For many movies, weekend work or night shoots were necessary in order to get access to locations. So there wouldn't be much movement outside of Pinewood for the next four weeks or so.

I had asked if that was normal for a film shoot and Lin had said average, though as Ross was in almost all the scenes to be shot here – either directly or as cut-aways or reaction-shots to other actors – it was very concentrated for him. Still, the upside seemed to be that once I had got him to the studio, the rest of the day was my own until I had to take him home. Therefore, my priority would be to find where the rest of the drivers went to snatch a few hours' sleep. There was always a place somewhere on jobs like this, where you could hide away.

But only after you'd done the shopping, it seemed. According to Lin I was also expected to be available to shop for the basics of Ross's life – at least until he got settled into his rented place and Lin had appointed a housekeeper and cleaning staff. At least that was one thing I didn't have to worry about. I definitely did not fancy having to whip the Dyson over the carpets when I had a spare minute.

Apart from a shooting schedule, Lin had also prepared a list of clothes sizes and preferences for Ross, including boxer shorts in plain colours, no stripes, and the fact that he was allergic to pure wool next to his skin. She read all this out to me from the back of Armstrong and added that I needn't worry about cosmetics as that would be taken care of by Marcus.

I had asked: Marcus *who*? And she had said Marcus Moore, Ross's personal hairdresser on twenty-four-hour stand-by, as if I was clinically brain dead. But at least that reminded her that she ought to brief me about Kurt Valori, who was Ross's personal trainer and would be arriving tomorrow; and Christine Schwartz, who was Ross's personal publicist (though she had nothing to do with Tony Lovisi's public relations outfit); and Eugenie Pomeroy, who worked for Ross's agent's London office; and the catering company Ross always used if he wanted to entertain.

And there were dozens more. Lin droned on through the list, though I'd stopped listening. The point she was making was that all these people expected instant access to Ross, but wouldn't get it unless they went through her. All except Marcus the hairdresser, that is. He really was on twenty-four-hour stand-by whenever Ross was filming, and when his skills were needed, roads were cleared, sirens turned on.

All those on the list would get access to the Ross presence, of course, but it was Lin's job to know who, when and what they wanted. She was there to 'lessen the stress' on Ross, help him get through the day. Make sure everyone who should see him did so, but in an orderly fashion with the stop-watch ticking.

There was one exception, though. No matter how hard he pleaded, how low he grovelled or how much he offered in bribes, one individual was not allowed anywhere near Ross, on-set or off – Walter Wilkes Booth.

'The scriptwriter,' I had said proudly, showing off that I did know something after all. 'Why not him?'

'Because he's the scriptwriter,' Lin had said, as if that explained all.

'Oh, yeah, right, I see,' I had said but I just felt stupid again.

I parked Armstrong slap bang outside the front door of the apartment block on double yellow lines about five feet from a 'No Parking' sign.

'You can't park here,' said Lin primly.

'I'm a black London cab. I can park anywhere.'

We got out and I locked Armstrong before following Lin into the building. She was hefting a set of keys in her right hand as if she might throw them at somebody.

In the entrance hall she strode over to the lifts and pressed the call button and then swung her head imperiously from side to side, sniffing the air for a target. In the corner of the hall was a wood and glass office with a door marked House Manager. It appeared empty but I thought I heard the scrape of furniture at one point. Lin obviously picked something up on her radar.

As soon as we were in the lift and she had punched the button for the third floor, she said:

'I bet he was in there all the time. That toe-rag of a house manager, Foster. He's hiding from me.'

'And why would he do that?' I asked, thinking of no more than a thousand reasons off the top of my head.

'He's the one who told the tabloids about Ross not spending

New Year's Eve here. He's almost certainly on somebody's pay-roll, the bastard. I'm supposed to hand these keys in when we leave. I do hope he's there to accept them.'

For the moment she had to make do with inserting the keys into the apartment door rather than the unfortunate Mr Foster. I don't know what I had been expecting to find in the flat, apart from the luxury fittings and fitments you would expect if you were paying as much rent as Ross was. These were there in spades to be sure, but apart from clothes in the wardrobes, a couple of paperback novels, a pile of scripts (unread) and five bottles of malt whisky, all unopened and still in their Christmas box wrappings, there wasn't much else. It could have been a hotel room almost anywhere in the world.

'He hasn't exactly made himself at home, has he?'

'He can't afford to,' said Lin, opening a closet door and pulling out two very classy leather suitcases. 'This place has cleaners and laundry service every day, plus the bastard Foster snooping around. Somebody in Ross's position can't afford to leave any-thing lying around, not unless he wants to read about it in the papers tomorrow.'

We were back to the trust theory of life and I wondered why Ross trusted Lin, or rather, what had made him trust her in the first place. Somebody had said they had worked together for several years, so what had he seen in her back then? Of course Ross could not have known how big a star he was going to become, though being an actor he had probably assumed it. Maybe she worked for peanuts in those days and Ross was rewarding her loyalty. Maybe she had something on him, but then if she had she would probably have gone for the lump sum down payment and an easy life rather than running around after him, learning his shoe size, answering his mail, soothing his ego, packing his underwear like she was doing now. Maybe he had made a pass at her. Maybe she was waiting to make a pass at him. Maybe it was just me who found her humourless, paranoid and not a little scary.

I followed her into the bedroom where she slammed the suitcases flat on the made-up double bed and began to undo the straps.

'I'll do his clothes,' she said. 'You check the bathroom. There should be a wash bag in there. Don't leave anything, and I mean anything, that that bastard Foster can sell to the souvenir hunters.'

I didn't ask if that included hair in the plugholes as that would only have got her worried about somebody trying to get hold of Ross's DNA. As it was, there wasn't much apart from aftershave and deodorants because he would have taken an overnight bag down to Julius Cockburn's place. I did find the wash bag, though, a silk affair decorated with Chinese characters and dragons, and in the bottom of it was an unopened packet of condoms on which the 'Use Before' date was five months previously. Maybe this superstar life was not all it was cracked up to be.

Back in the bedroom, Lin had filled one case and was reaching into a wardrobe for a pair of red silk pyjamas on a hanger. She squirreled them into the second suitcase as if embarrassed. I did the diplomatic thing and ignored them, not that I have anything against red silk pyjamas – Amy looks really good climbing out of hers – but what sort of man hangs them up on a coat-hanger?

'Check the living-room,' she ordered briskly, 'and make sure you get every scrap of paper in case he's written a message or anything.'

'Will do,' I said cheerfully, beginning to feel a bit like a spy or the suave skiing detective Ross played in *White Cut* and, more recently, in *Side Edge*.

It was while I was snooping around the CD and DVD players, which seemed to come as standard fittings for the flat, that I happened to glance out of the window overlooking the front of the block.

Armstrong was parked where I had left him, but now there was a blue Ford Granada parked with its engine running just down the street in one direction and thirty yards in the other direction was a guy sitting on a parked motor bike, reaching behind him into the carrier box for a long lens to attach to the camera slung round his neck.

I guessed that Mr Foster was not only in the building, but had been busy.

Lin did a final scout of the room trying to sniff out any stray strands of hair or incriminating stains. I thought she might have checked inside the lavatory water tank to see if Ross had a secret supply of dope taped around the ballcock, but she didn't. (I had; there wasn't.)

'I think that's everything. You know where to go?' she said when she was satisfied.

'You've told me twice and drawn me a map,' I said. 'What about you?'

'I've got to hand the keys in, give Bastard Foster a piece of my mind and then I've got things to do here in town. I'll get a real cab from here. See you tomorrow.'

I had my marching orders and picked up the two suitcases into which all trace of Ross Pirie had been crammed.

'Have you been given a mobile phone yet?' Lin said as an afterthought.

I shook my head.

'Then see Alix first thing. Everybody carries one except Ross, and I mean everybody. You keep it switched on at all times. All the key numbers will be punched in for you.'

'Right. It's good to talk,' I agreed and she gave me that look again, somewhere between pity and despair.

We took the lift down together and then, without a word, she headed off towards the house manager's office. If Bastard Foster was in there, hiding under the table, I almost felt sorry for him. She left me to struggle with the spring-loaded doors to get the suitcases out on to the street.

I had taken no more than two steps when the cameras started clicking.

Two guys were coming towards me from the parked Ford, one holding a camera to his face and clicking first me, then the front of Armstrong. The guy on the motor bike took an automatic whirr of shots with the camera round his neck, then climbed out of the saddle and he too walked towards me. They were all badly dressed, cocky and younger than me, which would help.

They assumed I was the cab driver, so I gave them their money's worth.

'Oi! What the fuck you tossers think yer doin'?'

'Just doin' our job, mate,' said the one out of the Ford without a camera, while his mate with the camera glared at the bike-riding photographer. 'You working a fare?'

I walked by him, close enough to see the white patches on his face where he'd put on too much Clearasil, and put down the cases so I could unlock Armstrong. His mate immediately photographed the luggage.

'No, mate, it's my day off. I'm collecting for Oxfam,' I said with a sneer.

'Whose is that luggage?' said the even pimplier youth under the crash helmet, twisting his lens grip to zoom in on the designer label.

'I neither know nor care, son, and neither should you,' I said, piling the cases into the luggage space next to the driver's seat.

'Do you know where you're taking it?' asked the first guy.

I closed the side door and turned to him, hands on hips.

'No, 'course I don't. This guy just says get on the road to Damascus and sooner or later this big finger'll come down from the heavens and point the way for me. What the bleedin' hell d'you think?'

The non-photographer one bit his bottom lip to keep his temper.

'Yeah, right, sure, fine. Do you know who ordered the cab?' he tried.

'The bloke I'm taking the cases to,' I answered as if he'd asked: Are frogs waterproof? 'It's a personal delivery.'

'Did you get a name?' asked the biker.

'Yeah, a Mr Ross or something like that. Why? What's it to you lot?'

'Double fare if you take me along,' said the first guy, reaching for his wallet.

'Bugger off,' I snarled. 'Get me done for double-booking in the kipper season? You must be joking.'

I wasn't sure whether they understood that the kipper season for cab drivers was January and February, when trade went flat after Christmas and New Year, or if they were aware of the latest clampdown by the local authorities on cabs picking up people whilst on their way to a booked job. But they got the gist.

I got into Armstrong and made to close the door.

'What if I gave you the fare, but made my own way there?' he tried.

I sniffed loudly and closed the door, staring straight ahead of me for about five seconds before I pulled down the window.

103

'Twenty quid's the fare,' I said.

'What's the address?' the first guy said with a sickly smile.

'Each,' I said.

He produced two £20 notes from his wallet but kept a firm grip on them.

'He's not with us,' he said, jerking the money towards the lad in the crash helmet.

'All or nothing,' I said.

The guy turned on the biker.

'Come on, Jacko, fucking cough up. No freebies on this one. You're not following us on your push-bike for nothing this time.'

That was what I had been worrying about. I could have lost the Ford no sweat in the lunchtime traffic, but if you want to follow a black cab in London, you need a motor bike.

Reluctantly the biker dug into his leather jacket and produced two crumpled £10 notes.

When the money came through the window, I palmed it and started Armstrong's engine.

'Number 9, Stuart Street, Hackney,' I said.

They were off and running towards their vehicles like a Grand Prix start and didn't even bother to hang around and watch me turn south towards Wandsworth Bridge and the river.

I stopped for a pie and a pint in a cracking Young's pub near Dorking and then pressed on to find Julius Cockburn's house while there was still daylight. Lin's map was spot on, though. I went through Horsham and out into St Leonard's Forest where St Leonard's Grange nestled between the golf courses.

It was quite an impressive pile, the sort of house you see in a BBC costume drama where they spread sand over the driveway for the horses and carriages. But there was a very modern BMW Series 7 parked outside.

I pulled Armstrong up right behind it and unloaded Ross's cases, carrying them up to the impressive oak front door complete with bell-pull. I must have looked like a travelling salesman of old, or an evacuee child from the East End during the Blitz.

I began to feel like an extra from a porn movie when the door creaked open to reveal, and I do mean reveal, a middle-aged blonde wearing only jewellery and a badly tied white bathrobe. Her toenails were painted gold and she wasn't a natural blonde.

'Yes?' was all she said, putting her head on one side. She seemed to be having trouble with the word, probably because she was as high as a kite.

'I've brought these for Ross Pirie,' I said, hoping that wasn't too difficult for her.

She leaned on the door to open it wide and she leaned with it until she was at roughly the same angle as the leaning tower in Pisa.

Now if we had really been working to a porn film script, this would have been the place where she said: 'He's not here, so come on in, Big Boy' or similar, and we'd have cut immediately to the bedroom or the jacuzzi or the billiard table, depending upon the budget.

Instead she just pointed a finger to the floor of the hallway, which was made of dark red square tiles and seemed to go on forever, and said: 'Put them there.' And as soon as I had, she let the door go and I had to step back smartish as it slammed shut.

And there I was outside again. So much for my career in porn films.

I took a step back towards Armstrong and stopped in my tracks as the BMW in front of me started to hum in stereo as the passenger side window came down and the driver's seat came up from the recline position. The driver had been doing what drivers do when they're not driving; having a kip.

And this was a professional. I could tell that immediately from the dark suit, white shirt and thin dark blue tie, plus the new box of Kleenex on the dashboard.

'She anywhere near ready, mate?' he asked me.

'Ready for what?' I said.

He chuckled at that.

'Don't get me started,' he said. 'Are you this Angel we've been warned about?'

'Sounds like me,' I answered honestly. 'You with the studio?'

'For my sins, mate, for my sins. I'm Dave, Mr Cockburn's driver.'

'He has a driver too?'

If he did, and Ross was staying here, why was I on duty at 5 a.m.? Some people were so selfish.

'Has to,' said Dave, making drinking motions with his right hand.

'He's not alone, is he?' I nodded towards the house.

'Oh, she's a terror, that one. I'm supposed to take her up to some do in the West End and then bring the lot of them back here.'

'That include Ross?'

'Yes. He's a nice man, that Ross. Never had any trouble with him.'

'Driven him before?'

'Once or twice. Frank Shoosmith was his regular though.'

'You know Frank?'

I checked myself from saying 'knew' as if he were dead.

'What, old Spiderman? Sure, known him for years.'

'How is he?'

Dave the Driver pursed his lips, exhaled and shook his head. He looked for all the world like a garage mechanic about to give me an estimate.

'Not good. No broken bones amazingly but something's gone up here.' He tapped his forehead. 'He can't remember anything about what happened, doesn't even know why he was out at the studio that day. Should have been Christmas shopping with the wife.'

'So he remembers he's got a wife?'

Dave gave me a you-taking-the-piss? look, then grinned.

'Oh yeah. Spiderman was never that lucky. The doctors say it's selective amnesia. They're doing tests and scans and stuff.'

'Did they test for drugs and booze?'

Dave jutted his chin, pulling himself up to his full seated height. I could almost hear his feathers being ruffled.

'Steady on, Mr Angel. You don't know Frank. He wouldn't –'

'I'm not saying he did, I'm just asking if they tested. It might be something hanging over him, that's all. The cops weren't involved, were they?'

'No need. Frank wasn't on the public highway.'

'And they got him into a private hospital as quickly as they could, didn't they?'

106

'That's why they've got medical insurance. It's a nice place. It's called The Oaks, over in Slough.'

'You've seen Frank?' I said, not really knowing why I should be surprised.

'Sure. He's bearing up, all things considered. Feels terrible about letting Ross down, mind you, and 'course he's worried about his rating with the fleet.'

'The fleet?'

'Oh yeah, I forgot,' said Dave with a superior air, 'they did warn me you were a freelance. The film company gets a fleet deal on the cars.'

He took a business card from the top pocket of his jacket and handed it over. It read: CHILTERN CARS OF AMERSHAM – HUNDREDS TO CHOOSE FROM, and there was an address and phone numbers and an e-mail address.

'Chiltern. Hundreds. Nice one. I like that,' I said.

Dave looked at me blankly.

'What?'

'Never mind. Will the fleet have Frank's car?'

'I suppose so, for the insurance. If it's a write-off then Frank won't be flavour of the month.'

I knew enough from knowing people like Duncan the Drunken for many years to know that no car is ever a write-off as long as somebody had a welding torch and enough incentive, but I didn't go there with Dave. He might have been shocked. I pocketed the card.

'So, let me get this straight. Chiltern rents the cars to the film company – Last Ditch in this case – but the studio hires the drivers. Drivers they know and trust, that they've worked with before. That's the way it works, is it?'

'Yeah, that's about it.'

Dave made a sort of snorting noise down his nose.

'They warned me you'd be asking all sorts of questions,' he said smugly.

'Who's been doing all this warning you about me, Dave?'

'Everybody,' he said honestly.

Everybody seemed to know about me, that was for sure.

The next morning, as I drove into Pinewood, I was greeted

107

with smiles, waves and mock salutes. This time I took a map from the gatekeeper and he told me I could find Ross in his trailer parked outside Studio 7.

I had presumed the security guard meant trailer as in 'caravan' or 'mobile home' but I wasn't prepared for how big the thing was. This wasn't a mobile home, it was a mobile housing development and it had more rooms than my old flat in Stuart Street, a bar, a bigger hi-fi system, a bigger TV with video and DVD players, leather armchairs, pictures on the wall (real, painted ones, not ones cut from magazines), fresh flowers and no cats.

'Like it?' asked Ross from way down the other end near a pair of Bang and Olufsen speakers.

I waited a second just to see if there was an echo in there.

'Impressive,' I said. He had this and we were going to spend the rest of the day finding somewhere for him to live? What a life.

'It goes everywhere with me,' he said proudly. 'I designed it myself with a feng shui expert out in LA. Do you know anything about feng shui?'

'I know you should never put the rock near the hard place,' I said, keeping eye contact.

It took him about a minute. Like I said, actors were easy.

'Oh yes, very good. I'll remember that one.'

No he wouldn't. Nobody was paying him to say it.

'Lin'll be here in a minute. She's collecting the estate agent from Paul Brettler's office.'

'You're having him security-cleared?'

I only asked out of interest, though I privately thought a strip search and an internal examination were a wise precaution when dealing with estate agents. They might not achieve much but at least you felt you got your money's worth that way.

'She. It's always a "she" or so it seems. And Paul insists on a security check. You wouldn't believe the people who try to get in here.'

'Like the provisional wing of the Caravan Club,' I said looking around me.

But he didn't get that and I didn't have time to explain as there was a knock on the trailer door and Lin arrived with a Miss Maggie Vinall in tow.

*   *   *

108

I imagined that Maggie Vinall had won the Ross Pirie sweep-stake in the office where she worked, which was probably called Short Lets For The Filthy Rich or something similar. First prize: a drive in the country in the back of a cab with the object of her lust. Business didn't enter into it. Ross could have asked her to show him a treehouse on Mars and she would have given it a go. Apart from giving me directions, she didn't notice I was there, and she sat so close to him in the back of Armstrong that you couldn't have got a cigarette paper between them.

Ross was genuinely more interested in reading the printed particulars of the houses on the agenda than he was in looking down her cleavage, so I did that for him whenever I got the chance. She didn't mind because she didn't notice me, only having eyes for Ross. I was starting to get an idea of what it must be like to be invisible, though at one point, between tracks, she did say that she had never ridden in a black cab which played music so loudly before, and certainly not Ian Dury's 'Mr Love Pants'. Ross smiled at me in the mirror at that. I took it as his way of saying thanks for the distraction.

The first place we saw was out near Chesham. Miss Vinall told us it had six bedrooms, three bathrooms, one en suite, servants' quarters, a fully equipped gym and sauna in the cellar, stables and paddock out back.

We got out of Armstrong and stood there looking at it, and at the open driveway with no gates, fence, barbed wire or machine gun nests. I shook my head. Miss Vinall didn't notice me, but Ross did.

'This is actually owned by a well-known British film pro-ducer,' she gushed. 'And it actually has a water bed . . .'

'But no helipad,' I said.

'Good point,' said Ross. 'Next.'

The next on her list was a converted barn, with eight bed-rooms and the rest, between Chesham and Berkhamsted. Virtu-ally all of one side was glass, showing the split-level rooms and spiral staircase inside. With a decent lens you could pick out Ross's blackheads without getting out of your car.

'The master bedroom has a four-poster,' said Miss Vinall.

'No barbecue pit,' I said. 'And the weather's bound to improve.'

Ross nodded, catching on.

'Next.'

In a village outside Great Missenden, a lovely Georgian pile very tastefully modernised with A1 security including CCTV. Which shared a tennis court at the rear with the neighbouring girls' boarding school. Another time, in another life, perhaps.

'The feng shui's all wrong,' I warned Ross.

'You've got a point, Angel,' he said deadpan. 'The rock here is so close to the hard place it's not true.'

'You got that right.'

Then we found it, out towards Chinnor on the outskirts of a hamlet called Eight Ash Green. It was actually called Eight Ash House – a 200-year-old farmhouse with seven bedrooms, a servants' annexe, four bathrooms, jacuzzi, sauna, a barn and stables, a lake big enough to hold alligators without upsetting the eco-system, parking for up to eight cars as long as only two were Rolls-Royces, a stone terrace at the back reached by two sets of french windows with wonderful empty views of the Chilterns.

Best of all, the house was a mile away from the next nearest one in Eight Ash Green and was itself set back a hundred yards from the road to the village. A five-foot wall edged the property along the road and behind it, somebody had planted those really boring leylandii trees which grow like Triffids. They were at least fifteen feet high, waving in the breeze, an eyesore to serious gardeners but a delight to anyone who wanted more than their fair share of privacy.

Maggie Vinall told us that the gate had been opened for us by the lady from the village who came in to clean. Normally it was linked to a state-of-the-art alarm system in the house, which also controlled motion-sensitive floodlights. It was a condition of the lease that the alarm was set on every occasion the house was left empty.

'Who owns the place?' I asked as I steered Armstrong up the driveway.

Maggie Vinall ignored me. She only had eyes for Ross. So Ross repeated the question.

'I'm not at liberty to say,' she protested sulkily, implying that she would do anything for Ross normally. 'But I can tell you he's in the Diplomatic Service and he's away a lot.'

Whoever he was, he was certainly well connected.

His cleaning lady had arrived with a police escort.

There was a perfectly reasonable explanation for it, of course, as I told Amy later that night just before I went to bed.

Actually it wasn't very late that night, it was around 8 p.m. and Amy still couldn't get her head round the fact that I was going to bed even though I had set two alarm clocks, the timer on the CD player and punched in an alarm call on the phone, all for 3 a.m.

'The cleaning lady is a Mrs Winter and she's married to a PC Winter, the local copper. Well, actually he's a copper over in Aylesbury but he lives in the village. And he had to be there anyway.'

'To drive his wife in a police car?' Amy asked with a fair pinch of sarcasm.

I don't know why she was getting at me, she had been the one who had insisted I told her *every* detail of my day out with Ross.

'No, because of the guns.'

'What guns?'

'Half a dozen antique shotguns. The house owner likes to blast away at the wildlife whenever he's home.'

'He's leaving guns on the property and he's renting it out? You're making this up.'

'No I'm not. The guns are in a steel cabinet in the wine cellar, all locked up and kosher and PC Winter was there to read the Riot Act as to why Ross had to be responsible for them even though he wasn't allowed to use them.'

Amy snorted.

'Pah! I bet he just wanted to meet Ross.'

'No, I don't think so. He was just doing his duty.'

PC Winter had whispered to me: 'He's smaller than he is at the pictures, but the wife likes him.'

'So this house with its own armoury is the one then?'

'Yep. We move in tomorrow after the second unit's done the scenes where –'

I didn't get any further. Amy's face became a mask.

'*We*? What's with this *we* shit?'

9

SET DRESSING

'Frank always used to have a selection of newspapers for me to read,' said Ross from the back of Armstrong, over the music.

'Did he now?' I said through clenched teeth.

'If I didn't have any script to learn, that is.'

Oh well, Frank would have thought of things like that. Frank probably knew where to get freshly ground coffee and dough-nuts at 5.30 a.m. in the middle of a dark wood thick with frost in the middle of Sussex. Then again, Frank probably drove a car where the heater worked properly and almost certainly wouldn't have been half an hour late.

'Got much to learn?' I asked, feigning interest on the grounds that I'd read somewhere that keeping talking was a good way to stave off hypothermia.

'This morning is mostly make-up tests and then the second unit gets some establishing shots. I've actually only got one line of dialogue today.'

'Then I'll let you get on with that,' I said, turning down the volume on some remixed Chaka Khan. After all, Pinewood was less than two hours away and he had a whole line to memorise.

After a minute or so, he said:

'You're not really a morning person, are you, Roy?'

'You're not wrong there,' I agreed. 'But this doesn't count as morning. This is still night. Mornings involve daylight. Hey, how about that as a title for the movie – *Daylight*, instead of *Daybreak*?'

'It's been done. A Sly Stallone action flick.'

'Oh yeah, you're right,' I said, annoyed with myself for missing that one. 'You ever fancied doing the big budget blockbuster?'

'Sure. It's always a challenge to make yourself heard above the

112

explosions. They say no movie should cost more than $4 million as long as you don't want explosions.'

'Tell that to George Lucas next time you see him.'

'Nice thought, but I probably won't,' he laughed, leaning forward now to talk to me through the sliding panel.

'No, best not. You'll never work in this galaxy again.'

He chuckled some more at that, his teeth reflected in the headlights of oncoming traffic. What was it that website had called him? The old 'pants charmer' himself. I was beginning to see why.

'You're OK to move into Eight Ash House?' he asked.

'Yeah, sure. How about you?'

'I'll be glad to. I'm kind of in the way down at Julius's house.'

'You mean you get in the way between Mrs Julius and the gin bottle?'

'Something like that. I guess I just like the bachelor life.'

'Me too.'

I could feel him looking at me.

'How did Amy take the news that you were moving out to the country?' he said carefully.

'Very well. She was really pleased when I told her. Over the moon. Then she realised I said "out to the country" and not "out of the country".'

'And?'

'And then she was really pissed off. It's just jealousy, really.'

I couldn't tell in the dark whether he was blushing or not at that. Being an actor, he probably wasn't.

'You sure you don't mind spending the next six weeks or so out at the house? There will be time off, of course.'

'For good behaviour?'

'When I'm away, I meant,' he said.

'No sweat, we're cool. I'm ready to move in. Got all my gear.'

I reached over and patted the Adidas sports bag I had thrown into the luggage well where the front passenger seat would have been if black cabs had one.

'Is that it?' asked Ross. 'Just the one bag?'

I was hurt.

'I had trouble filling that.'

Pinewood. My first day working on a movie. I'd had two breakfasts and it still wasn't properly light. I hadn't seen an actor I recognised (apart from Ross who had been whisked away by the make-up department), nor anyone from the production company. I hadn't seen a camera, nor heard anyone shout, 'Lights! Roll over! Action!'

In fact the only thing I did recognise was the mini fire engine I had seen the other day, and only then because it almost ran me down as it negotiated a corner between two of the sound studios. The driver gave me a friendly toot on his horn and a wave as he drove by me, so close he cooled the coffee in the styrofoam cup I was carrying.

There were plenty of people around, wandering from studio to office to canteen to one of the many mobile tea trolleys which also did bacon sandwiches. The average age seemed to be about twenty-two and the regulation uniform seemed to be jeans, with fake-fur parkas for the women and bomber jackets for the men. Some jackets advertised films on the back, as did the baseball caps which seemed to be almost compulsory. *The World Is Not Enough* seemed to be the most popular and I made a mental note to ask Ross to get me a *Daybreak* one. Most people wore scarves and gloves against the cold and everybody, but everybody, was talking into a mobile phone or a walkie-talkie, probably to people less than fifty feet away.

Nobody seemed to be actually doing anything except drinking coffee, shouting hello to old friends and swapping Christmas horror stories or boasting about the last film they were on – which invariably had a bigger budget, better locations, regular free supplies of Class A drugs and expense claims to die for. It was like the first day back at school after the holidays, which for most of them was exactly what it was.

As I mooched around scrounging coffee and cigarettes (they all seemed to smoke) I tried to chat up several of the younger female 'runners' as they called themselves, casually dropping into conversation that I was Ross's personal driver and I knew just how much he was looking forward to doing this film. It didn't seem to cut the mustard as they all showed total disinterest and suddenly remembered they had to call somebody on their mobiles or their radios.

'It's not that they're not interested, Angel,' said a voice behind

114

me, 'it's just that it is *so* uncool to *show* an interest. Most of them would sell you their virginity just to find out what colour underwear Ross put on this morning, but they'd never admit it.'

It was Burgundy Dulude and it worried me that she had come up behind me so quietly.

She was wearing a scruffy US Navy-issue parka with the hood up, the fur trimming forming a double halo with her hair.

'You sure they've still got something to sell in the virginity department?' I asked.

'Oh yes,' she said seriously. 'And they're all from good homes and putting in unsociable hours in sub-zero temperatures for peanuts and the chance to say they've worked in the movies.'

'So are you,' I observed.

'But only until the right casting director comes along and I can sleep with him.'

She looked me in the eye and didn't flinch. She was good.

'Or her,' she added with perfect timing.

She was damned good.

'I have the ear of the big star of this picture,' I said reasonably. 'I could always put a word in for you.'

She made like she was working out a complex mathematical formula, arguing with herself.

'So, if I'm prepared to sleep with a casting director and you say you can perform the function, so to speak, of one, then the question surely has to be: would I be prepared to sleep with you?' She paused for effect. 'Well, I'm not against charity per se but . . . But you'll be too busy. Alix Tse wants to see you over in the admin building, then Paul Brettler, though I can't think why I'm running around after you.'

'You forget, Burgundy, I'm a friend of the family.' I smiled my best smile.

'As if I could.'

I followed her down the narrow streets between the hermetically sealed studios and promised myself that one day I would have a look inside one, see if I could see a movie being made anywhere. I said as much to Burgundy.

'Making a film is like sex,' she said calmly. 'Lots of talk beforehand, numerous lunches, mountains of money involved and promises of great things afterwards, but the actual thing gets done in three-minute bursts.'

115

We had arrived at the admin block and she held the door open for me. I could see the diminutive form of Alix Tse standing in an office doorway waiting for me.

'Three minutes, huh?' I said to Burgundy as I walked through, not giving her the chance of a comeback.

Alix Tse was wearing a different trouser suit today, this one light brown with a wide stripe, which didn't make her look any taller.

Her office had a desk on which sat one of the new see-through AppleMacs and a keyboard. There was nothing else on the desk except a Nokia cell phone and a charger unit, a BT pager and a sheet of paper.

'These are for you, Mr Angel,' Alix said, moving behind the desk.

There was one chair on this side of the desk so I sat down. Burgundy slumped into an armchair near the wall. Alix remained standing.

I picked up the sheet of paper first. It was a list of names:

1 Lin
2 Gloria-Maria
3 Burgundy
4 Paul Brettler
5 Tony Lovisi Associates
6 Eugenie Pomeroy
7 Christine Schwartz
8 Marcus Moore
9 Kurt Valori

'Those are the numbers already programmed into your speed-dial memory,' said Alix. 'All those people have your number and your pager number.'

'Remind me,' I said, 'who is Eugenie Pomeroy?'

'She works for the London office of Ross's agents, Walt Roscow Global,' said Alix.

'And Christine Schwartz?'

'Ross's personal publicist.'

'She mostly organises photo-shoots for Ross,' Burgundy chipped in. 'People who get invited to the set want their picture taken with the big star. Pain in the ass really.'

'Marcus Moore and Kurt Valori?'

'Ross's personal hairdresser and physical trainer,' said Alix, glaring at Burgundy, expecting another comment from the sidelines.

'Oh yes, I've heard about Marcus, I think.'

'You'll warm to Marcus,' drawled Burgundy. 'Trust me on that.'

I ignored her, smiling instead at Alix, trying to win her over as I pocketed the phone and the pager and folded the sheet of paper. It was as effective as breathing on an iceberg. I might as well have saved my jaw muscles the effort.

'That all seems clear,' I said politely.

'You'll take your daily instructions from Lin,' she said, then paused as if waiting for this to sink in.

'That has been made abundantly clear,' I said.

But still she waited and I had no idea what it was I wasn't doing.

'I think Lin would expect you to turn the phone *on*,' said Burgundy drily.

'Ah, yes.'

I smiled a 'silly me' apology at Alix and took the phone out of my pocket and pressed the On button. It rang immediately. The chirping electronic ringing tone was the first three bars of the theme from *The Great Escape*. Burgundy burst out laughing.

'Hello, Lin,' I said. It was a good guess.

'I have your schedule for today. Come to Ross's trailer when you've finished over there.'

Before I could say anything she had cut the connection, but I kept the Nokia to my ear just for the hell of it.

'Yes . . . If I can spare the time . . . I'll see if I can squeeze you in . . . Missing you already.'

Then I closed the phone and slipped it back into my pocket, but I knew I hadn't fooled anyone.

'I need you to sign a contract,' said Alix, pushing a button on her keyboard. Somewhere under the desk a high speed printer hummed and she reached down and began to hand four pages of small print, one after the other across the desk.

'This is our standard consultancy agreement which is valid for two months. You will be paid pro-rata direct into a bank account of your choice on a fortnightly basis, but being self-employed, you are responsible for all tax, National Insurance and so on. This is a short-term contract which does not entitle you to any health benefits or pension scheme. It can be terminated without compensation at twenty-four hours' notice on either side. As, I understand, you are providing your own vehicle, your fee reflects that. We will cover any out-of-pocket expenses including fuel and modifications to the vehicle. The contract also includes the standard confidentiality agreement. Please read it all and sign at the bottom of each page.'

'When you say "modifications to the vehicle" – what exactly does that mean?' I said as I flipped through the pages, thinking I might be able to get a new set of tyres out of them.

'In this case, those would be any modifications deemed necessary by Ross Pirie by the transportation sub-clause in his head contract.'

'I see,' I said, though I didn't.

'It means Ross can insist you install a cocktail cabinet in the back of your cab if he needs one,' Burgundy said sweetly.

'Seems reasonable,' I mused.

'Richard Widmark in *The Last Wagon*,' said Burgundy almost as a reflex.

'Very good,' I muttered, partly at her but also because I had just seen the figure of £5,000 typed in the section under 'remuneration'. 'Anyone have a pen?'

'Don't you want to read it properly?' asked Alix, although a felt-tip pen had materialised in her hand.

'I'm cool with everything,' I said.

'Then sign the bottom of each page and fill in the details of your bank account in the section on page four.'

I signed 'R. Maclean', which was one of the advantages of having a name like mine. I could be, and had been, Roy Maclean, Fitzroy Angel and Roy F. Angel when it came to official documentation. I even had one of the new European Union-approved photocard driving licences and a bank account in the name R. Maclean, which neither the taxman nor Amy knew about.

'Leave that one with me and I'll run off a copy for your files,' Alix said, counter-signing each sheet as I passed them back to her as the printer hummed again somewhere underneath her.

'You mentioned expenses,' I said.

Now when you say that to an accountant, the next thing you

usually hear is a sharp intake of breath followed by a drumming of fingernails on the nearest hard surface. I don't know why they have to make such a thing of it. I've tried to explain it simply to them, that if there weren't people like me trying to claim expenses, they wouldn't have a job. But they don't see it that way. I'd read somewhere that it was the right frontal lobe of the brain which was responsible for the sense of humour and could only assume that the operation to remove it had been perfected on accountants.

'You wish to make a claim already?' she said with steel in her voice.

'Not just yet,' I said reasonably. 'But I did want to ask you about petrol receipts. Frank Shoosmith's petrol receipts actually.'

'What about them?' she asked quickly.

'Did Frank make any claims for petrol?'

'Of course he did.'

'I'm only interested in the week before he had his accident.'

'What have they got to do with his accident?'

'Nothing as far as I know. I just wanted to have a look, see what his routine was.'

Alix didn't look as if she believed that for a minute, but then neither did I.

'I can't give you access to our computerised accounts –'

'I don't want that. I just want to see the receipts or the credit card slips. Whatever it was he handed in to get the cash back.'

'Oh, the paper copies,' she said almost to herself, as if bits of paper were somehow distasteful. 'The same applies. I cannot open the books without some authorisation.'

'Not even for Ross Pirie?' I tried.

Burgundy shrieked another laugh.

'Especially not for Ross! Jees-us, he might find out that they're paying Zina Ray more than he's getting!'

'Are they?'

'I dunno,' she grinned.

Alix Tse's expression had not changed.

'How about Paul Brettler?'

'He works for Pinewood Studios, not the production company.'

119

'Try Gloria-Maria,' offered Burgundy, head down looking at the floor.

Alix looked at her. She didn't stare, didn't say anything, just looked. I had no idea what she was thinking.

'How about Miss van Doodler?'

'Yes, she can authorise access to the petty cash accounts.'

I waited but she wasn't going to offer anything else.

'I'll give her a ring, then, shall I?' I reached for my new mobile phone. 'What was she on the memory?'

'I'll e-mail her,' said Alix.

'Well, that's fine then. Let me know what she says. We done here?'

She nodded once and handed me the copy of my contract.

'Then I'll say have a nice day and get out of your hair,' I said.

She just said: 'Yes.'

Outside her office in the long corridor again, Burgundy let out a long, low whistle.

'Well, you really got to her,' she said.

'I did?'

'Yeah. I've never seen her so agitated before.'

'You haven't?'

'I think she must have the hots for you.'

'As if.'

I had never seen anyone less agitated than Alix Tse, at least not anyone who was supposed to be breathing.

'You know where Paul's office is?' Burgundy flicked the hood of her parka up and over her blonde tresses and pulled a walkie-talkie out of one of the pockets. 'Keep going down this corridor to the end then take a left.'

'You're not coming?'

'No, I'm supposed to be working, not giving you the guided tour.'

'Then what were you doing in Alix's office?'

'Oh, I just had to see how you two bonded. Have a nice rest of the day.'

And with a searing flash of perfect American teeth, she turned on her heel and stomped off. She was yelling at somebody down the radio before she reached the doors.

I started down the corridor and realised I was still holding the copy of my contract. I began to fold it so I could stuff it in my jacket when I reread that magic line about the £5,000 fee.

'Shit!'

I looked around furtively but the corridor was empty, so I crammed the sheets into my inside pocket.

The contract said *instalments* of £5,000 *every* two weeks.

Amy was definitely not going to know about this. She might stop my allowance.

'I've been taking your advice,' Paul Brettler said.

That wasn't something I heard on a regular basis.

'I've been checking out the websites on the Internet like you suggested, and I think you're on to something.'

I did? I was?

I let him talk. He had offered me a comfortable chair and a fresh cup of decent coffee and turned the monitor of his PC so I could watch him surf the Net. I felt like we were two workmates chewing the fat at the end of the working day before deciding which pub to go to. The only trouble was it was still only 9 a.m.

'I've found twenty-five relevant sites and that doesn't include official ones like Last Ditch Productions or Walt Roscow Global, Ross's agent, or the official Ross Pirie Fan Club one. There are also over forty links to other sites where Ross gets mentioned, making about 1,200 pages in all.'

I settled back in my chair. I didn't mind flipping through them. After all, I was getting paid for this.

'Now most of it, we can live with,' said Brettler. 'Some of the sites are so amateur and take so long to download that they'll never get looked at.'

'Why not?'

'Because if a site doesn't come up within something like eight seconds, the average surfer moves on to the next. You've got to be slick and you've got to be quick these days to hold the young browser with the attention span of a piece of roadkill. That's why the big commercial sites hire web jockeys now to keep people talking in the chat rooms.'

'The Left Click Culture,' I agreed, 'but didn't I read somewhere that about a third of web users are over sixty-five?'

'They may well be but they don't buy stuff electronically. They use the Net for research or to educate themselves, things like that.'

I tut-tutted at the very idea as Brettler clicked on to the site which Amy had found for me, the one with the picture of Ross, the cover of the book of *Daybreak* and the headline 'This Movie Sucks'.

'I must say I like that catchline,' I said. 'They should use it on the posters when the film comes out.'

Brettler grinned.

'You could mention it to Gloria-Maria or Don Sager if you ever see him again, but don't do it while Julius Cockburn is in earshot.'

'Sensitive, is he?'

'Oh yes. Creative geniuses are, aren't they? He's convinced he's got a shot at an Oscar or two with this one. The people who did this site agree with him, but then they think Wesley Snipes should have had one for *Blade*.'

'This would be the vampire fan club, would it?'

'Yeah. We call them the Goths. In fact they call themselves that, or Gothics. These people are really into vampires – it's not just a fashion and black eye make-up thing – it's the whole life-style.'

'Shouldn't that be deathstyle?'

'Maybe,' he nodded agreement. 'But generally they're harm-less. The vast majority of them are women, funnily enough, and they come out of the woodwork and on to the Net whenever there's a new book or movie or computer game about vampires. This is the *daybreak* site and it was set up when the book came out in the States, but now it's concentrating on the movie. And it's very well informed. Look at this.'

He read from the screen: ' "Second unit filming starts at Pinewood Studios, England, this week and one of the first appointments for stars Ross Pirie and Zina Ray will be costume fittings with British fashion diva Amy May, who has been brought in as a consultant on the production." Pretty up-to-date, huh?'

Brettler didn't look at me – which was good of him – he just stared at the monitor.

'I've no idea how they got that piece of information,' I said, making a mental note to check the Outbox on Amy's computer when I got home.

'I wouldn't lose sleep over it,' Brettler said, clicking his mouse back to the search engine. 'This one is more serious. This is *Pirie's Pets*, the site you printed some pages off.'

'The one that knew about Frank Shoosmith's accident.'

'And a lot more. It's clear to me that *Pirie's Pets* is used as a trusted source by all the other sites interested in Ross. It is very well informed and up to now has been totally loyal to Ross. But since he signed up to do *Daybreak*, the tone has changed. This site does not want Ross to do a vampire picture. It wants Ross to be a role model for Christian values, not mess with this 'Satanic trash' as it calls it. And it says that Ross's loyal fans will desert him in droves.'

'Don Sager called them Moral Minority stalkers.'

'And don't underestimate them. These are the sort of people who can get Harry Potter books banned from schools and never forget, this little baby –' he tapped the console – 'goes world-wide.'

'So who are they?'

'I don't know. It may just be a sad and lonely fan with a crush on Ross.'

'You're going with the Lone Nut theory, then?'

'The Internet certainly breeds them in abundance. This looks like a private site, the sort somebody does for a hobby. It doesn't carry any advertising. All the news updates are credited to somebody called Pat and they're done in the style of the old Hollywood gossip columnists. "Pat, the Premier Pirie Pet", she calls herself.'

'Or himself,' I said. 'As in Patrick?'

Brettler shrugged his shoulders and sighed.

'You could be right. Nothing should surprise me any more. Whoever he or she is, "Pat" seems to have a good track record on gossip on Ross and lots of the other sites feed off this one, according to Chrissie.'

'Chrissie?' I asked.

'Christine Schwartz, Ross's personal publicist.'

Ah yes, Number 7 on speed-dial on my new mobile phone.

'I haven't met her yet,' I said.

'You should. She's a good kid and on the ball. To be honest, she's the one who brought this to my attention.'

He turned the monitor fully towards me so I could see the home page of *Pirie's Pets* with the picture of Ross with Frank Shoosmith and the BMW in the background.

'I was going to ask you how they got that picture,' I said.

'I don't know, but I'm checking it out, but don't look at that, read the text in the main box, there.'

When he took his finger out of the way, I read:

Despite thousands of letters from anguished fans begging our lovely Ross not to soil his career with material which goes against God and Christian teaching, one of the finest film actors of his generation seems committed to damning himself on the horror flick Daybreak. Romanticising the black arts and fuelling the fantasies of sick individuals is not . . .

'Yeah, yeah, yadda-yadda-yadda. I've been through this.'

'No, keep reading,' said Brettler, scrolling down the page.

. . . even as Ross makes himself comfortable in his fabulous new country mansion, Eight Ash House, there is still time for him to stop and think about what he is doing. It is not too late for the sake of Christian values, to think of the impact on young, impressionable fans . . .

'Bugger me,' I said. 'They are quick off the mark, aren't they?'

'Did you tell anybody about Eight Ash House?' asked Brettler softly.

'Absolutely not,' I lied.

10

KEY HAIR SUPERVISOR

As soon as I got to Ross's trailer, Lin asked me if I knew how many times she had tried to call me since I had turned my phone off, but I didn't think she seriously expected an answer.

There was a man in the trailer with her, relaxing on the sofa, his arms out along the edges of the back cushions. From his clothes and his teeth as he smiled when Lin yelled at me, I could tell he was American. From his muscle tone and tan, I guessed Californian.

'This is Kurt Valori,' said Lin. 'Ross's personal trainer.'

''Meet yer,' said Valori making no move to get up.

'Back at you,' I said, real hip.

'Your one and only major task of the day – if you think you can manage it – is to get Kurt and his equipment out to Ross's new house at wherever it is,' Lin ordered.

'Eight Ash Green,' I said. 'I think I can manage that.'

'Without getting your picture in the paper?' she growled.

'What?'

'You'd better check in with Chrissie Schwartz. She's got the daily press cuttings. But don't let that delay you. Find Marcus and get out there –'

'Marcus? Marcus Moore? Ross's hairdresser?'

'There's only one of *him*,' she said pointedly. 'He's going to be living at the house, so is Kurt here. Ross likes to be surrounded by things he's comfortable with and that means Marcus and his hairdryer and Kurt with his weights and his exercise bike.'

'I've got everything in a truck out on the lot,' said Kurt. 'You lead, I'll follow.'

'So I'm going out there to set up a gym and a hairdressing salon?' I said.

This was the movies?

'And I want you to keep an eye on the agency people.'

'What agency people?'

125

'The decorators and the cleaners and the caterers that the leasing company have put in there this morning to make the place liveable. There's some local cleaner as well, a Mrs Winter. She'll be around too. They know what to do, just make sure they don't take any souvenirs and that they're all out of there by the time Ross wants to come home tonight. He'll stay there this evening, learning his script for tomorrow. You get him here for 6 a.m. That's it. Any questions?'

'Do I have his supper ready for him when he comes home?'

Kurt Valori cracked a laugh at that. If he kept smiling like that I was going to need sunglasses.

'Leave all catering issues to Marcus. You may have to take him shopping, though.'

'What about cash?'

'Everything's on account except what Marcus decides he needs. He's got a company credit card.'

'Oh he has, has he?'

'Yes,' she said dead seriously. 'We trust *him*.'

Kurt Valori offered to help me round up Marcus Moore, who was over in Special Effects or 'SFXs' as Kurt said it. He'd done Ross's hair for the shots the second unit wanted and now he was busy blowing up a head.

'Of course he is,' I said with total British restraint, thinking I'd misheard him. 'I'll get the cab.'

'We can walk,' said Kurt.

'This is a movie studio, nobody walks.'

'Unless they need the exercise. You do.'

There was no point in arguing with someone with so many muscles, several of which were probably between his ears, so I fell into step alongside him.

I know we turned right after we left Ross's trailer and then left and then right again, through the narrow streets as I thought of them of this confusing factory city. Cars were parked every-where with gay abandon and the social meeting places were either around the numerous steaming tea trolleys which appeared as if by magic, or by the large rubbish bins on wheels where the smokers gathered. Everybody seemed to be busy, but doing nothing except talking into cell phones or radios, clearly the ultimate status symbol. And despite the variety of designer clothing they wore, the chill January morning gave everything a grey, washed-out aura. It was as if the place had been filmed by Ridley Scott with a hangover.

No one gave me a second glance, but most of them – second assistant assistants, runners, best boys, assistant gaffers, whatever they were – at least nodded at Kurt as he padded by them. The females nearly all smiled at him, some of them whilst talking on their phones, just to show they could do two things at once. He seemed a popular fellow.

'You've not met Chrissie Schwartz?' he asked me, as a pair of girls marking up a script in red pen smiled weak-kneed smiles at him.

'Not yet,' I said, but remembered I had her number on my new phone.

'She's quite a looker,' said Kurt. 'And very fit, if you know what I mean. She could put her shoes under my bed any day.'

If she could find room for them among the empty cartons of steroids, I thought, but it was not the sort of thing I would say out loud to someone who bulged like that in all the right places.

'I'll be happy to introduce you . . .' Kurt was saying, but I had my phone out and was punching #7.

It rang. Very loudly and very close.

'Hello?'

I didn't have to have the phone next to my ear and risk all that damaging radiation. Chrissie Schwartz was standing about a yard away, having just helped herself to a cup of coffee from one of the urn trolleys.

'Er . . . Hi, I'm Angel.'

'I recognised you from your picture,' she said through a cloud of smoke as she pulled a cigarette from her lips.

We both slipped our phones away sheepishly.

'That bad, was it?'

'Tony Lovisi's people were up all night . . .'

Suddenly she realised that Kurt was standing behind me. In one fluid movement she dumped the cigarette into her coffee cup and the coffee cup into a nearby rubbish bin. Her voice melted to body temperature and her eyes widened, her eyelashes taking on a life of their own.

'Hello, Kurt,' she purred. 'Happy New Year.'

'Happy New Century, Chrissie,' he said politely and I swear her legs started to go at the knees. 'You been exercising over Christmas?'

'I've slipped badly, Kurt, and the chocolates have taken their toll.'

She looked fine to me; very fit. If she'd put on a few pounds over the festive season, they'd all gone on the right places. And Kurt was right, she was attractive in a round-faced English way, her short red hair cut the way Vidal Sassoon used to do it, curving around her cheek bones.

'You'll have to design me a new training circuit,' she said in a voice which sounded as if she had let half a pound of chocolate dissolve in her mouth. 'After work, whenever you have a gap in your schedule.'

'Take it as read, Chrissie. It'll be a pleasure. God, I love this job!'

'You won't when you see me in a leotard,' Chrissie laughed while she blushed.

I was totally forgotten, but if this was going to go on much longer I was quite prepared to put my fingers down my throat and throw up over the lovebirds.

That might get their attention.

'Lin said you had some press cuttings to show me,' I said instead.

Chrissie Schwartz turned her big round eyes on and I saw the pupils shrink as I came into focus. I've seen Springsteen do that until the only sign of life left there are two little vertical lines, a bit like when you switch off a television. In his case, it's a sign that you should get out of range.

'Yes, I have,' said Chrissie. 'Excuse me, Kurt.'

Kurt excused her as she unzipped a lime green quilted jacket so she could get at a DKNY bum bag strapped to her hip. From it she produced a couple of sheets of paper folded to no bigger than a cigarette packet and handed them over.

They were photocopies of press cuttings done for Tony Lovisi Associates by an agency at 6 a.m. and they'd been through a fax machine, so no wonder the picture wasn't a good likeness.

There were seven or eight stories pasted up on the sheets, all about Ross or *Daybreak* and mostly fairly standard stuff taken from press releases probably penned by Chrissie Schwartz herself. One of them, I noticed, was a paragraph in a diary column about Alec Walters, the British thespian of the old school now called upon to play a gay American lawyer vampire, and it pointed out that he had in fact played Dracula himself off-Broadway a few years back. That one, I suspected, had been lifted from the Internet by some showbiz reporter who then bunged in an expenses claim for travelling to Stratford-on-Avon to interview Walters at the RSC.

The relevant one was about me. Or rather about an unnamed cab driver who was pictured coming out of the apartment block in Chelsea with a pair of suitcases. The picture showed me and the front of Armstrong across two columns and was about four inches deep. The accompanying 'story' took up about ten per cent of that area.

He might not have Ross Pirie in the back of his cab, but he's got his luggage!

Superstar Ross, filming at Pinewood Studios this week, moved to a secret location yesterday to concentrate on his new blockbuster. He sent a London cab to pick up his luggage from an exclusive Chelsea apartment where the rent was rumoured to be £1,500 a week. Too rich for Ross's blood? He should know, he plays a vampire in his new movie!

'Well, that's harmless, isn't it?'

Chrissie was too busy smiling at Kurt to register that I had spoken. She noticed he was looking at her legs encased in black opaque tights under a short black leather miniskirt. She moved her right leg through ninety degrees, stretching the leather.

'I've been working on my muscle tone,' she was saying.

Kurt diplomatically averted his eyes.

'Have you tried step-aerobics?' I suggested helpfully and suddenly she realised I was on this planet too.

'Tony Lovisi's PR company spent most of last night taking calls on this,' she said. 'The stories were getting wilder by the minute. Ross had been thrown out of his flat in Chelsea. Ross had walked off the movie and was leaving the country. Ross had a secret lover in some hideaway over in Hackney . . .'

'What happened with that one?' I was genuinely curious.

'Seems to have been a total cock-up. Some mad Scottish guy decked a photographer, said he'd never heard of Ross.'

That was a result then.

'So where's the problem?' I asked.

'As it turns out, Ross and Julius were at a charity dinner last night along with two cabinet ministers and three newspaper editors, so we had no trouble issuing a blanket denial. The problem was we weren't expecting anything to break last night. You could have warned us. You should have warned us.'

'Now I've got your number, I know who to call,' I said as sincerely as I could. 'Should it happen again – which it won't.'

'Make sure you do,' she said, quite strictly.

Then she melted again as Kurt said:

'And *I'll* be sure to call just as soon as I get my weights unpacked. We'll work out a new regime for you.'

She went starry-eyed at the very thought.

'I'm sure Kurt'll make you sweat,' I told her.

'Mmmm . . .' she agreed.

On the rest of the way to the SFX department, Kurt was accosted at least four times, all by women, all wanting their biceps felt or their thighs admired, all wanting to look good, feel good, be felt. For the first couple, I made an effort to hold in my stomach and walk on the balls of my feet but it made no difference, I might have been invisible. By the time we had walked half-way across Pinewood, I was dying for a cigarette and ready to put my feet up with a mug of hot chocolate.

I'd worked out that all the studios, or 'sound stages' as some of the older hands called them, had red and green lights outside them indicating when you could or couldn't enter. Special Effects just had a red light, but as we approached it snapped off.

'What exactly is Marcus doing in SFX?' I asked Kurt.

'Blowing up a head,' said Kurt, or at least that's what I thought he said.

That's what I hoped he'd said.

'Reckon we can go on in,' Kurt said, levering open the metal door.

I stepped into the gloom and quickly realised it wasn't gloom, but a film of smoke which smelled of cordite and something else I couldn't identify. I could make out a long bench table, a bit like the chemistry laboratory at my old school, with two or three sinks and taps set into the surface.

Along the bench top at regular intervals, each on a square box mounted like a trophy, was a human head. Five of them.

'Good God! That's Bo Jay Roberts,' I spluttered. 'And so's that. And that, and that.'

'See!' somebody shrieked. 'Instantaneous recognition. You have so little faith in me it's just not true.'

The heads were very lifelike, or rather deathlike, for the expressions were tortured, the eyeballs rolling upwards, the tongues lolling out. I had seen at least two movies featuring the black American actor Bo Jay Roberts – a totally cool dude in all of them – but this likeness had definitely caught him on a bad day.

The fifth one, at the end of the line, was even more grisly. It looked as if that head had been burned from the inside out, almost collapsing in on itself, and despite the wisps of smoke rising from the singed hair, it was still recognisable as Bo Jay.

'It's Howard, isn't it?' I said aloud to no one in particular. 'Bo Jay plays Howard and Howard gets decapitated by the bad vampire.'

'It's the only way to be sure – with a vampire,' said a voice.

'And when a vampire's head comes off it bursts into blue flames,' I said, proud that I could remember that from the script I had read months before.

'But blue is *such* a harsh colour, we've been experimenting with pastel shades.'

'You must be Marcus Moore,' I said to the voice.

There was a gay pub I knew in Hackney which didn't take itself too seriously, where the regular drinkers had got up a petition demanding that the pub's name be changed to the Screaming Queen. They almost got away with it until the local council refused planning permission for them to change the pub sign on the grounds of good taste (they did have some pretty whacky designs) and the rather dubious assumption that the Royal Family would be offended. The disgruntled clientele had settled instead for printing their own spoof car stickers which looked just like the standard European 'GB' stickers, except they read 'GBB' – which stood for Gays Behaving Badly.

I don't know what made me think of that when I saw Marcus Moore.

Perhaps it was the white wool suit with the almost-matching off-white waistcoat, complete with fob watch on a gold chain, and the white cowboy boots. It could have been the Tony Curtis haircut, last seen in retro documentaries about the Swinging Sixties but without the blond highlights. It might have been the jewellery – a chunky gold ring on six out of eight fingers, a dangling gold bracelet and one (gold) stud ear-ring. He also wore a copper bracelet on his left wrist. I know, so did John Wayne. Proves nothing.

'I certainly must,' he said, 'but who be you?'

'This is Angel,' said Kurt before I could answer, 'standing in for Frank.'

'Ross's new friend, I do believe,' said Marcus in a duff Southern accent.

'You'll have been warned about me,' I said.

'Oh yes.' Marcus pursed his lips as if he'd just caught the lemon in his gin and tonic. 'And I've told Zandra here to stay well away from you.'

I had been so spooked by the row of dead heads and then dazzled by Marcus Moore that I had not realised there was another guy, this one half Marcus's age with black hair slicked back and ponytailed.

'It's Alexander, actually,' he said, 'and I'd be grateful if you all got the fuck out of my way now, as some of us have work to do.'

Marcus breezed over towards me and touched me lightly on the wrist, pretending to lean in and whisper in my ear.

'Zandra can be quite touchy but he's ever so sweet really. Anyway, I just *had* to see if Bo Jay's hair stood up to decapitation and then spontaneous combustion. It does!' He clapped his hands with a clinking of jewellery. 'Even in death and immola- tion, a Marcus Moore hair design shines out! Just look at that widow's peak I did for Bo. That will start a trend.'

'They said you did good head,' I said, admiring the line of models, not looking at him.

His jewellery stopped tinkling.

'And I was warned you had a smart mouth,' he said huskily.

'Take it outside, girls,' Alexander said loudly. 'I'm going to blow another head and, no, Marcus, you can't watch.'

'Killjoy!' said Marcus, sticking his tongue out at him.

'Come on, Kurt, flex those muscles and keep all those freaky women away from me.' He linked his left arm through my right. 'And you, Mr Angel, you can take me for a ride in this twee little taxi I hear you own. Where is it?'

'Behind Ross's trailer,' I said, falling into step beside him as we emerged from the SFX building.

'If I stand on a corner and whistle, will you come for me?'

There was a distinct twinkle in his eyes, though it could have been something to do with the plastic surgery, which in turn made it difficult to guess his age. I would have said fifty-five trying to look forty-five but I wasn't going to go there, not with someone like Marcus.

'You know how to whistle?' I said innocently.

As we walked back through the maze of studios, females would wave to Kurt or pantomime the lifting of weights or even break into a jog as if they were worried about him catching them slouching. Every time it happened, Marcus would make a point of shouting to some unsuspecting young male, most of whom tried to cross the street when they saw us coming arm-in-arm, and whether they acknowledged him or not, he would say to me: 'Had him. Almost had him. Coulda had him.'

He had kept his right arm free because around his waist he wore a gun belt but in the holster on his hip, instead of a gun, he had a short-barrelled hairdryer which he would occasionally fast draw and blast a passer-by with hot air. I guessed he had a battery pack on the back of the belt under his coat.

'Hairdryer, will travel?' I asked.

I was rather enjoying the attention we were getting. It was a taste, albeit a strange one, of the sort of fame real movie stars enjoy or suffer depending on the mood they're in. And anyway, when I had walked through the studio with Kurt, nobody had noticed me.

'Never travel without it, that's for sure,' said Marcus. He looked at the top of my head and reached out with the dryer, giving me a whoosh of hot air. 'Don't tell me, Toni and Guy had a fight over who would do you.'

'Something like that.'

I grinned because Amy had said almost exactly the same.

'Be nice to me, Angel, and I'll do you a freebie,' he said, then he saw another poor sod who had pulled up his anorak hood just a second too late. 'Hey there, Simon! Don't be a stranger, you hear?'

He picked on several others along the way, yelling outrageous greetings and then telling me, without lowering his voice, that they were sad fuckers, wannabe actors, wannabe directors, wannabe human beings and, in one case, a poor soul who 'double parks on the wrong side of sexuality street'.

Marcus had long ago decided to become larger than life and, judging by the reaction of everybody we ran into, he had succeeded. Only Kurt seemed unruffled by his sheer presence.

When we reached Ross's trailer, Kurt said he would collect the rented van with all his gear and meet us by the gatehouse.

'How far is it to this place?' he asked.

'About twelve miles,' I said.

'OK if I follow on in convoy?'

'Sure,' I said, then looked at Marcus.

'Oh, I'm going in style in the company limo, with you, ducks,' he trilled. 'You don't mind me calling you "ducks" do you, Angel?'

'Not if you don't mind me calling you Dick van Dyke.'

'Oooh, ain't we so sharp. You can be in the shower scene, ducks.'

He squeezed my arm playfully.

'I've got to get my necessaries out of Ross's bedroom . . .' His fingers dug into my flesh as he rolled his eyes. 'The inner sanctum, as we call it. Don't wait for me, Kurt. Angel will look after me.'

Kurt smiled weakly at the prospect of leaving me to my fate. Then promptly left me to my fate.

As he walked away, Marcus shouted after him:

'Me, Angel and a bedroom. Deal with it, Kurt, just deal with it!'

Even from where I was, I swear I saw Kurt's ears start to go red.

I retrieved my arm from Marcus's and tried the door of the trailer. It was locked.

'Don't worry, ducks, I have a key,' he said, pushing by me. 'Do you really think we leave Ross's private stuff unlocked? Don't you know anything?'

His face was six inches from mine as we stood on the trailer steps.

'I know you're not gay,' I said.

He held my gaze for several seconds, then jerked his head in the direction Kurt had taken.

'No, I'm not, but *he* is.'

'I knew that,' I said quickly. Perhaps too quickly.

'But you won't tell anyone, will you?' Marcus pleaded. If he fluttered his eyelashes any more he'd take off.

'Would you give a shit if I did?'

'I wouldn't. Who the fuck would believe you?'

'Good point.'

'But Kurt might.'

'Then your secret is safe with me.'

I thought right then that this would be a really bad time for someone to come round the corner and find us there, Marcus and me standing on the steps of the trailer, him putting a key in the lock, both of us seemingly staring deep into each other's eyes, our faces inches apart, the rest of our bodies not even that. So I shouldn't have been surprised, the world being what it is, when somebody did come round the corner.

In a way, I was rather relieved that it was Alix Tse. I had nothing to lose there.

She was walking with a tall, handsome Chinese man in a dark suit and tie and sheepskin coat of the style no one except football commentators have worn since the early Seventies. I had seen forty years of fashion come and go in about an hour at Pinewood and I hadn't been inside a studio yet.

Alix and her escort may have been heading for the trailer but when they saw the two of us almost in a clinch on the steps, Alix veered away and kept on walking, averting her eyes. Her partner followed in step but he didn't look away. In fact I got the distinct impression we were getting his killer look for some reason I couldn't work out.

'Hi there, Alix!' Marcus shouted as he turned the lock and the door opened. 'Hey, you too? Isn't it just raining men?'

'Get inside,' I hissed, slapping him on the backside.

'Ooh! Gad, sir, you're a character!' he mugged in a terrible English accent.

I followed him in.

'Sidney Greenstreet in *The Maltese Falcon*,' I said.

'I'm impressed,' he said, and he looked it. 'Most of the kids I have to work with these days have never seen a movie in black-and-white. Anyway, why're you so keen not to be seen with me by Alix Tse of all people?'

'She pays the wages,' I said. 'It never pays to get on the wrong side of someone like that.'

'Dream on, Angel. That is a stone bitch who has no other side except wrong. She gives me the heebie-jeebies. And the kissin' cousin double spooks me badly.'

'The guy's her cousin?'

I walked down the trailer to one of the bay windows – it had bay windows – and caught a glimpse of them rounding the corner. Alix didn't look back, but the Chinese guy did and from his face, he was not a happy bunny for some reason. I was pretty sure he wasn't looking directly at me, but it felt like it.

'Either hers or Lin's,' Marcus said from the bedroom at the other end of the trailer, no more than half a mile away. 'I forget. They're all thick as thieves. He's called Terry or Tony or Tommy. Whatever. He was hanging around all the time we were shooting *Side Edge* over in Europe. These are mine. I'll get Ross's back-up.'

He put two large metal suitcases down near the door, went back into the bedroom and came out with two large leather ones.

'These contain everything our boy needs for seven days camping out in the woods. They're packed and ready to go at any time. I hear the President does the same.'

He put his hands on his hips and posed.

'Don't you just hate living out of suitcases?'

'I could live *off* that luggage for a week,' I said. 'Quite comfortably.'

'Now, now,' he wagged a finger, 'don't let the green-eyed demon of jealousy rise up. That ain't what we want to see rise. Is there a TV in this stately home we're going to?'

'At least two,' I said.

'Then you'd better get his Gameboy and some games together. He's lost without it. It's in that unit under the VCR.'

'There's a VCR there too,' I said hopefully. 'Shall I bring some tapes?'

I had noticed a bank of video tapes which included several movies I had yet to see, some which had only been out in the States a few weeks.

'No tapes. The voting for the Academy's over so he doesn't actually have to watch movies any more. Not until next year's Oscars, anyway. You'd better bring some music though, he likes listening to shit when he's learning lines. There, down there with the Gameboy stuff.'

I bent down and opened the unit to find a pair of plastic racks of CDs. The first one I pulled was a Shania Twain.

'Don't ask,' said Marcus, 'and don't make me touch it. Just bring them along. I'll get you a bag.'

He disappeared into the bedroom and emerged with a black leather shoulder bag.

'I'll bet he's got a Bryan Adams in there as well,' he clucked, throwing the bag. 'He has no taste. No taste at all.'

'Except in stand-in chauffeurs and hairdressers,' I said, pulling CDs out by the handful and stuffing them in the bag.

Marcus cocked his head and smiled down at me.

'You know, Angel, I think this could be the beginning of a beautiful friendship.'

That was so easy I ignored it.

'So why the camp act, Marcus?'

'Because Warren Beatty gave us all a bad name, that's why. To be a hair stylist in Hollywood these days, you have to be gay. We all know that hair styling is just a cover for one large beaver hunt, but we play by the rules. The husbands can trust their wives, the wives get what they want. Everybody knows it's an act but they play along.'

'It's a cliché.'

'It works.'

'Well, if it ain't broke, don't fix it.'

'My sentiments exactly.'

That one almost threw me for a minute, but I got it.

137

'Randolph Scott in *Ride the High Country.*'

'Damn,' said Marcus, 'if you ain't as good as they said.'

With Marcus enthroned in the back of Armstrong, his feet on one of Ross's suitcases, I rendezvoused with Kurt's hire van, a white Ford Transit, and led the way down the entrance road to the gates.

One of Brettler's uniformed security men appeared, waved us to slow and went to open the gates himself. As he did so, I could see him talking to a small group of four or five figures out on the road, telling them to stand back. He then waved us through as the gate opened.

Hanging from the gate, tied to the upright iron staves, were what appeared to be a necklace made of chicken bones, several bunches of red feathers, a lifesize but obviously plastic skull of the sort they sell in pet shops to put in with tropical fish, two crucifixes hung upside down and about a dozen small leather spell pouches.

The people who had put them there watched us in silence as we drove out, looking in the back of Armstrong just to make sure no one incredibly famous was trying to sneak by them. They were all dressed in black and I think I identified three as female, but couldn't be sure. They all wore more black and white make-up than a racoon in heat and they all had long fingernails painted black. One male, I think, wore a monk's robe and cowl and all I could see of him was his hands and fingernails as he described cabalistic symbols in the air over Armstrong. Or maybe he'd just had bad experiences with London cabs.

'They . . .'re . . . here,' said Marcus from the back, just like the kid does in *Poltergeist* as the spooks come through the television set.

The only trouble was, they were waiting outside Eight Ash House as well.

11

CHECKING THE GATE

'Hey, you've organised a riot to make me feel right at home,' said Marcus, leaning forward in his seat as we approached the entrance to Eight Ash House.

'Hardly,' I said. 'Legally you need twelve to have a riot in this country.'

'Is that true?' I nodded that it was. 'Shit, you only need one in Alabama, if you're black.'

There were five of them in a picket line across the gateway. Four were female and teenagers, all with jet black hair either long and straight or short, curly Afro styles, which made me suspect wigs, lots of white face paint and black eye make-up. They wore black tops, black skirts, black boots and between them about a ton of metal in the form of crucifixes, moon and star symbols and Zodiac signs. They all looked pinched with the cold except for the one male, who was dressed as Count Dracula, complete with tuxedo, bow tie and a red-lined cape to keep him warm. Behind the make-up and the slicked-back hair, I guessed he was in his late teens as well, though technically speaking, of course, he was well over 600 years old.

I hit Armstrong's horn and flicked the indicator on so that they, and Kurt in his Transit behind me, could see that I wanted to turn into the gateway. The picket line very politely moved to one side to let us through, Count Dracula even gracing us with a low bow and a bullfighter's flourish of his cape.

'Where's Buffy when you need her?' said Marcus. 'Who are these punks?'

'They're not Punks,' I said, deliberately misunderstanding him, 'they're Goths.'

'Is it a lifestyle thing?'

'I think it's more a fashion thing. You must have them in the States.'

'Hey, there are parts of New Jersey where everybody looks like that. Friggin' freaks.'

This from an ageing hair stylist who dressed like the Man from Del Monte and pretended to be gay.

'I think they're fairly harmless,' I said. 'Worst they'll do is drink the local pub out of tomato juice this lunchtime.'

Which reminded me, it still wasn't lunchtime yet I seemed to have been on the go for hours. This working for a living was definitely going down in my estimation.

I checked in the mirror. The Goths had resumed their peaceful vigil across the gateway.

'I guess they're just waiting for a sight of their hero Ross,' said Marcus. 'Don't they have tombs to go to?'

'You wait until after dark.'

I was only half joking. There was no doubt in my mind that their ranks would swell as more of them checked the Internet. We hadn't even moved into Eight Ash House and already it was under siege. So much for Ross's 'secret location' as the tabloids had put it.

'How do you think Ross'll take this lot camping on his doorstep?' I asked Marcus. 'You know him better than I do.'

'It goes with the territory,' he said, 'but he won't like it. As long as they keep their distance, he'll be cool about it. Hell, for the percentage points he's getting on this movie he can deal with it for four or five weeks. Funny thing is we came here to make this movie to keep a low profile, stay out of the limelight. But not because of these guys, because of the other guys.'

'What other guys?'

'The Christian Centre, the Righteous Right, whatever. The Holy Joes who have God's direct line on speed-dial. Mothers Against Demon Worship.'

'You made that one up.'

'Nope, straight arrow. Lot of feeling Stateside that this movie is unholy and messing with dark forces.'

We were almost at the house where two cars, two small vans and another Transit were parked near the open front door. The side of the Transit advertised the cleaning company Stains of Staines.

'Why this picture?' I asked Marcus. 'They're always making vampire films.'

'Sure, but in this one the vamps are the good guys. They're all cool, have aspirational jobs and lifestyles and live happily ever after. There's also some shit about the story being an allegory for the War of Independence, you know, shaking off the colonial chains of Olde England and mad King George. So that got the Daughters of the Revolution and suchlike worked up too. Coupla hired hands in the Senate making speeches about moral decline, the good old Stars and Stripes, fundamentalist values, yadda-yadda-yadda, and it all makes people nervous. It doesn't take much to make Hollywood nervous and then the money dries up.'

'It's only a movie,' I said, which was probably heresy.

'Thank heavens the Chinks think that way,' said Marcus as I pulled on Armstrong's brake.

'The Chinese? Chinese what?'

'The Chinks love vampire movies and they like Ross, so they're bankrolling the movie, just like they did with *Side Edge*.'

'What? The Chinese government?'

'Christ, no. It's some venture capitalist or banking consortium operating out of Hong Kong, getting into film production big time. Didn't you know that?'

No, I hadn't known that but I knew that if I wanted to find out what was going on, I'd ask the hairdresser.

Stains of Staines had almost finished the housework. Two guys from a company probably called Alarms of Amersham had checked over the burglar and fire alarms, presumably at the request of the production company. In the kitchen, two ladies from Waffles of Windsor, or similar, were loading the freezer and the fridge with goodies ranging from tubs of Ben and Jerry's ice cream, to hand-made pizzas, a whole roast ham and a roast turkey, a giant bowl of salad spiked with lobster claws, dips, cheeses, you name it. I was delighted to see they had also brought a case of champagne, a mixed case of wine and a mixed case of malt whisky and Stolichnaya vodka. If we really were in for a siege, we were in good shape.

All this was going on under the watchful eyes of Maggie Vinall, from the leasing company, and Mrs Winter, the policeman's wife, both of whom recognised me from yesterday and both of whom immediately looked over my shoulder to see if Ross was with me.

'Everything under control, ladies?' I asked cheerfully.

'Well, the caterers aren't sure what to freeze and what you might need tonight –' Maggie Vinall started.

Neither she nor I got any further, as Marcus took command. 'Allow me, ducks. Did you get the quails' eggs? Good. The fillet steak ground to burger meat? Excellent. I asked for any six cheeses as long as they weren't American. Yes, you've managed that. Coffee? I said Mocha and Mysore *blend*. I suppose it will do. Oh my.' He plucked a small bottle out of one of the boxes the caterers were unpacking and held it like it was contaminated. 'I know I said dressing, but who mentioned Paul Newman own brand?'

He went on, and on. At one point he paused and surveyed the women staring at him open-mouthed, then he reached out a bejewelled hand and gentle stroked Maggie Vinall's hair just above her left ear.

'I could do something with that, you know,' he said, then went back to checking groceries.

I drew Mrs Winter out of the kitchen and into the hall. Through the open oak door we could see Kurt unloading weights, a cycling machine, a rowing machine and numerous other instruments of torture from the back of his hired Transit. Some of the things looked quite heavy, but he had the muscle tone to handle it and didn't seem to have broken sweat.

'Are the bedrooms ready?' I asked Mrs Winter.

'Yes,' she said, nodding enthusiastically. 'Mr Pirie has the master bedroom at the back of the house. Well, if that's acceptable to him. The others are all made up just in case. I wasn't sure how many people were going to be sleeping here.'

'I can tell you one who is,' I said, 'right now.'

Kurt woke me after two minutes. Actually, it was more like three hours and the afternoon light was already slipping away over the Chilterns.

'Marcus wants to know what you want for dinner,' Kurt said as he shook my shoulder.

'Dinner?' I mumbled, trying to sit up. Apart from my Doc Martens and my jacket, I was fully clothed under the duvet which formed a cocoon around me and it was tempting to stay there. Then I remembered I was hungry.

'You mean lunch,' I said to Kurt.

'No, dinner. Marcus insists we eat on American time. Cocktails at five, dinner at six. He's planning something with lobster tails and pasta.'

'Sounds good to me.'

I swung my legs out from under the duvet and shook my head to clear it.

'Ross! Shit! When am I supposed to pick Ross up?'

'I dunno,' said Kurt going through the door, 'but if you switch your phone on, I expect Lin will tell you. She's called me twice in the last hour trying to find you.'

'What did you tell her?'

'Marcus said to say you'd gone shopping.'

'Thanks. And tell him thanks.'

'No problemo. He hates her as well.' He paused, reconsidering. 'No, actually he hates her dress sense.'

I bit the bullet and fished the mobile out of my jacket, which seemed to be all sleeves and have a mind of its own, and turned it on then pressed #1.

'Where the fuck have you been?'

She must have her phone programmed with caller ID. On the other hand, maybe she answered all her calls like that.

'Shopping. Just checking in to see what Ross's schedule is for the rest of this very long day,' I said. 'Do I get overtime, by the way?'

She ignored that.

'Ross is almost finished here. He's got a meeting with some people at five then he's free. Pick him up from the trailer at five thirty sharp, understood?'

'Got it,' I said, sitting to attention on the edge of the bed. 'Then what?'

'Straight to the house, no detours. Tell Kurt to cut his session to half an hour tops. Tell Marcus to have him fed by seven fifteen at the latest. Bed by eight thirty. He's in make-up at 7 a.m. tomorrow. Got that?'

'I think so.'

'Then do it.'

She hung up and I spent a minute or two making faces at the phone. Then I pressed #8 and heard a ringing sound downstairs in the house.

'Hello.'

'Hi Marcus, I'm gonna miss dinner. Can you do me something to go?'

Now there was a stupid question. By the time I had grabbed a quick shower and run a battery-powered Ronson over my face, there was a delicious smell of frying coming up the stairs mingling with the gentle strains of what sounded like a Herbie Hancock track.

Marcus was at the kitchen stove, wielding a heavy iron frying pan over one of the burners, wearing an apron which advertised something called The Cotapaxi Smokehouse, Colorado. He had split a sesame seed bun and had it under the grill, a slice of white cheese on one half, red cheese on the other. In the pan he was frying a burger about an inch thick and from the mixing bowl he had used I could see he'd added onion, capers, red chilli, black pepper, sea salt and tomato purée to the mixture.

'Looks good . . .' I said but he held up a metal spatula to cut me off.

'Cooking, not talking,' was all he said.

He turned the burger and increased the heat under the pan. The top was still pink, the bottom in the process of getting charred. He took a teaspoon and pressed it into the meat then he carefully cracked a quail egg into the depression he had created. From one of the fitted cupboards he took a pack of thick paper napkins and counted off three, placing them on the work surface next to the stove. He switched everything off, plucked the two halves of the bun, both bubbling with melted cheese, and put them on the napkins then he scooped up the burger, the quail's egg now set, and slid it on to the base bun, then flipped the top one on to it.

'That'll be $3.95. Please pay at the second window as you drive thru. Have a nice day and enjoy your meal.'

'I am so impressed,' I said genuinely.

'But not surprised, huh? It goes with the territory. Gays can cook, style hair and do interior decoration.'

'You going to persist with this act?'

'Worked so far.'

I left him opening a bottle of a Napa Valley Shiraz and listening to Herbie Hancock. There was no sign of Kurt but the door under the stairs, leading down to the wine cellar, was open and I thought I could hear the metallic clank of equipment. I decided that personal exercise regimes are something best kept private.

I finished my Marcusburger outside, walking to Armstrong which, with Kurt's van, was the only vehicle left there. It wasn't dark enough yet to trigger the exterior lights, but the winter gloom was coming down fast and I could only just make out the shadowy figures at the bottom of the drive by the gate. I couldn't work out if there were more or less of them than earlier in the day and made a mental note to get a pair of binoculars just to keep an eye on them in case they tried to jump the wall or sleep in the trees.

I didn't think they would. The January ground temperatures would put all but the foolish off the idea of camping out. Perhaps if they got a glimpse of Ross, that would be mission accomplished and they could all go home to a nice, warm, comfortable coffin. How would I know? I could always ask them.

I started Armstrong and turned on the gravel circle until I had him pointed down the long driveway. I didn't put the lights on until I was about twenty yards from the gateway, illuminating a chorus line of very white faces blinking in the beams.

Dazzled though they were – and there were more of them than there had been, perhaps a dozen – they moved to either side to let me through. I slowed down and stopped on the edge of the road and pulled my window down. The nearest Gothess was about a foot away from me, small enough to be at eye level. She wore a black curly wig, had studs in her nose, eyebrows, ears and lips, and her black and white make-up made me think of two giant ink spots blobbed on the white cliffs of Dover. Count Dracula hovered behind her – not literally – shivering under his cape.

'Excuse me, darlin', but what are you lot waiting for? The next Millennium?'

'We're waiting for Jason Neville,' she said seriously.

145

The character Ross played in *Daybreak*, but I was a cab driver. How would I know that?

'Nobody here by that name, love,' I said helpfully.

'He will come when it is dark,' said the Gothess with absolute seriousness.

'When it is dark,' the others said as an echo.

'When it is dark; when it is dark.'

They were swaying and shivering and it became a chant. And all this without the obvious aid of either drugs or drink.

I shook my head and muttered, 'Fucking nutters . . .' just like a real cab driver would, pulled out on to the road and headed towards Pinewood.

At least there they got paid large amounts of money for dressing up and pretending to be vampires.

The Goths outside the studio gates probably knew that and were auditioning. Their ranks had swelled to about thirty, some of them holding black candles, others with torches which they held under their chins and shone upwards. Didn't these people have better things to do; homes to go to? The really sad thing was that they probably did, they just didn't know it.

Paul Brettler had doubled the number of security officers on the gate and had either given out Armstrong's number or just issued a standing order about cabs, because I was allowed straight in. I had to slow down to get through the Goth vigil and as I did so, they surrounded Armstrong, pressing their faces up against the windows trying to spot a passenger. As their faces blurred in passing they reminded me of the white-faced clowns which plague Covent Garden when it's rained and their faces have run.

I negotiated the narrow suburbs of Film City, mostly empty of parked cars now, until I got to Ross's trailer. There was one car parked there, a BMW, and leaning against the bonnet was Dave the Driver, a cigarette cupped in his hand. I stopped Armstrong behind the Beamer and nodded to him as I got out. He flicked a thumb towards the trailer, where the lights were on.

Purely by chance I looked into the BMW as I walked by. There, across the back seat, was the woman I assumed was Mrs Julius

Cockburn, fast asleep, mouth open, head resting on two Harrods shopping bags.

'Hard day at the office?' I asked Dave, nodding back at the BMW.

'You could say that. Pissed out of her mind, rat-arsed, shit-faced. You could say that too.'

I was impressed. I'd not had him down as a philosopher.

'Is She-who-must-be-obeyed around?' I whispered.

'No, thank God, she knocked off early,' he confided. 'Unusual that, for Lin. Normally she's first in, last out. The rest of them are in there, having a pow-wow.'

The rest of them were: Ross, Julius, Gloria-Maria and Paul Brettler. Burgundy Dulude was there as well, mixing drinks at the little horseshoe bar for everybody else, a victim of the pecking order. She glared at me, daring me to mention the fact or order a cocktail.

Ross was relaxing in one of the leather chairs, nursing what looked like a weak scotch and water. I thought for a moment he'd had an allergic reaction to it, then I realised he was still wearing make-up.

'Hi, there, Angel!' he called out, giving me a smile which could have been sponsored by his orthodontist.

Except any normal orthodontist would have surely raised an eyebrow when, as Ross kept smiling, the two top middle teeth of his most illustrious client began to grow, lengthening and nar-rowing to points.

'What's up, Doc?' I said cheerily.

'Oh, fuck!' Ross spat and his smile disappeared, which was a bit of mistake on his part as he couldn't actually close his mouth with the teeth extended.

'State-of-the-art SFX and he thinks I look like Bugs Bunny,' he said, putting a hand over his mouth and wrestling with the plate which covered his normal teeth.

He held it up between forefinger and thumb, two whiter than white teeth on a thin, clear plastic plate which must have had some form of pressure pad which his tongue could operate. The sharp fang teeth came out and then retreated. I was glad to see they'd gone for the two front teeth, like in Bram Stoker's orig-inal, and not the extended canines which are only used for

147

skewering moving prey, not hypodermic incisions. You don't believe me, ask a cat.

'Does anyone actually give a flying fuck what Angel thinks?' asked Gloria-Maria. Then when she realised we were all looking at her, she added: 'Of the special effects, that is?'

'The effects are cool,' I said, 'especially the exploding heads. I caught them this morning.'

'There you are, then,' said Gloria-Maria. 'One satisfied customer already.'

'He's easily pleased,' muttered Burgundy, 'so I hear.'

'So how's the first day's shooting gone?' I asked to be friendly and also distract from the fact that I was nearly an hour late.

'Tell you tomorrow when the real work starts,' drawled Julius, examining his fingernails.

'Julius doesn't count second unit work as serious directing,' said Ross, holding his vampire teeth in his hand and making snapping movements towards his director. 'He gets to crack the whip tomorrow morning at 8 a.m. and for the next four weeks he's God.'

'It's only a part-time job . . .' Julius flicked a hand dismissively.

'We kinda wanted to know how your day had gone,' said Gloria-Maria, clearly itching for a cigarette.

My day? I'd caught up on some sleep, eaten a great burger, met Marcus and Kurt and Chrissie Schwartz, and had my picture in the paper. From their expressions, I guessed this wasn't the sort of thing they wanted to hear.

'Er . . . well, everything's ready for you out at Eight Ash House,' I said weakly.

It didn't seem to impress them.

'Have you managed to follow anything up?' asked Paul Brettler.

Follow up what?

'Well, all my plans were rather thrown by the Goths,' I said as if I knew what I was talking about. 'They moved much faster than I thought they would.'

'This is the movies, darlin',' said Gloria-Maria. 'There are fans and there are groupies. Get used to it. They always hang around the studio gates.'

'Sure, but I didn't expect them to have Eight Ash House surrounded so quickly.'

That got their attention. They hadn't realised that the Goths had established another picket line out at Ross's country hideaway almost before the ink was dry on the lease. That was probably because I hadn't bothered to tell them.

'Shit!' said Ross, shaking his head. 'What do these freaks want?'

'And how did they know about the house?' asked Burgundy quietly.

'It was posted on the Internet last night,' said Brettler, 'but I didn't think they would find it so quickly.'

'How did these . . . these . . . Goths . . . get hold of that?' Ross demanded. He was trying to look tough but it didn't quite work as he was still holding his vampire teeth in his hand.

'I don't think they did,' I said. 'I think they read it on the *Pirie's Pets* site, like Paul and I did this morning. Where *they* got it is the good question. Anybody got an answer?'

'What do you mean, Roy?' asked Ross.

'He means: who knew?' said Burgundy.

'No he doesn't,' snapped Julius, 'he means who told these damn website people. Well, I didn't.'

'And I didn't know where the fuck the place was until this afternoon,' Gloria-Maria spluttered. .

'Hey, hey, cool it. We're family here,' soothed Ross. 'Roy's only doing his job.'

I was?

'So who did know? That site was updated sometime last night,' I said, having no real idea where this was leading me.

Ross ticked them off mentally as he spoke.

'Me, you, Paul of course. I told Julius last night, but he was with me all night.'

'Thank you very much,' said Julius with heavy sarcasm.

'Lin knew, so did Alix, as they both dealt with the letting agents. Marcus and Kurt were told, and Chrissie Schwartz and she would have told Tony Lovisi's people and my agents at Global.' He stopped counting. 'Quite a few, I guess.'

'Not to mention the housekeeper, the local police, the fire brigade, the security alarm people and the caterers,' said Paul.

That was why he was Head of Security.

'So how you gonna find out who blabbed?' asked Gloria-Maria in such a smarmy way that if I'd had a cigarette I would have lit up in front of her and to hell with the smoke alarms.

'Why do I have to? You're the one who said get used to it. They're fans, groupies. Pretty strange ones, I grant you, but essentially harmless.'

'What happened to Frank Shoosmith wasn't harmless,' said Julius.

'There's nothing to suggest that had anything to do with anything that's going on now,' I said.

'He's right,' said Brettler, clutching at straws.

'Except that Frank's accident was posted on the Net as well,' I said gently. 'So at the very least you've got a leak somewhere here in your little movie family.'

'But Don Sager thinks it's more than that, doesn't he?' Ross leaned forward in his chair, full of concern or what he reckoned passed for it. 'That's why he asked you to sniff around.'

I heard Burgundy stifle a snigger at that, but before I could say anything, Gloria-Maria waded in.

'Come on, Ross, you know Don. He just doesn't want the picture getting bad publicity before it starts. Don likes smooth waters, no waves. But he has the attention span of roadkill. He flew in, calmed a few nerves and flew out. He'll have forgotten about *Daybreak* somewhere over Greenland and be on to his next project by now. He wants everything on schedule, that's Don's bag. He doesn't want another *Side Edge*.'

'What's happened with *Side Edge*?' I asked.

'They're having to reshoot some of the scenes – and a new ending,' said Julius, cheering up suddenly. 'As soon as we've finished with Ross here, he's got to go back on the ski slopes and do it all again. It wasn't one of mine, I hasten to add.'

'But it means *your* schedule is now ultra-tight, Julius,' Gloria-Maria came back. 'But if you work weekends, we can wrap here by the end of the month, do Europe and then move to the States for completion.'

'So you see our position, Roy. This schedule is already tight and now it's being squeezed even more. We need a problem-free shoot and we're looking to you to minimise our problems.'

Ross spoke as if he were auditioning for the role of a young, idealistic President. I had a feeling that one would be a long time coming.

'So how are *you* gonna help *us*?' drawled Gloria-Maria, fixing me with a stare.

I thought this a bit rich. Here I was, expected to save their movie from no one knew what, and I hadn't even seen a camera turn in anger, let alone bé offered so much as a walk-on part. Maybe this was my audition; it certainly felt like a job interview from what I remembered of them.

'Well, I can certainly make a few enquiries about the stuff that's appearing on the web, see where that's coming from. But I think at the end of the day it'll be just some of your dedicated fans going over the top.'

'It's surely a bit more serious than that,' said Paul Brettler, all concerned.

'It may not be. It might just be the price you have to pay for fame, fortune and trailers that are nicer than most people's homes. Your fans out there in the real world don't have lives like this, so every move you make is absolutely fascinating to them.'

'But somebody is telling them things, like about Ross's house,' said Brettler.

'Yes, but maybe not intentionally,' I said, though I wasn't convincing them. 'Loose lips, careless talk, gossip on the set. There's not necessarily any malice behind it.'

'What about Frank?' asked Ross.

'What about him? He had an accident. It's not got to be connected to you having a couple of stalkers on the Net.'

But it was odd that a picture of Ross at Pinewood, with Frank Shoosmith in the background, had been posted on the *Pirie's Pets* site. A photograph that somebody had taken shortly before the accident had happened.

'I'll go and see Frank, though, and I'd like to see the wreck of the car.'

I looked at Brettler. He flicked a glance at Ross, who nodded his head ever so slightly.

'I'll fix that for you. It will be with the leasing company unless they've tried to repair it or scrapped it. I doubt they've done either until they've claimed on their insurance.'

'And nothing much will have been done over the holiday,'

I agreed with him. 'So there may be something to see. I'll also check up on Bernie Brooks.'

For a second they all looked blank. They'd forgotten about Frank's passenger. As far as they were concerned, the only thing poor Bernie was famous for was being in the car when it could have been Ross. Frank had been 'family', Bernie was only recently hired help. Just like me.

'He's still in a coma,' said Brettler. 'I don't know whether you can actually get to see him.'

'We ought to send flowers or something,' said Ross and at least he had the decency to look embarrassed that he hadn't done so far. 'Could you make a note, Burgundy?'

There was a drop in temperature in the trailer.

'You mean make a note to tell Lin to do it?' said Burgundy and I could tell without looking round that she had her teeth clenched.

'Er . . . yeah, that would be . . . fine,' said Ross nervously.

'Where is Lin?' I asked.

'She needed some personal time this evening. Problems at home, I think,' said Ross. 'Why?'

'No particular reason. It's just that I might have to reschedule my working hours if I'm going to be sniffing around for you.'

Burgundy sniggered when I said 'sniffing'.

'Oh, relax, Roy,' said Gloria-Maria. 'Ross'll be working a fourteen-hour day from now on. You get him here by 7 a.m. and pick him up about 9 p.m. and the rest of the day's your own.'

'Oh. That's OK then,' I said deadpan, wondering if my contract said anything about overtime.

'Thanks for the reminder, Gloria,' said Ross. 'That's a very polite way of telling me I should be heading for my new home, learning my lines and going to bed. You ready to roll, Roy?'

I didn't think I had any choice in the matter.

'Whenever. I was hoping to pick up a coupla things which might be useful.'

'Such as?'

'Some binoculars,' I said. 'To keep an eye on our Gothic picket line out at the house.'

'There must be some around here, Paul?' said Ross. 'I had a really great pair of Zeiss on *Side Edge*, with night vision enhancement.'

'They'll be over in Props. All the props from *Side Edge* came back just before Christmas,' said Brettler. 'They won't even have been unpacked yet.'

'And a wig,' I said.

'A wig?' Ross asked, his eyes widening.

'A blonde one. Long.'

'You want a long, blonde wig?'

Had I stopped talking English or something?

'No. You do.'

A few years back there was a court case at, I think, Islington Magistrates, which has entered legend. Up on a charge of handling stolen goods was one Ignatius Francis McGuire, better known as Iffy McGuire, who had his own bookmark tab on the Police National Computer. The prosecuting copper described to the Bench how the forces of law and order, acting upon information received (from one of Iffy's disgruntled wives), had raided a pair of lock-up garages rented by said Iffy to discover hi-fis, computers, VCRs, silver plate, jewellery, antiques, paintings, two cocktail cabinets, 106 lava lamps, thirty-six cases of fine wines and eighteen food processors. It was, said the case for the prosecution, 'a veritable Aladdin's cave of stolen property'. Iffy's solicitor – acting for the defence, mind you – then stood up and opened his plea of mitigation with the immortal words: 'It may have been an Aladdin's cave of stolen treasure, your worships, but it's going to take more than a genie to get him out of this one.'

I knew how those coppers on that raid must have felt when Ross and Paul Brettler took me into the props store.

There was everything you could have possibly wanted if you were looking for a fun time. There was also stuff you knew you didn't want, but just felt you ought to have. Until, on closer inspection, you realised that half the things were made out of cardboard or fibreglass.

They would still have been appreciated by some of the people I knew, but then I knew people who would really like to give house room to an eight-foot fake cactus, or a Browning .50 calibre machine gun on a tripod which had a barrel that had exploded and peeled back like a banana, or a four-foot model of a Tudor man-of-war for the bath, say, or a lifesize model of a trooper from the Horseguards complete with horse, or a penny-farthing bicycle, or a statue of just about every Roman god you could shake a stick at.

And that was just the stuff piled in one corner by the entrance, waiting to be logged and filed and stored or whatever it was they did with it. I knew where I was coming for my Christmas shopping in future.

'The *Side Edge* stuff is over here,' said Brettler, his voice echoing in the cavernous warehouse, which I guessed had been a sound stage at one time. 'See, most of it's still unpacked.'

Ross and I followed him over to three metal containers, each big enough to have doors in the side where you could walk in. All were open, one was empty.

'They must have started unloading,' said Ross, 'though we'd better put a stop on that if we have to do a reshoot. Everything might have to go back out to Switzerland. Which one's got the skiing gear?'

'This one,' I said, peering into the nearest container which was crammed with skis, poles, snowboards and racks of ski wear. 'But you could rent all this stuff, couldn't you?'

'Continuity,' said Ross. 'We have to have the same equipment we used on the shoot or someone will notice the joins.'

'Yeah, right. I knew that.'

'Look for some of the smaller boxes of hand props. The binoculars will be in there.'

I started to throw things out of the way so we could actually get inside the container, trying not to think how much this amount of skiing equipment would fetch retail.

My shins grazed up against something which I couldn't kick out of the way. It was a pair of suitcases, both very heavy as I discovered when I tried to pull one free.

'Careful with those,' said Ross, 'we'll need them if we have to reshoot the last scene. They're crucial to the plot.'

'Who have you got in here?' I asked, straining under the weight of one of them.

Ross grinned and took the case from me, pushing stuff out of the way with his foot so he could lay it down flat and flip the catches. The case had a sticker on it saying 'Side Edge scenes

119–131'. He knelt down next to it and held the lid with both hands, pausing for dramatic effect.

'I won't bore you with the intricate plot of *Side Edge*, just go with me on this. The hero, that's me, goes hand-to-hand with one of the baddies over one of these babies, which is not only rigged with explosives, but contains . . .'

As he flipped the lid he made a 'Tah-dah' noise. Inside were row upon row of purple banknotes, bound in bundles, the top one displaying the numeral 500 in at least six different places.

'Mickey Mouse money,' I said.

'Not quite,' said Ross. 'They're euros, 500-euro notes.'

'What are they worth, then?'

'One euro is about one dollar US, I think. How the hell should I know? You Brits are the ones in Europe, the single currency, all that shit.'

I shook my head.

'Not us, mate. We're only in Europe for the cheap booze and cigarettes. All that financial stuff, nothing to do with us.'

Ross scowled at me like it was my fault. Then got back to the plot.

'Anyhow – there I am killing one bad guy while two others get away by car, driving down the mountain, having set off an avalanche to trap me.'

'With you so far,' I said, trying to look interested.

'So I remove the skis from the dead bad guy, strap the suitcase to one and send it down the hill towards the other bad guys' car, whilst I strap on the one remaining ski and go for the big jump to safety. The suitcase explodes just as it lands on the bad guys' car sending up a big cloud of burning money through which I come jumping, kinda surfing the air actually, with the avalanche in the background. Great shot or not. What d'you think?'

'Let me guess,' I said carefully. 'As you land, on one ski, perfectly in control and strangely out of range of the avalanche, the burning money starts to come down around you. Dead casual, you grab a burning note out of the air, and take out the cigar stub you've been saving from a pocket in your Armani ski suit. With a suave, ultra cool glance into camera, you light the cigar. End credits.'

Ross let the suitcase lid fall and clicked the locks down with his foot. He put his hands deep into his pockets and appeared to be counting to ten before he spoke.

'You've read the script of *Side Edge*, haven't you?'

'No I haven't. Did I come close?'

'I'm wearing a tuxedo, not an Armani ski suit.'

'Of course you would be. Why didn't I think of that?'

He glared at me, then pointed to a carton marked 'Hand props–RP'.

'I think the binoculars are in that one,' he said.

They were; a very tasty pair of Zeiss glasses in a leather case which would have cost over £400 even if you'd bought them from a man in a pub down Woolwich.

'They'll do fine,' I said, trying them out on the approaching figure of Burgundy Dulude.

In magnificent, precision-lensed close-up, she stuck her tongue out at me as she walked towards us, a long, straight blonde wig in one hand.

'I liberated this from Make-Up,' she said. 'I don't think they'll miss it.'

She tossed her head so her own fair locks shimmied under the strip lighting, as if saying: If you want the real thing . . .

Ross took the wig and put it on, bending his head, then snapping his neck back so the blonde hair fell about his shoulders.

He squinted out from beneath the fringe, then pulled a comb out of his jacket.

'Just let me settle this down.'

As he combed, I noticed he was looking into Burgundy's eyes at his own reflection. He didn't have a mirror to hand, but she had nice big eyes and he was a professional.

'I still don't know why you want me to wear this,' he said, flicking a couple of strands behind his ears with the comb.

'You will, but promise me one thing.'

'What?'

'You'll take it off before Marcus sees it.'

As we turned a corner to where Armstrong was parked near Ross's trailer, he jabbed an elbow into my ribs and hissed, 'Sssh.'

I had no idea what was going on but walking unsteadily towards us was a tall, thin man wearing aviator sunglasses and a suede safari jacket. From one of the pockets of the jacket protruded the neck of a bottle; Jack Daniels at a guess. The thin man clutched a leather briefcase to his chest and was concentrating on looking straight ahead and putting one foot in front of the other.

Ross, still wearing the blonde wig, kept his head down and quickened his pace, with me keeping up. The thin man walked by without saying a word.

I heard his boots behind us. Five, then six paces, then Ross grabbed my arm.

'Let's get out of here. Move it!'

'What's the matter?' I shot back, fumbling for the keys to Armstrong. 'Who is that guy?'

'The writer,' said Ross, as if that explained everything.

12

TRACKING SHOT

It was still not seven o'clock when we left Pinewood. The rush hour would be dying down, the pubs filling up, the restaurants chalking up their menu specials, the crowds starting to drift through the streets to mid-week football matches. And here I was driving an international sex symbol in a tarty blonde wig through a picket line of teenagers whose main ambition in life was to be the walking dead.

'This isn't going to work. This isn't going to work,' he was muttering as we approached the gate.

'Relax. Sit in the middle of the seat and look down.'

A security man opened the gate for us and as I made to move off one of the Goths, a young girl wearing a short skirt and black stockings with luminous green stripes down the side, rushed forward to peer into the back of the cab.

Even before I had got into first gear, she had turned away disappointed and was shaking her head at the other Goths and Gothesses gathered in the road.

'Go, go, go!' whispered Ross from the back.

I edged forward until I was almost on to the road, turning left, then I stood on the brake and pulled my window down so I could yell at the girl who had eyeballed me.

'Oi, darlin', who you after?'

'We are waiting for Ross Pirie, to seek his blessing,' she said without thinking.

''E's long gone, darlin'. Haven't you heard? He's got what he calls a stealth house over in Hackney, gets a cab to take him there. The last sort of place you'd expect a film star to live. Number 9 Stuart Street so I 'eard. It was in the papers this morning.'

I pulled away and watched in the mirror as the other Goths surrounded the girl to find out what I had said. I could imagine two or three of them saying yes, there had been something in the papers this morning and it had involved a cab somehow. Then Ross, in his fright wig, sat up and blocked my view.

'Do you have many friends?' he asked.

About fifteen minutes later I went through the same routine at the gateway of Eight Ash House, but with one added refinement: I waved the photocopied press cuttings Chrissie Schwartz had given me to add authenticity to my story, though I didn't hold it out long enough for Count Dracula to read it properly.

As we drove up the driveway, the exterior security lights came on but they didn't reach as far as the gateway. One on each side of the house and one above the front door covered an arc not more than fifty feet from the house. If Ross had been thinking of permanent residence here I would have advised him to stake out some ground lamps in the shrubbery and invest in CCTV. Given the sort of fans he was attracting, I would have told him to throw in a minefield and stock the lake at the back with piranha.

'You enjoyed doing that, didn't you?' said Ross. 'Blowing the breeze up their unsuspecting ass.'

'I think you mean "winding them up" and yes, I did,' I said. 'You can take off the wig now, though I have to admit to becoming strangely attracted to you in it.'

'What would you have said if one of those zombies had asked who I was?'

'I would've said you were a prostitute hired to slake Marcus's carnal lust for the evening.'

'You mean Kurt,' he said, pulling the wig off and looking at me in the mirror.

'I know what I'm talking about.'

He nodded, impressed.

'You are sharp. You got it on day one of meeting him. Most husbands don't realise until it's too late.'

'You can say that about a lot of things.'

Marcus scolded Ross for being late for dinner; Kurt scolded him for being late for his evening work-out on the instruments of torture he had assembled in the cellar.

I wished them all a happy evening, said I would take one of

159

the keys to the back door and that I may be gone for some time.

None of them asked where I was going or whether it would involve risk to life or limb. The superstar had to be fed, watered, exercised and put to bed. Nothing else mattered.

None of them noticed me opening the switch box on the wall by the front door and turning off the power to the security lights front and back of the house. Once out of the back door, I crossed the large brick patio to go round the house clockwise. There was enough light from the two sets of french windows in the lounge to make sure I didn't wander down into the lake and to make out the stable buildings about fifty yards away which had been converted into garages though I hadn't yet got around to exploring them. At the corner of the house, I turned to edge my way along the blank wall – all the windows in the house were front or back, none at the sides – until I reached the front wall. I didn't want to go too far in case I crunched on the gravel driveway as I knew the sound would travel. That was the trouble with the countryside; it was quiet. Too quiet.

My eyes had become accustomed to the dark by this time and the Zeiss glasses helped me pick out the young Goths bunched at the gateway more easily than I had expected. I had half expected them to start sneaking up the long drive just for the sake of something to do. After all, the night was still very young, except in Eight Ash Green, that is, where the only source of amusement was staring at a lonely streetlight. There was the trouble, you see. Nothing for the young folk to do in the country-side except go stalking their favourite movie star.

I couldn't make out too much detail even with the binoculars, but one of the group – Count Dracula perhaps – moved apart from the rest and seemed to be leaning his head over to the side. It was a safe bet he was using a mobile phone. After all, even vampires had to get with the twenty-first century.

He could have been ringing the other group of losers waiting outside Pinewood, or he could have been phoning home to see if his mum had his dinner ready, but after a couple of minutes it became clear he had been calling a cab.

It was a minicab, a family saloon of some sort, and probably the only car to come down the road since Armstrong. The odds were it was a local firm looking for a nice little run into London.

None of the London firms based around Heathrow would be keen to come out here when there was better business to be had in town at this time of day.

Three or four of the Goths gathered round the cab and the passenger door opened and the interior light came on. They had a protracted discussion with the driver and I could guess what was going on. There were seven of them, but only one cab. The other, no doubt, was on its way. Honest.

Eventually, after much negotiation, four of them got in the cab and three stood at the side of the road as the cab turned round and headed off towards the M40. As the lights and the engine noise of the minicab disappeared into the night, the three Goths stood looking anxiously down the road, beating their arms around themselves to keep warm. Cold, alone and more than a bit pathetic. Bless.

I packed the Zeiss away and pulled Armstrong's keys out of my pocket.

They wanted a cab; I had one.

They all lived in Harrow-on-the-Hill. Did I know it? I was supposed to be a cab driver so I just grunted, plotting a flight path straight down the M40 and on to the A40 as far as the Greenford roundabout. It wouldn't take that long as I would be going against the flow of any late rush-hour traffic and if the worst came to the worst, I'd just drop them near the Bakerloo or the Metropolitan lines.

Armstrong was cruising down the motorway before one of them noticed that I didn't appear to have a meter running.

'Private hire,' I said, quick as a flash.

'So how much is this costing us?' said one of the girls, though in the dark with all those dark clothes and the make-up, I couldn't distinguish them.

I did some quick calculations based on what a black cab would charge from Heathrow to the West End, increased it to take account of the greater mileage, then halved it.

'Thirty quid, this time of night,' I said reasonably.

That seemed to get the thumbs-up from them. They relaxed visibly, all squashed in one black shadow across the back seat, and I heard one of them say that now they had enough money to go to the pub. After a few minutes of whispering, one of them asked:

'Do you know the George and Dragon on Harrow Road?'

'Big pub, on the way to Wembley, sure. There isn't a match on, is there?'

'No, no,' one of them said, 'we just use the place for meetings.'

Of what, I thought, the coven?

'You in some sort of society, then?' implying that whatever it was, I would have an opinion on it. I was a cabby. It was my job.

'No we are not,' said one of them sullenly.

'What you all doin' out in the sticks then? You protesting about something?'

'We wanted to see Ross Pirie, the actor. He's making a film here and we wanted to wish him luck.'

I still had no idea of which of the three witches had spoken.

'But I told some of you lot earlier on. He ain't out there, he's supposed to be over in Hackney.'

'So who's in that big house then?'

'Some American ponces – pardon my French. Special Effects people, not actors.'

'Not Ross?' It was a plaintive cry. It was pathetic.

'No way. I should know, I was chatting to him this morning.'

'You were? What's he like?'

I felt them all lean forward in anticipation.

'He's much taller on the screen,' I said, 'but the wife likes him.'

They didn't speak to me again until we reached the car-park of the George and Dragon where they counted out four £5 notes and one ten, handed them over and each of them said 'Goodnight' as they climbed out, proving that deep in their black hearts they were nice, polite, middle-class girls, albeit lousy tippers.

Once out of Armstrong, they couldn't stop talking, putting their heads close together and chattering away as they walked towards the pub without looking back. I watched them in the wing mirror until they entered the main doors and turned right at an illuminated sign saying 'Lounge Bar'. The windows of that part of the pub were throbbing with green and red flashing lights, so I assumed it was disco night down at the coven.

I pulled Armstrong into the last parking space before the exit and switched off the engine. In Armstrong's boot I always kept a sweater – an ex-RAF job with shoulder and elbow patches – and a baseball cap bearing the California Angels logo. I took off my leather jacket and pulled them on. It wasn't a great disguise, but then, who pays any attention to the taxi driver?

At the pub's front door, I turned left into the saloon bar, pausing only to try and identify the low-volume thumping of the music coming from the lounge. I couldn't make it out as it was being played fairly quietly. Obviously the friends of the undead didn't want to disturb the living in the next bar too much.

The saloon was about half full with regular punters mostly minding their own business, nobody paying much attention to the TV slung from the ceiling in the corner which was showing a sit-com. I picked a spot at the bar near the door where I could see into the lounge bar via the mirror behind the back-fittings which held the spirits bottles upside down on their optics, pulled up a bar stool and sat down. I took a fiver from the young Goths' taxi fare, slotted it between index and middle fingers and put my palms down on the bar until the barman noticed it. When I caught his eye, I ordered a bottle of Pils which he served without asking if I wanted a glass. After feeling the sticky bar counter and noticing the puff of dust from the bar stool as I sat down, I wasn't going to ask for one. But I did ask him what was going on in the next bar when he brought my change.

'Black Sabbath Appreciation Society or something, I dunno,' he said offhand. 'Landlord lets 'em use the lounge when it's a quiet night. He calls it his Fright Night. They sit around listening to shit music. You know, the stuff that says "Kill the Pope" backwards. Bloody strange if you ask me, but they're harmless. Go in if you like, it's not a private party.'

'I'll stay in the land of the living,' I said.

I sucked on my bottle of beer and concentrated on what I could see of the lounge. The first thing I noticed were three crates of bottled tomato juice stacked on the floor behind the bar there. No prizes for guessing that the most popular drink in the pub tonight would be a Bloody Mary and no wonder the landlord didn't mind the Goths, given those profit margins on a quiet night.

I didn't have much else to think about as I was working on the assumption that everything comes to he who waits, including an idea of what to do next. All I really needed to do was get one of the Goths on their own and persuade them to tell me the source of their information on *Daybreak* and whether their intentions towards the production were honourable. On the basis that anyone will tell you anything if you only ask the right question, all I had to do was hang on until I could get one of them on their own. They certainly didn't give anything away when they travelled in threes, but maybe a lone straggler would be looking for a taxi ride home, or perhaps I could chat up Count Dracula when he went to the Gents. Even vampires had to go sometime, didn't they?

I took my beer in slow sips, making it last. If I hadn't been driving I would have had far too many and come up with a really stupid plan, like going into the lounge and putting 'Monster Mash' on the juke box. As I didn't even know how many of them were in there, they would probably all turn on me and it would be like the final scenes of a Sam Raimi film.

As it turned out, all I had to do was sit there and stare into the mirror. Unlike vampires, Goths did show up in them as they came up to the bar to order more tomato juice. And, of course, so did I. So I shouldn't have been surprised to see one of the Gothesses – black Afro wig, white face paint, black lipstick and a six-inch metal pentacle in a circle hanging from a chain around her neck – clocking me as hard as I had been clocking her zombie friends.

I raised my beer into the mirror in salute. She slammed some coins down on the bar and disappeared from view.

I heard a door slam, then the door to the saloon opened behind me and a faint whiff of incense announced her arrival at my shoulder.

'Good evening,' I said politely.

'You fucking following me?' asked Chrissie Schwartz.

On the drive back to Eight Ash Green I turned on my mobile phone and rang Amy's mobile. She answered on the fifth ring

and I got an earful of disco music, a remix of the Blondie hit
'Atomic'.

'Hi there, it's me.'

'Who?'

'It's me!' I shouted.

'Oh yeah. Right. What's the problem?'

'No problem, just a question.'

'Go for it.'

'Have you been e-mailing anybody on the Net about the
movie?'

'I might have.'

'Talk to me, Amy.'

Talk? We were both shouting above the background music.

'OK, then. I did e-mail the *daybreak* site just pointing out the
credit due to the costume designers, but that was it.'

'You didn't give out the Eight Ash Green address?'

'What?'

'Did you e-mail anybody else?'

'No I didn't. I've been busy working for a living.'

That was a low blow.

'OK, fair enough.Where are you now?'

'I'm in a client meeting.'

She hung up.

Eight Ash House was in almost total darkness when I got back.
I assumed they had all gone to bed – and the pubs not even shut
yet – leaving me to an empty, lonely evening. It was just like
going home to Hampstead.

Except that there I wouldn't have found a note on the long
pine kitchen table telling me that there was a lobster 'po-boy'
sandwich, some cherry ice cream and a bottle of Chardonnay
in the fridge for me. This was better than going home to
Hampstead.

The sandwich was a small baguette with lettuce, mayo and
three or four lobster claws. By squashing it on the table I just
about managed to get a corner of it into my mouth and I was
munching merrily and pouring out a glass of wine when I heard
a squeaking noise coming from somewhere. Sandwich in one
hand, glass in the other, I went to investigate and found the

source of the noise to be the basement with the door open and the light on.

I had automatically assumed it would be Kurt, toning his muscles or polishing up his tan, but it was Marcus on a bright chrome rowing machine, bulging out of day-glo purple gym vest and shorts. Whoever invented Spandex had a lot to answer for.

'Thanks for the sandwich,' I mumbled, spraying crumbs over a rack of shining weights.

Marcus nodded, gritted his teeth and did three more strokes on the handles of the machine then released them, exhaled, and began to wipe his face with a towel.

'Been busy?' he asked me.

'Chatting up the Goths, as you do.'

'Successfully?'

'I think so. I reckon I've put them on the wrong trail. With a bit of luck they'll be staking out Ross's secret hideaway in Hackney tomorrow.'

'Does Ross have a secret hideaway in wherever?'

'Nope. All quiet here?'

'Ross and Kurt sleeping like babes.' He stood up and stretched, looping the towel around his neck. 'Separate rooms of course.'

'So what's the plan for tomorrow? We actually going to make a movie?'

'Ross is. And I'll be doing his hair, so we both need to be at the studios by seven. Kurt's gonna hold the fort here, see the cleaner lady in, keep an eye on things. I guess Lin will want to move in tomorrow sometime.'

'Lin? Here?'

I thought it was going too well.

'Sure, she likes to be close to Ross. We're gonna need a fax machine put in here, for the overnights.'

'Overnights?'

'The script changes for the next day's shooting.'

'The script's going to change?'

He looked at me like I was brain dead.

'Daily. That's Burgundy's job, to get the script changes through. She might as well move in here too, there are rooms spare. We're gonna need a coupla more cars here.'

'That's good thinking,' I said. 'So you don't have to rely on me.'

Marcus gave me the evil eye.

'Don't go disappearing on us, now, Angel.'

'I'm only a phone call away,' I said, thinking: Note to self – turn phone on. 'But I do have some errands to run. What's the security like on this place?'

'You expecting trouble?'

'No, but there are some pretty spooky fans out there. What's to stop them coming here looking for souvenirs?'

'The local cop, Winter, the housekeeper's husband, he said he'd drive by when he could and the alarms are state-of-the-art. All ground-floor doors and windows are wired and linked to the nearest police station and there are smoke alarms with a link to the nearest fire station. If all else fails and we have to reshoot The Alamo, we come down here and break out the shotguns.'

'Excuse me?'

'Over there.'

The cellar doubled as a utility room for the house, with a washing machine and dryer and the boiler which powered the central heating. There was also a floor-to-ceiling wine rack, which had been wisely emptied before the house was let, and an old-fashioned upright, grey metal filing cabinet with double doors. Just about every other square inch of space was taken by Kurt's mobile gymnasium.

'Securely stored in a locked metal container – my ass!' sniffed Marcus. 'Thought you Brits had gun laws.'

'Who has the key?'

'The policeman, Winter, has one. I used this.'

Marcus pulled a long thin hairgrip from behind his ear. One end was bent into a serrated shape ending in a right angle.

'You snooped?' I asked.

'I snooped,' he said.

The cabinet had a crude tumbler lock built into the handle, the sort of lock that was designed to keep the doors shut and the racks of bulging paper files in, rather than a snooper out. Marcus's hairgrip key had the door open in four seconds. Inside the bare metal cabinet were three double-barrelled shotguns, standing on their butts, leaning drunkenly from bottom left to top right.

'They're not worth anything,' Marcus said, casually picking one up and breaking it open to peer down the empty barrels. 'I thought the guy who owned the house might have a Purdey or something interesting and Italian. These are cheap horse pistols, made in Belgium or somewhere.'

'You a gun freak or something?'

'Of course I am,' said Marcus with a smile, 'I'm an American. Don't worry, there's no ammo for them.'

'That's a relief,' I said, though I still had no intention of touching them.

'But they'll do to scare off any unwanted guests.'

I pretended to take a sudden interest.

'Does that include Lin?'

But I didn't have to worry about Lin moving in the next day – she phoned in sick to the studio. Not that anyone really noticed or commented on that very much.

The sole topic of conversation around the tea trolleys was the fact that Ross's luxury trailer, equipped with every mod. con. known to man, had been burnt to the ground during the night.

13

STORY EDITOR

The security guard on the gate at Pinewood the next morning said, 'Good morning, Mr Petrie' and 'Good morning, Mr Moore' and then scowled at me and told me to drive direct to Make-Up, straight away, no stopping. Miss van Doodler's orders. It was 6.50 a.m., cold, wet and dark, and I'd only had one cup of coffee. I wasn't about to argue.

'My, my, early call for Gloria-Maria,' Marcus camped it up from the back seat. 'It must be serious for her to be out from under her latest toy boy at this time of the morning. I bet the old hooker's suffering withdrawal symptoms . . .'

'Can it, Marcus,' said Ross, trying not to laugh.

It was serious enough for Gloria-Maria to be waiting for us outside the Make-Up building, standing underneath a sodium arc light chain smoking. She waved as if hailing a taxi, which I suppose she was, so I pulled up alongside her.

But instead of us getting out, she got in, pulling down one of the rumble seats and sitting opposite Ross until their knees touched. Marcus drew himself as far back into the corner of the seat as he could.

'Good morning, Gloria,' said Ross, all charm. 'What's the problem?'

'I've been trying to call your cell phones for the last hour,' she started, defence being the best form of corporate attack.

Marcus showed her the palms of his hands.

'You know I don't take calls when I'm cooking breakfast,' he lisped.

Breakfast? Why had I missed breakfast? Because Kurt had had to throw me out of bed at six twenty, that was why.

Gloria-Maria swung on me, waiting for an answer. I remembered that Ross was the one person in the world who didn't carry a mobile phone, which left me. I tugged the Nokia out of my jacket and switched it on.

'Sorry. Why didn't you call the house?'

'Nobody gave *me* the number.'

'Lin has it,' said Ross.

'*That's* one of the problems,' she snarled. 'Lin left a message at the office. She's sick. She's not coming in today.'

'Lin's never sick,' said Marcus. 'Humans get sick, but that's because they're weak.'

'Marcus!' Ross snapped. 'It's not like her, though. She took some personal time yesterday. That's not like her either, not on a shoot.'

'What's the other problem?' I asked, trying to get them back on message.

'Oh yeah, your trailer burned down last night,' said Gloria-Maria as if suddenly remembering. 'Paul Brettler's talking to the local Fire Chief right now.'

Everything was under control, of course.

The fire had been discovered at about 10 p.m. and by the time a local fire engine had arrived, the trailer was down to its wheelbase. No one had been hurt, though, and the fire had only spread as far as a nearby rubbish bin. The trailer didn't use gas cylinders, so there had been no explosion. No one had, or was admitting to, a theory yet as to how it had started. Gloria-Maria had already left instructions at her office to get a replacement as soon as possible, but that might take all of twenty-four hours. She'd try for an upgrade, too; which as far as I could see would mean the new one had a jacuzzi as the old one had everything else.

It began to dawn on me that the reason for Gloria-Maria's agitation, and her turning out at this time of the morning, was due to the fact that the star of the film now had nowhere to go to relax in private between takes. I hardly called that life-threatening. There were far more important issues of the moment, like when I was going to get breakfast.

To give him his due, Ross took it all very calmly. Gloria-Maria must have been used to the kind of movie star who threw a wobbler and stomped off set if the freshly squeezed orange juice had bits in it. I'd heard that some of them could be quite moody, not to mention temperamental.

Ross just said:

'As long as nobody got hurt, that's the main thing. I know you'll look after me, Gloria, you always do. There was nothing personal in there, was there? Marcus got my luggage out yesterday and I haven't had time to accumulate anything else yet. What about those videos from the Academy?'

'I left them there,' said Marcus. 'Thought you'd seen them all.'

'Most of them,' said Ross. 'But it's too late to vote now anyway, isn't it?'

'Relax,' said Marcus, patting Ross's knee. 'We voted on time.'

Then he saw me grinning and added:

'*You* voted on time.'

'Then I guess we just keep a lid on it. I presume that's what Tony Lovisi will say.'

'Dead right,' said Gloria-Maria, 'though I haven't been able to raise Chrissie this morning.'

I kept quiet. My guess was that Chrissie Schwartz was either catching up on some beauty sleep or organising a Gothic vigil over in Hackney right now, even though she knew it to be a waste of time. That had been our deal.

'And does Lin know?' Ross asked her.

'Can't get her either. It was just dumb luck I checked the office machine before I came out here. Look, Ross, we can get you one of the make-up rooms to yourself for the rest of the day and I'll get Burgundy to assign a couple of the runners to you. Get you anything you need.'

'I'll survive, Gloria,' he said charmingly, 'for a day or so. Now let me and Marcus get to work. I don't want it said I delayed the shoot.'

What a trooper! Prepared to rough it with only Burgundy and two of the young, female runners to cater for his every whim like that. Still, at least it meant I could sneak off and find the tea trolley which handed out the excellent bacon butties.

'Roy, get a big bouquet of flowers and some fruit or something and drop it round to Lin's, will you?'

'I don't know where she lives,' I said plaintively.

'You can get the address from Gloria's office,' he said, glossing

171

smoothly over the fact that he didn't either. 'Or from Paul Brettler when you see him.'

'When I see him?' I said pathetically.

'Find out if we have anything to worry about with this trailer fire, would you? Talk to Paul so you can fill me in tonight. You can pick us up here at six. If we wrap any earlier, I'll call you.'

'And remember, we've seen you turn your phone on,' warned Marcus, wagging a finger.

They climbed out and from nowhere a crowd of young runners and gophers and second assistant assistants appeared waving clipboards, or script pages, or offers of help or mostly just themselves. They didn't mind the dark and the damp and the unearthly hour, they were making movies. I had to go find a florist.

Fortunately I found a tea trolley which had a couple of Danish pastries left and I was clutching them in one sticky hand with a cup of black coffee in the other when I shouldered my way into Brettler's office.

He was sitting at his desk across from two burly men in county fire brigade uniforms. Given the setting, it could have been a scene from *Carry On Burning*, which never got made.

'I'm nearly finished here, Roy,' he said, 'if you could give me a minute?'

'Actually, Ross Pirie sent me over.'

Admittedly, I probably didn't look like a film star's personal assistant: the leather jacket, the jeans, the trainers, badly shaved and the fingers of my left hand stuck together with apple Danish. But dropping the Ross Pirie name seemed to help. In fact, the two firemen stood up as if the royal presence was about to follow me in.

'Mr Pirie is here?' asked the elder of the two officers, and much the senior one given the decoration on the shoulders of his jacket.

'He's in Make-Up,' I said hoping that I sounded suitably professional. 'The cameras are waiting for him. But he asked me to come here and make sure, because he is very, very concerned, that no one was hurt fighting the fire.'

The senior officer's chest swelled with pride.

'How thoughtful of him; how charming. Please assure Mr

Pirie that all my boys are fine and unscathed and only sorry that we couldn't save his caravan, but it was well ablaze by the time we got here. Though I think we can be rightly proud of our response time.'

'No complaints there, Mr Linscott,' said Brettler diplomatically.

'Any idea what started it?' I asked.

Linscott glanced at Brettler who nodded that it was OK to let me in the loop.

'We're checking, of course,' he said as he pulled on his peaked hat, 'and as gas supply is not an option in this case, we'll have a look at the electrical wiring. But the most obvious candidate at the moment is a cigarette end in a chair plus the added fact that there seemed to be a lot of booze lying about. We found bottles and glasses scattered about. We'll keep looking into it.'

'I know Ross would appreciate that,' I said, looking for somewhere to put my coffee down.

'Tell him next time he wants to have a bonfire, do it on the day shift. Barry here is on hand most days.'

The other, younger fireman smiled at me and introduced himself.

'Barry Hood, Pinewood liaison.'

He seemed to think it should mean something to me. Then I remembered.

'I've seen you driving that dinky little fire engine around here, haven't I?'

The senior man bristled at 'dinky' but Barry Hood grinned.

'That little appliance has been in more films than I could name,' he said cheerfully, 'but we've never got a credit. We're in this new one with Ross Pirie.'

'You are?'

I'd read the script and I didn't spot anything involving a fire engine and certainly not a British one. The film was supposed to be about vampires in New York unless they'd made some really drastic changes without telling the writer. Of course, that was perfectly possible.

'Well, our water is,' said Barry Hood. He could see that he had lost me completely.

'We spray water on to the floor of the set to saturate the

atmosphere. It improves the quality of the colour film, giving it a much deeper texture. We do it on all the Bond films.'

'I knew that,' I said, too quickly.

The senior one, Linscott, eyed me suspiciously.

'We'll be off now, Paul,' he said. 'I see no reason to put this call out into our daily round-up for the local papers, do you?'

'Absolutely not. We appreciate that,' said Brettler, relieved.

As the firemen made to leave, Linscott looked down at me from under the peak of his hat.

'You actually work for Ross Pirie?' he said.

'Oh yeah, I'm his driver. And personal assistant,' I added.

Linscott leaned in towards me, his back to Paul Brettler and Barry Hood.

'What's he like?' he whispered.

'Shorter than you'd think,' I whispered back.

'Thought so,' he mouthed silently.

As the door closed behind them, I put my coffee down on Brettler's desk and began to peel the Danish off my left hand.

'So how's your day going so far?' he said.

'I'll tell you when I wake up. But my evening was quite productive. I went out drinking with our Goth friends last night and hopefully they'll be camping on somebody else's doorstep for a while. You'll still probably get a hard core here at the studios whilst they're filming, but hopefully they'll leave Eight Ash House alone.'

'How much did this cost, then?'

'A large tomato juice. One other thing, they never posted the Eight Ash address on their website. They read it on the *Pirie's Pets* site. That's where the leak is . . . er . . . leaking.'

'Have you a lead on them?'

'Give me a break! I haven't finished breakfast yet.'

'Sorry. It's just I'm not too sure what it is Ross wants – expects – you to do about all this.'

'Don't worry, that makes three of us – you, Ross and me. But I have an idea about this web thing. I know a guy over in Islington, right up his street.'

'Let's call him,' Paul said keenly.

'Get real. This time of night?'

'E-mail him?'

'No way. This guy is so paranoid he has his e-mails sent to a safe house in Latvia or somewhere. He's convinced the cops are bugging everything he does.'

'Are they?'

'They probably should be, but I doubt it. But he does a lot of hot-desking or the other thing – what do they call it? Wildcarding, that's it, just to make it difficult to find him. No, I'll do it the old-fashioned way and get some face time with him.'

Brettler looked puzzled.

'Face time,' I said. 'Non-electronic discussion.'

'How you going to do that?'

'I know where he lives, I'll pop round and knock on his door, he'll never expect that. Scare the shit out of him. Probably hasn't spoken to another human being for years, unless you count phoning for pizza. Can you do pizza on-line yet?'

'I expect you can.'

'Me too. Anyway, that reminds me. Ross wants me to take some flowers round to Lin, so I need her address.'

Paul leaned towards his computer and began to key in a password.

'She not in then?'

'Phoned in sick to the production office. Where's that, by the way?'

'Last Ditch? It's in St Anne's Court, off Dean Street in Soho. There's Lin.' He turned the screen so I could see his address book program. 'Gerrard Street,' he said. 'That's Soho too, isn't it?'

'Chinatown, just down the end of Dean Street,' I said automatically. 'One other thing, the hospital where Frank Shoosmith and Bernie Brooks are convalescing.'

'The Oaks,' Paul said, reaching into the top drawer of his desk. 'I've got a map for them.'

He handed over a leaflet advertising The Oaks private hospital which included a map showing its position on the outskirts of Slough and boasted ample car-parking. It made no mention of trains or bus stops on the natural assumption that if you didn't have a car or a chauffeur to get you there, you probably couldn't afford the operation.

I unstuck it from my left hand and stuffed it in a pocket.

'What's the score on this Bernie Brooks?' I asked.

'No change. He's still in a deep coma and it's been – what –

twelve or thirteen days now, though I'm told by the medics that that's not unusual and the chances of him pulling out of it are still –'

'No, I meant Bernie the man. Who is he? What do we know about him?'

'To be honest, not a lot. He came with excellent references, ex-Met, ex- a very well known risk management company. Fit guy, martial arts man but not freaky that way. Seemed to get on with Ross – and Frank. Quiet guy, did his job.'

'What about relatives?'

'I don't know for sure. None close, like a wife or anything. Somebody said something about parents in the North.'

'I presume *somebody* was told that he's at death's door in Slough?'

Even as I said it, I realised how scary it could be describing somebody as at death's door in Slough.

'I'll check that,' said Brettler uneasily and he tapped a reminder on his keyboard.

'The BMW crash happened on Christmas Eve, right?' He nodded. 'When both Frank and Bernie should have knocked off for Christmas. They weren't needed, not with Ross on a plane to Switzerland, were they?'

'No, that's been worrying me,' said Brettler.

But he didn't sound worried, or at least not about that. Maybe about something he'd just thought of.

'I asked Alix Tse to dig out Frank's last lot of expenses receipts,' I said.

'Why did you do that?'

'If I was a driver taking the car home for Christmas, the first thing I'd do is fill it with gas I could claim back from the company. I just wanted to see if Frank had done that. We were expecting him to go home for the holiday as soon as he dropped Ross at Heathrow. That's all. Is Alix around?'

Brettler clicked his computer mouse several times in rapid succession.

'I doubt if she's here yet,' he said, as if he had to remind me it wasn't yet eight o'clock. 'But I've got everybody's diary here on our Intranet. There you go, Alix will be in meetings at the production company this morning. She'll be here after lunch.'

'That can probably wait, though I could have done with some petty cash.'

'Keep your receipts,' he said.

'I do,' I said. 'I hope Frank did. Useful way of remembering what you did the night before, receipts are. Or so I've found.'

'I think Frank's condition is a little more serious than simply tracing which bar he was in last.'

I shrugged off his snooty attitude. Tracing which bar I'd been in the night before had been a matter of life or death for me on several occasions, but I left it unsaid. I drank the rest of my coffee and left the styrofoam cup on his desk, along with a couple of ounces of crumbs.

'You haven't asked about the fire,' Paul said.

'According to Fireman Sam it was an accident. Bottle of booze with the top off, cigarette left burning – we've all been there.'

'You don't think it was anything else? I mean, two accidents in two weeks involving Ross?'

'Neither actually involved Ross,' I pointed out, 'just Ross's driver and Ross's mobile home. Not quite the same thing. Chill out.'

'I can't, they were both on my patch – here. You wouldn't put your friends the Goths in the frame for last night?'

I shook my head.

'They'd gone by then, but even if one came back for a bit of after-hours arson – why? They want Ross to do the picture. They love the idea of him as a vampire. It might – just might – be a publicity stunt for the other side. You know: tangle with the forces of darkness and a bolt of lightning torches your caravan.'

'There won't be any publicity,' he said forcefully. 'We've put a lid on it.'

'Let's keep an eye on the *Ririe's Pets* site, shall we? See how long it is before they break the news.'

I left him staring at the screen of his PC. Not a happy man.

Out on the lot, I sniffed the air to try and detect if the caterers were circulating any more bacon sandwiches. All I got was a whiff of melted plastic and wet, burnt wood, which must have pricked my conscience as I wandered round to where Ross's trailer had been parked just so I could say I had shown an interest if anyone asked.

Somebody had ringed the remains of the trailer with red and white traffic cones, though I couldn't see why they bothered. What was left could have been scooped up and dumped in a skip. The trailer had burned down almost to its chassis and metal frame, the roof supports leaning at a crazy angle as if a giant foot had stomped on it from above. A few pieces of furniture were still roughly recognisable but anything not completely burned had been smashed by the water used to put the fire out, as was always the way. There was nothing I could see to interest the most desperate of souvenir hunters, which was probably why there were none hanging around. In fact, the entire Pinewood population seemed to be avoiding the site as if it had a hex on it.

There wasn't much point me just staring at the wreckage, it wasn't going to tell me anything. But what Brettler had said about two accidents in two weeks – within a couple of hundred yards of each other if you thought about it – did niggle away at the back of my mind.

I rummaged through my jacket until I found the card Julius's driver Dave had given me for Chiltern Cars. The fire brigade had crawled over the remains of the trailer, but had anybody looked at the wreck of Frank Shoosmith's car?

I was flicking the card with a thumbnail and weighing up whether or not to sneak back to Eight Ash House and go back to bed or not, when I heard a loud moaning sound.

Standing at the corner of the block was a figure frozen in anguish, mouth wide open, staring at the trailer pyre.

'Noooooooo!' he wailed like an animal in a trap.

He had a leather briefcase in one hand and a plastic carrier bag from Oddbins which clinked as he moved in the other. He was dressed as he had been the night before when he had walked by Ross in the blonde wig without recognising him. It was the scriptwriter – Booth; Walter Wilkes Booth, that was it.

'Did anyone get it out?' he moaned.

I looked around. There was no one else in sight, so he must have been talking to me, but he wasn't looking at me, just glazing over at the sight of the wreck.

178

'There was nobody in there when it burned,' I said. 'Everybody got out in good time.'

That hadn't been what he meant.

'My revisions – the new Scene 96 – I wrote it for Ross. Did anyone get it out?'

'Er . . . you left it in there?'

'I left it with Ross's assistant last night. The Chinese girl.'

He had a deep American accent which could have been Arizona or New Mexico, somewhere like that, but it was difficult to tell with him sobbing.

'Lin? Lin was here last night?'

'Yeah. Late. I was working late on the revisions. She said she'd get them to Ross. I had to work in one of the editing suites. They won't give me an office. Where is Lin?'

He asked me, but it was like he didn't quite believe I was there.

'She's not here today. Call her tomorrow,' I said, backing away.

'They won't give me a phone,' he wailed. 'They won't let me talk to Ross.'

I wanted to say 'There, there' and put an arm round him. But then he started crying and I thought no, life was too short, and I left him standing there.

A keen young man in a suit came out on to the forecourt of Chiltern Cars of Amersham as soon as I pulled up. Black cab drivers were probably bad news for a car hire company, most likely calling round to complain about unfair competition or their drivers pinching their pre-booked fares. When I said I was from Pinewood and hinted that I worked for Ross Pirie and Last Ditch Productions, he softened. When I said all I wanted to do was look at Frank Shoosmith's wrecked Beamer, he became really helpful, as he could get rid of me on to someone else. He told me to ask for Stan, round the back in the workshop. Oh, and would I mind parking the cab out of sight round the back as it didn't fit their image?

Stan, the wizard of the workshop, wiped his greasy hands down the front of a set of green overalls which said Chiltern

Cars on the back, and told me that Frank's BMW was 'still on the truck'.

The breakdown truck, parked down the side of the workshop. Stan walked with me just in case I pinched a hubcap bearing the blue and white BMW propeller logo (dating from the days when they made aircraft). And because he was a highly skilled, highly trained mechanic, he just had to give me his professional opinion on the state of the wreck.

'Well fucked, that is,' he said philosophically.

From what I could see, I had to agree. The right offside wheel was bent at a right angle and in fact the whole right front of the car was squashed, as if it had gone up against a giant cheese-grater and the corner had been shaved off.

'Good job these things are built like Panzers,' said Stan, my technical consultant. 'There's many a car, the engine would have been pushed through right into the driver's goolies.'

'Did you find anything inside?' I asked Stan. 'Any personal stuff?'

'Haven't looked inside,' said Stan, hands deep in his pockets. 'We just checked for the basics, see if there was a mechanical fault in the brakes or the power steering.'

'Was there?'

'No, nothing wrong mechanically. And we checked it all again for the guys from the insurance company. They were a bit pissed off nobody had cut the brake lines or drained the fluid. Didn't happen, though.'

'Insurance company?' I said. 'Were they the regular assessors you use?'

'We don't normally see anybody, they mostly take our word for things, but this time they sent a pair of lads round. I suppose if it's a write-off, there's a few quid involved for them. They were bloody quick off the mark, though.'

'How quick?'

'They turned up first day back after Christmas. What was that, the Tuesday? The 27th, something like that? The day we brought it in, as a matter of fact. It had been sitting at Pinewood over Christmas and it's been sitting right there on the back of the recovery ever since.'

If I remembered correctly, Frank Shoosmith's accident had happened sometime late on the afternoon of Christmas Eve.

Chiltern Cars probably couldn't have picked up the wreck before the Tuesday, the first working day after the Christmas weekend, because no one had told them about it until then. So for the insurance assessors to turn up the same day really was going some.

'Did the insurance people look inside?'

'Probably. Would have checked the air bag at least. But they seemed more interested in the brakes.'

'Mind if I . . .?' I pointed up at the wreck.

'Help yourself. It's not locked,' said Stan. Then he added: 'We've taken out the radio and the CD-player, but there's some CDs in the rack. Nothin' worth listening to, though.'

I climbed on the back of the recovery truck and edged along the side of the BMW until I could open the driver's door, which screamed on its hinges. The interior of the car reeked of leather and petrol and damp and cold and the deflated air bag hung from the steering column like a lolling tongue. I climbed in, kneeling on the driver's seat and leaned over into the passenger side.

It didn't help. As Stan had said, there were some CDs in the rack – Bryan Adams, Shania Twain again, Oscar Peterson – which I deduced were all down to Ross feeling homesick. Apart from that, nothing.

I checked the glove compartment and the ashtray: both empty, as if new. In fact the only obvious sign that anyone had ever been inside the car at all was the condition of the rubber floor mats, which had the usual ground-in layer of mud and muck and crumbs.

Now I looked at them, especially the one on the passenger side, there did seem to be quite a lot of crumbs, as if somebody had been eating a packet of crisps during an earthquake. It was probably nothing, but it jarred. I had seen myself how house-proud the Chiltern Cars drivers were.

I reached down and ran my fingers over the mat and under the lip of the passenger seat. I scooped up a fistful of crumbs and let them trickle through my fingers. They weren't from a packet of crisps, they were crushed Chinese fortune cookies, because there was one intact under the seat-positioning mechanism.

No doubt about it, it was a fortune cookie and I didn't have to crumble it, it fell apart in my hand. Inside was small scroll of paper. I unrolled it and read the single line of typescript:

The man who never does anything wrong has never done anything.

That was probably true, but I bet he died old and in bed.

I drove due south out of Amersham and stopped at a garage near Beaconsfield to fill up with diesel and buy a red flower plant in a fat plastic pot.

Ross had given me the idea when he told me to buy flowers for Lin. Before I went anywhere near her, I was going to pay a call on Frank Shoosmith and the pot plant made me look like a bona fide hospital visitor. This working in the movies was starting to rub off. I was realising the value of having the right props.

I went over the M40 at Dorney Hill and took the old Farnham road to the outskirts of Slough, then followed the map printed in the advertising brochure for The Oaks which Paul Brettler had given me.

Looking at the hospital, I guessed that the free brochure was the closest I would ever come to being a valued customer there. The size of the car-park alone indicated a substantial piece of investment in real estate in this neck of the woods. It was also very convenient for Eton and Windsor Castle, should anyone there fall ill.

I carried the pot plant like camouflage into the entrance lobby, which was big enough to hangar a small aircraft and had more furniture than the average showroom. The reception desk was a Mission Control of white plastic, two computers, switchboard and PA system with a microphone on a flexible metal stalk. Behind the desk was a fresh-faced redhead in a starched green uniform which stretched in all the right places. She had a soft Edinburgh accent and a smile that was more effective than the in-house security system.

'That's a nice plant,' she said. 'What sort is it?'

'A red one,' I said and I put it down on the desk in front of her, quickly removing the price tag from its cellophane wrapping.

'It's for you. Please give it a good home, but remember, a plant is for life, not just Christmas.'

'Christmas has been and gone,' she said with a smile.

'Don't you think I feel guilty about that? That's why I bought you the plant.'

The name tag over her left breast said Siobhan.

'And the other reason you dropped by . . .?' she said.

'To see Frank Shoosmith, if I may.'

'One moment, sir.'

She turned to her keyboard and started hitting keys. She kept the heels of her hands on the plastic keyboard guard, her fingers splayed out, floating over the keys so that she didn't have to press down and risk her nails, which were long, painted red and perfect. Whatever she called up seemed to satisfy her.

'That's fine. Mr Shoosmith isn't scheduled for anything this morning. Take that lift over there to the first floor, turn right and it's Room 106. No mobile phones allowed in the hospital.'

I had expected to be asked for some identification or authorisation or at least have to wait while Siobhan phoned Frank's room. But this was the relaxed private sector. Frank was a guest, not an inmate.

'Don't worry, it's not switched on,' I said, flashing my best smile at her. 'Whilst I'm here, is it possible to see a Mr Brooks, Bernie Brooks?'

Her hands hovered over the keyboard again.

'No, I'm sorry. Mr Brooks cannot receive visitors because of his condition. If you were a member of the family, then we could arrange something.'

'No, I'm not. But thanks anyway.'

'Don't forget your plant,' she smiled back.

We were having a smile fight and I was prepared to surrender.

'It's yours, if you'll give it a good home.'

'Well I'll certainly do that,' she said, picking it up and tentatively sniffing one of the large red flowery things.

'This good home you're giving it,' I said, 'would be where exactly?'

Frank Shoosmith's room was fifty per cent bigger, a hundred per

183

cent more comfortable and a thousand per cent cleaner than any hotel room I'd ever stayed in.

Frank was wearing blue silk pyjamas and was propped up in bed reading the *Daily Express*. He peered over the pages as I knocked on the open door.

'Hello, Frank, remember me?'

I almost bit my tongue when I realised what I'd just said to a guy suffering from amnesia, with a vivid purple bruise stretching from above his right eye to almost over his ear, where his hair had been shaved in a semicircle.

But Frank seemed not to take it amiss.

'Sort of,' he said, folding the paper away. 'Pinewood?'

'Yeah, friend of Ross Pirie's. Saw you a couple of times before Christmas. Angel, Roy Angel.'

'So what do you do?'

He settled himself in among his pillows. He probably didn't get many visitors, or maybe he got loads but just couldn't remember them.

'Mostly your old job,' I said, pulling up a chair to the side of the bed, 'driving Ross around. Until you get back on your feet, that is. Frankly, the sooner you do that, the better as far as I'm concerned.'

He laughed at that.

'Not being a bit precious, is he? Not Ross, surely. He's a pussy cat compared to some of them I've driven.'

'Such as?' I tried hopefully.

'Couldn't say, could I? I'm saving it all for my memoirs.'

'So you . . .' I started, then stopped myself as it was going to come out stupid.

'Yes, I can remember things,' Frank said angrily, 'like my name and what I did for a living and who the wife is and where I live. Anyway, what bloody business is it of yours?'

'Steady on, Frank, calm down.' I was about to tell him not to burst a blood vessel but he'd already done that. 'Ross sent me because he's ever so guilty nobody's been to see you.'

I had a flash of inspiration. I usually do when I'm lying.

'And now there's a problem with the filming so he's not going to get away for a month or more, so he's feeling even more guilty and asked me to come out and see you, see if there's anything you need, make sure they're looking after you here.'

He relaxed back into his pillow, his cheeks pink with pride.

'Tell Ross that's very nice of him and I'm fine. They're looking after me nicely here. What's the problem on the set?'

'Oh, something about having to do reshoots on the last film he did. Nothing to do with this one, but, naturally, he's worried about what happened to you.'

'He's thoughtful that way, always was. Always remembered things like the wife's birthday . . .'

He must have read my face.

'Yes, I can remember the wife's birthday,' he said wearily. 'There's only a few things I can't remember.'

I didn't think it appropriate to tell the story of the Scottish footballer who got knocked out in a First Division match after going head to head with his marker. The guy was unconscious for a good two minutes and when he came round the trainer yelled to the manager 'He doesn't know who he is', and the manager had shouted back, 'Tell him he's Pele.'

'Like what happened on Christmas Eve?'

'Yeah, that's what everybody wants to know. Like I told the others, I can just about remember taking Ross to Heathrow that morning but after that I don't remember a thing, honest. Not until I woke up in here and found I'd missed me Christmas dinner. And the wife's not going to let me forget *that*.'

He smiled disarmingly as he said that, but it niggled at me because it sounded so rehearsed. It was like a sound-bite he'd been practising, suitable for most occasions and all audiences. It was too pat, too well thought out.

His eyes gave him away.

'That's the way it was, straight up. I don't even know what I was doing out at Pinewood that afternoon. And don't think I don't feel bad about what happened to Bernie.'

He was looking anywhere except at me.

'What others?' I asked.

14

ADDITIONAL DIALOGUE

Back in Armstrong in The Oaks' car park, I dug out the list of phone numbers Alix Tse had given me. I was carrying so many bits of paper around my jacket was becoming a filing cabinet.

I switched the phone on and hit #4 to talk to Paul Brettler.

'Did you know that Lin Ooi-Tan had been to see Frank Shoosmith in hospital?'

'No. Should I?' he asked.

'Three times in fact.'

'She never said anything. Is it important?'

'I don't know. Would you know if there are any insurance assessors on the case? Two of them were snooping around the wreck of Frank's Beamer and they've been here asking Frank questions.'

'News to me, but that's not my area. Insurance is done by the production company, Last Ditch. Alix would be the person to ask.'

'I might just do that. Keep an eye on the *Pirie's Pets* site, won't you?'

'I will.'

I checked my personal telephone directory again and punched #3 for Burgundy.

'What?' she yelled in my ear.

'Hi there, it's Angel. How's the wonderful world of movie –'

'Angel, we are going for a take here, so make it short and sweet, but mainly short.'

'Is Ross nearby?'

'Yes. Clock's ticking.'

'Does he still want me to get him some fireworks for Chinese New Year?'

'Oh, Sweet Jesus. Hold it a minute.'

She covered the phone then came back loudly in my ear.

186

'Yes, a definite yes. Spend what you like, he says. Now will you get out of my hair?'

'About your hair, Bee. Have you ever thought of asking Marcus . . .'

She was gone.

I switched my phone off again and started Armstrong, waiting at the entrance to the car-park while a new Rover 75, a red one, turned in, then I headed for the M4, Chiswick and the West End.

I looked at my watch. If the traffic went in my favour I was on schedule for a nice spot of lunch in Chinatown.

I stashed Armstrong in the car-park behind the Charing Cross Road and walked round into Shaftesbury Avenue, taking my life in my hands as I crossed it to Greek Street.

I got a window table at Ming's, which wasn't as busy as I had expected, and watched the world go by as expensively dressed media types piled out of taxis and into Soho House to one side, while local residents with charge accounts at the Oxfam shop squeezed into the Coach and Horses on the other.

The good thing about Ming's was that they remembered you no matter how long ago your last visit. That was also the bad thing about the place, but they served me, so I must have behaved myself last time out. My waitress was short, almost spherical and very jolly. She brought everything on a large tray and arranged it in front of me, then pointed to each dish in turn.

'That's your crispy Mongolian lamb, that's your Singapore noodles, that's your Ma Po bean curd with chilli sauce, that's your Tsingtao beer.' She turned her pointing finger on herself, aimed at her breasts. 'And I'm your waitress. Will there be anything else?'

'Actually, yes, since I'm here. Where can I buy some fireworks?'

She held her chin as if thinking about it.

'No, not on menu. No call for them lunchtimes,' she said with a twinkle in her eyes.

'Where round here? I need some for the New Year.'

'Chinese New Year? You a Dragon? Yes, you are, I can see.'

'Does it show?' I grinned, putting my chopsticks to work on the bean curd.

'I'm a Snake. Dragons and Snakes go well together. Dragons are very lucky.'

I wasn't sure if any of those statements were connected and I grabbed my beer because I'd just discovered how hot the Ma Po was. I hoped she didn't take it as a sign of weakness.

'So was Mao Tse-tung,' I croaked.

'What?'

'A Snake. So was Greta Garbo.'

Even I wasn't quite sure what that proved.

'So, you having a party?'

'A friend is,' I said quickly before she could con an invite. 'He's a Dragon too, so he wants to celebrate. With fireworks.'

'You could try the supermarket,' she said.

'I don't think Sainsbury's sell them,' I snapped, thinking she was winding me up.

'*Chinese* supermarket,' she said slowly, as if long words were something you had to use sparingly to Dragons. 'Mr Chung's on Gerrard Street. He sells everything.'

She was not wrong there.

On the pavement at the front of Mr Chung's there were barrows of fresh fruit and vegetables, but of the sort you wouldn't find on your average television soap opera set down the rub-a-dub, cor blimey East End. In fact even your highly paid organic food buyer from Sainsbury's would have been hard pushed to name everything on display there. Some of the vegetables wouldn't have looked out of place in the Ann Summers sex shop round the corner. Some of them looked like reject designs from the set dressers of *Star Trek*. Some were probably hallucinogenic if cooked the wrong way. At least one was illegal in tablet form.

Inside, the shelves groaned with cans and bottles containing everything from mango purée to squids in their ink, plum wine to Tiger beer, sacks of countless types of rice, dried noodles, dried mushrooms, chillies in bottles, as paste, as powders and probably (somewhere) as a suppository. Cold cabinets bulged with guava juice, passion fruit ice cream, spring rolls and smaller oyster rolls. Other shelves held dry goods ranging from teapots with matching cups, intricate jade 'pillows', incense sticks and rice wine flasks to frying pans and woks. There were also racks of silk shirts and trousers and, in a glass case near the counter, fireworks – indoor ones for use on a plate or a saucer and boxes of Black Cat brand 'for outdoors only'.

A middle-aged, balding Chinese wearing half-rim glasses was sitting on a bar stool by the cash register, reading a Chinese newspaper.

'Excuse me, I'm looking for fireworks.'

He looked over his glasses at me as if I'd just asked to buy a mating pair of gremlins.

'We got what you see,' he said, waving his paper at the display case.

'I was looking for some Chinese fireworks, rockets and crackers. It's for the New Year.'

The authentic Chinese rocket – and the Chinese military were using rocket-launchers while the Anglo-Saxons were sharpening sticks – is built for speed and sound, not rainbow-colours display with the crowds going 'Oooh' and 'Aaah'. They go up screaming and then stop, scaring the hell out of you, and even the little ones get to impressive heights.

'The home-made ones,' I added when he didn't react.

'Who told you to ask here?'

I could understand his suspicion. There were probably a dozen illicit firework factories within a hundred yards this time of year and it was only a matter of time before some interfering busybody started asking questions such as where did they get the gunpowder? But I couldn't see a downside to an honest answer.

'Ming's restaurant, across the road.'

'That's OK then. I've got some out back.'

He locked the cash register with an electronic key on the end of a chain attached to his belt and disappeared into the back of the shop. Apart from locking the till, I was quite flattered that he trusted me alone in his empty shop.

Once he had moved I could see a small wooden-framed abacus on the shelf behind and I thought good for him, who needs microprocessors? Then I noticed the bell jar next to the abacus. At first I thought it was empty except for some short dark strands of, say, vanilla pods or cinnamon bark on the bottom but then the strands started moving and I realised that I was eye-balling a spider. This wasn't a house spider or one of the minuscule 'money' spiders which are supposed to bring you good luck. This was a substantial beast, gently bouncing on eight very hairy legs and no doubt eyeballing me with however many eyes a spider has.

Mr Chung, if that was his name, reappeared with a bundle of five small rockets no more than ten inches long including the stick, held together with a rubber band. There were no markings on the yellow rocket tubes of any sort. No 'Best before' date, no maker's mark, no safety instructions.

'Those are they,' I said. 'Just the job. How many can you let me have?'

'How many do you want?'

I hadn't a clue, but Ross wouldn't want me to be a cheapskate.

'Ten packs?'

He shrugged and went out back again. I looked at the spider. The spider ignored me.

Ten packs didn't look like a lot of fireworks and I said so.

'How about crackers?'

'Oh yes, must have some of them.'

'What about bigger rockets? Bit expensive.'

That sounded good.

'Money's no object,' I said rashly. 'What do they do?'

'They're bigger,' he said flatly.

'Fine, then, let's have some of them.'

He left me again and I decided I was bored with looking at the spider, so I turned to scan the other shelves behind the counter. I spotted two more smaller jars with spiders in and one with what, though I couldn't be sure, looked like a scorpion and then, on the floor, a small glass tank with a plastic lid which contained a lime green snake about eighteen inches long.

No wonder Mr Chung didn't worry about leaving the store unattended, his pets were more effective than Dobermen and he didn't have to house train them.

He staggered back under the weight of a deep cardboard box which had once contained melons from Spain. The 'bigger' rockets were a foot long with a three-foot stick, fat and coloured red. For danger, presumably. The crackers were long strings of continuous brown paper firecrackers, concertinaed together in five-foot long strips with blue waxed fuses and red ribbon tapes to tie them to roof awnings. There was enough ordnance in the box to start a small war and I realised that the 'No Smoking' sign stuck to the cash register had nothing to do with food hygiene.

'All this lot, £200.'

I wasn't sure whether I was supposed to haggle or not, but it wasn't going to be my money at the end of the day.

'Fair enough,' I said, pulling out my wallet. 'Do you take plastic?'

'You got debit card?'

'Yes,' I said reluctantly.

'Then you buy something else and I'll give you cashback.'

The cunning old sod. That way he avoided registering any sale at all.

'I could do with some fruit,' I said, thinking I ought to take Lin something more than a potted plant from a garage, 'but only if I can get a receipt.'

'OK.' He held out his hand.

'Can you wrap the box up with something?'

I didn't fancy walking through Soho looking like the poor man's Guy Fawkes, not whilst the pubs were open. But good old Mr Chung produced a black plastic rubbish bin liner and began to slide the box in while I wandered out to the fruit and veg display at the front of the shop and started to fill two large brown paper bags with fruit.

I chose a pineapple on the basis that everybody likes pineapple, some lychees, a mango, some passion fruit and a durian, which is ugly and smells of open drains in a hot climate but makes unbelievably delicious ice cream. I know that if I'd gone to a big store they would have done it all up in a presentation basket, but then I'd probably have been given something boring like apples and grapes. Even in brown paper bags, it was the thought that counted.

Mr Chung had my fireworks packaged and tied with string and he added £7.50 to my debit card slip for 'fruit' underneath the £200 'cashback'. He made me initial the £200 box and sign the slip, and then presented me with a handwritten receipt in Chinese, which could have said anything. He even shook my hand and wished me a Happy New Year.

I pointed to the spider in the jar on the shelf behind him and said:

191

'You really do sell everything, don't you?'

Mr Chung took it as a compliment.

'Oh yes. Spiders and snakes very popular. Scorpions, not such a good line. Sell them for pets. Very popular, very profitable. Get them free.'

'You do?'

'Oh yes, they come in from overseas with the fruit.'

The fruit I'd just been hand-picking out front.

'Are they poisonous?'

'Oh yes. Mostly.'

I staggered back to the car-park with my shopping and locked the box of fireworks in Armstrong's boot, then set off again into Soho clutching my two bags of fruit, but only after I'd shaken the bags carefully to make sure I didn't have any stowaways.

Instead of heading back to Gerrard Street to look for Lin's flat, I opted to stroll up Dean Street to look in on Last Ditch Productions Inc. There was a time when such a journey could have taken me up to two days unless I avoided the temptations of the French House (still known by a few diehards as 'Gaston's'), the Groucho Club, where I was not a member, Gerry's Club, where I was, the Nellie Dean, which used to be a film cameramen's pub, and the Toucan, otherwise known as the Irish Club off Soho Square. I seem to remember there being some half decent restaurants down there as well, though its main claim to fame of an evening these days was for the passing craze of bicycle rickshaws, whose unfit drivers tried to sting tourists for ten quid a head for a hundred-yard ride.

However, I was on my best behaviour, carrying fruit on a mission of mercy, and in any case, it wasn't three o'clock so Gerry's wouldn't be open yet. I felt quite good about it all and I would feel even better once I screwed £207.50 out of Alix Tse and her petty cash box.

Last Ditch had their offices in a mews which had been modernised as a small pedestrian throughway to the parallel Wardour Street. I remembered it when it was just a series of open doorways with staircases leading up three flights to rented rooms. The door frames would be peppered with small holes which were not woodworm but where thousands of postcards had been drawing-pinned over the years telling customers which girls were in residence on which floor.

It had all changed. The mews had its own glass-fronted tapas bar and the new office suites were glass and steel with combination locks and double-entry doors like they have in banks. There were flower baskets hanging from the lamp posts and litter bins sponsored by multinational corporations, but there were still a few signs of the old Soho. The empty cans of Special Brew and the broken bottles of Thunderbird in the gutters, for instance.

Last Ditch had a brass plaque and an electronic keypad with an intercom button. I pressed it and a distorted voice said: 'Yes?'

Through the armoured glass door I could see another glass door and a motorised CCTV camera hanging from the ceiling.

'My name is Angel, here to see Alix Tse.'

'You have an appointment?' said the disembodied voice.

The camera moved silently up and down, getting me in full frontal clutching two brown paper bags of exotic, and hopefully spider-free, fruit.

'Not exactly. I work for her out at Pinewood.'

'Sorry, she's not here. Would you like to make an appointment?'

'No, never mind.'

I realised my mistake: I'd been honest. I should have pretended to be from fruit.com making a delivery.

It was no big deal. After all, Brettler had told me Alix would be out at the studio after lunch so she was probably there by now. So I was quite prepared to bite the bullet and go and see the dreaded Lin in her sickbed. Maybe she had something infectious so I would have to push all my exotic fruits through her letter box.

I was still standing outside Last Ditch, on the pavement, mulling this over, when I thought they'd had a change of heart. There was a loud metallic click as the inner door snapped open and then an echoing click as the outer door unlocked. But it wasn't to let me in, it was to let somebody out.

It was the tall, good-looking Chinese bloke who had been with Alix and who had given Marcus and me the killer look when we were going into Ross's trailer to get his luggage.

He didn't seem too keen to see me then and he hadn't changed his mind.

I was about to say something and I was quite happy to make

it something polite and even throw in a smile, but I never got a chance. He came through both doors and out on to the pavement and would have walked right over me if I hadn't taken a step backwards to get out of his way. It wasn't that I was frightened of him, it was just that I had fruit to think about.

By the time I had realised he was threatening me, he was ten yards away, crossing Dean Street towards Soho Square. Had it been a threat, or just downright rude? No, he had done it deliberately, though I couldn't think for the life of me what I'd ever done to him. I hadn't even been introduced to him, which is when I normally get up people's noses.

I pressed the intercom button.

'Yes?'

'Can you tell me who that was who just left?'

'I'm sorry, but we cannot give out personnel details. If you wish to see someone, please make an appointment.'

'How about nine thirty tomorrow?'

'No, sorry.'

'How about February the 12th?' I said at random.

'That's a Saturday, I'm afraid, and the office is closed,' said the voice.

'March the 8th?' I tried, a complete shot in the dark.

'That could be possible. Nine thirty?'

'Great, look forward to it.'

'What name shall I say?'

'Spielberg. Steven Spielberg.'

I cut down through Wardour Street and across Shaftesbury Avenue again to get back into Chinatown and started looking for Lin's flat.

The flat's entrance was at the west end of Gerrard Street, just a big brown door between a newsagent's shop and a restaurant with a series of bell-push buttons and another intercom. Against the bottom button, which I guessed meant the top-floor flat, was written the name Ooi-Tan. There couldn't be any other Ooi-Tans in this part of Chinatown, could there? Knowing my luck, hundreds.

But it was the right place, just the wrong voice on the intercom. Or at least the wrong sex, which said:

'Who is it?'

It had never occurred to me that Lin might have a husband/live-in lover/father/uncle/whatever. The little I knew of her was of an independent, single-minded career woman dedicated to looking after Ross. Why shouldn't she have a family outside the film studio?

'I've come from Pinewood Studios to see Lin,' I said into the intercom grille. 'See how she is.'

'Lin can't see anybody. She's not well. She will phone in tomorrow.'

I thought the voice had an American twang but it's always difficult to tell through those crappy voice boxes.

'Ross Pirie sent me.'

There was silence. Obviously the one time in living memory when using Ross's name didn't open a door as effectively as saying 'Open sesame'.

'Ross is very worried about Lin. It's not like her to be ill.'

'She is ill!' the voice shouted. 'She wants to be left alone!'

There was a click as something switched off and then more silence.

I had never faced so many locked doors in Soho before in my life, or at least not before dark.

I stepped back from the door and looked up and down the street trying to work out the geography of the place and whether there was a back door or a fire escape or something. If there was, it was round the back out of sight.

Then I thought: what the hell was I doing?

If I had found a back door or a window open or a lock I could pick, then what? Risk a breaking-and-entering charge just to deliver some fruit? The hell with that. I was here on a mission of mercy, charity, goodwill.

I rang the bell again.

Big mistake.

'How many fingers can you see?' said a voice.

'Nine,' I said, batting the hand away from my face. 'What's that smell?'

There was something soft under my right hip, something hard under my head. The soft thing was one of the bags of fruit, the

195

hard thing was Gerrard Street. The smell was crushed durian fruit.

Two men wearing suits and dark blue raincoats were leaning over me, one of them waving three fingers across my eyeline, the other wrinkling his nose at the stench.

'Christ, he's ripe,' I heard him say.

'It's not me, it's my fruit,' I said, which made perfect sense to me.

I sat up and gingerly felt the back of my head. There was a bump the size of a seagull's egg but no blood in my hair. My shoulder hurt and so did my chest, right on the breast bone, and I couldn't work out why.

'Can you remember what happened?' the guy with the fingers asked.

'I must have slipped,' I said.

I was about eight feet away from the door to Lin's apartment block and I had no problem remembering how I had got from there to flat on my back on the pavement.

When I had pressed the bell the second time, the door had opened immediately, almost as if he had been waiting for me. I should have been expecting it as the same thing had happened not fifteen minutes earlier at the offices of Last Ditch, and with the same bloke! Only trouble was this time I didn't get out of the way and he steamrollered right over me. Or at least, that was what it felt like from down here on the pavement.

'Did you bollocks slip,' said the second Good Samaritan, 'that Chinese bloke belted you. I saw it.'

'I didn't,' I said, and I meant it. I could guess that my moody Chinese nemesis had thumped me in the chest, but I hadn't seen it coming.

Fingers offered to help me to my feet by hauling at my arms.

'He was bloody fast,' he said. 'He used that kung fu shit, you know, martial arts. He only hit you the once.'

'That's usually all it takes.' I nodded my thanks gently so as not to rattle my brain any more. I looked at the scattered and crushed fruit smeared over the pavement. 'Fruit salad,' I said.

'Leave it. Let the locals clean up,' said the second guy.

I looked up and down the street. There were shoppers going by, two waiters from a nearby restaurant standing in a doorway, cars going by, light vans parked at the kerb delivering and collecting. Maybe forty or fifty people. Nobody said anything and apart from my two helpers, nobody saw a thing.

'Where is he?'

'He's long gone,' said Fingers. 'Didn't break step, just came at you and then kept going, bit like swatting a fly.'

Gee, thanks. I wondered if this guy was a professional counsellor or whether he'd won a do-it-yourself book in a raffle.

'I'm OK,' I said as I felt first one and then both my arms being held.

'You want to take it easy, you know. Your head didn't half bounce when it hit the road.'

'I'll be fine.'

We were walking down the street now, even though I didn't want to go.

'We've got a car just round the corner,' said one of them.

'You ought to sit down for a bit, or maybe we can drop you somewhere,' said the other.

'Really, I'm fine,' I insisted, though my head was throbbing like a piston and my vision was definitely blurred.

The grips on my arms tightened and I was sure that if I lifted my feet off the ground they would still propel me along. I could have been an early casualty of a late liquid lunch, but this was Soho so none of the passers-by gave us a second look.

'Do you know the guy who hit you?' asked Fingers.

'Yes . . . no . . . I don't remember.'

The curse of Frank Shoosmith was upon me. What was it he called it? Selective amnesia? Christ, if I couldn't remember what it was called, I must have it.

But then I could remember who Frank Shoosmith was and what I had been doing that day, at least up until about five minutes ago. I could remember visiting Frank at The Oaks and I could even remember, as I was leaving, a new, bright red Rover 75 pulling into the car-park.

'This is ours,' said Fingers.

There was a new, bright red Rover 75 parked illegally on double yellow lines and only a yard from the junction with Wardour Street.

'Why don't you just sit in the back for five minutes, get your breath back?'

Fingers had to release his grip on my arm in order to put a key in the Rover's lock. I leaned into him as if punch drunk, pressing him against the door so he couldn't open it.

'Who are you guys?'

'We're the guys who picked you up off the floor,' said Fingers.

I held up a finger in front of his face.

'Technically correct, but philosophically vague. Let me guess, you're insurance assessors.'

'He's rambling,' said the one on my left, 'he needs a doctor.'

'Help!' I shouted at the top of my voice and both of them shuddered with surprise. 'Help me! I'm being kidnapped by insurance assessors.'

'Just get in the back, Angel,' said Fingers, 'and stop fucking about.'

I got in. Fingers gave the keys to the second guy and told him to drive, then he walked round the Rover and got in the back next to me.

'You spotted us at The Oaks, didn't you?' he said. Then he tapped the driver on the shoulder and told him: 'Just do a circuit 'till we're done. Where's that cab of yours?'

'Just round the corner,' I said. 'Did you tail me from Slough?'

'We lost you near Fuller's Brewery down in Chiswick, but we knew you'd end up here or hereabouts.'

'Brettler,' I said and he didn't dodge it.

'Yes.'

'He didn't know when I would be going to The Oaks. I didn't know myself.'

'It was a good bet it would be sometime today and when you got there you were greeted by a very nice redhead, right?'

Siobhan with the smile. Who didn't even ask my name, because she'd been expecting me and seen me arrive in Armstrong.

'She phoned it in, eh?'

'Sent us an e-mail actually,' Fingers said modestly, 'whilst you were standing there, chatting her up. Said she quite fancied you.'

The one driving laughed at that and turned the Rover towards

Cambridge Circus. I decided it would be more dignified to ignore him than respond.

'So who the hell are you?'

'We're not insurance assessors,' said Fingers.

'I guessed that. Insurance companies don't send out claims assessors for anything less than the torching of Windsor Castle. It's all done through call centres these days and to hell with your no-claims bonus. Especially over Christmas.'

'Yeah, well.' Fingers looked a bit embarrassed. 'We're actually from the National Criminal Intelligence Service.'

'Isn't that a contradiction in terms?' I asked innocently.

'Watch it.'

The tone of his voice persuaded me to behave, for all of about five seconds until he said:

'My name's Carter and that's Inspector Regan.'

I burst out laughing even though the effort made my head throb even worse.

'I don't believe it!' I spluttered. 'Regan and Carter, the Dynamic Duo! Pride of the Met! Are they still doing reruns of *The Sweeney* on satellite?'

Actually, I knew they were and that it was a cult programme with off-duty policemen. In fact it was still, twenty-five years on, the only TV cop show regularly watched by real policemen.

'I told you this guy was a clown, guv,' said 'Regan' from the front as he indicated and turned right into Charing Cross Road.

'Come on,' I giggled, 'you're not really called Regan and Carter, are you? That would be totally bad.'

''Course we're fucking not, but it'll do for you.'

'I'd have gone for Holmes and Watson myself,' I spluttered, 'just to blend in.'

'Give him a slap and chuck him back on to the street where he belongs,' snarled Regan.

'Shut it!' I yelled, melting into the upholstery with laughter.

'That's quite enough of that,' said Carter. 'Just tell us what Frank Shoosmith told you and you can be on your merry way.'

'Why?'

'Why should you tell us? Because we can make your life even more miserable than it already is, that's why.'

'No, why do you want to know?'

'I can't tell you that.'

'But I'm supposed to co-operate with two pretend policemen just like that, am I? Without knowing what's going on?'

'That's about it. And we really are policemen.'

'Not insurance assessors at all, then?'

Carter just blanked me. Regan manoeuvred the Rover into the traffic jam leading into Trafalgar Square.

'But you've been sniffing round the wreck of Frank's car, haven't you?'

'Yes.'

'Find anything?'

'Nothing wrong with the car as far as we could see.'

'But you want to know why Frank decided to test out the air bag for no good reason.'

'Yeah, we'd like to know that.'

'So would Frank. Says he don't remember a thing.'

Carter frowned, working out whether or not it was worth him throwing some crumbs of information into the water to see if he got a bite.

'But you reckon it's not connected to what's going on with this film they're making?'

'Frank's crash? I can't see it. The geeks who are putting stuff up on the web are just geeks. The really weird ones want the film made. It's an everyday story of vampire folk, right up their street.'

'What about the trailer fire last night?'

'I dunno. Somebody left the gas on?'

'It was all electric,' said Regan. 'Haymarket, guv?'

'That'll do,' said Carter.

The traffic was solid now and we were moving in inches rather than yards.

'So you've got that down as an accident, have you?' he asked me.

'You tell me different,' I said.

'I'll give you a little scenario if you like. Sometime before Christmas you, Mr Angel, join Ross Pirie's little entourage, even go away on holiday with him. His driver ends up in hospital and look who steps into the breach. You do. Day One of filming out at Pinewood, guess who's seen sniffing around Ross's trailer?

And where exactly were you when it was torched? Guess who gets his picture in the paper moving Ross Pirie to a secret location which then appears on the Internet? And then guess who's seen having a lover's tiff with Tony Tse? See where I'm going with this?'

'Whoa, hold up there.' My brain hurt and it wasn't just down to the lump on the back of my head. 'Who's Tony Tse?'

'That very nice man who kung-fu'd you on Gerrard Street,' said Regan helpfully, tapping his fingers on the steering wheel in frustration at the traffic.

I had an unselective flashback to that brown door opening and the tall Chinese I had seen only minutes before at the door of Last Ditch, and the look of thunder in his face, and then his right hand, palm first, shooting out like a piston towards my chest.

'Actually, it was Tang Sou Dao,' said the one who called himself Carter.

'What was?'

'What he hit you with. It's a martial art, "way of the hand" or something. Tony Tse is a black belt.'

'That's a comfort. I'd hate to have been decked by a novice.'

'Humility and respect are supposed to be part of the Tang Sou Dao doctrine, but I think Tony had a sick note the week they did that bit.'

'So who the hell is he?'

'You're his sparring partner, you tell us,' said Regan, grimacing at the traffic backing up from Piccadilly Circus.

'I've only seen the bastard three times in my life. I've never spoken to him and now he's thumped me in broad daylight.'

'I would have thought that was par for the course for somebody like you,' said Carter.

'Hang on, haven't you got this wrong? Shouldn't one of you be a Good Cop?'

'Stop pissing about, Angel. You're a chancer and you think you're on the gravy train with these film people, don't you? Have you got any idea what you're into?'

I held up my hands.

'I'll 'fess up now, not a clue. Why don't you tell me what's going on so we can all get on with our lives?'

Carter pretended to think about this.

'No,' he said finally.

201

'No what?'

'No, I don't think you need to know. Just do what Brettler and the film people want you to do and stay out of our way.'

'That could be difficult if I don't know which way you're going,' I said and I thought it a perfectly reasonable thing to say.

'That's your problem, sunshine,' said Regan over his shoulder.

'Hey, look, lads, all I've been told to do is sniff around the bad vibes on the *Daybreak* production, most of which are coming from one chapter or the other of the Ross Pirie fan club. It's just like a public relations job, that's all.'

'Well you do that, then,' said Carter. He looked out of the windscreen to see where we were – coming into Regent Street.

'You're not interested in *Daybreak*, are you?'

If I was going to get something out of this meet I would have to do it quick. They were looking for somewhere to dump me.

'I'm sure the wife'll go and see it when it comes out,' said Carter, looking at the street. 'She's a big fan.'

'So it's to do with Frank Shoosmith, then?'

'Nobody likes a dangerous accident where there's no obvious reason for one,' said Carter, reaching out to tap Regan on the shoulder.

The best I could hope for was that they slowed down when they ejected me.

'Police investigate accidents, yeah, I can handle that. But that's a job for Traffic not the National Crime Squad. And certainly not pretending to be insurance assessors to get a look at the wreck.'

'We like to keep a low profile.'

'Bollocks. If you were really doing a number on Frank's Beamer, you'd have dragged it down the Transport Lab and X-rayed it. Anyway, nobody called the cops and the accident was on private property. Nobody *asked* you to check it out, so why did you?'

'We have our reasons,' said Carter, but he had hesitated and we were still moving.

'So if you didn't want to look *at* it, you wanted to look *in* it, right?'

They said nothing.

'Find anything?'

'Did you?' Carter shot back.

'Apart from a fortune cookie, not a bleeding thing, but I was –'

'A *what*?' snapped Regan, and Carter winced when he said it as if he'd suddenly given something away.

'Oh, I get it,' I said, bullshitting wildly. 'Crashed car littered with Chinese fortune cookies, let's go suspect a Chinaman. You got this Tony Tse in the frame for something?'

'Forget about Tony Tse, he's way out of your league,' Carter warned.

'League? What league? I don't even know what game we're playing!'

'Then find another game,' said Carter and this time he did tap Regan on the shoulder. 'Anywhere here'll do.'

'Come on, give me a clue,' I pleaded. 'You won't tell me anything, Frank can't remember anything and this Tony Tse character prefers to bruise his knuckles on me rather than give me the time of day. I'm running out of people to annoy. What do I have to do, go and sit by Bernie Brooks' bedside till he comes back down to planet . . .'

That got him. Carter definitely winced at that.

'It's Bernie, isn't it?' I said. 'It's not about Frank or the film or this Tony guy. It's about Bernie Brooks. I'm right, aren't I?'

The Rover pulled into the kerb.

'Get out,' said Carter.

He opened his door and climbed out on to the kerb, holding the door so I could slide across the back seat. When I was upright, he slammed the rear door and opened the front to climb in next to Regan.

'Sorry to have wasted your time, officer,' I said loudly just in case any of the passing January sales vultures were listening.

'Don't worry,' said Carter, 'you haven't wasted our time at all.'

The Rover pulled away into the traffic, leaving me to wonder what he had meant by that.

A few of my remaining brain cells must have been working, because it didn't take me too long. My two Good Samaritans hadn't been worried at all about blowing their cover when they picked me up off Gerrard Street. This Tony character, whoever he was, had no compunction about slugging people in the street and walking off like he owned the place. Therefore it was fair to assume that by now he would have been told about me being marched arm-in-arm to safety by two of the National Crime Squad's finest. They hadn't been bothered about my welfare, they had wanted to finger me as one of their own on Tony Tse's turf.

I started walking back to Armstrong, taking the long way round, down Oxford Street to Tottenham Court Road and then down Charing Cross Road, dodging into the doorways of bookshops to check the coast was clear, and avoiding Chinatown like the plague.

15

HAIR IN THE GATE

I made it back to Pinewood by the skin of my teeth. Six o'clock, on the dot, outside the Make-Up block. I was there, no one else was, although I could see Burgundy Dulude on the corner being chatted up by a guy wearing jogging gear, Nike trainers and sunglasses. He was also listening to a personal CD-player, which I didn't think would endear him to her.

There was nobody else around and it took a while for it to dawn on me that the working day was probably over. I had almost forgotten that there was a film being made around here. I hoped they'd had a better day than me. I had been grassed up by a smiling receptionist, beaten up by someone I'd never been introduced to, threatened by two pantomime cops and, I was beginning to suspect, conned by a selective amnesiac, among others. At least I'd had a good lunch and had managed to buy Ross his fireworks.

The jogger was still leaning, one hand on the wall, as if he was hanging on Burgundy's every word. He still had his stereo headphones on and I couldn't see Burgundy putting up with that sort of rudeness for very long. They'd had five minutes when I flashed Armstrong's lights at them and pulled down my window.

'Are you going to be long, Ross?' I yelled.

He made an 'aw, shucks!' movement with his arm and stamped his foot, then began to stomp over towards me. Behind him, Burgundy put her hand to her mouth then put her head down so that her hair tumbled forward and hid her face.

'When did you spot it was me?' he asked, pulling off the sunglasses.

He was in full make-up now that I could see him up close, and Marcus had done his hair up and swept back and there was a half-inch streak of white going back from above his right eye.

'Straight away,' I said.

205

He went into hangdog mode, or more accurately, pathetic puppy. I hadn't given the right answer, but then again I hadn't told him that nobody wears sunglasses in England in January without a labrador walking with them.

'Not even a Marcus Moore make-over can hide such a famous profile,' I said diplomatically and he cheered up instantly. 'Good day at the office?'

'Yes, I think so. Julius seemed pleased. We wrapped the exterior scenes with Bo Jay first time.'

'That would be where you, as Jason, go jogging with Howard whilst you're hunting the rogue vampire down near the Brooklyn Bridge,' I said confidently.

'That's right. We put the Brooklyn Bridge in later.' He reached for the door handle. 'I'm really impressed. You know the script as well as I do.'

Behind him, Burgundy stuck her tongue out at me for being a nerd.

'That reminds me,' I said, because it did, 'the scriptwriter, Walter Wilkes –'

'Where?'

Ross spun round in a panic, eyes rolling like he was checking the rooftops for snipers.

'Relax, he's not here, it's just I saw him this morning. He was trying to get some rewrites to you last night.'

'There are always rewrites on a picture,' said Burgundy.

'I guessed that. Walter said he gave them to Lin in your trailer last night.'

'He may well have, Roy, but Lin's not been in today and my trailer is a pile of ash,' Ross said in a sing-song voice. 'Actually, Gloria tells me I'll have a new trailer tomorrow, so life is looking sweet.'

I realised what it was. Ross had turned in a good performance today, which had got his adrenalin flowing and there's nothing worse than a hyped actor who knows he's good and has finished for the day. He needed something to distract him, something to worry about. I was pretty sure I could think of something.

'I think Roy is trying to tell you something, Ross,' said Burgundy.

'He is?' Ross was turning his head to look at her then back to me and shuffling his feet. From a distance, with those clothes, he must have looked like a junkie going for a score.

'Take him home, Angel, let him work it out of his system,' said Burgundy, who was on the same wavelength I was.

'You ready to roll?' I asked him.

'Sure. Kurt's got himself a hire car so he and Marcus have gone on ahead.' He paused as if he was remembering his lines. 'Marcus is cooking lamb and Kurt has got some judo mats so he wants to fight me before dinner.'

'Excuse me?'

'Training. It's in my fitness programme. He's a judo black belt.'

'Of course. It's not Tang Sou Dao, is it?'

'No, it's a Japanese style called Aikijitsu. It develops long, lean muscles. Do you know martial arts?'

Intimately, I thought, as of today.

'Go, get out of here,' said Burgundy, shoo-ing him into the back of Armstrong.

'Are you moving out to the house with us?' I asked her.

'Tomorrow, maybe,' she said.

Ross jerked a thumb at her.

'She's got a date with Bo Jay Roberts.'

'I'm having some dinner with him, that's all,' she said, spots of colour flashing in her cheeks. 'And we're meeting up with Gloria-Maria and Zina later.'

'Zina Ray?' I said, discovering that my voice seemed to have gone up an octave.

'Gloria's meeting her at the airport,' said Ross.

'How come she gets all the good jobs?'

'Because she's an associate producer and you're a driver,' said Burgundy.

Accurate; but cruel, I felt.

On the journey down the M40 I tried to give Ross edited highlights of my day and he listened in silence, or so I thought. Foolishly, I mistook silence for attention. It wasn't until around Junction 5 that I caught a glimpse of him in the mirror by the light of following headlamps. He was sitting back in the seat, turning his head, his mouth moving but no sound coming out.

He was either rehearsing tomorrow's lines or reliving the good ones he'd delivered today. Whichever it was, his attention span was working on credit.

After I had given up and gone quiet for a few minutes, Ross stirred himself to say:

'Oh, by the way, Paul Brettler was trying to find you this afternoon. Something about a website.'

'I'll catch up with him,' I said, trying to keep the edge out of my voice as I realised he hadn't taken in a word I had said.

'So how was Lin?'

I felt like bashing my forehead on the steering wheel but that would just make my head hurt in two places.

'I didn't get to see her, but I left her some fruit.'

'That's nice. Fruit's good when you're ill.'

There was no getting through to him, so I gave up.

'I hear Zina Ray is really looking forward to working with you,' I said. 'What's it like working with an actress who really fancies you?'

And from there until we turned into the (Goth-free) driveway of Eight Ash House, he talked about his favourite subject. Himself.

At the house, I showed Ross the box of rockets and Chinese crackers in the boot and for a minute or two he was like a kid on Christmas morning, enthusing about how he would have them strung from the stables and on poles around the lake. And did I know where I could lay my hands on a couple of hundred paper boats and candles to decorate the lake?

I mentioned that I had spent two hundred quid on them.

He didn't bat a heavily made-up eyelash, just said that was fine, get the cash from Alix out of the public relations budget, and when I'd finished securing the fireworks in one of the outbuildings, I should come and watch him training.

I knew my place: driving and heavy lifting.

Ross jogged into the house while I drove Armstrong round the side of the house towards the stable block beyond the edge of the lake. Security lights came on as I approached the double swing doors which had been installed to turn the old stables into garages. One was occupied by a new BMW Z3 sports car, which I presumed was Kurt's hire car of choice and gave me a new perspective on what a personal trainer could earn. The other garage was empty and I parked Armstrong inside.

I opened the one remaining original stable door and flicked a light switch to find enough space to park Armstrong again without disturbing the ride-on lawn mower, the workbench and the rows of pristine gardening tools neatly stacked on racks nailed to the walls. The place was dry, dust-free and came furnished if you counted the stacks of tubular-steel framed plastic chairs in two piles as high as the roof. I presumed they were for laying out on the brick patio during the summer and there were enough to accommodate an entire orchestra should one be passing by and feeling the need to perform a lakeside concert.

I stashed the fireworks on the workbench, turned off the light and closed all the doors behind me. There didn't seem to be any locks on the stable or the garages, one of the advantages of living out in the country.

Another advantage is that you can put half a dozen judo mats out on your patio on a chilly January evening and then have one of your employees knock seven bells out of you, without anyone calling the cops.

Ross and Kurt had changed into judo pyjama outfits and were stretching and running on the spot to warm up. Marcus was standing in one of the sets of french windows, wearing a leather jacket zipped to the throat, and holding two huge glasses of red wine.

'A drink before dinner?' He offered me a glass.

'Before, during and after. Thanks.'

'Bad day?'

'I've had better.'

Ross and Kurt started to make guttural noises and circle each other on the mats, bobbing from foot to foot. When they went at it, it was more sound than fury as the kicks and the punches snapped out but stopped inches short of their targets. It was still enough to make me wince.

'Is there anything on television?' I asked Marcus, moving inside, leaving the karate kids to it.

'Your call,' he said. 'The only shows I recognise I saw last year back home. Put some music on if you want – some of mine, not the crap Ross likes. Or you can open some more wine while I get dinner.'

'That sounds like a plan.'

In the kitchen Marcus busied himself steaming couscous and spiced vegetables and carving a large leg of lamb spiked with rosemary and oregano, which, like most Americans, he mispronounced. Then he squeezed harissa sauce out of a tube into a small dish and made me promise to say it was home-made. I got busy with a corkscrew. Apart from the Ninja warriors out on the patio, it was a scene of perfect domestic bliss.

'Who's Tony Tse, Marcus?'

'I don't talk business when I'm cooking or eating,' he said, 'just like Nero Wolfe. But I'll tell you something for free: he is the most bad-tempered, evil-minded, mean son-of-a-bitch I've ever met and in this business you get up close to the cream of that particular crop. Trust me.'

'But what does he do? What's his relation to Alix?'

'He's a money man and he's her cousin twice removed or something. He's also got some sort of dominance thing going with Lin as well.'

'Dominance? As in sexual?'

'As in pulling the wings off flies. Keep out of his way, Angel, he's rich and he's mean and he's more or less untouchable round these parts.'

'How come?'

'Because he's a money man, like I said. He put money into *Side Edge* – a lot of money according to the scuttlebutt – and *White Cut* before that. He's also got a stake in *Daybreak*. You think movie stars get away with murder? It's nothing to what the money men get away with. And he's Chinese. That helps.'

'Helps how?'

'China only allows in thirty foreign films a year for distribution in potentially the biggest market in the world. Anybody who can help get you that Jade Oscar, you need on board.'

'He's into martial arts as well, isn't he?'

'Oh yes,' said Marcus. 'I saw him beat up on a waiter who spilled his drink when we were shooting *Side Edge*. If Alix hadn't been there, he might have killed the kid. If the kid hadn't been Turkish, and we hadn't been making a movie, young Tony would have been in big trouble with the law. Stay clear of Tony, young Skywaker. The Force is strong in him.'

Marcus wiped his hands on a length of paper towel and set a timer shaped like a giant egg for fifteen minutes.

'Call the children in from the yard, would you, dearest?' he slipped into full high camp. 'It's getting dark and they need to shower before dinner.'

'They seem to be enjoying themselves.'

'Amateurs,' scoffed Marcus. 'I could take them both.'

'Oh yeah?'

'Could so. But don't tell 'em.'

I walked through to the french windows and yelled out:

'Hey Ross, Marcus here says he can take you! One arm tied behind his back.'

Next morning, I fell straight into my established routine. I overslept, Kurt had to threaten to throw me out of bed and I missed breakfast, although Marcus had got a selection of doughnuts from somewhere and I grabbed the one he called 'Bavarian Cream' but I called custard, and munched it as I got Armstrong ready for work.

On the way to Pinewood, Ross did his silent talking-to-himself routine, rehearsing his lines. The steely glance I got from Marcus told me not to comment on this ritual, or offer to help.

We got to the studio just after seven, the miniature streets of Pinewood busier than ever; stage hands moving scenery, props people carrying furniture of all descriptions, runners running, cameramen having a quick cigarette by the coffee urns, the whole scene like a Far Eastern street market.

Burgundy, clipboard in hand, ran up to Armstrong and ushered Ross out and into Make-Up like the Secret Service move a President around. At the door, Marcus turned and made the gesture of putting a phone to his ear, then he pointed a finger sternly in my direction. I got the message and made a mental note to turn the thing on. Sometime. Later. I had things to do, like getting some coffee inside me.

I drove to the end of the block, turned right and spotted one of the mobile tea trolleys on the next corner. Julius Cockburn's driver, Dave, was standing there, warming his hands around a steaming cup.

'How's it going then?' he greeted me.

'Hectic. It's nearly as bad as working for a living,' I said, helping myself to a black coffee and four sugars.

'Not as glamorous as it's cracked up to be, is it?'

'Tell me about it. Up before dawn, bed before ten, no wild orgies and not a sniff of a drug anywhere. I reckon I've got a case under the Trades Descriptions Act.'

'It isn't what it used to be, but it will just have to do.'

I almost said: Edmund O'Brien at the end of *The Wild Bunch*; but it wasn't close enough and, anyway, Dave the Driver wasn't in on the game.

'Did you get out to see Spiderman?' he asked between slurps from his plastic cup.

'Who?'

'Frank Shoosmith, your predecessor.'

'Oh, yeah, sends his regards,' I lied. 'Going to pop in on him again, actually. Might do that this morning.'

Before the silky smiling Siobhan came on duty, I thought to myself.

'Why do you call him Spiderman?' I asked, realising that I was probably going to regret it.

Dave chuckled as if it was the richest thing in the world.

''Cos he's totally shit-scared of spiders, that's why. Totally screaming paranoid about them. Supposed to have a little mesh grille over the plughole in his bath, stop them climbing up. A real big girl's blouse when it comes to spiders is Frank.'

In fact I was half tempted to nip into Soho and ask Mr Chung to sell me one of his stowaways so I could dangle it in front of Frank until his memory came back or he decided to tell me what was going on; whichever came first.

I had either guessed right, or was just lucky. Siobhan wasn't at her desk in the foyer of The Oaks, nobody was. But there was a steaming cup of tea on a bone china saucer next to the telephone which meant that whoever was on duty wasn't far away.

On the way there I had stopped at a 7–11 and bought a box of Belgian chocolates as a bit of a cover story. International movie star sends round chocolates by taxi to faithful retainer – happens all the time. As it turned out I didn't need them to help blag my way in. I just strode across the foyer and into the lift and I was outside Room 106 within twenty seconds of entering the building.

Frank was sitting up in bed, glasses on the end of his nose, reading the *Daily Mail* racing section. He'd had his breakfast in bed on one of those trays on wheels which go over the bed and had pushed it towards his feet. From the debris on the tray, he had enjoyed grapefruit, scrambled eggs, bacon and grilled kidneys, toast and honey and a pot of coffee. Any sympathy I had ever had for him went out of the window.

'What the . . .?' he said as he saw me, his face remembering me.

''Morning, Frank,' I said, closing the door behind me. 'Brought you a present.'

I dropped the box of chocolates, a deep, gold-coloured box done up with a red ribbon, on to his breakfast tray. I hadn't expected thanks or dying devotion and I certainly hadn't anticipated that he would start howling like a banshee.

'Shit! Shit! Fucking shiiiiiit!'

He screamed it, threw away his paper and started to lever himself out of the top end of the bed, grabbing the tubular metal of the bed head for purchase. He was half in, half out of the bed, his legs tangled in the sheets, kicking and shouting, trying to get away from something. He shook his head violently and his glasses flew off, clattering to the floor. He would have climbed the wall if he could have found a way of doing it without taking his eyes off the gold box which seemed to hypnotise him.

I had given women boxes of chocolates before now and never got this good a reaction.

'What's the matter with you, Frank? Calm down, for God's sake. They're only chocolates.'

He looked at me with wild eyes, then he looked at where he was, virtually standing on his pillow, and he began to take deep breaths.

'Jesus, but you startled me. You shouldn't do that. I just can't take it.'

He began to relax, let his head fall back against the wall and he almost slid down it back into the bed, his eyes closed.

'You know, don't you?' he said with his eyes still closed.

'Tell me about it, Frank,' I said gently.

I had no idea what was going on, but I slid the box of

chocolates off the tray and out of his sight. If he told me a load of old cods, I'd show it to him again.

'There was a box like that in my car, Christmas Eve,' he said quietly. 'Waiting for me on the seat. A Christmas present, from Lin, I thought.'

'Fortune cookies,' I said confidently.

He nodded, prepared to give it up now.

'Bernie picked it up as we set off, asked if he could have one – see if it would tell him what he was going to get for Christmas, some such bollocks. So he opened the box and he said "They're moving" and, 'course, I looked over and there's this fucking tarantula, big as a plate, climbing out on to his hand.'

Frank opened his eyes again. They were moist with tears.

'Next thing I know, I'm eating air bag and then I pass out and then I wake up here with the wife at the bedside moaning 'cos I missed Christmas dinner.'

There was a sharp knock and the door behind me clicked open. Frank and I looked at each other and then, sheepishly, he brought his left hand out from under the covers. He held a panic button which he let slip so that it dangled down the side of the bed.

'Are you quite comfortable, Mr Shoosmith?' a female voice said. Then: 'Oh, it's you.'

'Good morning, Siobhan,' I said without turning round. 'Early morning call to bring Frank a present.'

I held up the chocolates to show her. In the bed, Frank winced.

'I'm fine,' he told her.

'Very well. Don't forget that your consultant's coming at nine.'

I turned my head to smile at her and sneak a look at her legs for the first time.

'I'll be out of his hair long before then,' I said graciously.

She glared at me.

'Chocolate?' I offered.

She closed the door behind her. I didn't know how long I had, but the clock was ticking.

'I heard about the Spiderman name,' I said gently, sitting on the end of his bed as part of my caring, sharing bedside manner.

'It's a phobia,' said Frank. 'Had it since I was a kid. I can't help it. I see one, I freak out if I'm in a confined space. I suppose that's what I did when Bernie opened the box and that thing crawled out.'

He shuddered and wrapped his pyjama sleeves across his chest to hug himself.

'You haven't just remembered this, like just now, have you?'

If he had, I was going to apply for a job as a consultant here. A couple of miracle cures before lunch then out on the golf course; that was the life.

'No, I never lost my memory, I just said I had. How could I own up to something as daft as that? Not with Bernie lying next door in a coma. How do you think I felt? I'd have been a laughing stock. If Bernie comes round, I'll have to deal with it, but if he does make it I won't feel so bad anyway. That make sense?'

'Some of it. What were you and Bernie up to anyway? There was nothing happening at Pinewood on Christmas Eve.'

'That's why we were there, we thought we would have had the place to ourselves.' His eyes flickered up to mine. 'Bernie told me he was an undercover policeman. I suppose you're going to tell me I was being a right prat on that as well.'

'I think that's solid, Frank. What was his interest in *Daybreak*?'

'Nothing at all. He was interested in *Side Edge*, the film they just finished in Europe. And the one they did before that, *White Cut* or something. The ones they did in Europe.'

'He was?' I tried to conceal my surprise. 'What was his angle?'

'The money, of course,' he said sulkily.

'It's always money, isn't it,' I said sympathetically. 'Was it a profits scam? The film costs $10 million to make, takes $30 million at the box office but still ends up making a $5 million loss. That sort of thing?'

If I'd been in a glider I couldn't have gone further over his head, but he looked at me like I was the idiot in the room.

'No, *the money*. Euro notes, banknotes, currency. They've got suitcases of the stuff – 500-euro notes in the props department. They used them for the films.'

'Frank, they're props. They blow them up in the final scene.'

'They can afford to, they're fucking printing them.'

'What?'

'They're not just props, they're *counterfeit*. Bernie Brooks told me they'd been doing 200-euro notes for over a year and now they're going into the 500-euro note. They've used them to open bank accounts and launder money and set up the finances for the films with them. The ones in the suitcases are, like, a first run of the bigger denomination.'

'Bernie Brooks told you all this?'

'Yes, he did. I caught him snooping around the lot one evening, checking out stuff that had come back from the *Side Edge* shoot.'

'And he took you into his confidence, did he? Just like that?'

'When I told him about the paper, yes he did.'

I gritted my teeth.

'Frank, you've had two weeks' bed rest to get your story straight. I've got maybe two minutes to hear it, so cut to the chase, will you?'

'Like I said, I caught Bernie snooping around the props boxes which had all come back in the same shipment as the technical gear and Ross's trailer.'

'Ross's trailer? He has his trailer on location?'

'Well, he did on this one, it was built into his contract. Easy enough through the Channel Tunnel, with most of the locations on the French/Swiss border. Anyway, the stuff started arriving back at Pinewood a few days before Christmas. There was nothing much going on there, but Ross asked me to have a look and make sure nothing got lost or nicked. There's a lot of souvenir hunters out there. That's why Ross always has Marcus cut his hair 'cos he can trust Marcus not to sell it off.

'So I go to put an eye over things and there's Bernie ferreting around already, says he's looking for anything out of the ordinary it being part of his job at Pinewood Security. I go and open my big mouth by telling him that I've already seen something a bit iffy in one of the containers which is supposed to have filter screens – you know, for the lights – but in fact there's packs of paper in there that wouldn't filter sewage let alone daylight.

216

Polymer paper too, the stuff they print banknotes on. Reams of it.'

'How did you know that?'

'That's exactly what Bernie asked me and I told him. I did twenty years as a printer before I got made redundant. When it comes to paper, I know what I'm talking about. So then Bernie says take a look at these and he shows me a couple of 500-euro notes he's taken from the props box and asks me if they're real or not and I say how would I know? I've no idea what a 500-euro note's *supposed* to look like – who does? But it's a damn good print job, I tell him.

'So then he fills me in. He reckons there's a well-organised counterfeiting ring using the production company to shift dodgy money into Europe, especially the countries where they're using the euro already and those that don't care where money comes from. All the paper I found, that's coming into this country for printing. It was top whack quality polymer-based stuff that, like the Australians use. State-of-the-art, somebody must know what they're doing.'

'There's an empty container in the props area,' I said, 'but the money in the suitcase is still there.'

'Best place to hide it, Bernie said. You know there's nearly a million dollars in one of those cases? A 500-euro note is worth about three hundred quid.'

'Except you can't spend them in this country.'

'Exactly. Bloody worthless over here, so leave 'em in plain sight. Everybody thinks it's Mickey Mouse money only good for special effects.'

If I'd had a hat I would have taken it off. It was a wonderful bluff. If anyone had questioned all that cash being dud money, well it was supposed to be. It was only a prop after all.

'So on Christmas Eve, you were out at Pinewood with Bernie – doing what?'

I looked at my watch, trying to guess how much time I had left.

'Just a final check. The paper was still there and the place was closing up for Christmas so we figured that nobody would be collecting it until after the holiday. You know what it's like when a film's on, there are people coming and going all the time. We didn't think anything would happen until the New Year.'

'Was that all you did that day?'

'Not much else to do, nothing happening out there.'

Except somebody watching the watchers armed with a box of fortune cookies containing a surprise free gift. Somebody who knew about Frank's 'Spiderman' nickname.

'Did you do anything? See anyone?'

'No. There wasn't many people about. I did a few chores in the trailer, 'cos that had just come up from Dover that morning, then we decided to call it a day and I offered Bernie a lift into town.'

'What sort of chores?'

'The usual. Whenever it's moved something gets broken – a bottle of booze, cups, that sort of thing. I also do a sweep for Ross's personal stuff – books, scripts, CDs, underwear – put it somewhere safe. You'd be amazed what the fans will nick for souvenirs.'

'Yeah, you said, like his hair. Did you find anything?'

Frank shook his head.

'No, but I wasn't looking for anything special. Certainly wasn't looking to have a fucking great spider planted in the car.'

'It never occurred to you to let on about this?'

He started to blush.

'How could I? Grown man frightened of bloody spiders, crashes fifty grand's worth of car and puts a decent bloke in hospital? I didn't want to have to 'fess up to that. Anyway, nobody asked except you.'

He was wrong there. Nobody had asked the right questions except me, and that by a combination of a basic distrust of human beings and sheer dumb luck.

'What about Lin? You said she came to visit.'

'She asked what had happened, sure. I just said I must have lost control of the car and I didn't remember anything. She didn't push it. Nice of her to come really.'

'And what about your other visitors?'

He had to think about that.

'What others? The wife? I didn't tell her anything. I'd never have heard the last of it if –'

'No, the insurance assessors.'

'Oh, them. They sniffed around, didn't seem to know what

they wanted. Asked if anybody else was involved in the accident, when did I last service the car, that sort of thing. They did ask what Bernie was doing in there with me but I just said I must have been giving him a lift. I pleaded amnesia and they left it at that.'

They would. Carter and Regan playing their cards so close to their chest they could get nipple rash.

'Those two will be back, Frank, probably in the next few minutes. They're not from the insurance company, they're police and so was – is – Bernie. I suggest you tell them everything you've told me and anything you haven't.'

I stood up and picked up the chocolates. Frank wouldn't ever pluck up the courage to open them anyway.

'What's your interest in all this, anyway?' he asked me.

'None at all now,' I said. 'I'm not into counterfeiting, conspiracies or sending people spiders. Let the professionals deal with that. I'm in public relations.'

16

BEST BOY

I made it out of The Oaks without running into the Dynamic Duo, though I was sure it was only a matter of time before they were kicking down the hospital door to find out what Frank had been telling me. I was relying on Siobhan to e-mail them and I'd left her the Belgian chocolates on her desk as a reminder. I hadn't had time to find a spider.

I had meant what I said to Frank. There was nothing I could do about money-laundering scams, that was out of my league. All Don Sager had asked me to do was look into what was going on with the Goths and the suspiciously well-informed *Pirie's Pets* website. I had warned Chrissie Schwartz that her private life-style was her business as long as she kept it away from the set, the alternative being unemployment. She'd seen it my way. And there was something I could do about the website. Or rather, I couldn't, but I knew a man who could.

His real name was James but everybody called him J. and knew him as the Junkyard Geek. He got the name, and a regular income, by trawling refuse dumps and recycling centres rescuing old computers, particularly ones dumped by offices or the Civil Service when they upgraded. He would rescue information from the hard drives of machines long thought wiped clean by the former owners. But that was the beauty of modern technology: nothing actually ever went away.

Once the Junkyard Geek had identified the company, he would e-mail their IT manager and suggest that, for a small fee, he would make sure that last year's pay rises were properly wiped clean and not e-mailed to all the company's staff or, say, next year's profits forecast be not e-mailed to a City stockbroker or two. His best ever had been 'resurrecting' the patient records of a very well-known private clinic in Harley Street, which had some even better-known patients consulting on very high profile diseases. His offer to help them make sure the records didn't fall into the wrong hands set him up with enough new hardware to ensure he didn't have to leave his house ever again.

But of course he did, if only to go fishing through another junkyard or an unguarded dumpster, though that was usually in the evenings. It had taken me over an hour and a half to get across to Highbury and Islington, which made it just short of ten thirty. That was good. The Junkyard Geek would still be in his pit after a hard night's surfing the Net, downloading gay porn from an anonymous server in Roumania and charging it to a non-existent credit card account he himself had created. J. had several credit card identities, all using the initials KMM, such as Kevin Michael McGeer or Kathleen Mary Moon. It was his trademark joke as KMM stood for 'kiss my modem'. He maintained it was his way of sabotaging the capitalist exploiters on the web and he wasn't really interested in the porn at all. Yeah, right. He never did it when his mum was around, though.

I knew his phone number and that he would never answer it. He didn't do well in face time, or 'non-electronic discussion' as his last school report had said when they expelled him. So that was my plan. Park Armstrong more or less anywhere (no problem around there as the majority of real London cab drivers are Arsenal supporters) and go and beat on his front door. See if he remembered the sound of a hand knocking instead of clicking.

After the fifth knuckle riff I heard a voice from the other side of the door of the two-up, two-down terraced house.

'What do you want?'

'It's Roy Angel, J., come to get into bed for a capture on a heavy site.'

I thought he would respond to this babblespeak, which, roughly translated, meant: I want your professional advice on gathering more information on a website claiming to get many hits.

But just in case he didn't, I added:

'And I won't tell your mother about your rewritable CD collection.'

The door opened and the Geek stood there, tall, thin and wearing a Cotton Traders T-shirt. I wondered which name he'd used when he'd ordered that.

'Don't even try and talk the talk, Angel, you're useless. Everyone's moved on to Super Disks now, not CDs or Zip Disks. What do you want?'

'I want you to make me a cup of tea and find a website for me.'

'Why should I?'

'Because I saved your life once.'

'Hardly.'

'All right then, I gave you a lift at a crucial time.'

J. had been sifting through a skip parked outside a house in Camden which the yuppy owners were renovating. He had chosen to do it whilst the yuppies were having a dinner party and he'd been spotted. Quite why the yuppies were so possessive about their rubbish puzzled me, but they gave chase as J. legged it down the street with a Pentium II processor under his arm and I just happened to come round the corner in Armstrong.

I suppose it was the fact that he was wearing school uniform and was outnumbered six-to-one that made me let him climb in and drive him out of harm's way. Of course he didn't have any money on him, but he was quite open about what he was nicking the hard drives for and I was so impressed I took my 'fare' in credit time for his expertise should I ever have a problem with computers in the future. That had been two years ago, so he must be sixteen by now, and I had borrowed his skills on numerous occasions. So many in fact, that if he ever worked them out in relation to the cost of a cab from Camden to Highbury, he would realise he had been done and could have had a real cab ride to, say, Edinburgh.

'I'll put the kettle on,' he said with a sigh.

I followed him up the stairs to his bedroom, which he called his office, where there were the component pieces of about twenty computers including one which worked. I could tell that because it had a Simpsons screen saver on. Every conceivable square inch of space in the room was occupied by a piece of computer hardware or accessory, boxes of disks, joysticks, computer manuals or back copies of *What Computer?*, *Which Computer?* and similar magazines. If there had been a computer centrefold, it would have been pinned up.

He really did ought to get out more.

'So what do you want me to do for you?'

222

'Find me a website and tell me who put it up there.'

'Could be tricky if it's a naughty one. The server's most likely outside the European Union.'

'Don't worry, it's not one you're likely to have book-marked.'

He stared me full in the face. It was good to see his acne was clearing up.

'There's more on the Net than porn, you know,' he said defensively.

'I'm told it's still the single most popular hit by miles.'

'But medical advice comes next,' said J. peevishly. 'That helps millions of people. I was looking at a site this morning. Did you know that only thirty per cent of men regularly check them-selves for testicular cancer?'

'Yeah, but sixty per cent try and get somebody else to do it for them. You one of the self-checkers?'

He furrowed his forehead in youthful confusion.

'You calling me a tosser?'

'No, but it'll do until I think of something better. Now why don't you boot up your machine or whatever it is you do and let's get to work.'

'Nobody 'boots up' any more, grandad,' he said, pushing a pile of magazines off a typist's chair and sitting down in front of his monitor. 'What's the site?'

'It's called *Pirie's Pets.*'

J. clicked up a search engine and typed it in, clicking on Search Now. It took about five seconds to start to come up on the screen, but he was already bashing his mouse up and down and mutter-ing: 'Come on, come on. This is so *slow.*'

It was said that the average attention span of a dedicated web-surfer was 7.5 seconds, which is two and a half times that of a goldfish and only slightly less than some barmen I knew.

'There it is. Anything you want to see?'

I looked over his shoulder. There was the home page and the picture of Ross at Pinewood. The menu running down a sidebar offered various options including 'News'.

'Hit News,' I said.

The screen dissolved and reformed into a box with NEWS . . . NEWS . . . NEWS across the top.

'Updated yesterday,' said J. as I read.

A mystery fire destroyed Ross Pirie's beloved on-set caravan last night at Pinewood Studios on the first day of shooting on a new film which this site will no longer dignify with a name. No one was hurt in the fire which happened after shooting ended for the day but Ross is thought to be upset at the loss of what has been his second home while working in Europe. Some unkind souls might call this a judgement on Ross's choice of material which this site has always advised against . . .

'They're on the ball as usual,' I said to myself rather than J. 'Can you trace it for me?'

'There's usually an e-mail address at the end of these amateur sites. That's funny, there isn't. Still, there'll be a chat room unless it's real amateur night and this is done from some sad bastard's bedroom.'

I looked around us and knew what he meant.

'No, no e-mail address, no advertising either. Must be some sort of ego trip. Doesn't seem much point to the site.'

'It's a labour of love,' I said.

'I can try a few variations on the domain address. Seems to be somebody called Pat putting the stuff up. Pat says this, Pat says that, it's odds on Pat at the domain address will get there. Is this some little old lady running a fan club?'

'Very probably, but hang on, I don't want to send them an e-mail.'

'You don't?'

'No, I want to go and see them, like face-to-face, and I don't want them to know I'm coming.'

If I'd asked J. to post a picture of his mother on one of the infamous 'water sports' sex sites, he couldn't have looked more gobsmacked.

'You want to . . . visit them? I mean visit as in go there, rather than *visit* . . . electronically?'

'Got it in one. It's a bit strange, I know, but there's a few of us in a sort of underground movement who prefer to actually meet people. We have to keep it pretty quiet for obvious reasons. It's not something we're proud of.'

J. gave me a withering look, shook his head and turned back to the monitor.

'Whatever you say. There's the address, bottom of the last page: aurora-dot-com-forward-slash-piriespets. You're in luck, it's a dot-com.'

His finger picked out 'aurora.com/piriespets' on the screen.

'I am?'

'Piece of piss. It's a beta site of whatever aurora.com is and . . .'

He saw my expression, the one damned people use.

'A beta site is like a secondary site, something tacked on to the main website put up by aurora, whatever that is. It'll be some sort of business with its own server so that makes it easier to trace. Anything at 'aurora.com' would work as an e-mail address. We could try littleoldlady@aurora.com if you want.'

'Or littleoldman, just to be politically correct,' I said, still bemused. 'Go for it.'

He clicked out of the site and began to type.

'I'm going into Network Solutions,' he said, 'but it might be a bad time of the morning. Lots of people going on line about now.'

The ones with jobs and offices and free access to the Net.

'What's Network Solutions?'

'It's a service I subscribe to.'

'What is it?'

'About $35 a year. Oh, I see. It registers u.r.l.s – unique resource locators.'

'You mean addresses.'

'If you like,' he said sulkily. 'Here we go. We just pretend we're from aurora.com and we want to make some alterations to our service agreement.'

On the navigation bar at the top of the screen he clicked Make Changes. The site then asked him if he was used to forms and documentation and did he want the easy route, the medium route or the Full Monty. Naturally, he clicked on Expert and then, given a choice of things, on to Service Agreement.

'Right, let's try littleoldlady@aurora.com as my e-mail address and here we go: do we want to Manage Your Account? Yes, we'll have some of that. Now, do we want to make Administrative, Technical or Billing Changes?'

'Billing,' I said. 'Follow the money.'

'Good call. There you are.'

'What am I looking at?' I asked. He had done it so quickly, I was having trouble keeping up.

'There.' J. pointed to the bottom right corner of the screen. 'Registered Organisation Name. That's where the server sends the bill for putting up this site. You're in luck, it's in London.'

'I knew it had to be close,' I said, more confidently than I had any right to.

'It doesn't tell you who designs and edits the site, but that's who pays for it. Aurora Corona Residences, Eastern Avenue. Do you want the phone and fax numbers?'

'No, that's OK. I know it.'

'You do? What are the odds on that?'

'Staggering I should think, but it's true. It's an old people's home out at Redbridge. You were dead right with the little old lady tag. I used to know one of the nurses who worked out there, called Zaria. It's a small virtual world, isn't it?'

Zaria Inhadi, who was some sort of second niece twice removed of my landlord in Hackney, Naseem Naseem, and an old relationship with her was the reason I still paid a peppercorn rent on what Ross called my stealth house at Stuart Street.

'Hello, Earth to Planet Angel. You receiving me?' J. was saying. I must have been daydreaming. 'Is that it then? That all you wanted to know?'

'Absolutely. I won't stay for the tea. Isn't this modern technology wonderful,' I said with a smile.

Stalkers on the Net? Pah! You could find them in the time it took to boil a kettle.

'Sugar?' asked the Matron, whose name badge said 'Mrs McKendrick'.

'Just the two. Thank you. It is good of you to see me.'

On the drive east over to Redbridge, through Leytonstone and beyond Wanstead Park, almost as far as you could go across London from Pinewood and still be within the M25, I had worked out a number of scenarios for getting into the Aurora Corona Residential Home.

My old flame Zaria was long gone, now something big in the property development market and never likely to go back to a job where she had to wear a badge. So I had run through the idea of saying I was conducting a survey on computer use among the over-65s, or the Grey Panthers as the marketing men call them. Or that I was from the Computer Police investigating a complaint about hacking. Or British Telecom, to talk about putting in more lines. But all those options had the same basic flaw in that I wouldn't know what I was talking about and it would show. After all, I was looking for someone who knew how to put up a website, which was more than I did.

So I stuck to what I knew would work. I played the movie star card and said I was from Pinewood Studios, acting on behalf of Ross Pirie, no less.

'Ah, then you'll have come about Pirie's Pets,' Mrs McKendrick had said proudly. 'We just love Ross to bits here. Come into my office and have a cup of tea. Our webmaster is having physio at the moment but she won't be long.'

Webmaster?

I followed her black stockings and sensible shoes into her office and we made ourselves comfortable on a small sofa covered in a Laura Ashley print while a white-coated male nurse brought in a tea tray with drop-down legs. Mrs McKendrick said she would be mother, poured the tea and offered me a chocolate digestive, taking one herself and eating it so that crumbs fell on to the bosom of her blue uniform. Every time she mentioned Ross, though, her bosom heaved and the crumbs slid off and into her lap.

'There's quite a fan club for Ross Pirie here,' she said, 'has been for a number of years. The residents always turn out for his videos when we show them and quite a few of the ladies are in his official fan club. It's mostly the ladies. Our gentlemen quite like his action movies but they don't understand how he can stir a woman. Do tell me, what's he like in the flesh?'

'Stirring,' I said, but I could see she wanted more. 'And very, very charming. And genuine. Generous, too. In fact, exactly like the characters he plays on screen.'

I thought that was a safe bet, as Ross had never played the bad guy that I could think of, but Mrs McKendrick looked disappointed. Her bosom sank visibly.

'Not, I hope, like this recent part he's playing,' she said primly.

'Ah, the vampire,' I said, catching on. 'I think you'll be pleasantly surprised when you see the finished movie. It's quite a moral love story really. I've read the script.'

Well, I had read *a* script. God knows if the final movie would bear any resemblance to it.

'I, of course, will reserve judgement, but some of our group have already made their minds up about it, I'm afraid. The Christian ethic is quite strong among our residents and this new film sounds anything but Christian in either tone or content.'

'The "group"?' I asked. 'You said "group". Are you a member?'

'Oh yes, I'm one of Pirie's Pets, as we call ourselves. I told you, we're all great fans here and it seemed logical to put our interest on the World Wide Web when we became computer literate here. The computers are wonderful outlets for many of our residents who don't get out much these days.'

'I've heard that said about web users,' I agreed, keeping a straight face.

'But Mrs Hood is the ring-leader, she's the one who said we should get our own site, or borrow part of the official site. She's our webmaster. And here she is. Come in, Pat, and meet Mr Angel. He works for – get this – Ross Pirie!'

I wasn't sure what I had expected, perhaps some shy, retiring old dear in a wheelchair with a secret cache of bags of sweets for passing children.

Maybe Mrs Hood's mother was like that, because she wasn't. She wore a purple shell suit and light blue Reeboks and she had a white sweatband fanning hair which Marcus would no doubt have had something to say about. She held out a hand to me, a hand which seemed to have at least two rings on each finger, then changed her mind and launched into a big hug.

'He's sent you to ask me to have his children!' she shouted in my ear.

'Pat, really! Behave yourself. If boxaerobics excites you like this I'm going to cut down your sessions.'

Mrs Hood released me but I felt that her hair spray would stay with me for a while.

'Only kidding, Rita. I'm sure Mr Angel wouldn't begrudge an old woman her private fantasy, would you, pet? Now he is staying to lunch, isn't he?'

Mrs McKendrick looked slightly perturbed but not angry.

228

'I hadn't actually got around –'

'Then I will. It's Friday, so it must be fish. That OK with you? They don't give the Protestant carnivores much choice round here,' said Mrs Hood, linking an arm through mine.

'I really didn't plan on staying –'

'Pat's right,' said Mrs McKendrick politely. 'Chef has made a lobster bisque and has done a very nice deal with the fishmonger on some sea bass.'

'Well, I –'

'And they let us have a gin and tonic before lunch,' said Mrs Hood, eyes sparkling. 'Only one, but it's this big.'

She held her hands up, one about nine inches above the other.

'And we've got so much to talk about,' she added, pleading.

'That's true enough,' I said, although I hadn't said why I was there in the first place.

'I knew Ross would send somebody after he'd seen our site and see how we care about him. That's the power of the Internet, you know.'

I looked into her flashing blue eyes and wondered how many people were in there with her.

'Well, I did want to talk to you about the site, that's true.'

'Then we'll do it over lunch, but you'll sit with me. I won't let any of the others get you. You're mine and you're going to tell me all about Ross, aren't you? I call him my "Best Boy" because you see that on the credits of films, don't you? I don't know what it means though.'

'Neither do I,' I said, 'but it's a deal only if you tell me a few things about Pirie's Pets.'

She looked surprised.

'Why, of course I will, but I can't think what could possibly interest you in us. Now come through to the dining-room. Angel did you say? What do you do on the film?'

'I'm sort of –'

'Don't tell me, I know.' She held up a hand to silence me. 'You're Ross's new driver, aren't you? Standing in for that nice man called Frank, who had the accident.'

'Why, yes I am,' I said, showing her my best smile. 'Now how did you know that?'

I reckoned we had a *lot* to talk about.

* * *

And did we talk. In fact, I ended up more or less giving a seminar involving the whole dining-room of about thirty residents.

I was safely seated in maximum security conditions between Mrs McKendrick and Mrs Hood, who only let go of my arm to wield her spoon, on a table set for eight. There was almost a fist fight for the remaining five places.

My reputation had gone before me, or at least a reputation for being an expert on the movie business in general and Ross Pirie in particular, and I was expected to sing for my lobster bisque, which was good, and sea bass, which was excellent. The dining-room also had a healthy stock of white burgundy, which I could really have done some damage to if it wasn't for the fact that I had to get Armstrong all the way across London that afternoon.

So I told them about how good a skier Ross was, which I knew to be true as I had seen him, albeit from the safe distance of the cocktail bar in his Swiss chalet, and how he did his own stunts. And how kind he was to animals and how courteous to women and what a pleasure he was to work for. And they started asking questions ranging from was it true that he had used the same hairdresser for seven years (absolutely), how did he feel about never being nominated for an Oscar (watch this space) and did he really eat nothing but carrots as one of the trashier magazines had suggested? (I couldn't possibly comment, but he did have 20/20 night vision.)

Most of the questions raised about Ross were answered by Mrs Hood – 'call me Pat or Patsy' – who lost no opportunity in telling me about how she had been running the *Pirie's Pets* website ever since she'd moved into the Aurora Corona and realised that the facilities included access to the Internet. She'd had to learn about computers – 'didn't know my mouse from my elbow' – but now she was up and running and the next step would be to establish a chat room, if they would let her.

When they started asking about *Daybreak*, it started to get a bit tricky. Not only were most of the residents firmly in the this-is-unholy-material camp, but I somehow had to get round the fact that I hadn't actually seen a frame of film shot in anger yet. So I said that Ross was really looking forward to working with Zina Ray, and who wouldn't want to sink their fangs into her? But that didn't go down well, so I turned to Alec █████ Ross's co-stars and not only a thorough gent but su███ British actor-knight if there was any justice in the Quee██ day Honours.

'So why is he wasting his time doing this rubbish?' one of them muttered and I thought it might be time to leave before the bread rolls started flying. But Mrs McKendrick persuaded me to stay for the double nut *torte* and perhaps just half a glass of a 1988 Sauternes, as I was driving. I wondered if the residents had to have a nap in the afternoon. I could certainly do with one.

While Mrs McKendrick was organising dessert, I tackled Patsy Hood head on.

'Ross asked me to pass on his regards to the webmaster. He was quite specific about that.'

'Really? He visits the site?'

'Not as often as he'd like.' I refrained from adding that he had a life, but it gave me an idea. 'But not when he's working.'

'Oh.' Patsy Hood's eyes dropped. 'We had hoped to try and persuade him not to do this *Daybreak* film. Vampires, the undead, werewolves, that sort of thing. We don't like that here.'

'Too close to home?' I said before I could help myself.

Fortunately she laughed at the thought.

'Honestly, don't worry about it. It's very tastefully done and the word is that Ross –' I looked around the table and lowered my voice, though they were all looking at me and could probably lip-read – 'could be in the running for an Oscar next year for it.'

'Really?'

There was not so much a twinkle as a flashing strobe light in her eyes. She was itching to get to her keyboard to update her news page.

'But, of course, that mustn't get out,' I said seriously.

'It mustn't?'

'Oh no, the Academy takes a very dim view of actors who promote their own nominations, especially ones who are members.'

'I see. But what if an independent source suggested it, like our website?'

'Oh no, that wouldn't do. You see, this is really why Ross

come over here. I'm on a sort of mission, a
ssion for him.'
it,' she breathed, reaching for a bottle and filling her
glass.

The entire table went quiet. The room went quiet. You could
have heard a set of dentures click at twenty paces.

'Ross doesn't look at your website because he doesn't look at
anything when he's filming. I mean it. He allows himself absolutely no distractions, it's the only way he can work and put in
a quality performance. And, you know, Ross *is* the film. Without
him, it would be nothing.'

Patsy Hood nodded in total, unquestioning agreement. The
rest of the table were nodding. The whole room was nodding.
Either nobody here needed a hearing aid or the daily Viagra
dose was working.

'Which is why I've come here to ask you to close down your
website for the duration of the filming. I know it'll be hard for
you, but for Ross's sake it's the only way. I'm afraid there is so
much going on on this set that we have to shield Ross from any
distraction. All of us have to work together for this. Ross said he
knew you'd understand, being such loyal fans, and all of you
will be in his prayers.'

I wondered about that last bit, but Patsy looked suitably
touched and one or two of the old dears on our table positively
beamed.

'Ross knows you don't like the sound of this film, but he asks
you to do him one really big favour and that's lay off it on the
Net, for the next month anyway.'

Mrs Hood made as if to say something but I held up a finger
to silence her.

'In return, once filming is finished, he would very much like
you to invite him to lunch.'

Somebody in the room dropped a fork on to a plate. The
clatter was deafening.

'Here?' squeaked Mrs Hood.

'Absolutely.'

There was a beat when you could hear the pulse of the room.
Then the pulse became a roar as the room broke into spontaneous applause. It was the nearest I was ever going to come to
winning an Oscar.

'What can we say, Mr Angel?' said Mrs McKendrick. 'You've not only made our day, as they say, but you've managed to make Patsy speechless.'

'Then my work here is done,' I smiled. 'Is it a deal?'

'Yes, yes, yes, oh, yes!' shouted Patsy Hood. Then she cracked a huge grin. 'And I haven't said *that* in a fair few years!'

When the laughter subsided, which took a while as it had to be explained to a couple of the diners, I found Mrs Hood's arm through mine again and, under the table, Mrs McKendrick's hand on my knee.

'Your Barry will have to do some work for once now,' Matron said across me to Mrs Hood.

'I suppose so,' she replied.

'Barry?' I asked.

'My son Barry,' said Patsy. 'He's a fireman out at Pinewood. He tells me all the gossip. He's my – what d'you call them? He's my mole, that's it.'

She would probably have told me if I had asked her straight out when we'd been in Matron's office, she was so proud.

But then I wouldn't have got such a good lunch.

No day is wasted.

17

STUNT CO-ORDINATOR

It was mid-afternoon and already getting dark when I found the M11 and then turned on to the M25 to cruise around the skull of London in an anti-clockwise direction until Junction 16 which was more or less Pinewood's doorstep. Once out of Essex and into Hertfordshire, I fished out the Nokia and turned it on. Black cab drivers could usually get away with using a mobile whilst driving, but the Essex police had been having a blitz recently and I had had a drink. Cabbies with alcohol on their breath are shown no mercy.

I didn't have a schedule for picking up Ross – I couldn't believe I was almost missing the super-efficient Lin – so I pressed #8 for Marcus and got him on the second ring on a connection crackling with static and a deep background hum.

'Marcus? It's Angel. Where the hell are you?'

'I'm in a cab.'

'No, I'm in a cab. Where are you?'

'Just clip the lip, will you? I'm in a cab on my way out to the house. We've got a problem out there, which you would know about if you kept your fucking phone on and not up your ass!'

I held the Nokia away from my ear. They say you can get brain damage from them but I didn't realise they meant the bad language.

'Is it Ross?'

'No, he's strutting his stuff in front of the cameras. It's Kurt. Somebody jumped him out at the house.'

Marcus was shouting into his phone and I wondered what his cab driver was making of it all, especially somebody jumping Kurt.

'Is he OK?'

'He says he'll survive. I think his pride's hurt, though. He reckons he disturbed a burglar. Fortunately, *he* remembered how to use a cell phone.'

'Who else knows?'

'Just me. Now you. I'm doing damage limitation. You coming to give me a hand?'

I checked the traffic, most of which was going the other way at the moment, but that would change if I hit the M40 in rush hour.

'It could take me an hour, hour and a half.'

'Well, punch it, boy, I might need some local knowledge. Where the hell you been all day anyway? Brettler's been turning over stones looking for you.'

I bet he had.

'I've been busy. What about Ross? Am I supposed to pick him up?'

'You're cool until 7 p.m. He's looking at some rushes after they wrap and then he's having a new trailer-warming party. You just put the pedal to the metal and get out here.'

'Ten-four, good buddy,' I said.

And I switched off the phone again.

Kurt had done his morning work-out in the make-shift gym in the cellar while Mrs Winter, the cleaner from the village, had done hers with a Dyson in the rest of the house. After lunch and while the light held, Kurt had climbed into his 'sweats' and gone for a run out in the grounds of the house, having estimated that four times around the perimeter of the lake out back was worth six miles on the running machine, the rough ground giving added toning to his calf muscles.

And while he swore he had locked the doors, he did admit to not bothering to set the alarm. After all, this was the British countryside.

On his second or third circuit, heading back towards the house, he thought he saw a shape flit between the two sets of french windows on to the large brick patio. Going into his Special Forces crouch – just like he trained Ross to do in *Six Men Dead* – he approached the house via the stables and garages, putting him on the blind side of the house.

Sneaking round the front – or 'approaching using the natural angles of cover' as he put it – he found the front door open. The tongue of the Yale lock was still in the locked position, but the hasp which held it to the door frame was half-way down the hallway.

Kurt's first mistake was not getting into his newly hired sports car and getting the hell out of there. His second was going into the house. His third was believing everything his Aikijitsu instructors had told him when he graduated.

He couldn't remember exactly how many times he had been hit. The first blow, maybe a kick, was to his kidneys, then there was one to the base of his spine and others to the back of his neck. Then he was grabbed around the neck and, he swore, lifted off the floor and held there while a black-gloved fist worked on the pressure points in his neck until he passed out. He had worked out subsequently that the livid blue-to-purple bump in the middle of his forehead had been acquired when he'd been thrown unconscious down the cellar steps and one of the weights anchoring the rowing machine had broken his fall.

Marcus had filled a white towel with ice cubes and twisted it into a pack so that Kurt could hold it against his head. By the time I got there, he was in need of a refill.

'Why don't you have ice machines in this country, for Christ's sake?' Marcus stormed, for the sake of something to yell about. 'There's one plastic tray in the freezer. One! What the hell am I supposed to do with that?'

'Calm down,' I told him. 'Get a pack of peas out of the freezer.'

'Peas?' He looked at me as if I had just landed from Mars.

'We use frozen peas in this country,' I said. 'And you can eat them afterwards.'

He stomped off grunting, but at least it gave him something to do.

'No way you saw this guy, right?' I asked Kurt.

'There could have been ten of them for all I saw.' He winced as he blinked.

'There was no vehicle around?'

'Not that I saw. Nothing out front.'

'And your car was in the garage.'

He nodded and regretted the movement immediately.

'So he probably thought the place was empty. You disturbed him and he reacted badly.'

'Sounds like you know who it was,' he said suspiciously.

'If it was who I think it was, I've had some negative inter-action with him.'

'Does that mean a fight?'

'Oh no, I wouldn't go so far as to say that. What was he after?'

'I dunno. When I came round I called Marcus then I think I blacked out again. Oh yes, I also threw up somewhere.'

'Don't worry, we'll find it,' I said reassuringly but with no intention of going looking. 'Do you know how long you were out?'

'First time, maybe ten minutes. Second time, maybe five.'

'Is that good?' asked Marcus, returning with a pound bag of frozen *petits pois*.

'I don't know,' I said. 'It's just something the paramedics always ask. We should think about a doctor, maybe an X-ray.'

'I'm fine,' Kurt protested, wincing as he gently applied frozen vegetables to his forehead. 'Really, I'll be OK. Don't want to make trouble for the movie.'

'How long is it since you were on your feet?'

'Coupla hours,' he said.

I didn't think that was good. When I'd had my head cracked in Gerrard Street, I was out for a few seconds only. I had probably just fainted with the shock. It had happened before, like when opening a credit card bill.

'I think we should get him into The Oaks, where Frank Shoosmith is,' I said. 'The insurance'll cover it.'

'I guess we'll have to clear it with somebody,' said Marcus. 'Lin?'

'Did she show up on set today?'

'Nope. Burgundy's still covering for her. We could try Alix.'

'No,' I said quickly. Then I changed my mind. 'OK, why not? Just say Kurt's had an accident with his weight-training gear.'

It couldn't get us into any more trouble than we were already in.

I let Marcus make the call to Alix Tse and she told him to phone

The Oaks and quote a group insurance policy number. The Oaks agreed to send a private ambulance immediately, no questions asked. There are times when you really appreciate private medicine; mostly when you're not paying for it yourself. I was sure that the Junkyard Geek could have found us medical guidance on the Internet, but then I didn't have the time to look at all the sites dealing with headbanging.

While Marcus was using his mobile I left Kurt, telling him not to move just in case (though I wasn't sure in case of what), and went into the living-room to see what there was to see. Which was nothing much, or nothing immediately obvious.

Then my foot crunched on something brittle and plastic. It was a CD case from Coleman Hawkins' *Bean and the Boys* compilation, the one recorded in France with Roy Eldridge on trumpet. I guessed it belonged to Marcus as it didn't square with anything I'd seen or heard of Ross's taste in music, but the CD wasn't in the by now useless case.

I spotted it in one of the armchairs as if it had been casually thrown by a mad frisbee player. Then I saw another case on the floor, then another under a chair and then a CD – Sarah Vaughn's *The Divine One* – over by the right-hand set of french windows. At first I thought it was lying on the carpet but as I picked it up, I had to pull. It was about an inch off the carpet, actually embedded into the wooden frame of the windows. Whoever had thrown the Divine Sarah that hard may have a World Series pitching arm, but they had absolutely no taste.

I checked the stack near the giant hi-fi where the CDs should have been. About half a dozen were piled behind one of the speakers, all out of their boxes. I couldn't tell if any were missing.

'What the fuck?' said Marcus behind me. 'We been visited by the Music Police?'

'Something like that. You know what was here. See if anything's gone walkabout.'

I turned, holding handfuls of discs. Marcus was holding one of the 12-bore shotguns from the cabinet in the cellar. He held it professionally, broken, over his crooked arm. In the breech I could see the brass ends of two cartridges.

'What are those, Marcus?' I asked with a sense of dread.

'We deal in lead, friend.'

238

'Yeah, yeah, Steve McQueen in *Magnificent Seven*. Where did you get them?'

'Props Department. They're blanks, relax.'

'This is not a good idea, Marcus. This is west of London not the Pecos.'

'Hey, like they say, the West wasn't won with a registered gun.'

'It's not registered to you and the British police take a dim view of armed vigilantes, even armed with blanks. Go put it away. It's supposed to stay under lock and key.'

'Just taking precautions in case the scumbag comes back. You'd better go get Ross. I'll stand guard over Kurt until the paramedics get here.'

'Marcus, seriously. Put that thing away. On no account let the paramedics see it. I mean it. That is seriously not a good idea.'

'I'll be discreet.'

Oh, great. Lock, stock, two smoking barrels and discretion.

But as I left by the front door and I saw how far the hasp of the lock had been smashed down the hallway, I began to think that maybe Marcus had a point.

The security man who opened the gates for me at Pinewood started speaking into his walkie-talkie even as I drove by him, so I wasn't surprised when I found Paul Brettler waiting for me on the steps of the admin block. The fact that Carter and Regan were standing like bookends astride him didn't take my breath away either.

'Does your phone actually work?' Brettler asked as I climbed out.

I patted the pocket of my leather jacket.

'Off and on,' I said. 'I'm here to pick up Ross.'

'He's watching the rushes in the editing suite, then he's having a small drinks party in his new trailer. You've got plenty of time.'

'For what?' I asked, as if I didn't know.

'For a chat,' said the one who called himself Carter.

'I'm actually quite keen to see these rushes . . .'

'It's not optional,' said Carter.

'We can use my office,' said Brettler.

I followed him down the maze of corridors, with the Dynamic Duo half a step behind me to make sure I didn't run away. I let my eye roam over the framed film posters on the wall, desperately hoping we would pass *Carry On Constable*.

Carter couldn't wait until Brettler's office.

'You've been a busy boy, Angel,' he said in my ear. 'What've you been up to since you called on Frank this morning?'

'Social work,' I said over my shoulder. 'Visiting the frail and elderly and entertaining them. It's a side of me you rarely see.'

'Chopsy little git,' muttered Regan. 'Where've you been all day?'

'Doing what I'm being paid to do, which is more than I can say for you.'

Brettler unlocked the door to his office and I made to follow him in.

'What d'you mean by that, smartarse?'

'Oh, like where were you two when Tony Tse was burglarising Ross Pirie's house this afternoon, and damn near killing Kurt Valori in the process?'

I knew I shouldn't have baited them like that. In fact a general Rule of Life should be never to bait someone *behind* you, especially not if there are actually two of them.

One of them cuffed me across the back of the head. It wasn't a punch or a slap, it was a definite cuff and nobody had done that to me since a certain Geography teacher, whose pride and joy was a souped-up Ford Capri. His second mistake had been underestimating the number of ways a thirteen-year-old could disable the basic Ford engine.

It hurt like hell, because it caught me on the bump – now down to the size of a pigeon's egg – I had acquired, literally, on Gerrard Street. But I wasn't going to cry and let them know.

Brettler held up his hands for calm and tried to make peace.

'Let's not get silly here, people. We need an exchange of information, not a fight. We have been trying to contact you all day, Roy. Where have you been?'

'Mostly sorting out your *Pirie's Pets* problem and I think it's fair to say it's well and truly sorted. You shouldn't get any more surprises from that source. But just to be sure, have a word with the local Fire Chief and suggest that Fireman Barry Hood be transferred to other duties. Rescuing cats up trees, that sort of thing.'

'Barry Hood? But he's been around for ages.'

'So has his mother and she's the Ross Pirie stalker on the Net. But she has her price. Trust me on that.'

'Why should we trust anything you tell us?' Carter said with a half-snarl. 'What's this about Tony Tse?'

'You tell me.'

It was petty, but I enjoyed it.

'You,' he pointed at my chest, 'are in no position to play silly buggers. You are in well over your head.'

'So are other people, and you're the one who's been hiding the life-jackets on the *Titanic*.' I looked at Brettler. 'Though you had help there.'

'Just what's your problem, Mr Smart Mouth?' said the Regan character.

'You hung Frank Shoosmith out to dry, didn't you? All of you. And by playing undercover cops, you've put other people at risk.'

'Only you,' said Carter reasonably.

'What about Lin Ooi-Tan? And Kurt Valori?'

Carter shrugged his shoulders and parked a buttock on the edge of Brettler's desk.

'As far as we're concerned, Lin Ooi-Tan is off work sick. Nobody's suggested anything else.'

'Anybody seen her the last few days?' I pointed out.

'No, but nobody's reported her missing or in danger either. If you're worried about her connection with Tony Tse, well, she's a grown woman and she's been screwing him for over a year, so she should know what she's getting into. As for this Kurt – what, Valori? – whoever he is, that's news to us. You going to tell us about it?'

'Valori is Ross Pirie's personal trainer,' said Brettler before I could answer. 'He only came over from the States last week. He's moved into this house in the country Ross has rented.'

'He's now in residence at The Oaks hospital,' I said, 'after being jumped by a burglar this afternoon.'

'You reported this to the local police, I take it?' asked Carter casually.

'No we didn't.'

'But you think this burglar was Tony Tse, do you?' Carter said it like he was giving an example of sarcasm to an English as a foreign language class. 'Does this Valori think that, or does he leave all the detective work to you?'

'He didn't see who it was, and before any of you ask, Kurt will survive. But thanks for your concern. Feel free to show it any time.'

It was water off a duck's back.

'But *you* think it was Tony Tse?'

'We've never been officially introduced, but if I was looking for a sociopath with superhuman strength and an interest in the film business, I'd start with him.'

'But you've no proof it was.' Carter's eyes wandered around the room, trying to look disinterested in the answer. He was a rotten actor.

'What is this, *Who Wants To Be A Millionaire?* Do I have to phone a friend to get some answers? I'm the one who doesn't know what's going on.'

Carter looked uncomfortable and pushed his fists deep into his trouser pockets.

'How much did Frank tell you this morning?'

'Probably about as much as he knew. Somebody is shipping in printing paper – he called it polymer paper or something – and shipping out counterfeit euro currency, using Ross's last film as a cover. Gives a whole new meaning to the expression "European co-production", doesn't it?'

'That's not the half of it,' he said. 'What's been done through this movie *Side Edge* is no more than a dry run; a quality control test. They've opened bank accounts, established lines of credit, paid wages with fake euros. They've even bought sterling and dollars with it, not to mention fund the movie.

'But it's nothing to what is going to happen. By the end of this year, the eleven countries using the euro are supposed to print 13 billion – yes, billion – euro banknotes. It's going to be a nightmare. Nobody knows what they're supposed to look like, there are no agreed security printing measures and with existing currencies like the franc and the mark still around until 2002 or

2003, there will be maybe 30 billion notes circulating in euroland. Who the hell is going to check them?'

'Frank told me about a 500-euro note,' I said. 'That's about 300 quid. Now somebody's gonna notice if I buy a round in the Dog and Duck with a 300 quid note. It's the old music hall joke isn't it? The guy who prints a £9 note and nobody will change it for him, so he goes to Ireland and the first barman he tries says, 'Will three threes be all right?''

Brettler snorted a nervous giggle but Carter's face didn't crack.

'You wouldn't use a 500-euro in a bar or down the post office to buy a stamp. But you could move over a million pounds sterling in a small hold-all and open a bank account in another country. Easy. You could buy a million quid's worth of drugs in Spain and pay for it in Germany, breaking the money trail. Not to mention laundering on a grand scale. Up to now the $100 bill has been the launderers' note of choice. The 500-euro is going to take over.'

'And they're being printed here, in the UK? Even though we're not in the Emu?'

I had often wondered which bright spark in Brussels had come up with European Monetary Union without realising that the initials conjured up a picture of one of the most stupid, ungainly, flightless birds since the dinosaurs threw a genetic wobbler. Why didn't they opt for the Dodo and be done with it?

'The Royal Mint has contracts to produce euro coins for seven countries to date,' said Regan. 'But that's legal.'

If that was a joke, no one laughed.

'Put it this way,' said Carter, 'this is a Europe-wide scam and the franchises for printing the stuff are, shall we say, currently out to tender.'

'And Tony Tse is putting in a bid, right?'

'It seems so.'

'So why don't you pull him in?'

'We were watching him,' he said defensively.

'You mean Bernie Brooks was?'

'He was watching for what came back from the shoot in France and Switzerland. See who came to collect it. Frank got involved when he found some of this new polymer paper

243

they've developed in Australia. He knew what it was used for straight away.'

He looked down at his shoes.

'We didn't know Frank had been a printer.'

'If you'd known he was frightened of spiders you might have saved yourself two weeks . . . Hang on a minute . . .' I had an unexpected rush of clarity to the frontal lobes.

'What?' Carter was instantly suspicious.

'None of you has asked me what Tony Tse was looking for out at Eight Ash House today. You didn't even ask if anything was missing. Now that's either because you already know what he was looking for, or because you're not worried that he found it. What was it?'

'I can't say,' said Carter.

'You don't even know if it was Tony Tse, Roy,' said Brettler patronisingly.

'Shut it!' I snapped at him. 'Let me think this through. What do you need to counterfeit banknotes? Paper – right, you've got that. Ink? Shouldn't think there's a problem there. London is the ink capital of the Western world for all I know. What else? I know: plates, engraved plates. One for the front and one for the back. Seen it in a thousand movies. Michael Douglas in *Black Rain*, for instance. Good film. Except today you wouldn't use engraved plates and printing blocks, would you? You'd use a computer and scanners and laser printers and your artwork would be on a Zip Disk or a Super Disk or a writeable CD. Am I getting warm?'

'I can't say,' said Carter again. 'This burglar, was he interested in your CD collection then?'

'Not mine. Ross's maybe, or Marcus Moore's.'

'And was anything missing?'

'I don't think so. What does that mean?'

'I couldn't say . . .'

'Oh for fuck's sake, people are getting hurt!'

'I think he's frightened, boss,' sneered Regan.

'So he should be. Unless he keeps his nose out, somebody could snip it off.'

Carter took his hands out of his pocket, linked his fingers and cracked his knuckles like gunfire.

'But if you do see or hear anything we should know, then we

expect to get to know it and pretty quick. OK? Mr Brettler here knows how to get hold of us.'

He eased himself off the desk and stretched his back.

'You waiting to catch Tony Tse in the act, is that it? You're waiting for him to go into production before you pull him, aren't you? What's the matter – got no evidence? Or can't you say?'

Carter shot out a finger and jabbed me in the chest. It was a tickle compared to what Tony Tse had done to me in Chinatown, but it startled me and I took a step backwards, off balance. Regan laughed but Carter didn't.

'You blundered into this, Angel,' he said in my face. 'I don't owe you an explanation. I warned you off, that was my favour to you.'

He prodded me again but I held firm and hardly flinched at all.

'I've done a bit of checking on you, sunshine. You've had a very lucky life so far and now you're mixing with movie stars and living with a fashion designer and yet you don't seem to have any visible means of support of your own or any credentials for doing so. Don't make it worth my while to dig any deeper. OK?'

I held my hands up.

'I get the message. I'm out of here and I'm history. I've done what I was asked to do. I'm just a driver from now on. I'll even turn my phone on.'

I took the Nokia out of my jacket pocket and made a show of beeping it on.

'There. Can I go now? I've got a movie star to drive home.'

'That's a very good idea,' said Carter. 'Knew you'd see it my way once you'd thought it through.'

I got out of the office and scuttled down the corridor, trying to breathe deeply.

I was thinking about what he had said. Especially the bit about me having had a 'lucky life'.

It was the way he'd said 'so far' that worried me.

245

18

GAFFER

By the time I got down to the main entrance of the block the rushes viewing had finished and they were all piling out of the stairwell in little groups talking quietly to each other or just staring blankly off into space. Ross had Julius Cockburn whispering in his ear, Gloria-Maria was scrabbling in her handbag for a cigarette, Burgundy Dulude had a clipboard and looked harassed, constantly raking a hand up and through her hair. I recognised Alec Walters, the British classical actor, as he emerged slowly shaking his head, but there were about a dozen I didn't recognise, though I guessed the ones wearing fleece-lined leather jackets were cameramen or second unit directors. There were also six or seven young women clutching scripts or giving out call sheets or pink pages of new dialogue, circling the group like pilot fish. Bringing up the very rear was the haggard vision of Walter Wilkes Booth, the scriptwriter, who looked as if he had slept in his clothes and given up razors for Lent. He held the swing door open as if to step through into the foyer, but paused and slowly and quietly began to slam his forehead against the edge of the door.

I fell in alongside Burgundy as we stepped out into the night air.

'Why so glum? Nobody liked the rushes?' I asked quietly.

'No, they were really good, but nobody ever says that at the first screening.'

'I knew that.'

'You coming to the launch of Ross's new trailer?' she asked.

'Sure.' I looked around at the size of the group. 'How big is it?'

'Oh, don't worry, only the select few.'

She looked over her shoulder back into the admin block where Walter Wilkes Booth was still gently bashing his own brains out.

'But not him?' I said.

'Christ no,' she shuddered. 'He's the scriptwriter.'

Half the group disappeared as we walked down the block to where Ross's trailer was parked, as if they had just melted into the studio walls. They knew their place.

The trailer itself looked to me like an exact replica of the original one. Maybe their insurance only covered like for like. It was even parked in the same spot and all traces of debris from its predecessor had been removed.

Inside, there was a mêlée in the centre of the trailer where drinks and canapés had been laid out on the horseshoe bar and a pair of waitresses in black-and-white were trying to open bottles of champagne. I spotted Mrs Julius Cockburn waiting impatiently in front of them, an empty glass tilted in her hand. Most of the men, including her husband, tried to give her as wide a berth as was possible in the confined space.

Ross finally acknowledged my presence and elbowed his way towards me.

'Grab yourself a drink, Roy, this won't last long. Fifteen minutes tops then I'm out of here. Early to bed again, it's another 7 a.m. start tomorrow.'

'It is? But it's Saturday.'

'No rest for the wicked,' he grinned idiotically.

I helped myself to an orange juice with ice and Alec Walters squeezed by me holding the same.

'Ah, a fellow sufferer,' he said. 'Doctor's orders for you too?'

'No,' I said deadpan, 'I'm driving.'

'Profuse apologies,' he said and turned away.

Burgundy tapped me playfully on the arm with the neck of a bottle of Budweiser.

'I'm about to make your dreams come true,' she said huskily.

'You are?'

'You're taking me home tonight.'

I almost said something I would possibly not have lived to regret, but I remembered just in time.

'Right. You're moving out to the house. I hope Marcus has remembered to make you a pallet on the floor.'

'He'd better do better than that,' she said firmly, then turned to flick her hair at one of the cameramen.

I stepped to one side to avoid someone's glass and the person behind me had to do the same. When Mrs Cockburn took a step, everybody moved to the side. I'd been to better parties in a phone box and at least there you couldn't fall down no matter how drunk you were.

Then two pairs of shoulders parted in front of me and I found Alix Tse looking up at me.

'I've been trying to reach you all day,' she said, her face small and round and hard as a cricket ball.

'I've been busy,' I said, determined not to be the one to blink first.

'I've got those petrol receipts you asked for.'

I blinked and she realised I had forgotten all about them.

'Frank Shoosmith's petrol receipts from before Christmas. You asked me for copies. I have them in my office.'

'Oh, yeah, with you now. Sorry, but I don't need them any more.'

I smiled at her but it got no reaction.

'Then why did you ask for them?'

'To see if I could piece together Frank's movements just prior to his accident. But it's OK, I talked to Frank this morning and he told me all I needed to know.'

'He did?'

There was still no expression in her face but I thought I saw something flash in her eyes.

'Absolutely. Got his memory back all of a sudden. Told me everything.'

Yes, there it was. A definite tremor in her throat. A shiver, not an earthquake, but a definite movement.

'He remembers everything?' she said in her usual monotone.

'Yes,' I said with a smile. 'And it's quite a story. It would make a good movie.'

I made a point of scoping the trailer over her head until I caught Ross's eye and he nodded.

'There's my cue from the boss,' I said cheerfully. 'It's time to leave.'

'Good advice,' said Alix.

But from the set of her face I had no idea if she was talking about me or herself.

*   *   *

248

Burgundy walked with me to collect Armstrong and her suitcase, which she stashed in the front luggage area next to my seat. Then she climbed in the back, pulled down a rumble seat and put her feet up.

'This is cool. First time I've travelled in a London taxi without getting a come on from the driver.'

'Day ain't over yet,' I drawled, starting the engine.

'Jack Palance, *City Slickers*,' she said instantly. 'Just drive.'

I stopped outside the trailer while she went in to get Ross. When he emerged, about half a dozen of the drinkers came out to see 'Ross's very own taxi' and to say 'how cute' and make simpering noises. Through the bay window of the trailer I could see Mrs Cockburn sliding behind the horseshoe bar.

They waved us off and we hadn't even made the Pinewood gates before Ross said:

'What did you think? Honestly, now.'

'They were great, Ross. You know it, I know it, everybody there knew it. Don Sager will love them. I bet he'll double the number of screens you open on after he sees them.'

I had to check in my mirror that it really was Burgundy talking. I had never heard that voice before: so soft, so deferential, so soothing.

'You don't think Alec was trying to best me in the sidewalk scene?'

Come to think of it, I had never heard Ross using such a mousy voice before. I wondered if *Pirie's Pets* would recognise this character.

'Face it, Ross, you're the star so they'll all try and best you,' soothed Burgundy. 'But I don't think Alec is doing an Alan Rickman on you, it's just his way. Stage training and so forth.'

'So Bo Jay is the one I have to watch, right?' Ross had gone into nervous mouse by now.

'You shouldn't worry about this, Ross. The camera loves you, and you know it.'

'He's younger and he's fit and sexy and cool. He has a wide fan base. This film will do a lot for him. He knows that. He'll go for it; big time.'

Nervous, wounded mouse seeing Springsteen for the first time.

I didn't know about Burgundy, but I couldn't take much more.

'Bo Jay Roberts' character gets decapitated in Scene 43,' I said through the open partition. 'The rest of the film's your own.'

'Just drive,' said Burgundy, closing the partition.

I had been going to tell them about Frank and about how their movies were being used for a multinational counterfeiting scam, and how Ross's personal trainer had been slugged in what they would call a home invasion.

But if that was their attitude, sod 'em.

However much Ross was paying Marcus Moore, it wasn't enough.

Not only had he hidden the shotgun, found and removed Kurt's vomit (I hoped), cleared the messed-up CDs in the living-room, screwed the front door lock hasp back in place, made up a bed for Burgundy and cooked a meal, but he had a jug of martinis waiting for us. And they were the genuine article. I could see that from the bottles on the kitchen table. The Gordon's gin was half empty, the vermouth bottle had perhaps a capful missing. And we had a choice: either an olive or a small pearl onion. Ross was only allowed one as he had lines to learn. I had three. They could have fuelled Armstrong for a month.

As soon as we had driven up to the house and the security lights had come on, Marcus had opened the front door just to make sure we were who we were. In the hallway, in an ancient hat and coat stand, I noticed an old leather golf bag upside down amidst a cactus of golfing umbrellas and I realised what he'd done with the shotgun. Ross and Burgundy walked straight by.

Marcus closed the front door and slid on the two deadbolts, top and bottom, then punched in the four-digit code on the electronic alarm pad on the wall. Handily, someone had written the code in felt tip pen on the plastic casing.

'I hope this works,' said Marcus. 'I don't know if it will after the kicking it took this afternoon. Maybe we should get it checked out. You said anything?'

'Not to these two.'

'Keep it that way.'

I did, so when Ross eventually realised somebody was missing and asked where Kurt was, Marcus strung him the line that Kurt had pulled a muscle or three while training and had been packed off to see a physiotherapist and would stay overnight.

Ross said that he must send him something, maybe a case of hi-energy drinks or a multipack of vitamin supplements. He said it out loud as if someone was there to take notes and make it so. We ignored him.

Marcus served up a huge steaming bowl of spaghetti with dishes of beef, lamb and veal meatballs and a thick tomato and basil sauce on the side. On the table he placed a grater and a chunk of fresh Parmesan big enough to require a second mortgage. I opened a couple of bottles of Valpolicella and we pretended it was a scene from *The Godfather*.

Ross talked about his characterisation in the coming scenes, about the lighting, the difficulty of working against a blue screen so the special effects could be put in later, whether Alec Walters really was trying to upstage him or not, whether Julius was getting the *texture* of the film right. When he had finally run out of things to say, he declared he was going to his room to learn his lines for tomorrow. Burgundy said she would have a bath and ring a few friends back home in the States. I told Marcus he was an A1 chef and helped him load the dishwashers. (The house had two; that was class.)

Then we checked all the doors and windows, hoped the alarm was set, and we went to bed. Him with a mug of coffee, me with the remains of a bottle of wine.

It was 9.35 p.m. and a Friday night.

This jet-setting, movie-star lifestyle was going to be the death of me.

Which made the stick I got from Amy the next morning even more difficult to take.

The day started routinely, as they seemed to, with me oversleeping. With Kurt missing in action, it was left to Burgundy to roust me out by shouting at me at point blank range, leaving a cup of cold coffee on the bedside table and muttering loudly about the clothes littering the floor and cursing when she tripped over an empty wine bottle. The words 'hog', 'happy' and 'shit' were used liberally.

As my feet hit the carpet I focused on my watch to find it was 6.24 a.m. I hadn't known until then that there was a 6.24 a.m. on a Saturday. Saturdays were for racing, football and going to the pub. Nothing else.

I didn't have time to shower or shave, but nobody noticed. Marcus had decided to borrow Kurt's hire car and follow us into Pinewood, not because he wanted to try out the BMW Z3 but because he had to go shopping after he'd done Ross's hair, though that didn't stop him overtaking us on the M40 doing, I reckoned, at least a hundred and ten. Neither Ross nor Burgundy, in the back of Armstrong, saw him or even realised he wasn't sitting with them. They were too busy going over the three lines Ross had to say on cue that morning, and they seemed to involve an awful lot of Ross rehearsing his profile.

It was only as I dropped them inside the studio that Ross acknowledged my presence.

'We'll wrap about four this afternoon,' Ross said after he had got out.

A platoon of runners, assistants and assorted hangers-on were already surrounding him, clipboards waving, mobile phones on stand-by, all wanting a piece of him.

'The plan for tonight is that Marcus will cook us something special then we'll have a night watching videos, bitching about people we know in the business. There's no need for you to stay over if you want to get home, Roy. I know you have a life.'

I did? I'd forgotten it.

'See how you feel. I've got two things to go to tomorrow but Marcus has offered to drive me. You can take the day off.'

'On the seventh day they rested, eh?' I said.

Ross creased his forehead.

'That's from *The Player*, isn't it?'

'Probably,' I said, just to avoid argument.

The Ross Pirie caravan moved off to work, blissfully unaware of anything else in the world other than what they were going to telescope down a very expensive camera lens a few centimetres wide over the next few hours.

I located a tea trolley and helped myself to coffee and an apple Danish, noting that they hadn't bothered putting out bacon sandwiches for the Poor Bloody Infantry, it being a Saturday.

It finally dawned on me that it was just after 7 a.m., it was cold, damp and still dark and I was standing outside in the elements with nothing to do when I should be tucked up somewhere nice and warm or at least with somebody nice and warm. I reviewed the options open to me and decided I should go home and get some clean clothes before it became a hygienic necessity.

I had consciously made that decision, my mind was set and there was sadly nothing else to distract me, so I got into Armstrong and headed for the main gates only to meet a very familiar Freelander being driven in.

I pulled over and flashed my headlights once. The Freelander drew up alongside me and the window came down.

'Never expected to see you up and awake at this time of the morning,' said Amy.

'One out of two ain't bad,' I said. 'I was on my way home, you must be psychic.'

'I didn't come here to see you!' she laughed, rather easily. 'I've got the call.'

'You have?'

I was always wary when people said things like that. Once, at one of Amy's fashion business booze-ups, I was chatting up a middle-aged woman who told me that her seventeen-year-old son had 'had the call and gone to Jesus' and I'd said how sorry I was and was it a car accident? She'd looked at me like I was dirt and said she meant Jesus College, Cambridge to read history.

'On to the set. They're doing some of the scenes with the costumes I designed today.'

'They are?'

'Don't you have any idea what's going on around here?' she wailed. 'I came in yesterday – but you weren't around of course – to do a fitting for Ross and Zina Ray.'

'Zina Ray's here?'

'Cor blimey! Do you go around with your eyes shut?' She shook her head in pity. 'Anyway, the mouthy American chick asked me back to see the filming today. You know, the one with the *Charlie's Angels* haircut.'

'There were three haircuts in *Charlie's Angels*,' I said just to be picky.

'There was only one that mattered to men,' she said primly.

'What's her name? Beaujolais or something? She was talking about you as a matter of fact. Offered to send you to pick me up. I think she's got the hots for you.'

'Ha-bloody-ha. Did she know who you were?'

'Oh she knew who I was, she just didn't know I knew you.'

'And you didn't tell her?'

She smiled at that.

'Thanks,' I said. 'Will you be back home later?'

'Dunno. I'll have to see how the shoot goes. Why? You got laundry?'

'No,' I said quickly, 'I just wanted to spend some time with you.'

'What have you done?' She scowled down at me from the Freelander.

'Nothing. Just feeling a bit guilty about not calling. Marcus and I have been running around like blue-arsed flies the last –'

'Marcus Moore? Is he on set?'

'Yes, he's just arrived but he's living out at the house as well.'

'He is?' Amy's eyes turned to lasers. 'Why didn't you tell me? I could have come over and visited. Do you think he gives freebies?'

'Well, contrary to the image he has on set . . . Oh, I see. You mean haircuts.'

'Of course I do. Have you any idea who is on his client list in Hollywood?'

'Like, you mean, who *isn't*?' I bluffed, not having a clue. 'You could always try being nice to him, I suppose.'

'I can do that,' she snapped. 'When I want to.'

She checked her watch.

'I'd better move it. It doesn't look good to be late in front of all these big shots.'

'Absolutely,' I agreed.

'Oh, by the way, if you go home, check the answerphone, will you? You've got about sixteen messages all from Stuart Street. Your friends there seem to be after your blood. Something to do with a crowd of punks sitting outside not going away, waiting for autographs or something . . .'

*   *   *

254

Amy had been exaggerating of course. There were only fourteen increasingly obscene messages waiting for me at her Hampstead house.

I pressed the Erase key on the phone for the required three seconds and wiped the lot. Then I drew myself a bath using liberal amounts of some of Amy's expensive herbal bubbles, made myself a mug of decent coffee and settled in to read the latest Harry Potter novel, which Amy had given me for Christmas.

I was just finishing a shave when the phone rang and I wandered down the stairs wearing a towel as the Call Screening programme kicked in. It was Amy.

'Angel, pick up if you're there. If you're not just make an effort to wear something decent when you pick up Ross this afternoon. He's invited me – us – to have dinner with him tonight, after we wrap. It'll be early – you know what Americans are like – but we could go on somewhere afterwards. But try and look half reasonable for once, will you? Don't show me up. You never know, you might score with your American admirer. What's her name, Bergerac? She mentioned you again this morning. Oh, yes. I've been told to tell you you've turned your fucking phone off again. 'Bye.'

I made a face at the phone and Amy's ability to nag by remote and started back upstairs to find some clothes. I had a green Paul Smith jacket Amy had bought for me and a red roll-neck sweater which I could wear with a new pair of khaki combat trousers. The last time I had worn that combination Amy had said I reminded her of a set of traffic lights. Serve her right.

But I was only on the second step when the phone rang again and so I waited for the recorded message to do its work, half expecting it to be Amy with an extra insult.

I couldn't have been more wrong, or more surprised when I heard the incoming voice.

'I'm trying to contact Roy Angel. This is Lin. Lin Ooi-Tan. And it is very, very important . . .'

I picked her up on Shaftesbury Avenue, at the side of the Ambassadors Theatre.

I stopped at the kerb only long enough for her to open

Armstrong's door and throw in her bag. I was moving off by the time she was in and seated and we were going across Cambridge Circus before she had the door shut. That was as near to China-town as I was going, thank you very much.

I swung Armstrong round the back of Centre Point, cut across the bus lane and waited at the lights to turn left so I could head west down Oxford Street. It was only then that I got a good look at her in the mirror, but what I saw made me turn my head for a proper look.

'You've been through it,' I said.

It was the sort of thing a real cabby might have said: accurate to the point of stating the bleeding obvious, non-judgemental and just the sort of thing she didn't want to hear.

She wore a plain blue baseball cap with the peak pulled down but I could see that she had bruises around both her eyes and on her jaw, her lips were puffed and cracked and I suspected that her nose was broken from the difficulty she was having breath-ing. When she saw me looking at her, she put her right hand up to cover her face. The middle and fourth finger of the hand were taped together with blue adhesive plasters, the sort chefs and restaurant staff have to use. She kept her left arm across her midriff which made me fear for either her forearm or her ribs.

'So it's Heathrow, then, is it?'

'Yes,' she said with a lisp and I realised she had a front tooth missing.

I hadn't noticed on the phone, where it had been difficult enough to cope with her mounting hysteria without picking faults with her diction.

'We had a deal,' I reminded her, pulling away as the lights changed.

The deal had been that I would get her to the airport for a flight to a destination she would not reveal on condition that she told me what the bloody hell was going on. I also had a supple-mentary question: why had she picked on me?

In the mirror I saw her turn and look out of the back window, then turn back into her seat, her face contorting with the effort. She took a deep painful breath.

'It's Tony, he's out of control,' she started.

'Tony Tse, right?' I asked, like we had a choice of them.

'Yes, Tony Tse. He was in my flat when you called round.

256

He's been keeping me there. He's insanely jealous and he suspects every man I look at or who looks at me. These last few days . . .'

I indicated left and pulled over to the kerb. We hadn't even reached Oxford Circus Tube station.

'Goodbye. Have a nice flight.'

'OK, OK, keep going, I'll tell you.'

I moved off again.

'I believed you as far as when you said 'Tony'. Start from there.'

After a pause, she said:

'How much do you know?'

'I know Tony's into counterfeiting in a big way, using Last Ditch Films as a cover to ship in printing paper, which he's probably got stashed away somewhere, and something else – something on a CD maybe? – which he's still looking for. Going to tell me what it is?'

'I don't know. I'm really not involved . . .'

I indicated and began to pull over again, drifting to a halt near the Hog in the Pound, the pub where I first met Amy, though they hadn't put up a plaque or anything.

'It's the artwork for printing a new banknote,' Lin said quickly, so I speeded up again. 'It was on a compact disc in Ross's trailer. Tony couldn't carry it himself because he was being watched.'

'Who put it there?'

'I don't know, really, I don't. It's some syndicate, based in Switzerland. This is a sort of test for Tony, see if he can do the printing on the scale they want. It's like an audition for him – to get in with the big players.'

'I'd heard the job was out to tender. Who else is pitching? The Russians? They're good at funny money, so I hear.'

'I don't know, I don't know. I knew Tony was involved in something but until this week I didn't know how deep he was in.'

I checked the mirror. The peak of the baseball cap had come down like a visor as she bent her head forward.

'You suspected he did something to Frank Shoosmith, though, didn't you?'

'When I heard about the accident, I thought he might have done something to his car. Frank wasn't exactly clever, trying to follow us around. Tony was on to him straight away. But Frank says he doesn't remember anything.'

'Frank was lying. Somebody put a spider in his car wrapped up in a box of fortune cookies.' I took my hands off the wheel and held them six inches apart. 'This big, Frank said.'

'Oh, no,' she breathed.

'Did Tony collect spiders by any chance?'

'No, but he knew about Frank's phobia and he could easily get things like that. He once threatened to put a scorpion inside a kid's crash helmet for taking too long with a delivery.'

I shuddered. Not even Domino's Pizza deserved that.

'Was Tony out at Pinewood on Christmas Eve?'

'Yes, he was. I think he was collecting the paper samples but he couldn't get into Ross's trailer without me. I think he would have tried, but Frank's accident stirred things up too much.'

The one thing Tony hadn't counted on was Bernie Brooks getting a sudden craving for a fortune cookie, making the surprise he'd planned for Frank come early. Tony had probably planned for it to happen on the motorway at seventy miles per hour or maybe over Frank's Christmas dinner. He was thoughtful that way.

'So he started hanging around as soon as the place opened up after the New Year?' I said. 'Trying to get into the trailer.'

'I had to let him in the other night, after we thought everybody had gone.'

In the mirror I could see her in profile, staring out of the window into Kensington Gardens as we sped towards Notting Hill.

'Even then, that idiot Walter turned up.'

'The writer idiot,' I said, 'with his rewrites.'

'When Tony couldn't find the CD he went berserk, started smashing the place up. He poured vodka and brandy over one of the chairs and set fire to it. I had to drag him out of there otherwise I think he would have stayed to watch it burn. He's gone over the edge.'

'And he took it out on you.'

'He beat me up so I couldn't come into work even if he'd let me. Then after you turned up he was convinced I couldn't be trusted so he kept me tied up in the flat. Yesterday he came back and beat me again. I don't know why. He was beyond even

258

telling me why he was doing it. I had to draw a line. I can't face Ross and the others. My life to date is now finished. It's a wrap. I've got to get out.'

'Don't say that. Ross needs you.'

'Like a hole in the head he needs me,' she said. 'I'm nothing but bad luck.'

'Tony's the bad luck, surely, and he's still on the loose, out there somewhere. How did you get away?'

She unzipped the shoulder bag she had on the seat beside her and produced a Sabatier carving knife, holding it up so I could see it in the mirror.

'I made it to the kitchen. I had to drag a chair with me. I won't go through that again. He won't touch me again. Ever. Next time I'll kill him, or he'll kill me.'

That's what I called a balanced view of life.

I wondered how she was going to explain the knife when the metal detectors went off at Heathrow.

'Put that away,' I said. 'People will think you're hijacking me.'

Who was I kidding, expecting the population of Notting Hill to notice anything like that?

'Where's Tony now?'

'I don't know. Probably with Alix.'

'How deep is Alix in?'

It was obvious she had to be in it with him. There was no way they could move funny money through the film company without her say-so.

'Do you know what a tong is?' Lin asked, which threw me for a minute.

'A Chinese tong – you mean, like a Triad?'

'No, not a Triad, they're professional criminals. A tong is a secret society of Chinese who live outside China. There have been tongs for centuries, ever since the Chinese spread out from the homeland, where the members band together for self-help and to send money back to relatives in China. They're usually based around a trade or a business. Tony is in a tong called the Wood Block Red.'

'Printers,' I said. 'Wooden block printing, paper money. The Chinese invented it.'

If she was impressed, she didn't show it.

'That's why he got involved. He thought it was his destiny.'

She made a snorting noise which passed as a laugh.

'He already owned a small printing company out in Essex. It seemed a natural progression to go on to printing money.'

'And Tony Tse is the boss of this Wood Block tong?'

'Oh no, not the boss. His cousin Alix, she's the boss. It's a very enlightened tong – there's no discrimination against women.'

She made me drop her at Terminal 3 but she had no intention of telling me where she was headed. All the way down the Great West Road from Brentford she had repeatedly turned to look out of the rear window and when I asked her what she was looking for, she simply said, 'A white Mercedes.' That got me going and I was on maximum alert, seeing them everywhere in the wing mirrors, in side streets, on the opposite side of the road going in the other direction. None of them seemed to be following us.

As we approached the airport I asked her why she had called me.

'I needed transport,' she said, 'and someone who could get to Ross and tell him I'm so sorry for everything. I didn't want to risk ringing the studio and I had Amy's number.'

'So if I hadn't been there, you'd have had to get a minicab, I suppose. Maybe even had to leave a tip.'

'No, there was another reason. I needed to warn you.'

'About Tony? He did a good job of that himself on Gerrard Street.'

'No, now it's worse. Alix spoke to him last night. Told him that Frank had got his memory back and had told you everything. She wants to cut and run but Tony won't let it go. It's a sort of matter of honour now and he's really out of control. He won't take orders from her any more.'

I slowed as we turned into Heathrow, glancing up at the planes circling overhead and wondering if maybe I should be thinking of getting on one. Any one would do.

'Are you saying that Tony thinks I've got his CD?'

'I think so. And I'm afraid he's going to do something really bad.'

She was afraid?

19

FIGHT CO-ORDINATOR

As the automatic doors hissed behind her, I reached automatic-ally for my mobile phone only to find I had left it in my leather jacket back at Amy's house. Typical. The first time I really needed it, the damn thing had got lost.

Still, Pinewood was only about ten miles away around the M25 and Ross and Amy would be in the middle of a movie set where surely nothing could happen to them before I got there.

Not that I was really interested in protecting them. I needed someone to protect me.

The security guard on the main gate didn't know if Paul Brettler was in his office today, it being a Saturday. Nor could he remem-ber if a white Mercedes had come into the studios. Naturally, he had no idea who Tony Tse was as he was only doing relief work at week-ends to cover for the regular guys. He didn't have a gun I could borrow either. Fat lot of good he was.

I parked near Ross's new trailer and tried there first. It was empty and locked but I did find a teenage girl runner scrunched inside a fur-lined anorak having a secretive smoke on the corner of the block. She told me that everyone who mattered was on Sound Stage 9 rehearsing for the final set-up of the day. But it was cool, I could go in as long as the red light was off.

At last, I was going to get to see a movie being made.

The red light was on. I went back to the girl in the anorak and bummed a cigarette off her. Then another, which would have to substitute for the lunch I had missed. When the girl realised I wasn't an agent or a producer, she remembered she had an elsewhere to be and took her cigarettes with her.

When the red light eventually changed to green, the doors opened but instead of the usual rush of runners, assistants, electricians, clipboard-holders and general hangers-around, only about half a dozen people emerged.

Burgundy was in the lead, followed by Ross, with an arm around Amy's waist. Amy was wearing black trousers and a jacket designed by Stella McCartney. Ross was wearing the dress uniform of a US cavalry officer circa 1864, complete with sword, hat and white gloves, designed by Amy.

'Roy! How yer doin'?' Ross greeted me loudly as if he hadn't seen me for eight years instead of about eight hours.

'Struggling on,' I said.

'You? Struggling? Get outta here.' He hugged Amy in closer. 'We've done good work today. Half a day ahead of schedule I would say.'

Burgundy asked if she could check something with Ross and one of the continuity girls and while he was distracted, I peeled Amy away from his side.

'So, what's it like making movies?'

'Making stills,' she said out of the corner of her mouth. 'All my designs are for photographs which appear in the background on a fucking shelf or something. We've been posing photographs of them, not filming. I may be in pictures, but not *moving* pictures.'

Unlike Amy I'd read the script, still it probably wasn't a good time to tell her that I had known her costumes were not needed for the main film action.

'Still, you'll get a credit out of it,' I said, trying to placate her.

'Damn right I will, plus a free haircut.'

She cheered up at the thought.

'That Marcus Moore is a very attractive man. What a waste he's gay.'

'Isn't that politically very incorrect?' I said, biting my tongue.

'Sod that. I did tell you we were having dinner with him – and Ross of course – didn't I?'

'Yes, and you told me to change.'

'Well, there's no time for that now,' she said brusquely. 'I promised I'd give Bermondsey a lift –'

'Burgundy.'

'Whatever. I promised her a lift out to this house where you guys do all your whoring and cocaine snorting and heavy drinking.'

'Hot chocolate before bed is about as good as it gets out there. Where is Marcus?'

'He went on ahead about an hour ago.'

'Marcus values his preparation time,' said Ross, muscling back into the conversation, his cavalry sabre clanking in its scabbard. 'But he is a good cook, don't you think, Roy?'

'A wizard in the kitchen,' I agreed. 'What's the plan?'

'I get myself out of this superbly tailored designer uniform –' he smiled at Amy – 'and then we're out of here. You two have some dinner at the house and then I'm out of your hair until Monday. Burgundy has next week's schedule.'

Burgundy joined us.

'We're clear here,' she said. 'Ready to rock and roll.'

'Ready when you are, sister,' said Amy.

'Do something for me,' I asked Burgundy. 'Before you get to the house, call ahead and just make sure Marcus is OK and expecting you. Just do it, right?'

'Sure,' said Burgundy, giving me a sideways look.

'What will you be doing?' Amy asked suspiciously.

'I'll be helping Ross out of his trousers,' I said loftily.

Ross didn't need any help getting changed, of course; he had Amy's closely researched and immaculately tailored uniform off and thrown in a bundle on the floor of his dressing-room in a few seconds. It took him about five minutes to dress in civilian clothes and then about fifteen to remove his make-up and comb his hair in front of a mirror.

I realised that the mirror was strong competition but I did try to explain what was happening around him. From all the reaction I got, I might have been explaining the rules of cricket. Eventually he turned to look at me as he shrugged into a long, soft, Ungaro leather coat.

'Does the media know any of this?' he said.

'Not from me,' I snapped back.

'I didn't mean it that way, Roy. You know I trust you. I'm seeing my agent and my lawyers tomorrow as it happens and I'm sure we can work something out in terms of damage limitation. As I see it, *Daybreak* as a production is not directly threatened, that's the important thing.'

263

'So the show must go on?'

'Something like that.'

On the way out to Eight Ash House he said only one other thing.

'Lin gave no indication of where she was going?'

'None at all, but I got the impression you won't see her again. She told me to tell you she was sorry.'

It was dark by now and there was little traffic on the motorway so it was difficult for me to judge his reaction in the darkened back seat. I would have liked to have seen his face to guess what he was thinking.

'She'll be difficult to replace,' I said.

I took his silence to mean I was spot on.

I had half expected a picket line of Goths on Eight Ash House, given that it was a Saturday and they didn't have to go to school or report to their probation officers, but Chrissie Schwartz seemed to have put the word round effectively and they were no doubt over in Hackney terrorising Stuart Street. In another life, no doubt, I would have to answer for that.

I turned Armstrong into the gateway and barrelled up the driveway, flicking my main beams on to pick up Amy's Freelander parked at the side of the house and Kurt's hired sporty BMW beyond it, outside one of the garages in the stable block. There were lights on in the house and everything seemed fine.

Except it wasn't. There was something wrong but I couldn't put my finger on it.

Ross must have sensed something. Maybe my personal feng shui was out of kilter.

'What is it? Something wrong?'

'The lights,' I said, suddenly realising, 'they haven't come on. The exterior lights are motion-sensitive. They should have picked us up by now.'

'What does that mean?'

'I don't know,' I snapped. 'A fuse has blown or somebody's reset them or somebody's turned them off, along with the alarm system.'

'And what does that mean?' he asked again, like he was

asking what his motivation should be in some scene in a movie.

'It means we go carefully until we're sure what's what.'

I turned off Armstrong's lights, dropped into second gear and turned off the gravel drive and on to the grass, feeling the steering going as the wheels scrabbled for purchase on the soft wet surface. I suspected I was leaving deep tyre ruts as we bounced along, but I decided Ross was wealthy enough to afford a gardener to sort it out before spring.

We passed the front of the house on a diagonal line, heading for a spot between the Freelander and the BMW. There was no reaction from the house and I killed the engine, coasting the last few yards on a slight downward slope.

'Stay here,' I said over my shoulder.

'But what –?'

'Stay here,' I said firmly. 'I'm just going to check things out. I'll be back in a minute.'

'Why not call them?' he said like it was the most obvious thing in the world.

'You got a cell phone on you?'

'No.'

'Neither have I. I'll leave the keys in.'

I opened Armstrong's door carefully and climbed out before he could argue about that.

In a crouching run I covered the gravel with barely a scrunch and fetched up against the stable block. For no good reason I could think of, I checked both garages, opening the doors slowly and peering inside until my eyes became accustomed to the gloom. Both were empty and the third, stable door opened on to the ride-on lawnmower, the workbench, the stacks of tubular-framed plastic chairs and the fireworks I had bought in Chinatown, exactly where I had left them.

From the stable block I skirted the edge of the lake, its surface rippling away into the damp, dark, cloudy night. I looked at my watch to find it was five fifteen – the cocktail hour out there in civilisation.

There was more than enough light streaming out on to the patio from the two french windows to make sure I didn't stray into the lake itself but I wanted to stay in the shadows as much as I could to get a look inside.

The first thing I saw was Amy and Burgundy sitting next to each other on one of the sofas. Nothing wrong with that at first, but they seemed to be sitting *very* close together, staring straight ahead of them. Neither held a drink and neither was talking. Both bad signs.

I moved position, almost crawling along the edge of the patio, inches from the lake, until I could see into the second set of windows. From that angle I could see what Amy and Burgundy were staring at. On another sofa opposite theirs lay Marcus, on his side, facing them. Even from where I was I could see that his hands were tied in front of him and that his face was covered in blood. And I mean covered. It was as if he had dipped his head into a bucket of it and it had splashed down his shirt, on to the upholstery and the carpet. They always tell you that scalp wounds look worse than they are, which is why American 'hardcore' wrestlers take barbed wire knuckle dusters into the ring with them, but it was of little comfort.

It wasn't much of a surprise either to see Tony Tse standing at the far end of the room near the door to the hallway, presenting arms with the shotgun Marcus had liberated from the cellar. Loading it with blanks hadn't done Marcus much good, although Tony Tse didn't know they were blanks or he wouldn't be holding it. Then again, he might have brought his own shells. Could it get any worse?

Tony took a step sideways to allow the door to open and Lin Ooi-Tan walked in like a ghost.

She had lost the baseball cap I had last seen her in and had let her hair fall down over her face to veil the patchwork of bruises. I couldn't tell if any of the marks were fresh but she nursed her right arm, where the hand already had fingers taped together, across her chest with her left hand as if she was breast feeding an invisible baby. The shoulder bag she had carried when she was in Armstrong was slung around her neck and over one shoulder, bouncing on her hip as she walked.

She said something to Tony and shrugged and he said something to her then turned his back on her as if she wasn't there. Lin hung her head, her hair a curtain to keep her from having to see or be seen.

If I read the situation right, they had thought they had heard us arriving and Lin had been sent to the front door to check. As she wouldn't have been able to see Armstrong from that angle, she had reported back that it was a false alarm. If I had read the situation wrongly, well, I just didn't know. I didn't have a Plan B.

Plan A wasn't up to much either.

I scuttled crablike out of the line of vision from the windows and ran around the edge of the lake and by the garages until I was grabbing for Armstrong's door handle.

'What is it?' said Ross from the back, scaring the hell out of me as I had more or less forgotten he was there.

'Jesus! Look, Tony Tse is in there and he's in full psychopath mode. I'm going to try and distract him so the others can get away.'

I thought it best not to mention Lin. I suspected Ross had a soft spot for her which might just cloud his judgement.

'Let me talk to him. Tony Tse wouldn't hurt me. He knows me. We've been in business meetings together.'

I was too late; his judgement had already disappeared in a storm front.

'Forget it. We need you to leg it to civilisation and get the police. Go across the grass until you get to the wall. Stay off the driveway. Once out of the gate, go left. The village is down there somewhere. Find a phone and scream for the police. The serious police, not the village bobby. Pretend you're a famous movie star, that might help.'

I could see him thinking that one over but he didn't rise to the bait.

'Look, Roy, I insist I talk to Tony. I'm sure we can work things out in a civilised way. He won't hurt me.'

'He's way beyond civilised and has gone through barbarian without collecting £200. Think of your contract. You're not supposed to be out after dark without a bodyguard. What's going to happen to the insurance cover on the film if the backers find out you walked into an isolated country house where we know there's a psycho waiting with a shotgun? Good God, man, if that was in a script even you would query it.'

He thought about that as a face-saving option.

'You have a point. Something like that could invalidate our backing.'

Not to mention getting you dead, I thought, so I brought him down to earth with a bump.

'Anyway, it's me Tony Tse's after, not you.'

That shocked him: somebody more important than he was, even if only on a homicidal wish list.

'You? Why?'

'I've got a nasty feeling he thinks I know where a certain disc is and he wants it badly.'

'And do you?'

'Not a clue.'

'So –?' he started slowly, but I cut him off as I leaned over to take my emergency disposable lighter from the glove compartment.

'And another thing,' I said. 'Have you got a cigarette on you?'

'No, but I've got a couple of very good Cuban cigars I was saving for after dinner.'

'That'll do nicely.'

I risked turning the light on in the storage shed once I had closed the stable doors. No one from the house could see the stable/garage block unless they took a step outside either front or back. A security design flaw I made a note to tell somebody about.

I stood by the door and sized up the situation. The workbench surface would be ideal for what I had in mind. It would have to be, there was no alternative.

The only thing on the bench was a can of petrol about half-full. I balanced that on the seat of the Snapper ride-on lawnmower and loosened the cap, in case I needed back-up. Then I pulled one of the plastic, tubular-framed chairs off the stack and with the aid of a pair of pliers which were neatly nailed above the workbench with an assortment of other tools, I prised off the rubber caps which tipped each of the tubular legs.

I laid the chair on the bench on its back, taking a claw hammer from the wall to rest on the plastic backrest to give it a bit of stability. The hammer might also come in handy if it was within reach.

Then I unpacked Ross's Chinese New Year rockets and selected four of the big fat red ones, inserting them down the tube legs of the chair. Because of the curve of the chair, even the two on the bottom would fly clear of the bench surface and straight at the doorway. If I got time to light them.

With the pliers, I cut the blue wax fuses as short as I dared and practised ramming Ross's unlit Cuban cigar into them: one, two, three, four. I was banking on the fact that to someone not actually expecting a home-made rocket launcher, it would look just like the clutter you would find in a garden shed or store-room. I had to bank on that for about five seconds I reckoned and I knew what Tony Tse could do in five seconds.

I went to the door, checked the positioning, then closed my eyes, took three steps until I came up against the Snapper and put my left hand out, straight on to the leg of the chair. I slid my hand up until I touched the rocket itself and my fingers found the fuse. Easy. I had just proved I could do it blindfold, which might give me the edge.

By standing on the Snapper I could reach the single light bulb hanging from the roof beam and I was about to unscrew it when the stable door began to creak open.

I didn't have time to react, I just froze.

'Nobody tells me to run. Nobody,' said Ross in tough guy mode.

I sighed, mostly in relief but partly because he didn't have a clue which movie he was misquoting.

'Ross, get out of here and get *help*. That's not running away. We're all depending on you. Go.'

His eyes widened as he realised what I had rigged on the bench.

'You're going to set fire to Tony Tse, aren't you?' he said stupidly.

'I'm certainly going to try.'

Maybe it was the realisation that he might become involved in a homicide by Chinese firework that persuaded Ross to go, or maybe he finally realised this wasn't a movie and he couldn't call for script changes because he didn't like his part. I wasn't worried about sticking to a script. I didn't have one. I was making this up as I went along.

I unscrewed the light bulb and did one more run through from the door in the dark, touching the unlit cigar to the four fuses one after the other, convincing myself I could do it without giving too much away to a homicidal target standing about four feet behind me.

My eyes were as accustomed to the dark as they ever would be. Outside the stables I bit the end off the cigar, which is not as easy as when they do it in the old Westerns, and lit up, puffing away but not attempting to enjoy it. Only when it was glowing like a hot coal did I clench it between my teeth and begin to stride across the brick patio to the back of the house.

Through the first set of french windows, little had changed. Amy and Burgundy were still sitting together like Siamese twins who had just had a row. Opposite them, Marcus lay inert except for his eyes, which flashed white in the red mask of blood which was his face.

Tony Tse was more or less where he had been, across the room near the open door to the hallway, shotgun at the ready. Only Lin was out of position in my mental blocking of the scene. She was on her knees at the end of the sofa on which Marcus lay, her head bowed, the top half of her body swaying from side to side.

None of them had seen me; were even looking my way. So it was time to announce myself.

Holding the cigar up in my left hand, so I must have looked like Churchill reviewing the troops, I rapped on one of the panes of the french window with the knuckles of my right and gave a little wave as all five of them, even Lin, snapped their heads in my direction. Particularly impressive was Amy whose expression changed from shock to delight as she recognised me. It was really rather sweet but it didn't last long. Within a flash she had adopted that bemused what-the-hell-are-you-doing-here? expression which I'd seen many times before, usually first thing in the morning. And then Marcus was moving his mouth, making the word 'Go' or maybe he was shouting it out loud, I couldn't tell.

But I had wasted precious seconds looking at them. I should have kept my eye on Tony Tse who had come across the room

270

like a train and now I was getting an eye-level view of the sole of his right shoe as he landed a kick on the central woodwork of the french windows.

The doors exploded outwards and I somehow managed to get an arm up before they hit me in the face. As it was, the force was enough to knock me flat on my back, my head bouncing on the patio.

I remembered that it was quite important to keep hold of the cigar in my left hand, but I couldn't remember exactly why.

Then my head bounced on brickwork again and I was moving and people were screaming and shouting and I was getting a carpet-eye view of everything as Tony Tse dragged me into the room by my left foot, like a dog bringing in a favourite chew toy. Casually, he let go of my leg and I relaxed into the pile of the carpet which was soft and comforting compared to being hauled across the patio and the sill of the french windows.

The comfort factor lasted about a thousandth of a second. Then Tony Tse rammed the butt of the shotgun one-handed into my stomach.

I spun into the foetal position on my right hip, clutching my guts, gasping for air, shaking the tears from my eyes. Nobody rushed to my aid. Marcus probably wasn't able to; Lin wasn't up for it; and Amy and Burgundy had Tony Tse's shotgun levelled at them.

He held it to his shoulder, pointing downwards, the barrels about two feet from their heads. The two women actually moved closer together as if they were trying to make it easier for him to blow their heads off. In the same situation, I would have been straining to give him only one target, preferably not me.

But I wasn't in that situation. I had problems of my own. One of which was I was having serious trouble actually breathing, the other being that Tony Tse had decided, for the first time, to talk to me.

'You have a disc of mine and I want it now, or nobody leaves here alive.'

Give him one thing; he didn't waste words.

I was still trying to catch my breath and remember how to make words come out of my mouth, when Lin of all people broke the silence.

'He needs it, Roy. He has to get it back to the people who franchised it to him. Give him it and he'll leave you all alone.'

She said this through the hanging garden of her hair, still kneeling, as if she was confessing. I sort of admired the composure that could still refer to her lover's little sideline to undermine the currency of Western Europe as a 'franchise'.

'He can have it,' I gasped, finding the power of speech at last. 'It's no good to me. If it gets him out of my face, he's welcome to it.'

Tony Tse looked down at me, the shotgun still aimed at Amy and Burgundy.

'Maybe you're not as stupid as you look.'

I could hear Amy thinking: Oh yes he is.

'Don't give the son-of-a-bitch the time of day,' croaked Marcus.

I rolled over on to my knees and started the long, painful process of getting to my feet.

'Don't be alarmed, Marcus,' I said, trying not to telegraph the 'alarmed' too much. 'I know what I'm doing.'

That'll be a first . . . I heard Amy in the back of my mind.

As I stood up, I scooped up the cigar which was happily burning a brown hole in the carpet. I made a point of letting Marcus see it but if he understood what I was getting at, he was clever enough not to show it. I cupped the cigar in my hand as I turned to face Tony Tse, not wanting him to notice it.

'It's out the back, where the cars are,' I said vaguely.

Tony Tse didn't look at me, he was sighting the shotgun at the two women on the sofa.

'Get it,' he said. 'You have five minutes.'

'Let them go,' I tried. 'You don't need them if you've got me.'

He swivelled his head, and the curious expression on his face I took to be a smile.

'Which one?' he asked me.

'What?'

'Choose one of them,' he goaded.

This was his thing; his game, the source of his kicks. Domination, pure and simple. That's what he got off on and like all obsessions, it was probably his weakness as well. It was a hell of a time to discover his weak spot.

'Don't play this game, Angel,' said Amy defiantly.

'Screw him,' said Burgundy, supporting the sisterhood.

'That one,' I said, pointing to Burgundy.

The look on Amy's face was priceless, but lasted only a micro-second as Tony Tse swung the shotgun full on at her.

'No,' he said gleefully, 'you can have this one.'

Of course, as I was to say constantly afterwards, I always knew he was going to do that, but it took a lot to get Amy to believe me.

As it was, the crunch never came.

'OK,' I said.

But then Lin intervened, and I never did figure out why. Perhaps it was some vestige of what she felt for Tony Tse, or that she was still under his spell. Perhaps she just couldn't help herself.

'That's his wife,' she said.

Tony Tse's face turned to thunder. Burgundy's face – staring wide-eyed at Amy and leaning away from her – was a picture as well.

'Get it – now,' he snarled. 'Two minutes.'

'Worth a shot,' I said to myself.

If my target wasn't going to come to the firework display, there was nothing else for it. I was simply going to have to burn the house down. I only hoped I had got my coded message through to Marcus and that the fire alarms linked to the nearest fire station were still working.

I almost choked puffing on the cigar to make the end glow as I ran across the patio towards the stables. I could have kicked myself for taking the light bulb out and I barked my shins on the front end of the ride-on mower.

I lashed out with a foot at the Snapper, swearing at it, then took another look at it, running my hands over it to discover an ignition starter with the key, mercifully, still in.

With my two minutes ticking away, I pushed the Snapper out of the shed and on to the patio, steering it round the rim of the lake until it was on a diagonal line for the french windows, one door of which hung open where Tony Tse had kicked it. The mower seemed easy enough to operate: an automatic lever offering Forward, Reverse, Cut and Park and pedals for brake and accelerator. I had no idea if it would start first time or how fast it would cover the thirty yards or so to the windows. These were variables I just didn't have time to worry about.

I tried to think of something to jam the accelerator down with and the petrol can I had balanced on the driving seat seemed to do the job – it would have to. I took the top off completely, smelling the reek of fuel through the damp night air, and squeezed it into place.

Then I ran to Armstrong, opened the front nearside door and grabbed the first CD from the rack I had fitted near the ashtray, slipping it into my jacket pocket. There was no sign of Ross. Hopefully he would be dialling 999 by now as long as he'd decided on the motivation of the character he was playing.

Back in the stable, I dived into the package of fireworks and produced four of the firecracker chains, each one five feet long, draping them around my neck like bandoliers of ammunition. I started to select some of the rockets and thought the hell with it, and grabbed the lot in the black plastic bin liner.

I tied the firecrackers to the steering wheel of the Snapper using the red ribbons which were supposed to tie them to lamp posts and roof beams, making sure that the blue fuses were as close to each other as possible, piling them into the well behind the engine cover where the driver's feet go. Then I dumped the bag with the rest of the rockets on to the seat, wedging it down as best I could. I was doing all this with the cigar clenched between my teeth, inches away from goodness knew how many tubes of gunpowder and a five-litre can of petrol with the top off.

If Tony Tse had moved to the windows and seen me, he could have taken me easily, I had no doubts about that. I just refused to think about it, banking on the fact that he thought I was harmless and anyway, he was having far more fun dominating two women. Three, if you counted Lin, but I reckoned he didn't see much of a challenge in her any more.

I ran back to the shed and picked the tubular chair off the table, holding it upside down by the plastic backrest so the rockets didn't fall out, and hurried back out to the Snapper, putting the chair down on the patio next to it.

To avoid flooding the damn thing, I held the petrol can off the

274

accelerator pedal and turned the key as casually as I could, working on the theory that you should never let machinery know you're in a hurry.

Amazingly, it started first time and gave out a deep, smokey roar as I jammed the petrol can back in place, pumping up the revs. I didn't look at the window to see if anyone had heard the noise. How could they not have? To me it sounded like someone kick-starting a Harley in church.

I blew on the cigar end and stabbed it at the blue fuses of three of the firecracker chains. I couldn't see the fourth. As soon as I got a fizzing spark, I whipped the cigar away and smacked the gear shift into Forward. The Snapper leapt across the patio as if it had been kicked from behind and made a beeline for the french window much faster than I had expected.

It was half-way there when Tony Tse appeared in the window frame and I was sure he could see the Snapper clearly from the light which spilled out of the room. He could see it, but he didn't believe it, as he made no move to do anything about it. He didn't even point the shotgun at it.

Then the first of the firecrackers started to go off and all hell broke loose.

The Snapper could never actually get into the room because of the lip at the bottom of the windows and even if the wheels had mounted it, the rotating blade in its circular metal case underneath the Snapper would not have. Ride-on lawnmowers are not known for their versatility in going up steps.

But even I was impressed when it smashed into the windows, taking out almost all the panes of glass in the left side door, and for a second stayed there, wheels churning as that first firecracker jumped and spat and exploded and lit up the whole of the back of the house. And then the other firecrackers started to go off and there was a dull *whoof* as the petrol can ignited and a small mushroom cloud of black smoke wafted into the air and out of it shot one of the smaller rockets, which screamed across the patio at knee height and disappeared into the lake with a fizz.

The firecrackers jumped and banged like flaying whips, some of them seeming to leap through the broken window and into the room. Rockets began to shoot off in all directions and a pall of cordite smoke wafted across the patio.

Holding my chair rocket-launcher out in front of me, I advanced through the smokescreen, the cigar between my teeth. I leaned forward and touched the shortened fuse of the top left rocket. It ignited immediately, almost setting fire to my hair.

It was also more powerful than I had expected and I only just managed to hold the chair level in order to ensure its horizontal flight path through the broken window and into the living-room.

I heard it as it started to explode and saw through the smoke as it ricocheted off one wall and then bounced off the ceiling. I put my head forward again to light the second leg of my artillery battery, jerking back just in time as the second rocket spewed flames and sparks and whooshed off after the first.

By now, even over the rockets' red glare and the machine-gun firecrackers cracking, I could hear screaming – human screaming – from inside, and then the shrill, constant beeping as the fire alarms began to go off.

Everything was going exactly to plan.

And then the second set of french windows – the set which weren't actually on fire – burst open and out spewed Amy and Burgundy locked in a bizarre and very deadly embrace with Tony Tse.

He had them in front of him, almost as a shield, the shotgun held over both their throats, snapping their heads back, like a crazy sort of milkmaid's yoke, both of them clutching and scrabbling at the barrel and the stock, both of them choking and coughing with the smoke and tears streaming from their eyes.

He was about twenty feet from me, holding the two women in front of him, and I could see his eyes bulging with fury in the light of the flames which now consumed the Snapper but if he said anything I couldn't hear it as the firecrackers continued to explode and the rockets screamed and from the house, the fire alarm shrilled insistently on its single, high-pitched note.

I turned the chair clockwise in my hands and touched the cigar to the third fuse.

The rocket flew straight at him and he could do nothing except react instinctively and throw himself sideways out of the way, but in doing so, he had to let go of the gun, releasing Amy and Burgundy, who dived forward, flattening themselves into the bricks of the patio.

'Run!' I yelled, but they couldn't hear me.

They just lay there, clutching their throats, not even attempting to pick up the shotgun. Another rocket went up from the Snapper, this time straight up as it was supposed to do, starbursting red and gold somewhere above our heads, giving the whole scene an even more hellish quality than it had already.

And the Demon King himself was determined to have his way.

Tony Tse hardly touched the ground when he dived out the path of my home-made missile. He went into a rolling dive and came up on his feet as if he were on springs.

I pointed my chair at him. Perhaps he would see the funny side and die laughing. Instead, he just ignored me and strode over to pick up the shotgun.

'Don't do it,' I shouted, the cigar wobbling dangerously between my teeth.

He ignored me some more and began to bring the shotgun up to bear on me at a range of no more than twelve feet. But then again, he was only twelve feet away from my last rocket.

He was staring at me, almost smirking, not worried at all, when I touched off the fuse. The rocket's blast scorched my face, in fact it did me more damage than it did him. All he had to do was swerve the top half of his body and the rocket shot by him at head height, curved upwards into the sky and burst in the first of a series of three balls of green light.

But neither of us were watching closely. I had only the plastic chair left, so I threw it at him.

And I missed with that as well.

Then he had the shotgun up and he pulled the triggers.

If anyone ever does an autopsy on me they'll find three unexplained lumps on the back of my skull, which are all down to Tony Tse. The first from Gerrard Street, the second from when he kicked the french windows into my face and the third when he shot me with a pair of blank cartridges close enough to blow me off my feet and I managed to break my fall with the back of my head. Again.

I think I must have had an idiot smile on my face when Tony Tse leaned over me and peered down. The poor guy was really confused. He couldn't understand why there wasn't a gaping hole where my chest should have been.

And then I heard a scream which wasn't a rocket and wasn't me; I didn't have the breath left in me for a squeak let alone a scream. The effect of two Pinewood blanks at close range was similar to what I imagined being kicked by a horse with red hot horseshoes was like. So I just lay flat on my back, which seemed to be what I did best, as another rocket went off above us and turned the sky red this time.

I watched as Amy jumped, still screaming, on to Tony Tse's back, wrapped her arms around his neck and attempted to bite his ear off. And I watched as he whipped the butt of the shotgun into her kidneys, flung it to one side and used his left hand to grab her by the hair and pull – almost peel – her off him, then straight-arm her so she staggered backwards and fell over into the shallows of the lake.

I continued to watch – it was all I could do as nothing much in my body seemed to work – as Burgundy's foot came up between Tony Tse's legs and for a minute I thought she had found his one weak spot. But with a howl audible above the still popping firecrackers, he swung around on his left leg and lashed out with his right, catching Burgundy in the stomach then straight-fingering her in the throat as she doubled over.

That was when – and it all seemed to be happening just for my entertainment, so unreal it was – Marcus came charging out of the house like a bull elephant, his hands out like claws, aiming for Tony Tse's throat.

Marcus never had a chance. Tony Tse went into a classic judo defensive stance and let Marcus's momentum do the rest. He flipped him off the ground and through the air, over where Amy lay gasping, and into the lake.

Then he turned back to me because I had finally done something to get his attention.

I had pulled the CD I had taken from Armstrong out of my pocket and opened the case, removing the disc and keeping it silver side up so he could get a good look at it.

It wasn't much of a bargaining position. There were four of us, all on the ground, all probably out for the count and he was still on his feet after we'd tried to burn, bite, strangle and castrate him.

Smoke and flames were billowing from the house now through both sets of windows, but at least the firecrackers had stopped. The shrill, ear-piercing bleep of the smoke alarm continued and I thought – hoped? – I heard sirens in the distance.

I could see Amy's face, white with desperation, as she tried to pull Marcus out of the lake. Through Tony Tse's legs I could see Burgundy in a heap where he had felled her. It was a surreal scene, lit by the flames from the burning Snapper.

Tony Tse held out a hand towards me.

'That's my disc,' he said and it wasn't a question.

'Told you you could have it,' I said, and I spun it like a frisbee out into the lake, the flickering reflection of flames from the house showing the splash.

The rest is hazy because the situation deteriorated somewhat after that and a lot of pain was involved.

The pain came as Tony Tse watched the disc skim into the lake and then turned and brought his foot down on my right ankle with as much force as he could muster. Suddenly I could see red rockets where there weren't any except behind my eyes and I could do nothing as Tony Tse grabbed Amy by the hair and pushed her deeper into the lake. Marcus, whom she had been dragging out, fell back and seemed to sink below the surface.

I don't know whether Tony Tse wanted her to dive for the disc or just drown her. I couldn't do anything about either.

Then a voice I didn't recognise said:

'That's enough, Tony. Leave them alone.'

It was Ross. He had his jacket slung over one shoulder, the other hand on his hip, standing there issuing a challenge. God knows what movie he thought he was in.

Tony Tse let go of Amy's hair and strode out of the lake, kicking my legs out of the way as he went by me.

I was too busy howling in agony to hear if they said anything else and by the time I had shaken the tears from my eyes, they had got it on.

Whatever styles they were fighting in, Ross was about three belts below Tony Tse. In fact he blocked most of Ross's early attacks so easily I began to fear that Ross had studied by correspondence course during a postal strike.

I wanted to shout out: *Not the face – don't hit him in the face*. But the opportunity slipped by, they were moving so fast. But then the entire fight lasted less than a minute.

Tony Tse blocked another kick from Ross, deflected a punch and struck once at Ross's throat, sending him staggering backwards like a drunk reeling from the cost of the last round.

He had his fist cocked, ready to let one go at virtually any part of Ross's body he wanted to hit, when suddenly there was more shouting and screaming and hell really did come to town, at least as far as Tony Tse was concerned.

'Rosssssss!'

Lin screamed it as she ran out of the house and slammed into Tony Tse's side, the force of her charge carrying them both backwards towards the lake. They were no more than eighteen inches from my head, so I got a good view.

The sight of her would have scared me if I'd seen it in a movie. In real life, and death, it was awesome.

Her clothes and hair were on fire when she charged. She must have decided to stay in the house and let the smoke and flames take their course. But then Ross had shown up and her boyfriend had started to take him apart and she knew he wouldn't stop. She'd seen how he had dealt with Amy and Burgundy and Marcus and me and she'd chosen to stay in the fire. But Ross was a different matter. Whether it was loyalty or love, he had to be protected.

And now that she had decided to ride to the rescue, she wasn't taking prisoners.

Amazingly, they both stayed on their feet and almost danced off the patio and into the lake. Neither of them was going anywhere else.

Tony Tse had his hands clenched around Lin's throat. Lin had both her hands on the handle of the knife she had shown me earlier that day out at Heathrow, the blade of which was buried in Tony Tse's chest.

They were about twenty feet out into the lake when they fell over and went under the surface.

Neither of them came up.

Ross had sunk to his knees and had his hands pressed to his chest, trying to regulate his breathing.

Five of us on the patio of a burning house, sirens in the distance definitely now, and not one of us could stand. From a distant planet it must have looked like we'd had one hell of a barbecue.

I sat up and held out a hand for Amy, who climbed, bedraggled, out of the water, pulling Marcus with her other hand. His early evening dip had at least washed the blood from his face and he began to retch and spit out water so I guessed he'd live.

Burgundy came to and made it to her knees before turning her head and vomiting to one side. It seemed to perk her up. She looked up and around, seeing Ross for the first time.

'Ross? What the hell are you doing here?' she said, as if he was on the wrong set with the wrong call sheet.

'Get him out of here,' I yelled at her. Then to Amy, whose hand I was still holding, I said: 'You OK to drive? Get them out of here. Take them to Hampstead.'

'You sure?' she said, tightening her grip.

'Absolutely. Fewer people here the better.'

'I can drive,' she said, 'and I don't fancy a press conference looking like this.'

'You were never here. Neither was Burgundy and certainly not Ross. Marcus and I can handle it, can't we?' I said to the retching Marcus.

He raised his head and looked at me.

'You came back. A man like you, you came back. Why?' he said in a cod Mexican accent.

'Eli Wallach in *The Magnificent Seven*,' said Burgundy, quick as a flash. 'Now can we stop playing this fucking game?'

20

WRAP

'Come on,' said Amy as the film finished, 'they're breaking for the bar already. Let's go or we'll never get a drink let alone anywhere near Ross.'

It was ten months later and we were at the premiere of *Daybreak* at the multiplex at Marble Arch.

'No, wait,' I said. 'I want to see the credits.'

Marcus and I had ended up in neighbouring rooms at The Oaks hospital, where they plastered up my ankle and told me to stay off my feet for a few weeks.

When I noticed Siobhan was on duty, I said that would do fine.

Amy was my first visitor, and she noticed her too.

When she'd been to see Marcus – to ascertain when he would be fit enough to do her hair – she came into my room and locked the door behind her, then took off her leather coat and draped it over a chair. She was wearing a knee-length grey woollen dress and black leather boots and she started off perched on the edge of the bed.

'Did you know that Tony Tse would let me go when you picked Burgundy?' she asked.

'I was banking on it. Reverse psychology. He was a psychopath, after all. It would have worked if it hadn't been for Lin,' I said confidently, because I'd had time to think it through.

'I suppose it was pretty brave of you coming in like that,' she said, her head on one side.

'Seemed like a good idea at the time. Actually, it was the only idea at the time.'

She smiled at that.

'I thought I'd thank you for coming to my rescue and take your mind off being in hospital at the same time,' she said, standing up.

She knelt on the end of the bed and began to edge her way up, straddling my plaster cast and hoisting her dress up until she was over my thighs. Then she began to pull the sheets off me.

'I see you're wearing your Christmas present,' I said, helping to get rid of the bedclothes.

'Mr Angel,' she said huskily, 'I'm ready for my close up.'

*

Last Ditch Productions
in association with
Red River Films
presents
Daybreak
a Julius Cockburn film.
Written by Walter Wilkes Booth
Produced by Don Sager

Cast

Jason	Ross Pirie
Norma	Zina Ray
Howard	Bo Jay Roberts
Sylvie	Charmaine Colvin
Ronnie	Alec Walters
Victor	Jack Palance
Cronin	John Cleese
Zupart	Walter Matthau

'These things go on forever,' said Amy. 'We ought to be networking.'

'Give it a minute,' I said.

The fire brigade arrived about five minutes after Amy drove Burgundy and Ross away from the house and managed to contain the fire to two rooms.

I was questioned once by the senior fire officer and eighteen subsequent times by people from various insurance companies. Each time I got the standard lecture about how dangerous it was to play with fireworks and how especially stupid it was to leave fireworks next to a can of petrol balanced on a ride-on lawn-mower.

No one ever asked me why I was trying to mow a lawn in England in January.

*

Script Editor	Philip Oakes
Script Supervisor	Ernie Bulow
Additional dialogue	W. Satterthwait
Associate Producer (UK)	Gloria-Maria van Doodler
Associate Line Producer	Burgundy Dulude
Second Unit Director	Hal Smithee
Art Director	Chris May

'Come on.' Amy pulled at my sleeve. 'We're missing the party.'

'Hang in there, will you?' I said.

Carter and Regan, with an embarrassed Paul Brettler hiding in the doorway, came visiting on the Sunday.

They had obviously had access to the version of events I had given to the local police – how Marcus and I had stumbled in on a lovers' quarrel which had turned violent and we had been hurt simply trying (and failing) to stop them killing each other.

In fact they seemed quite grateful that I had pitched it that way, keeping them and any whiff of anything bigger involving counterfeit euros well out of it.

For their end, they were willing to lean on whoever needed leaning on to make sure that Ross and the production company received the lowest possible profile and, as it turned out, they were as good as their word.

The local police trawled the lake at Eight Ash House and recovered the bodies of Tony Tse and Lin Ooi-Tan. She had drowned, he had the Sabatier kitchen knife in his chest. They were still locked together in an embrace when they were found.

A very polite man who said he was a coroner came to The Oaks and took a statement from me. Marcus pleaded that a blow on the head had resulted in temporary amnesia and he couldn't remember any details but whatever I said was OK with him. The coroner frowned at that but went away more or less happy.

Whatever the papers made of it, Tony Lovisi's people handled it well and the film continued on schedule and, I hear, actually came in under budget.

We'll hear about the Oscar nominations any day now.

*

Key Hair Supervisor	Marcus Moore
Costumes	Berman's
	Amy May of London

'There you go,' I said, 'your name in lights.'
'Yeah, right. can we go to the party now?'
'Not yet.'

Frank Shoosmith discharged himself from The Oaks as soon as he realised that Marcus and I were moving in.

Nobody stopped him and on the Monday morning he was picking up Ross for his early morning call.

Bernie Brooks came out of his coma in mid-February, after almost eight weeks. He had no loss of memory and seemed perfectly fit and healthy.

The first thing he did was ask for a phone in order to ring Carter and Regan to tell them that the missing compact disc with the design for a fake 500-euro note was in the CD rack of the wrecked BMW out at Chiltern Cars of Amersham.

Bernie had slotted it into an empty Shania Twain box after he had found it in Ross's trailer on Christmas Eve when Frank Shoosmith had offered him a lift.

Carter and Regan already knew this because I had told them it was the only place it could be. Tony Tse had looked – and wrecked – everywhere else.

I put in a claim to the film company for the perfectly good Ian Dury CD I had thrown into the lake.

As a quid pro quo for the information, Carter and Regan told me that Alix Tse had boarded a Heathrow to Brussels flight on that Saturday, using Lin's ticket. They reckoned Tony and his cousin had somehow known about Lin's plans to skip and had headed her off at the boarding gate.

They had no idea where Alix Tse was now and they didn't much care.

That made three of us.

*

Post Production Lawyer	Marcel Berlins
Key Grip	F. Lloyd Thursby
Best Boy Grip	Rob Hayward
Stunt Co-ordinator	George Harding

'Here we go,' I said, 'this is it.'

Beside me, Amy sighed, then relented and patted my thigh, as the credits continued to roll.

Stunt Drivers	Gwyn Lawrence
	Chas 'The Danger' Waudby
	Tim Props Prentice
	Roy Angel

'There you are,' I said gleefully, pointing at the screen as the cinema emptied around us. 'Fame at last!'